THE DANGEROUS EDGE

Lesley Grant-Adamson is widely acknowledged to be a leading writer of crime and suspense fiction. Critics have compared her novels with the best of Simenon, Highsmith, Rendell and Elmore Leonard.

D1149101

The
Dangerous Edge

LESLEY GRANT-ADAMSON

faber and faber

LONDON · BOSTON

First published in 1993
by Faber and Faber Limited
3 Queen Square London WC1N 3AU
This paperback edition first published in 1994

Phototypeset by Intype, London
Printed in England by Clays Ltd, St Ives plc

Lesley Grant-Adamson is hereby identified as author of this
work is accordance with Section 77 of the Copyright,
Designs and Patents Act 1988.

A CIP record for this book is
available from the British Library

ISBN 0-571-17020-X

1 3 5 7 9 10 8 6 4 2

ONE

1969, France

The scream is what people remember.

It seared the minds of those who heard it and it became part of the imagined memory of those who learned about it second-hand. Long after the death of the woman, her scream lingers.

There were no stars that night. The man who stood in the shadows of the poplars was a stranger. His cigarette made a prick of light, and when he had smoked it down to the butt he snuffed it out between finger and thumb and put it in his jacket pocket. They would find no more evidence than the soft pressure of his feet on the dry ground beneath the tree.

He shifted his weight from one sole to the other, eased his neck, which grew stiff sometimes as a consequence of the fall. A mile away a dog barked. In the branches a night-bird stirred. The man did not look at his watch although twice his hand pushed back his sleeve and touched the heavy gold band.

Across the drive and beyond a parterre the house was a black cliff. Lights on the ground floor had been turned out. He had ticked them off, room by room, along the broad frontage. Gradually other rooms blanked out until only one glimmered, high up.

Twenty minutes went by, longer than he had anticipated. He took another cigarette from the pack, put it to his lips, paused, replaced it in the pack. From a long way down the valley a faint sound, a mere disturbance of the summer air, reached him.

The light snapped off. The man moved forward, keeping to the tree line until the brief, exposed dash across the corner of the garden to the protection of the house. Rough stone snagged his sleeve. He inched ahead more carefully, avoiding the scaling wisteria and a jutting drain.

Coming to a window, he ducked and scuttled by. At the

second window he risked standing, peering in, making sure. Then the sash was gliding up, his leg swinging over the sill. For a fraction of a second he hung there, neither in nor out, head cocked. No sounds inside. And from the valley nothing but the barking dog and the indeterminate murmur that seemed little by little to grow louder.

The man threw the other leg across and disappeared into the blackness within.

Andrée was singing to herself as the car swayed through the bends. She had a fine voice that was trained to sing opera, although her career had been cut short by the twin discoveries that she would never be quite good enough and that she could marry a rich man. Without serious regret she had turned her back on La Scala and opted for a life of indolent comfort: the grand house in the Bois de Boulogne, the yacht that pottered about the Adriatic, and the château in the valley.

She sang now only when she was alone. Her favourite times were being alone, driving a very fast car through the night and singing. Arias she had once performed in public were wasted on sleeping farmhouses and unpeopled hillsides. Music no longer to be shared welled up inside her, flooded her whole being, overflowed in joy. Singing had become her tender secret.

This night, as other nights, she had left Paris late. Business pinned her husband to the city, but she wanted to be at the château. Her child was there. Once the dinner guests had left the Bois de Boulogne, Andrée had drunk a last espresso with her husband.

'You're sure you're not too tired to drive all that way?' he asked, as he always did.

'Not at all.'

'Well, be careful. You never know what lunatics are on the roads.'

'There'll be hardly any traffic. I shall enjoy it.'

And then she was behind the wheel and checking her speed through the damp streets of Paris. Once free of the city she pressed the pedal down and she began to sing. Her voice was light, with a touch of coloratura, a sweet sound for Mimi, the little milliner.

Andrée's child was two, a girl who had her mother's dark eyes and sometimes her look. Andrée was intensely proud of her. Tiny achievements seemed important hurdles crossed, and her charm and childish gibberings put all other children in an unflattering shade.

The child was infinitely precious because she was irreplaceable. A year after her birth Andrée was ill, there was an operation and there could be no more children.

The car went over the river, curving wide at the bridge rather than drop speed. Andrée pulled it back to the centre of the road, opened up the throttle ready for the long climb up to the head of the valley. To her left the water was a sheeny blur, to her right a scattering of houses merged in a pale streak against the scented darkness of pines. The car lights beckoned her on, parting the darkness. 'Come, do not delay,' sang Susanna, the bride of Figaro.

Andrée had left the house just as she was, in a black silk Balenciaga gown, a glister of diamonds on her fingers, her body breathing 'Escapade'. It was not her favourite perfume but it was a new one. When her husband entertained business people, she wore the newest, although she took scant interest in the conjuring act that created perfumes. The scent was rich, floral, too cloying for her own taste. She opened the car window a half-inch. Warm air stroked her skin, teased strands from her hair's neat coil. Andrée sped on, one hand on the wheel and the other winkling out the pins until the thick brown hair floated free about her shoulders. Marguerite, decking herself in Faust's devilish jewels, sang '*Ah, je me vois, si belle.*'

A tight bend came at her. She slowed, changed gear, jerked the car round, began zig-zagging up the hillside. Tree trunks, that was all she could see. Mile on mile, the trunks of trees and the flat-out road. Mile on mile, her delicate, sensuous voice

3

throbbing with the borrowed triumph and pain of the heroines of opera.

She reached the massive gates that stood open for her. Tyres sprayed gravel, headlamps floodlit the fairytale building. She looped behind the house and, humming softly, left the car in a paved courtyard and let herself in at a rear door. The narrow passageway opened into a broad hall where she clicked a light switch and illuminated a flourish of marble staircase. Andrée slipped off her pumps and ran lightly up, past the sleepers on the first floor, and on up to the top landing.

Often she would wake the child to prove she had kept her promise and come home. Sometimes she scooped her daughter into her arms and took her to her own bed for the soft comfort of the small body. Always she looked in on her. She would stand at the bedside, angling the lamp away so that the rush of light did not disturb her. Then she knelt and watched the subtle rise and fall of breath, the touch of sweat that on hot summer nights made the hairline glisten and the dark hair retract in corkscrew curls. She marvelled at the gossamer skin, the blue streak of veins through its translucence. She loved her with a deeper love than she had believed possible.

Andrée turned the rose-painted knob of the nursery door and let subdued light from the landing spill across the room. She made out the round table with the lamp on it, the form of the bed. Her hand went for the lamp but before she pressed the switch instinct stopped her. She snatched her breath. Without seeing, she knew she was alone.

Then she grabbed at the lamp, forced harsh yellow light on to the empty bed. She whirled to the doorway, shouting a name. Tried to leave the room but could not. The young English-woman who cared for the child burst out of the adjoining room, shocked from sleep, her nightdress hanging off her shoulder. There was a gabble of question and denial. Other figures appeared down marble corridors, converging on the hubbub. At first they could see nothing as Andrée and the nanny were in the child's room. So they crowded the doorway, disbelieving,

4

seeking soothing explanations. But Andrée understood. The agony broke from her. They never forgot that scream.

The local *gendarmerie* searched the grounds, the house and out-buildings and found no traces of the child. They quizzed the servants and the family, those who lived at the château and those who did not. They learned nothing. The examining magistrate for the district, a nervous young man with a wall eye and a tendency to stammer, dismissed the *gendarmerie* and called in the criminal police from the city. The family had been angered at the emphasis the *gendarmerie* put on events and personalities at the château. Their dissatisfaction was reported in the newspapers, and television cameras kept watch from the trees as the main actors in the drama arrived or left the château.

Welcoming the switch to the city police, the child's uncle, a rather humourless man in his late twenties, testily told a reporter: 'Now perhaps something will be done, although the *gendarmes* have wasted so much time it won't be easy.'

'Are you saying, *m'sieu*, it will be their fault if the case isn't solved?'

'Certainly they will bear a degree of responsibility.'

'But if they . . .'

'You must excuse me, I have to go now.'

When the uncle returned days later to the château, where he lived with his parents and several other members of the family, the examining magistrate, Judge Georges Laroche, was there. The judge had read the exaggerated reports and was annoyed, as it appeared the uncle was damning both the *gendarmerie* and the city police, and calling for the removal from the case of the man whose role it was to co-ordinate the inquiry: examining magistrate Judge Georges Laroche.

There was an opportunity for the uncle to withdraw, or at any rate explain the difference between his intended meaning and the resulting newspaper story. He did not take it. A child was missing, he protested, stolen at night from its bed, and the upholders of law and order were futilely aggravating the

5

distressed family instead of broadening the search. Worse, they gave the impression of fretting about personal prestige instead of concentrating on discovering the child. How many times had he picked up a paper or turned on the radio to learn that the police and the judge had been airing their views (invariably views critical of the ménage at the château) when they would have been more profitably engaged in appeals for information about strangers in the district, or a woman's sudden acquisition of a two-year-old girl, or . . . ?

'Ah,' said the judge. 'You b-believe the child to be alive, do you?'

'How should I know?' The uncle attempted to address the judge's good eye. 'All I know is, I was woken by my sister-in-law and the nanny causing a commotion and the child was gone.'

'So everyone in the house keeps saying.' Pedantic, the judge recited the story sing-song: 'Your sister-in-law says she called the nanny's name once and the nanny says she was roused by the sound of her name being called. They say the nanny joined your sister-in-law in the child's b-bedroom and the mother demanded to know where her daughter was and the nanny told her she was equally astonished at the empty bed. And then the rest of the household gathered in the d-doorway to find out what all the excitement was about.'

The uncle clapped his hands to his head. He wanted to throttle this stupid judge or anyone else who made him go round and round that shattering sequence of events. 'Yes, *yes*, That's what happened. You refuse to believe us but that's precisely how it was.'

'Ah, *m'sieu*, I need to understand how it can be that such a minor disturbance has you all on your feet and running upstairs to the child's room when none of you was disturbed by the child being removed. Is a child of two years going to be quiet if a stranger p-picks it from its bed and makes off with it? Isn't it going to howl the house down? Even if a stranger slinks into the house without any of you noticing, he cannot creep out again

6

with a screaming child without some of you being alerted. And yet you all, each one of you, claim that you were d-deep asleep until the moment the mother called out the name of the English girl.'

The judge raised an eyebrow, the one above his bad eye, but he was less questioning than triumphant. Suspicion of the family was vindicated, the eyebrow seemed to say.

The uncle wriggled his shoulders. 'What do you expect me to say? I can only speculate about how the child was taken from the house. Tape across her mouth to keep her quiet?'

'Perhaps. And perhaps she was never in her bed that night. Who says she was? The young Englishwoman, no one else claims to have seen her there.'

'But that's normal! Unless either of the child's parents was here, then no one else *would* go to the nursery.' Exasperated, the uncle appealed, anyway, to the man's common sense. 'Look, you know how distraught the nanny is. You have no grounds whatsoever for suspecting her of complicity.'

But he won no concession. They all remained under suspicion. The uncle ended the conversation by remarking, with considerable acidity: 'The sooner the ransom note arrives, the better. At least that will convince you that you and your police ought to look elsewhere for your child thief.'

A month had gone by, a month in which Andrée suppressed the horror with sedatives, her husband stayed away from the house in the Bois de Boulogne to be at her side, and the family drew in upon itself. There was an air of waiting, waiting for a second dreadful thing to befall them. Their cold, shut-down expressions discouraged conversation. Servants, especially the nanny who was conspicuously superfluous now the nursery was empty, were equally tainted with misfortune.

The nanny wrote to her parents who advised her to come away, that her presence could do nothing except emphasize the loss. But she stayed, sensing that departure might make her appear culpable or, at the very least, heartless. She hung on, keeping her tears private.

7

Andrée did not know of the rejected parental advice but valued the nanny's attention and loyalty. At no time did it flit across her mind that the girl had had a hand in the child's disappearance, and at no time did the nanny have doubts about Andrée. Their love and care for the child made such wonderings impossible. There grew between them a newer, deeper understanding. Although Andrée could not equate the girl's loss with her own, she credited her with sharing her feelings more keenly than the others did. Hadn't she been closer to the baby than anyone else except its mother? Hadn't she marvelled at the specialness of her charge, at her beauty and brilliance? Hadn't she appreciated, day after day, the depth and purity of the mother's love for her only child? All that rallied Andrée from her miasma of grief was the need to protect the nanny from the unkinder challenges of Judge Georges Laroche and the detectives.

With an outsider's eye, the nanny observed the gradual shifts in attitudes. At the start, the servants felt as violated as the family but this rapidly gave way to excitement. They had never expected to be fit subjects for reporters to pester, but they learned to cope. It was astonishing and thrilling to see themselves on television alongside Neil Armstrong and Buzz Aldrin creeping from the Apollo spaceship to take that giant step for mankind, on the surface of the moon; or to share a newspaper page with the old president, de Gaulle, and the next one, Georges Pompidou, or with the *Folies Bergère*, celebrating 100 years of artistic nudity.

Although they declined to give information about who was prone with grief and who was bearing up well, they were prepared to help in other ways, until they found the frivolous interest of journalists objectionable and they grew guarded. Within a few weeks they were pleased to escape from the château for an hour or two and relax, become their normal selves, turn their backs on gloom. And they began to whisper fantastical theories implicating one or other member of the family. Situations they had not alluded to over the years became

8

acceptable subjects for speculation. No one challenged the underlying assertion that, for all its wealth and fame, the family at the château was not a happy family and never had been.

The nanny's sharp eye noticed how the child's father grew restless at conducting his business on the telephone and then, about six weeks after the catastrophe, he declared it imperative to spend a number of days at the Paris house before flying to London. It was a hot, disgustingly hot, summer with lengthy periods of dry weather fractured by storms. Cities were more uncomfortable than the countryside and normally he contrived to avoid them. But he was desperate to get away.

The older couple were reduced to putting on a show of desolation in the presence of the child's parents but reverting to near normality otherwise. They had endured appalling tragedies in their lives and their spirits were hardened. Besides, the nanny could not entirely put out of her mind the evening she had overheard the grandmother, unusually querulous, complaining that Andrée was unhealthily besotted with the child, that it did a baby no good to be doted on like that.

A mere nanny, the girl took lunch but not dinner with the family and her opportunities of observing the child's uncle were curtailed. He seldom ate lunch, preferring to work in the room set aside for his office. He struck her as a chilly man, one who worked hard, *very* hard, and was perpetually striving to prove his worth. Both sons were directors of the family business but Andrée's husband was valued more, that was plain for anyone to see. The nanny felt sorry for, but slightly afraid of, the unemotional, industrious man who was not his father's favourite. She was not surprised when he imported another secretary to work alongside his personal assistant and made a great show of the amount of work he was handling. Not surprised, but disdainful.

Almost two months after the disappearance of the child, Judge Georges Laroche telephoned the château to speak to the child's father. The father was away and he was put through to the uncle. Impeded by his stammer, controlling it with breathy

9

pauses that made his delivery absurd, Laroche gave the news. '*M'sieu*, I regret . . . to inform you . . . that we have . . .'

What he had hoped to say without comedy was that the police had found the body of a little girl.

TWO

1990, Prague

Their circular escape brought them back to tease him. They forced him to lean out further over the bridge, his hands futile as the gulls swerved. He set a steadying palm on the parapet, flung the next fistful of crumbs into the air, nearer. He grabbed. Gulls sheared like sparks on the wind but his left hand had closed on leathery legs. Agitated wing beats stilled as he swung the bird upside down, lowered it to his bag on the ground, secured the ring around the leg. He looked into the eye, bright as a seed, and then launched the bird into the November air.

Then he noticed Rose. She was a few yards away, exactly where she stood the afternoon before and the one before that. Her good clothes and expensive haircut singled her out from the local women, her demeanour from the tourists. They held the gaze briefly, cut away from each other by language and custom. Then he turned to the clamouring gulls, there was a skein of crumbs, he lunged and the birds wheeled.

Rose drew her scarf closer. There was damp in the air, that and the unhealthy tang of smoke from soft brown coal. She knew the man was not coming, that he let her waste time and hope, and yet she allowed him five minutes more. She stayed motionless, watching the gull catcher in the dying of the light. Statues along the bridge grew indistinct, altering shape until baroque saints and kings were remade as beggars, each with an importuning hand.

The Vltava had changed from blue-grey to gun-metal and the frothy line of the weir was a smudge. Rose checked the figures traipsing towards her from the left. Seeing their gait was enough. Dawdlers were tourists. Locals sped on with no need to ogle the hilltop castle or gold-glinting roofline. Maybe a fishing boat swaying out from the shore caught an eye, or the pulsing

11

lights of the children's ride, the curiously named Loch Ness Monster, in the park on Kampa Island. But mostly they hurried on, intent on thought rather than scenery.

She saw no one with the hesitant, questioning approach of a fugitive man coming to meet an unfamiliar woman.

The murmur of a guitar, a girl's thin soprano. Rose looked to her right. The girl was a student, defying the cold in a home-made mini skirt and shining tights. Lamplight flashed colours from her legs, making them ripple like river water with her movements. Her guitar case lay open for alms. Passers-by passed her by.

Abruptly the gull catcher abandoned his quest to number and to know, he gathered his belongings and left. Rose also moved, towards the girl. The singer's head was tilted up, she might have been directing her song at a listener on the castle ramparts. Her voice was true but tender. Rose trickled a few coins into the empty case. She wished she could understand the words.

Across the bridge lay shelter and warmth, her favourite *kavárna*. Not the nearest one, she must walk as far as the square but . . .

'Rose!'

A fair man in an overcoat was in front of her, gabbling a greeting in accented English. 'Rose, whatever are you doing here? I expect to find you in London – Paris, maybe. But *Prague*?'

She gathered her wits. 'And you, Willi? Why aren't you in Frankfurt?'

He laughed. 'Yes, it's confusing when people pop up in the wrong places.'

'Come and have a coffee with me and tell me what you're doing in the wrong place.'

He did not tell her precisely. He said he was persuading writers from East Germany to let his company publish novels about life there as Communism withered. She did not blame him for being vague. Why offer details to a journalist?

She asked: 'Are they actually being written, these novels?'

12

A hand extended in despair. 'They tell me no. They say it's too soon.'

'I see.'

'Well, I tell you, Rose, I don't see. They have a story to tell, they have a publisher begging them to please tell it. At last they can have their say, there are no difficulties in their way. And yet . . .'

'They have a lot of experience to assimilate before they can take a novelist's view.'

'Oh, not you too, Rose. How fast do *you* assimilate your experience and write about it? Days? Hours?'

'Willi, you might just have pinpointed the difference between a journalist and a novelist.' She looked at her watch, calculating how soon she must leave.

Disappointed, he objected. 'And now, I suppose, you're going to behave like a journalist and run away? And I shan't see you again until we meet by accident in one of the capitals of Europe?'

She teased in return. 'No, I have plenty of time. Well, enough for you to tell me the rest.'

Caution crept in. 'The rest?'

'Yes,' she said, in the same light way. 'Non-fiction, for instance. Surely you're not only interested in novels?'

'Ah.' He leaned forward. 'You sound like a woman who's found something out.'

'I see I've made an intelligent deduction. There's good business for you if you can get those novels, but there's a fortune if you can buy the memoirs of certain other people who've been out of reach until now.'

'You're going to name names, Rose?'

'We both know them, Willi.'

With a gesture he conceded. 'OK. Well, I can forget the old one because he died in Russia in the eighties. That's genuine, not gossip. But if I can track down the other one, then . . .'

'And can you track him?'

13

He was about to explain when realization intercepted. Instead he said: 'No better than you can, Rose. No better than that.'

'And that, I'm afraid, hasn't been very successful so far.'

'So, do we go on together, seeking this unholy grail? Partners or rivals, Rose? Which is it to be?'

'Unless one of us succeeds, it scarcely matters.'

'Unless? *Until*, surely. We know he's alive, we believe he's in Europe. A man cannot disappear.'

'Willi, this one, I recall, was rather good at that.'

'To hop over a wall into sanctuary is not to vanish. And now there are no walls.'

They compared notes. They had both been drawn to Prague by the information that Krieger was there, that he slipped over the border with the hordes escaping the Honecker regime and was living quietly in the city. They had both acquired contacts who were to take them to him. And they had both been let down.

Rose asked: 'How much longer will you stay here, Willi?'

'Three days, then I must stop acting like a character in an out-moded spy story. I can return soon but I hate to go back to my office without a deal, you know. And you?'

'Until Friday. Then it's Rome.'

She had already described how much she was enjoying the new job, setting up a weekly news magazine based in Paris. In a few weeks' time it would be different, she would write again as she had for the London papers, but in the meantime she was travelling, hiring staff and stringers in key cities, organizing offices and lines of communication, smoothing the path ahead. And always, inevitably, seeking stories. An exclusive interview with one of the most mysterious figures from the Cold War years was the perfect prize, the certain way to ensure the magazine's reputation from the outset. And she was close to it, she sensed she was indeed close.

Willi said: 'Then perhaps we have time for dinner?'

They referred the matter to their diaries but could not match

14

spare time. Impish, she said: 'A walk in the park, then, early tomorrow morning? That's all that's on offer.'

She was more than half-surprised when he agreed.

Rose crossed the bridge alone. Upriver, downriver, cars blinked across the chain of bridges. Floodlight on towers, domes and spires made the evening city a fairytale. But it was that, anyway: a decorative delight designed, surely, by a *pâtissier* rather than an architect. She leaned on the sandstone parapet beside the figure of St Wenceslas, where the gull catcher had made birds fly round and round.

Until Friday. Then Rome. Until Friday she would enjoy Golden Prague, then wrench away to the pressures and pace of Rome. Her diary for next week was full. The magazine had established an office there, she was spared the minutiae of that, but there were people to meet: politicians, businessmen, a film director. If she bumped into another old friend, as she had bumped into Willi, she would have no time for him either.

A pity, she thought. A pity about Willi, one of the more appealing men who recurred in her life. Friendship was tempered with flirtation that teetered on the brink of something deeper, and it was nice that way. There was much to be said for a relationship as speculative as that one.

Rose reached the Old Town Tower at the end of the bridge. The enterprising young, trading in costume jewellery, paintings of the bridge, and Red Army uniforms 'liberated' from the barracks on the hill, were packing up for the night. She joined a couple of them, burdened with their fold-up tables and their bags, at traffic lights beneath scaffolding. Listening, understanding not a word, she fancied they were comparing the day's takings, swapping the daft remarks made by tourists. Then the lights changed and she sauntered away from them, into the traffic-free lanes. Dvořák's *Slavonic Dances* drifted from a *vinárna*. People clustered outside a theatre promising an evening of Mozart. Melodic Czech conversation mingled with the harshness of German and once, only once, she plucked out a phrase of English. She loved it.

'Rose, you'll hate the job,' John Blair had warned her. 'It sounds all right, of course it does. But you won't be swanning around Paris or Rome all the time. You'll spend most of it in airports trying to get in or out of places like Warsaw.'

She had seen through it at once. The job was tailor-made for him and he had not been offered it. But she sidestepped an argument about his motives and sought his opinion of a French politician with provocative ideas. Rose Darrow and John Blair could still talk on professional matters although the rest had fizzled out.

She was twenty-eight, had made her name fast as an incisive questioner who cut through flummery, a tough reporter with physical and moral courage. Not that she had claimed any of this for herself. Complimented, she mumbled about luck. A bit of that luck was running into John Blair on one of her first assignments. She stuck close and learned, the best way a journalist can learn the job, from someone who is good.

'Partners or rivals?' Willi asked her just now. With John Blair the question was never put and the situation sometimes seemed one thing and sometimes the other. Sharing a flat for a year – spaşmodically, when he touched base in London – she intended a partnership and was angered when she met rivalry. It was a disastrous love affair but it improved her work. When the competition is hard to beat, you raise your game.

'What's she like?' she once heard a reporter ask, thinking she was out of earshot.

And his colleague replied with simple praise: 'She's a good operator.'

Rose arrived at her hotel in Wenceslas Square. From a drab foyer stairs rose to an art deco restaurant. A squat man with pronounced Slav features sat over a beer. A young couple weighed the merits of apple strudel against abstinence. But the woman Rose had come to meet was not there. She went to her room, fitted in a telephone call to the magazine in Paris. The elfin Joelle, everybody's assistant, took the call.

'Having a good day, Rose?'

'Not at all bad,' she lied, skating round wasted time, broken appointments.

'Good. I could tell you what we've been doing here but some-one would kill me.'

There was the scuffle of the receiver being taken from Joelle's hand, a giggle. A man rasped: 'Rosie? Signed up that spy yet, have you?'

'Couldn't find my prey, Larry. Tomorrow, I promise.' She pictured him: flabby body, flushed bulldog face. A good thing the days of phone tapping by the Czech police were over. He was not a man given to discretion.

'Hmm. Well, quick about it. We don't want to be at the back of the queue on this one.'

'Sure, Larry, that's what I thought.'

He remembered it was her idea in the first place. 'Oh. Yes. Well, what's the hold-up?'

'He isn't walking the streets offering his services to passing journalists.'

'But you and Krieger are actually in the same city, aren't you?'

Rose drew a deep breath. Larry's tightrope act between jok-iness and outright sarcasm was wearing. She foresaw a future in which she slapped him down. Good God, she had been obliged to spell out to him the importance of Krieger, that's how much on the ball Larry was.

She said: 'The portents are good, Larry. But look, is there anything we have to discuss right now, because I'm supposed to be meeting a contact downstairs?'

'Well, er, Steve wants a word. Hang on.'

Soft spoken after Larry's brashness, Steve came on. Now she pictured whippet slimness, receding red hair. Straightaway she detected the tone of a man moving on to dangerous territory. The friendly greeting, the gently, gently circumlocutions. What the hell was he leading up to?

'Rose, something came up today. I thought we ought to men-tion it . . .'

And then her stomach muscles were tightening, ready for the blow, for the undefined attack on her composure.

'Crossfire,' she heard him say. And something about an ambulance. But the sense kept evaporating from his words.

'No!' she broke out. 'John Blair doesn't get *shot*.'

Steve's words again, explaining. And her mind's refusal to come to terms with facts. When the call ended, the conversation winding down in a mechanical way, she found herself rigid, listening to the throb of the empty line. Slowly, seen from a great distance, her hand lowered the receiver, relinquished it.

Her mouth framed the ugly word. 'Shot.' But it was inaudible and she did not believe in it. The people *she* knew did not get shot. Especially not John Blair, clever, lucky John Blair.

Rose poured a glass of water. The glass swayed on its way to her mouth. Steve's words were eddying, she needed them fixed and examined. He had said ambulance and he had said hospital and he had said critical. He had not said dead.

She clung to that. She snatched up the telephone, set it down again, afraid of appearing incompetent as well as shaken if she made Steve go through it again, and she was virtually sure he had not named the hospital. All right, the town then.

A small town, a nothing sort of place in Spain. Political frustration vented in war in the streets. Crossfire. Critical.

Douglas Somebody, that was who she needed. She dug details out of her contacts book, rang her former colleague in Madrid. The phone rang and rang without answer. He was probably in the no place town, anyway. She gulped the rest of the water, rang Steve after all.

'Hold on, Rose, I'll check.' But the fax did not say where the hospital was.

The woman who should have called at the hotel earlier arrived. Rose talked to her in the bar, then went with her to meet people who were potentially useful, took two of them to dinner, and all the while strenuously shoved aside the shattering news.

Alone, finally, walking back to the hotel, she crystallized her yearning to go to Spain. John Blair was a freelance, probably working alone. There might be no one with him if she did not go.

People were streaming from theatres and concerts, coming out of restaurants. They grouped around folk singers in the squares or gathered by shop windows. But she was unaware of them, her thoughts channelled into getting to Spain rapidly. Flying direct from Prague tomorrow? Via Paris? Any way it could be done, she would do it.

Young Germans, loud in horseplay, cut her concentration. And then: 'Willi!' she thought. 'He didn't give me a telephone number. I can't cancel our meeting.'

She kept it. The morning was bitter, the statues in the park rimed with the first frost of winter. Rose looked down the hill through flaring foliage. Gilded cupolas and red roofs floated on river-mist. A man and his dog drifted by her in the steamy cloud of their own breath. A woman in a dun-coloured coat limped along a lower path, an empty shopping bag slung over an arm. No one else came in sight until she saw Willi's fair hair and dark overcoat bobbing towards her. His eagerness touched her.

'Rose, you're inspired,' he said, undeterred by the ice. 'To make me meet you in a park by a castle on such a memorably beautiful morning. Now, all we must do is decide how together we may trap Krieger, force him to sign a book contract with me and grant you an interview, and the day will be perfect. Isn't that so?'

'John Blair died this morning,' she said.

THREE

Identity reduced to three words on a stone. Years of experience and dreaming distilled to just that. And the elements would smooth the words away.

Rose bit a lip and switched her attention from the headstone beside her to the funeral. She was off the tarmac path, damp earth sucking at the heels of her shoes. But she was not close enough to see what was happening nor to hear more than the occasional line of the service. Breath stained the air, mourners squeezed into gaps between graves, a bowing laurel became a screen.

He fleeth as it were a shadow, and never continueth in one stay.

The funeral director's men had lined the paths with wreaths, balanced them against graves, leaned them around the tree. John Blair was missed in all the offices of what was still sometimes inaccurately referred to as Fleet Street. He was lamented in all the anxious places of the world where reporters gathered.

In the midst of life we are in death.

Shoe leather scuffed on the path behind her. Rose allowed herself a backward glance. A photographer winked. Her glance took in a press of faces, youngish people (where *did* old journalists go?) and bulky layers of clothes that failed to keep the biting air at bay. She had felt on the periphery but discovered she was relatively near the front.

Deliver us not into the bitter pains of eternal death.

She wondered whose choice Highgate Cemetery was. Not John's, surely, but how could she know? That was not the kind of thing they talked about. There had been too much life to consider, the mechanisms of death never intruded. Asked to guess, she would have nominated the country churchyard in the village where his family had lived. Perhaps Christina, the ex-wife, knew better. It did not matter, anyway. All of it was irrelevant, unconvincing, because at any moment she would spot him among the unwieldy group, late as often before, side-tracked by the demands of news-gathering and scrambling to keep an appointment in the nick of time. But he always did manage it, with more luck than prudence.

Thou knowest Lord the secrets of our hearts.

Ahead of her people bent their heads and avoided looking at each other. Rose's hand clenched. The peculiar quality of the silence explained what she could not see, the business of lowering the coffin. Then the clergyman's voice again, the *ashes to ashes* bit, the *everlasting glory*, on to the final amen. And then the difficult, long hesitation before people felt free to break away, confess their vitality.

'The old words,' said a bundle of clothes Rose recognized as a fashion editor. 'They said the proper words over him. He'd have preferred that.'

'You know, Rose,' said the photographer who had winked, 'the most unbelievable thing about this is that he caught it in Spain. When you think of all the trouble spots he'd been to it's plain silly. Like the steeplejack who broke his neck falling out of bed.'

'What was he doing there?'

'Nobody knows. In fact, we'd decided he was working on something for that comic you're involved with.'

She let the gibe pass. 'No. We hadn't been in touch for months but I'd have known if he was on an assignment for us.'

'Bit of a mystery then.'

They drew close to the cemetery gate. Another hearse was entering. They stepped aside to let it by. The photographer laid his palm on a granite slab. 'Want a lift into town, Rose? I'm parked up the lane.'

'Thanks but so am I.' She read the stone words beneath his hand. Legible but the carving no longer sharp. In a few short years, oblivion.

Mourners from the graveside caught up with them. Christina

21

cut across to Rose. 'A few people are coming back to the restaurant, do join us.'

Christina had closed the business for the day, provided a buffet lunch. People stood in knots, self-consciously keeping their voices low as a sign of respect or seriousness or, in a number of cases, awe at their surroundings.

'Risky,' a sub-editor from one of the Sunday papers whispered in Rose's ear. 'This lot will drink her cellar dry.'

Rose summed him up as a creature who understood nothing about Christina. 'I'll back her to handle the situation.' On the other side of the room a waitress was already collecting wine glasses. Coffee permeated the air.

Rose was gauging how soon to leave. Not among the first because it might be interpreted as callousness, that she had done all that was required by turning up and was losing interest in the affair. But she was wary of lingering too long, fearing maudlin reminiscencers. She could guess who they would be, some of the hard-drinking old hands from the tabloids.

'Oh-oh,' said a man beside her. 'Here comes the Tiny Temptress.'

A very small woman with cropped black hair and long silver ear-rings bore down on them. People moved to let her through. She was small but she would never be insignificant. Rose was startled to be greeted with a hug.

'Maria, how are you?'

'Wonderful, Rose, but you know . . .' And her face was a sad comment on the reason for them being brought together that day.

Rose liked her accent, throatily Spanish. When she sang, which is what Maria did for her living, there was a haunting timbre. Rose had heard her sing at a charity gala. Several times she had seen her across a room. She did not claim to know her, not really, not enough to anticipate that hug.

'Please,' Maria was saying, her dark eyes wide, forcing Rose's

22

sympathetic attention. 'I would like a lift in your car when you leave. There are some things to say.'

Rose sensed the avid interest of the man beside her and disliked it. She did not want an audience if Maria were to lead her into discussing John Blair. Word had reached her months ago that Maria had taken up with John. This, then, was the time to leave, before she was embroiled in a scene with Maria. The woman was famously volatile, everyone told stories about her refusal to be anything but centre stage.

'Where do you need to go?' Rose asked.

'My flat's in Kensington.'

'Fine. I'll say goodbye to Christina.'

Other people were moving off, Christina accepting condolences or gratitude for her hospitality, whichever those leaving thought more appropriate in the far from clear circumstances. Christina was all well-bred poise topped up with professionalism. She turned to Rose. Rose had not reached her own decision about what to say but Christina spared her with: 'John and I were hopeless together but at least I always knew he was there. Now I don't.'

Rose squeezed her hand.

In the car Maria fumbled with the seat belt. She was childlike, not because she was five foot nothing but because of her apparent helplessness, her little-girl ways. Rose did not find any of this attractive. She started up the engine.

'OK, Maria. What are these things you have to say?'

Maria gave her the round-eyed look again. 'I want to talk about John.'

Well, obviously. Rose said 'Yes?' in an encouraging manner.

'Today some people were saying no one knew why he was in Spain.'

'But you think you know?'

'He went to France. I think he was investigating something in France.'

'Did he say what?'

23

'He said he had an idea about something and was going to ask around.'

Rose struggled not to sound exasperated. 'Do you remember where he was going to do this asking around?'

'Paris, for sure. He flew to Paris.'

'He might have flown there and picked up a car and driven somewhere completely different.'

'No, he was going to do some work in Paris.' A sidelong look at Rose. 'I thought he was going to see you.'

Rose shook her head. He had not done so. He left messages at her office but she did not return his calls. She shied away from thinking about the implications of that.

'Maria, did John say which newspaper or magazine he was working for?' She had never known him to finance a trip himself, an editor was sure to have commissioned the story.

Maria could not answer that either. They travelled a mile in silence before she said: 'He sent me postcards. Would you like to see them?'

Rose expected them to be produced from the bag on Maria's lap but they were at the flat. They might not add anything to the sum of her knowledge about John Blair's last story but they would allow her to satisfy her curiosity about a part of his life since they split up. She accepted Maria's offer.

'I'll make some coffee,' said Maria. 'Oh, please, Rose, stop here. I must buy some more coffee.'

Rose hovered on a yellow line while Maria took her time in the delicatessen. Through the window she could see her moving snail-like around the shop, joining the checkout queue, giving up her place to fetch another item, rejoining the queue which by this time had doubled. Rose gritted her teeth and thought about the things she would far rather be doing with her afternoon. She felt a fool to be going to Maria's flat, there was no reason for her to do it. The cards might embarrass her with their joking personal messages to another woman. What did she want from them? Hardly information. Perhaps the momentary pleasure of seeing his handwriting again, a final oblique contact?

Maria made a show of running to the car with her plastic carrier bag.

'Oh, the queue,' she moaned, oblivious of Rose's clear view into the shop. 'Did you have to battle with traffic wardens? They are devils here.'

Rose pulled out into the traffic. 'Where do I turn off?'

'First on the left. Then right.'

They had turned right and were crawling, seeking a parking space, when the world changed. Shards of metal ripped through the air. A young tree lurched at a crazy angle. A pall of dust and fragments obliterated the scene. As the thud reached her ears, deafened her, Rose felt the car buffeted, thrust sideways until it slammed into a parked vehicle and shuddered to a standstill. The last thing she heard was the long, thin howl of a woman, a woman in pain.

The passenger window was blown. Maria sparkled with jagged scraps of it. Rose nearly shook her to stop her screaming but drew back from the danger. The front of Maria's grey coat was darkened with damp patches, on her chest and her thighs.

Rose shouted at her to shut up. The scream dropped to a whimper.

'You'll be all right,' Rose said firmly, wishing it true. 'I'm going to undo your seat belt.'

Gingerly she fiddled with the clasp, picking shards out of the way before daring to grip. She kept her eye on the stains, measuring whether they were spreading, questioning whether it was safe to move Maria or whether she should sit there until an ambulance came.

A woman appeared the other side of the shattered window. 'Are you all right?' She registered the wet coat and Maria who was flopped back and moaning. 'Oh, God,' the woman said and withdrew.

Rose struggled out of the car, squeezing between the buckled door and the parked van. The street that had been empty was filling with onlookers. Cautious onlookers, though, who mostly kept a safe distance from the torn-up tree and the piles of tangled metal beyond it. Unlike lightning, terrorists were known to strike the same place twice. Above the undercurrent of quiet voices, a siren sounded.

Rose opened Maria's door, what remained of the window tipping into the road as she moved it. 'Maria?'

'Get me out, get me out.'

'No, don't move. The police will be here in a moment.'

'*Now*, let me out now.' She shifted in the seat, began to lift her feet over the sill.

Maria fell forward. Rose grabbed at her, catching her glittering shoulder and feeling glass embed itself in a fingertip. Maria's foot was caught around the carrier bag in the footwell. Her shoe skidded on its slipperiness as she attempted to sit upright. Rose steadied her, then lifted the bag. Milk spewed out of a slash in its side. She dumped it in the road.

'Oh, God,' said Maria, swinging her legs out after it. 'What a mess.'

She began shaking glass off her coat. In the damp areas it clung. 'Rose, help me take this off.'

Maria shrugged her way out of her coat. Her dress was unmarked. Open mouthed, Rose stared at the smooth green perfection of the dress. Maria was mumbling about the damage to her coat.

'It stains, milk. And I bought this coat only a month ago.'

'*Milk?*'

'I crushed the carton. It went all over me.'

'But it looked like . . .'

'I must take this to the dry cleaners. But the one round the corner's terrible. They ruined my skirt. No, I must take this to the Six Star dry cleaners. It's very expensive.'

The woman who had peered into the wreckage returned with a police constable and was disappointed to discover the victims unscathed and complaining about the exorbitant cost of dry cleaning.

Maria's flat was in a house next to the uprooted tree. The blast had turned the garden wall into rubble and mangled a car on the

26

drive. In spite of protests from the police, who were cordoning off the area, Maria clambered over the garden and opened the front door.

Her flat was on the ground floor. It had lost its front windows. The scene reminded Rose of photographs of the blitz. A heavy sliver of glass was wedged between pillow and duvet, where Maria's neck would have been if she had been in bed.

'We'll forget the coffee, Rose. I have some brandy.'

'And a plaster?' She had picked the glass out of her finger but it was bleeding freely.

Once the finger was dressed, Rose followed Maria into the rear room, a big square one opening on to a brick terrace and a shaded garden. A Christmasy robin hopped on to the arm of a Victorian cast-iron chair and made one of those characteristic robin twitches with its wings. Maria held out a tumbler into which she had poured a couple of inches of brandy.

Rose sank into the comfort of a fat, squashy sofa. 'This is turning into one hell of a day.' Nice British understatement, always handy to fall back on when events defy sensible comment.

She was leaden, muddled, unsure why she was in the flat. After a couple of searing mouthfuls she began to recover.

Sitting against the light, hands folded around her glass, Maria was talking, on and on, calmly but compulsively talking in her imperfect English about the experience they had shared. Rose let the sense elude her, listened simply to the rise and fall of the voice with its trilling 'r's and hidden aitches. The pictures in her mind were of the second before obliteration, when the explosion ripped at cars and walls and vegetation and the fragments that broke free were dancing in the air.

She realized Maria had dried up. Perhaps a question had been asked, at any rate a contribution was called for. Rose said: 'It's a nuisance about the car.' Ought she to ring her insurance company immediately? No, let it wait. What difference could it make?

'Oh, it was a terrible car.' Maria meant the one on the drive.

Rose's questions were cut off by a visit from the police. Whose car had been parked outside? Maria told them it was hers. Who lived in the other two flats? She said a television editor and his girlfriend were on the top floor and an engineer and his wife on the first.

The session was short and preliminary, the police said they would be back later. Maria explained she was working that evening at a club and they wrote down the times she was available.

While they talked, Rose telephoned the insurance company and then a reporter on one of the morning papers. 'The police say a bomb was attached to Maria's car. They have an eyewitness who claims it went up when a cat ran underneath it.'

'Who'd want to kill Maria?' And he added frivolously: 'Her voice isn't that bad.'

'Ha, ha. Listen, Colin, none of the people who live in the house now sound like candidates for assassination but have a look in the files for Linda Asprey.'

'The actress?'

'She owned the flat before Maria bought it. She married an MP.'

'Great. Any more, Rose?'

'Oh, come on. You've got to do some of it yourself.'

'Yes, but what about . . .'

'Over to you, Colin. Bye.' She hung up. She told Maria: 'I have to go. Will you be all right?'

Maria had replenished their glasses. 'You're forgetting the cards.'

And so she was. Rose sat down again, sipped, waited while Maria went into the glass-strewn bedroom and returned with two postcards John Blair had sent her on his last trip abroad.

One was a view of the Seine and postmarked Paris. The date was either the 13th or the 18th of September, his figures were unclear. Maria knelt by Rose as she read it. The message amounted to a quip about the weather and the suggestion that he was getting nowhere and was likely to return to London soon if things did not improve.

The second was from Nice on 20th October. He said every-thing was coming together very nicely and that he could be back in Paris before long.

But he had not been. He had gone further south, to Spain, and he had been lured to a town in turmoil and he had died there.

Both messages ended with 'love' and the squiggle that was his signature. But they were not special messages. There was no embarrassment to be endured. Rose smoothed the signature with the ball of her thumb. *Shot.* It made no sense, none of it did.

Maria sat back on her heels. 'Did he send cards to you?'

A shake of the head. 'Not this time.' She wanted to know whether Maria received telephone calls. If there had been no more contact than two postcards in a month, then her relation-ship with John was less fervent that the rumour stipulated.

Maria said: 'He expected to see you in Paris. He hoped you'd help him.'

She was saying things Rose had no wish to hear. Rose held the cards out to her. 'Sorry, Maria, I don't think we're going to get any answers.'

Maria's hands stayed on her lap. 'Take them if they are any use.' The eyes were compelling, she was a child gazing up at an adult and waiting for the world to be put right.

Rose was first tempted, then repelled. She wanted them, no, she could not bear to have them. She compromised. 'I'll copy the words down, in case there are any clues waiting to bubble to the surface. But, quite honestly, I doubt it.' She took out her notebook.

This time Maria accepted the cards and got to her feet. 'I'll call a cab for you.'

They waited, saying little. The things that had anchored them together were over. They would not normally have had any more to say to each other than they did now. Rose shut out all the thoughts that made it worse. She refused to speculate about John Blair sitting on the sumptuous sofa, sharing the wrecked bedroom with Maria. Above all, she resisted asking herself whether matters might have turned out differently if she had responded to his telephone calls when he had tried to reach her in Paris.

She said: 'The police won't let the cab right up to the house, I'd better walk down the road and meet it.'

They went to the front door. Maria paled and pressed a hand to her mouth. 'If we hadn't stopped at the shop, we'd have been killed.'

White tape cordoned off the front of the house, a section of the pavement and road. Uniformed police and others were searching, setting up lights. There were journalists with note-books, microphones and cameras. Before she reached them and gave the obligatory interviews, Rose had to climb over the churned-up garden, past the remains of Maria's car. Maria was right, the extent of the damage emphasized it. If it had not been for her maddening delay in the delicatessen, they would both have died.

FOUR

When Rose Darrow left the flat, Maria locked the door, drew the curtain, put a Bartók string concerto on her CD player, curled up on her sofa, shut her eyes and tried not to cry.

She did not answer the front door when the police returned. She was so far away inside herself that their clamour barely impinged on her consciousness.

Whatever went wrong with her (and things did, repeatedly, drastically) she knew of a deep place where her real 'I' was protected, undamaged. There, at the core, life could not hurt her.

She went in through the layers, sloughing off the immediate surroundings and demands; then the continuing pressures of her existence; and then the fundamental contradictions of her nature that made her way in life unpredictable and hazardous. And she arrived at that point where her true identity, her spirit, lived and sustained her.

Maria did not apply words such as identity or spirit, she dealt in emotion and nourishment rather than language. What she found when all the layers were stripped away was a tranquil, self-contained presence that preferred solitude to applause, that cared not very much what others thought.

The Bartók (it might have been any music, Bartók was what came to hand that afternoon) lifted and soothed her. The total experience was one of enrichment, encouragement.

The urge to tears disappeared. She relaxed, her hunched limbs freed and the puckering lines of her face smoothed away. An inner voice spoke to her in plain phrases of reassurance. She was safe, it said; she could not be harmed; everything would be all right; she was doing well with her life; she need not care about trivialities; she would thrive. The voice did not address her as Maria. There was another name, a baby name, a pet name for a girl child. Only one other person in all the world knew her by this name that she called herself, and she had never met him.

The music ended. She sat in silence for a while. The afternoon was unusually quiet because the sounds of traffic, changing gear at the end of the road and racing down the terrace, were replaced by the softer sounds of men exploring the aftermath of the explosion. Once or twice a voice called to a colleague further off but did not distract her.

She mouthed the private name, her secret since childhood. When she was very young she imagined that everybody owned an outside name and an inside name. And when she learned this was not so she wondered whether there might not once have been two of her, perhaps a twin sister who had died.

But her mother laughed off the idea of twins and remarked that one of her kind was more than enough.

Yet what was her kind? She was different from other children, she was aware of it from a young age. There was something, some*one*, within her that set her apart. She played in the Andalusian dust with her black-eyed peers and marvelled at her separateness.

Easter. A village cramped in a ravine, buildings forced in there under the pressure of a giant's heel. Thyme and papery cistus grow wild in the huge emptiness of the *serranía*, but it is Easter and the peace is threatened by the heartbreaking beat of a drum.

Maria is on her father's shoulders for a clear view as the procession trudges towards them. She is terrified. *Cristo* is leaving his church, tossed clumsily on a tide of penitential pointed heads. The sorrow and the blood are drawing closer to her with every swaying step of the cortège, and each step is marked with the thud of the drum, a thud that is amplified by the crushed-together houses and the rocky slabs that soar above. Each beat is a pain through her body. She feels her heart struck and shaken loose inside her.

People appear to be speaking. They are touching each others' arms and inclining their heads in the way people do as they hold conversations in crowds. But she cannot hear them and is unable to speak, to cry out, to demand to be carried away or set down and enabled to run free. All she can do is stare at the approaching horror. Because the road slopes up to where her father stands, she is level with the lurching blood-streaked face and the crown of thorns.

The crowd parts. She is astonished to discover the procession is led by a pair of hucksters. She recognizes them, they bring their wares to the village sometimes and set up stalls. But today their stalls are tiny tables that they can pick up and run with. They race a hundred feet towards her and drop the tables. People dart forward to buy nuts and sweets. Then, when the hooded monsters are three rhythmic steps away, the crowd falls back, the tables are picked up, there is a brief dash and the business of making a few *pesetas* out of the festival resumes.

Now that the procession is upon her, there are other sounds besides the drum. She can hear the *swish, swish, swish* as the shoes of the arm-linked penitents brush over the ground, and there is a gasp of their laboured breathing because the Easter burden is a heavy one.

'You're getting too heavy for this,' says her father, settling her down on a wall once they are past. He rubs his neck and then works the muscles of his shoulders. She clings to him, her hand straying over his harsh black hair. His best jacket feels rough too. It has reddened the backs of her legs.

The hooded figures stab their way into her dreams. For months she is afraid she might meet them, the streets become dangerous to her. But gradually she makes herself brave, echoing adult words from other times. 'Don't be frightened. Nothing is going to hurt you.' The comforting voice in her head does not call her Maria, there is another older name and she is more content with it.

The telephone brought Maria back to the present. The nightclub manager had heard about the bomb blast and wanted to know whether she was all right. She told him she was fine, she would be along at the usual time.

It was not one of her best performances. She was unsettled, tense. Kind questions about her near-escape kept it to the fore-front of her mind. Her throat was tightening and she feared losing her voice. For a time she hung around the dressing room but the mirrors troubled her. She was too short. She was too thin, scrawny like a sparrow. She was ugly with that wide mouth and large eyes. She hated her appearance and she would be unable to sing a note. She had to get away from those mir-rors.

Maria paced the corridor, peeped into the club. Pretty full, and all those people would be disappointed, and broadcast their disappointment, when she failed to find her voice. Ah, there he was again. Mike Lowry, the television presenter, was with a man she did not recognize and two actresses she did. It was almost time for her to go on but she returned to the dressing room and scribbled a note. Before she stepped into the spot-light, she handed it to a waiter.

Maria was into her opening number before Lowry unfolded the sheet of paper and read: 'Let's have lunch tomorrow.' When she was taking her applause, he nodded his reply.

Somehow she got through the evening. Her voice was not under her control, she was tremulous. An evening to forget.

In her dressing room Lowry's note awaited her. '*Christina's* at one,' he suggested.

Maria gave a wail that became a laugh. Of all the restaurants in London he had nominated the only one she wished to avoid because of its associations, the one owned by John Blair's ex-wife.

John Blair had been a mistake. He was attractive, he was a name, he was a success, exactly the kind of man Maria liked to be seen around with. Her mistake was to assume he would be around. In fact, she saw him intermittently, as often as he was in London, but that was seldom.

'Paris is an eye-blink away,' he had said. 'You can pop over.'

But how, when she was at the club in the evenings? When she needed to be in town? And she did need to be because she must keep herself in the gossip columnists' eyes and she had to develop those contacts that ensured that when the season at the nightclub ended there was another engagement to take up. The Kensington flat did not come cheap. She could afford to appear frivolous, a creature of whim, but she could not afford not to work. She did not go to Paris.

Maria allowed Mike Lowry to wait for her for ten minutes, then she left the shop across the road and joined him in *Christina's*. He raised his glass to her. 'To a new friendship,' he said. It could have meant anything.

She saw she was getting his professional act, the charm was indistinguishable from the variety he exuded on screen. Well, so be it. She expected professional favours from him. Whether or not he or his producer succumbed to her desire to appear on the chat show he hosted, she would be seen around with him. Her identity as one of London's magic circle would be enhanced because of her proximity to him. That was how she always chose her men.

John Blair had said to her on the telephone: 'I can't get back this weekend after all. The story is piecing together nicely but I have to catch a man who'll be in Nice on Saturday. I'll be thinking of you.'

She doubted it. He had more interesting things on hand than her opening night. Anyway, she picked up a rock critic who was in the audience and this led, by a circuitous route, to a profile in one of the quality Sundays. The quotes were tediously inaccurate and the photograph made her look fifteen, but no matter. Half a million newspaper readers, who had not previously heard of her, that day read her name. Good.

Mike Lowry gave her a fine lunch. He paid, of course. They always did, the men who accepted her invitations. No doubt they went into the relationships with their eyes open, knowing

35

there would be more to pay for than meals, that the currency would not always be cash.

Maria was pert and pretty, an eye-catcher. Throughout lunch she drew glances from other customers before they registered who her companion was. She was conscious of it all. It was a propitious start.

Over coffee Mike Lowry asked: 'Were you at Blair's funeral?'

She could not prevent a sideways look down the room. He said: 'It's OK. Christina doesn't appear in person at lunchtimes.'

'Yes, I was there. We came back here afterwards.'

'The ex-wife laid on the funeral meats? Well, well. I'm afraid I had to skip it. I intended to do my duty at the graveside but something came up.'

'Did you know John?'

'Since Oxford. I ran into him from time to time but it must be a year since I last saw him. Any idea what he was doing in Spain? Such a bloody silly place to get killed.'

She had refused Rose Darrow, had decided not to say to her all she had planned. Maria did not understand her decision, it happened without forethought. But she had no compunction about telling Mike Lowry.

'He said he was poking around among the Devereux skeletons. He went from Paris to Nice, but I don't know how he ended up in Spain.'

Lowry stopped dead at the name of Devereux. There was acute interest in his eyes as he asked her to confirm: 'The perfume family?'

'Yes. But he teased, he wouldn't say what the skeletons were. Do you know, Mike?'

He hunched his shoulders. 'Big business usually stinks, even the perfume business, I guess. Blair may have had an idea about a shady deal. Hardly worth dying for.' With a look he summoned the waiter and the bill.

The taxi dropped Maria at her flat and took Lowry on to a BBC television studio. The first thing he did there was pick up the telephone.

'Rose? Mike Lowry here.'

'A voice from the past if ever I heard one. How are you?'

'Fine. Listen, why was John Blair chasing the Devereux family?'

'Was he?'

'Oh, come on, everyone knows he was working for your outfit.'

'They do?'

'No keeping a secret in a little place like London, Rose. You ought to know by now.'

'I learn something new every day, Mike. Where did you pick this up?'

'A young lady whispered the name of Devereux in my ear over lunch. Now, please, what was John after?'

'Why are you concerned with the House of Devereux?'

'I have a little old lady aunt who's put her life savings into the company.'

'You're a liar, Mike.'

'So nothing's changed.'

'Try the truth, just this once.'

'Must I?'

'Dare you.'

He pretended to tussle with it, gave an enormous sigh of mock anguish. 'Well, if you insist. We're planning something on them for next year. Me fronting it, striding about among the petals and the pongs and discussing how they made their mega-millions and how they spend them. Or don't spend them, as the case increasingly is. If there's a problem, if we've got it all wrong and they're about to go bust or they've fallen foul of the law in a serious way, then the sooner we know the better. Between friends, Rose, what do you know?'

'Rather less than you hope, I'm afraid.'

'Right now anything would do. Give me the smidgeon you have.'

His persistence was intriguing. Then she got it. 'Hey, you're looking for a way out. You don't fancy striding about among the petals and the pongs, do you?'

He owned up. 'I think it's the most boring notion they've offered me in a decade. Apart from that, I love it.'

'But it's a better story if they go bust or go to jail.'

'Sure, but then it wouldn't fit my slot. They'd get someone else to do it. Promise me, Rose, if you hear something firm on this you'll give me a call.'

She said she would. Then: 'In anticipation of my future help, Mike, tell me the name of your lunchtime companion.'

'Oh, you wouldn't know her. She's a singer called Maria Flores.'

Rose choked back surprise and protest. Maria! So why had she . . .

Once Lowry rang off, Rose dialled Maria's number, determined to pin her down about John Blair and the Devereux family. There was no answer.

Maria was at her dining table, a pad of writing paper in front of her, twiddling a fountain pen in her hand as she sought a phrase. Her telephone was beside her but its trailing flex ended in a creamy coil a few inches short of the jack point.

She crouched over the paper and began to write again. There was no address to top the letter, only a date. She was writing about her singing, not the dire performance of the night before but about the joy and fulfilment of beguiling an audience.

Letters to him were always like this. Her life was dealt with elliptically, sensations taking the place of facts. She never talked as intimately as she wrote to him, baring her emotions, sketching her dreams. If ever they met, he would not know her. But they never had met and she was sure they never would. He never replied to her letters either.

FIVE

New York. An artist's loft. In the centre rose a giant bubble-pack half-finished. The thing was white plastic with twelve clear plastic bubbles. Nothing was in the bubbles, yet.

Ellie paraded around it, sniffed the whiff of adhesive in the air. She heard a sound. Sam had come to stand in the doorway.

'The Queen,' said Ellie.

'A computer.'

She tipped her head in agreement, sunlight gleaming on the bell of platinum hair. Then: 'How many do you have now?'

'Monroe. Mandela. A bar code. Charlie Chaplin. Er . . .'

'You're forgetting Presley and Che Guevara.'

'Yes. Maybe I'm not sure of those.'

'You can't quarrel with Che Guevara. Did you decide about the Dali soft watch?'

'Yes, it's in. What about Hitler, did we vote him in or out?'

'We? This is yours, Sam.'

He came across and slid an arm around where he guessed her waist to be beneath the cuddly sweater. They were both facing the bubble-pack. He said: 'And I was dumb enough to think it was going to be simple, picking twelve icons of the twentieth century.'

'It would have been. You'd have found it very easy indeed if I hadn't pointed out that all your first choices were American images.'

Sam moved away, running a hand through his springy hair. 'Hmm, I'm still sore about junking Mickey Mouse.'

Ellie told him she had just got in, that she was planning to put food in the oven and then do some work. He stayed by the bubble-pack, thoughtful.

39

'Hm? Oh, sure. You know, Ellie, I'm not convinced about Chaplin. I mean not at the expense of Kennedy.'

'I'll make some tea.'

The kitchen was downstairs. She expected Sam to join her but when he didn't she carried a tray up to the studio. Sam was prowling around *Icons of the Twentieth Century, sans* icons.

Ellie poured two cups and passed him one. He was not helpless or lazy but whenever she was there he expected every comfort provided. Ellie fully intended to change that. Somehow she never got around to making an issue of it. He was rather worse in this respect than her other men, but better in bed. Occasionally she challenged this, accusing herself of comparing each one unfavourably with his immediate predecessor. But it was true that he was a better lover.

'Sam, am I interrupting genius at work or can we talk?'

'Let's talk.' He rested his weight on a window sill, could not stop his eyes centring on the bubble-pack.

She was annoyed. Of course, it was his single-mindedness, which is to say selfishness, that enabled him to create the sculptures. She understood but it irked her to be accorded less attention than a sheet of white plastic with a dozen gaping spaces.

She said: 'Sam, I want to go back to London.'

That got his attention all right. He dumped the cup and saucer and stared at her with undisguised suspicion. 'You didn't say anything about this.'

'I'm telling you now.'

'Well, how long for?' His way of asking whether she meant she was leaving him permanently.

'I don't know. Maybe a month, maybe two. It's the book. You knew I'd have to go back for that some time.'

She was an art historian writing from a feminist viewpoint. Most of the research was complete before she joined him in New York. He had said: 'The flat's a big space. Three rooms apart from the studio. You'll find a place for your typewriter.' Doubtful, hoping to keep him in London instead, she was coaxed into it.

And it was more or less all right. She had never been to New York before, there were countless distractions and the book was taking for ever. She got stuck.

She went to stand behind the plastic sheet, looked through the clear film of a bubble at Sam against the window.

'I'm stuck,' she said.

'You said that before. You got unstuck.'

'I know. But it didn't come right and I have the feeling it won't until I sit down at my own desk in my own corner of London.'

'Two months?' He fingered the springy hair. 'You'd be back in February for my exhibition?'

'Wouldn't miss it.' She came from behind the bubble-pack, went to him and kissed him. 'Remember to miss me, Sam.'

He drew her to him but she knew that over her shoulder he was concentrating on that damned bubble-pack, focusing on the February show. Until that was over everything else would be purely incidental.

She disentangled herself, carried away the empty cups. 'I'm going to try for a mid-week flight.'

But there was no reply, not even one of Sam's absent-minded grunts.

He reminded her of someone. When she first met him, at an exhibition in London, she had the foolish sensation that here was somebody she already knew, an old friend. And exactly as if he were an old friend, they slipped into conversation and later into love. He was glamorous, exciting, she could learn from him.

The first time he invited her to lunch, they decided on a restaurant near her flat because they both had engagements to keep later. Sam called to collect her but as she picked up her bag the telephone rang. She was arguing with the Gas Board while he reached around her, stroked her breasts.

The man from the Gas Board was protesting in her ear about broken appointments to fix her cooker and Sam was nibbling her other ear while her nipples pressed against his palms. She wriggled away, to score a point against the Gas Board, but Sam's breath was in her hair, his teeth teasing her neck. The man from the Gas Board offered a new date for the fitter to call and she pulled away to reach her diary. Telephone cable wrapped around her, plastic coiling between her breasts. She was facing Sam. He leaned a little back from her and rhythmically squeezed her erect nipples.

As she turned to put down the receiver, she felt a hand slip inside the front of her waistband, Sam drawing her to him. They did not go to the restaurant.

When it was time for him to enter her, she shut her eyes and pictured another man's face, his skin against hers, letting the excitement of Sam's strokes inside her become his, making Sam's sighs and satisfaction his. It was an old game of hers.

All afternoon they made love, Ellie and Sam and the shadow who was there with them, in a way. They ignored appointments, mealtimes, the telephone and door bell. Outside birds sang and traffic built up to rush hour and fell away. Over and over they made love, Sam repeatedly eager, Ellie eagerly responsive. She felt full and soft, and pleasurably sore. The more he took from her, the more there was to give. She draped the quilt around her and knelt on the bedroom floor, her slanting grey eyes watching him dress and leave her.

London did not last long enough. He itched for New York and rather than lose him she tagged along. He was correct, it should not have made any difference to her at that stage of the book where the actual writing took place. It had, though. The same petty discouragements that forced him back to New York for his work were now pulling her to London.

There was an additional factor. The death of John Blair. She had received a call from a woman who understood she would care. John was gone, it made no practical sense to want to be in the city to which he would never return. And yet, and yet, Ellie did, she wanted very much to be in London.

'Life,' John Blair once remarked to her as he prepared to set out on one of his assignments, which she called his adventures, 'is one long inquiry. We're always looking for something we don't know or can't understand. Wouldn't you say so, Ellie?'

There should have been a neat reply but she fluffed it. He laughed at her and told her to finish her drink and have another one, that there was just time before his taxi came to take him to the airport. That was how she remembered him: his teasing, his laughter, the mock profundity that invariably caught her off guard.

To begin with it was the language that tripped her up but once she was committed to staying her English was transformed and she seldom betrayed a foreign accent. She had known John Blair as long as she had been in England. He was guide and instructor, an encouragement, a friend who made her laugh. She was fortunate in that lots of people helped her. But she knew, immediately the call came from London, that the space John Blair left in her life was one that would never be filled.

She took a mid-week flight to London and was settled in her flat for two days before she telephoned Rose Darrow.

'I'm back and I want to say thank you for letting me know about John.'

Rose sounded pleased to hear her, she always did. 'Ellie, I wish I'd thought of it sooner. It suddenly struck me no one else would have remembered either.'

'Or known where to reach me. I've been rather elusive, not the gay gadabout I once was.'

'The book,' said Rose. 'You just held your nose and dived into it. I remember saying how wonderfully disciplined you were.'

'Huh!' said Ellie, thinking about the time-frittering in New York, the getting stuck and then stuck again. 'Can we meet, Rose? I'd love to hear all the things I didn't hear because I was away.'

Rose flipped over the pages of her diary. 'Will tea do? I'm pushed, I'm going to Paris on Sunday. But if we can meet in the Strand this afternoon, I can fit it in before I whizz over to keep an appointment at the Law Courts. Any good?'

Ellie said it was fine. She suggested the café at the Courtauld.

43

She had the excuse she was looking for. It was not worth beginning any serious work with one eye on the clock. Instead, she pocketed a notebook and set out for the Witt library at the Courtauld Institute.

She dressed for the outing, exchanging everyday jeans for a short skirt and leather coat. Her hair was held back from her face with silver combs. Rose Darrow always looked so good, so expensive, and Rose was ten years younger, only twenty-eight.

'I'm being deliciously sidetracked on an idle inquiry about Frans Hals,' Ellie admitted to Rose.

'I didn't know you were interested in the Dutch painters.'

'No, not my field at all, not the seventeenth century, but a question has popped up and won't go away. I know what the Hals experts say but I'd like to see for myself.'

'Explain,' said Rose, sipping Earl Grey.

Ellie said it was a matter of the pendants, male and female portraits designed to hang side by side. In some instances, such as the paintings of Stephanus Geraerdts and his wife Isabella Comyns, there was no room for suspicion that they were anything but a pair. Their eyes speak love, his hand reaches for the rose she offers. No doubts at all.

'On the other hand, there are some unhappily matched pairs painted in varying styles and at different times. For instance, there's a dashing fellow in the National Gallery of Art in Washington, all cocked hat and swinging cape, who's been said for years to belong to a dreary female in the Louvre. Since he's been restored the experts who have doubts about the pairing have become more vocal. You see . . . But I mustn't deliver a lecture.'

'Go on, I'm interested.'

'Well, I've become curious about this mismatch. The names of the sitters aren't known – as they very often aren't in Hals's portraits.'

'The *Laughing Cavalier*, for one.'

'Perfect example. Strictly, he's *Portrait of a Gentleman*. Most of the other unknowns are sombrely dressed – lots of black relieved with touches of white at collars and cuffs – and they are recorded as portrait of a man or portrait of a woman. But look at this.'

She showed Rose a photocopy of the Washington man, saying: 'Companion pieces were very fashionable; whenever you see a portrait of a Dutch figure you're bound to wonder whether you're looking at one half of a commission. But various things suggest that in this case it's true.'

'Such as?'

'Well, he's shown three-quarter length, the way Hals usually painted pendants. And he's turned a shade to his left, the side on which female portraits always hung.'

Curls touched a pointed cambric collar, a high-crowned hat sloped at a jaunty angle, and a hand resting on a hip swirled a short cloak. A dashing figure indeed.

'OK,' said Rose, 'now let me look at her.'

Mousy, a motherly little woman, the lady from the Louvre was, to the untutored eye, no relation at all.

Ellie said: 'You see? The objection isn't only one of style. They don't correspond, there's no equivalent of the rose that Isabella Comyns offers and Stephanus Geraerdts accepts.'

Rose queried how they had ever been married up.

Ellie had the history off pat. They were not matched until earlier this century when an expert called Wilhelm Valentiner announced they were a pair. There is no evidence of them being linked in the past. The Louvre acquired the woman in a bequest from Dr Louis La Caze in 1869, all that is known of her history. The Washington man was probably bequeathed in 1820 by Lord Frederick Campbell to an ancestor of Lord Amherst, was sold in Paris in 1911 to a P. A. B. Widener of Elkins Park, Pennsylvania, and went to the National Gallery of Art as part of the Widener Collection in 1942.

She added: 'I've been amusing myself in the Witt library look-ing for a better wife for him.'

'You make it sound like a dating agency.'

'Once we've finished our tea, I'll show you if you like.'

But first they talked about John Blair, about the way Rose had

45

heard the news, about the funeral and his unexplained journey to Spain.

Ellie admitted: 'I'm glad I wasn't told in time to get to the funeral. I wouldn't have believed in it anyway.'

'I was there and I didn't. When did you last see him, Ellie?'

'Shortly before Sam and I went to New York. John expected to be in the States two or three months later and we were talking about what we were going to do when we all met up there. The trip was delayed and gradually we forgot about it.'

'Yes, I remember, there was a story he wanted to work on over there. He didn't always share, you know. He didn't spell out what that was all about. But either it didn't stand up or else he couldn't get a paper to finance the research.'

Ellie guessed it happened about the time Rose and John were splitting up. Or not splitting up, as he had hoped.

He said to her: 'Ellie, she'll be back. I don't think it's the end.'

'Hurt pride or is she important to you?'

'She's different and I expect her back.'

'Well, then, I wish you luck.'

He had not had much luck, not with women. Oh, journalists thought he was a lucky devil. She heard them refer to him as Lucky Blair. But that was professional, things were different on the home front. If Christina and he had stuck it out . . . But he was not dogged about his romantic relationships as he was about his work and eventually there was a sad but amicable parting.

The last time Ellie saw him, when he called in as she was packing for New York, they had that conversation about Rose. If anyone had asked her, Ellie would have said that yes, John Blair was in love again.

'Come and look at the Hals women,' Ellie said to Rose.

In the Dutch section of the library she lifted down one of the green A3 boxes of reproductions of unidentified Frans Hals women and compared each with the reproduction of the Washington man.

'You see?' she said. 'There isn't a good one, is there? Nobody who looks as if she was made for him.'

Rose agreed, adding that the Louvre lady seemèd too small.

'Actually, Rose, she can't be ruled out on size because he's changed his. When he was restored in the mid-1980s it was discovered that he's been on different-sized stretchers, one that made him her size. It's not known how big he was originally. But when Hals painted companion pieces the man and woman achieved equal importance. What he didn't do was a dominant man on one canvas and a feeble wee wifie on the other.'

Another of the green boxes contained photocopies of paintings merely attributed to Hals. 'What about these?' Rose wondered.

'There's nobody there for him either.'

Rose laughed. 'You have the gleam of the matchmaker in your eye, Ellie. How far are you prepared to chase around on his behalf, really?'

Ellie continued to place pictures beside the man, whisk them away as they failed the crude test of immediate visual compatibility. 'Oh, not very far. Perhaps another ten minutes in here.'

'But if you went on with it?'

'I'd be an idiot. This isn't my subject.'

'But if?'

'Haarlem for the Hals museum. Amsterdam for the Rijksmuseum.'

'And after that?'

Follow her nose, she said, it could lead anywhere. 'But without any serious chance of success.'

'Because the experts who object to the Louvre lady haven't succeeded? Well, don't be daunted by that, you could have an advantage they don't have: a fresh eye.'

Ellie laughed this off as preposterous. 'I'm amusing myself with it, that's all. At the most I'll get a footnote to my book. I should have known better than to mention it. If anyone's committed to a life of nosing around, then you are. Don't encourage me in my folly, Rose. I have a book to write and no time for this nonsense. Perhaps in my old age but for the present, no.'

They left the Courtauld together, Rose for the Law Courts, Ellie to walk down the Strand and take the Underground home.

After all these years it still gave Ellie's spirit a lift to be walking through London. To be walking and unwatched, free to do and say anything she chose. When she came to a travel agent's she went in on the spur of the moment and booked a flight to Amsterdam.

That evening, telephoning Sam, she told him about the trip, making it sound as though it were a piece of extra but essential research for her book. He talked for a while, then he said: 'By the way, I have to choose between Marx and Lenin.'

'What kind of a choice is that?'

'I don't think we can do the icons of the twentieth century without Communism.'

She let the 'we' pass. 'A hammer and sickle would work.'

'I know. I guess I'm afraid of it seeming like I'm making a political statement. I mean making one I don't intend. The thing's getting a rather leftish look, which would be sort of OK if Communism weren't passé.'

'Marilyn Monroe isn't left. *Hitler?*'

'I was thinking of Che Guevara and Mandela.'

'Too bad the devil has all the best tunes? Sam, if you're going for political balance as well as relevance, you're heading for disaster.'

'Yeah, thanks, Ellie. That's truly cheering.'

'Sam, I only mean . . .'

'I know, I have to give this some serious thought.'

'Return to Go. Pick out the most powerful images and never mind what they say.'

She left him to tussle with it. She had not told him she had talked to Rose Darrow about the mysteries surrounding John Blair's death. Sam had a way of shutting out everything in her life that did not directly relate to him. He lacked a layer of curiosity, a surprising failing in an artist, but that is the way it was.

She did her laundry, made ready for the day ahead and the trip to the Netherlands.

Her mind elsewhere, Ellie hung a blouse to drip dry, folded underwear into her travel bag, wrote notes to remind herself of last-minute tasks. She was thinking of her talk with Rose, of Rose telling her about John Blair and the nearly-story in New York and his final assignment involving the French perfume-makers, the House of Devereux.

There was a connection, she had seen it at once. But she had let the conversation flow on without saying so. She wondered whether it mattered.

SIX

Mike Lowry, the television chat show presenter, was not a man Rose Darrow cared to be seen around town with but his invitation was irresistible.

'Maria has a beautiful voice and I shall be accompanied by some beautiful people. You're to put your best frock on, Rose, and come.'

She did. She had heard Maria before, no need to satisfy curiosity about her talents, but Lowry was hinting at sharing information about the Devereux family.

'Oh, come on, Mike, tell me over the phone,' Rose pleaded. He refused to make it that easy and she set out for the club.

It was refurbished and in vogue again after a period in the doldrums. Lowry had one of the best tables. His companions, from television and publishing, were happily shredding the reputation of an actress in a soap opera.

He left them to get on with it and asked Rose: 'Do I take it you're picking up the baton John Blair so unfortunately dropped?'

'No, Mike, you don't.'

'Pity. My spies tell me a certain business journalist has filled you in on the workings of the Devereux empire.'

'Goodness, things *are* quiet at the BBC. Couldn't they find you a teeny little thing to keep you occupied? A spot on *Blue Peter*, perhaps?'

'Don't be caustic, Rose. Do you want to hear about the Devereux dirty linen or not? I thought you'd be interested.'

'Yes, sorry, Mike. *Please* tell me.' She aped avid attention.

'Of course, I'm not a journalist.'

'No. What *are* you, Mike?'

'A personality, dear. Where was I?'

'Not being a journalist but about to expose the Devereux family.'

'Very well. The researchers, the ones who think I'm going to make a programme about the perfume industry – which I shan't if I can wriggle out of it – well, they tell me the family's mightily at odds. The old man, Maurice, is being pushed aside by the son, Philippe. And Philippe's being pressured by *his* son, David. Clear so far, Rose?'

'I'm with you. But tell me why all this pushing and shoving is going on.'

'Why? The usual reasons: power, money. What else?'

'Hmm.' She thought there ought to be something else. If not it was an everyday story of family businesses. John Blair would not have been interested in it, neither would anyone else.

'A sceptical twist to your mouth, if I may say so, Rose. What were you hoping for? Blood on the carpet?'

'More detail, that's what. Is this family squabble about per-sonalities? Or are they each trying to move the company in different directions? Or is the company heading for the rocks with the contenders trying to save it?'

'Your conversation with a certain business journalist didn't enlighten you then?'

'We talked about company turnover, position in the market and so on. It sounded like good news, we didn't descend to board-room sniping.'

'Ouch! No, don't apologize. We all have our specialities. Yours is being frightfully determined and high-minded and mine's listening to tittle-tattle. So be it. You see, Rose? I knew you wouldn't have heard the juicy bits.'

'I freely confess to missing out on the juicy bits. That's to say, I know the old stuff, what the newspapers call the Curse of the Devereux, but I know nothing titillating about today.'

'Well, I can't offer you much. Don't get excited. What's hap-pened is that the old man – that's Maurice – has been caught with his hand in the till. Money that ought to be swishing around in the company isn't and there's hell to pay.'

She had heard nothing of this. 'What will happen?'

'Rose, remember I'm a mere personality. I thought *you'd* like to find out.'

'And let you know so you can scupper your producer's attempt to make a jolly little film?'

'That's right, Rose. Exactly right.'

'Wait a minute . . .'

'Hush, here's Maria. Now you're in for a treat, I promise.'

Swathed in a short clinging dress Maria seemed tinier than ever. Her dark eyes glowed, enhanced with elaborate make-up. She began in a whisper. What in everyday life could be irritatingly child-like, enraptured her audience. She was a waif who needed their encouragement and attention.

Rose had forgotten how fine the voice was, how expressive, how sure. Maria had gained in confidence since she heard her last. At the charity gala Maria had been overwhelmed by the scale of everything: the audience, the band, the occasion. Now it all fitted. The right music, the right setting, and people came specifically to hear her.

From a whisper the voice grew, melodic and sweet but with the timbre that English singers do not have and English audiences find fascinating. Maria beguiled them. No stamping and stomping about the stage, she was stillness. The sound flowed, seemingly without effort, rich and voluptuous. But with an undertone that was infinite sadness.

When she finished singing she stayed unmoving for a moment of spellbinding tranquillity. Then she stirred, her movement giving her audience permission to respond. There was a very special quality about her.

Lowry murmured to Rose Darrow: 'I can't help it, I keep coming to hear her.'

'Are you still wining and dining her?'

'It was only once but maybe I will.'

'You mean she hasn't asked you again?'

He cocked an eyebrow. Rose said: 'Don't be coy, Mike. She

has a wonderful line in picking up men, anyone would tell you. Is she going to be on your show?'

'Possibly. Are you warning me off?'

'Why should I? She's beautiful, talented and a natural performer. She'd be ideal on the show.'

'I didn't mean that. I wondered whether you were warning me off the wining and dining.'

'Oh, you're a big boy, Mike. I'm sure you can take care of yourself.' But she was not sure, not where a woman like Maria was concerned.

'Quite.' And then, before he realized how tactless it was, the next teasing line sneaked out. 'Did you warn John Blair?'

They kept coming back to John Blair. She said that. 'If he were alive and well none of us would be talking about him, only a few of us would ever think of him. As it is, he's on everyone's lips. Don't you find that strange?'

'Because of the way he went. He was always a man to do the unexpected. I remember when I got to know him, at Oxford, there was a time when he . . . Well, anyway, what I mean is, we like deaths to be explicable. There's sufficient mystery about the process without adding puzzles of the whatever-was-he-doing-there-in-the-first-place variety.'

He offered to top up her wine glass. She made a gesture to prevent it but he persisted and Rose relented. She had not drunk much, she rarely did. She did not see the point of becoming gloomy or confessional or being bleary the following day. But she hoped to talk a little longer before Mike gave his attention to the rest of his friends and she crept away early.

John Blair had always been jokily scathing about Mike Lowry and his richly rewarded career. They both went to Fleet Street from Oxford but Mike was a disaster and sloped off into television instead where, to general astonishment, he became one of the most popular presenters of the lighter programmes. Over the years he put the more embarrassing game shows behind him, successfully angled for the smarter stuff and was now entrenched as host of the longest-running chat show. He was a household word, a personality, all the things young men dream of when they opt for a life on the box. But John Blair knew, and a good many people besides, especially Mike Lowry himself, that it was a huge success born of failure. He still wished he was a journalist.

When Rose said nothing, he went on: 'I must admit, though, that I do enjoy mystery. Everything from detective stories through to real-life brainteasers like the puzzle about where all the odd socks get to. Or . . .'

But here he noticed Maria, a dark jacket thrown over her dress, crossing the room to join them. He switched the unspoken words for: 'Or even a mystery of this order. Who is she, Rose? Where's she sprung from? There's enough mystery in this *petite chanteuse* to keep me going a lifetime.'

'Dangerous words, Mike.' Rose spoke under her breath as Maria came close. 'Dangerous words, indeed.'

The morning papers carried a line about the bomb blast at Maria's flat, linking it with the previous owner of the property, as Rose Darrow guessed it was. An actress called Linda Asprey had married a junior cabinet minister who had been much involved in Northern Ireland and was therefore considered a target of the IRA. Although it was too early for precise details, the police suggested the bomb was the type triggered by a timer. This spoiled the story line provided by the net twitcher across the road who swore her cat triggered the explosion by running beneath the car. There was speculation that the incident heralded a new phase in the IRA's mainland bombing campaign.

Rose reread the piece, looking for hidden information as statements from police and government spokesmen frequently concealed as much as they revealed. Then her telephone rang. The foreign editor of one of the Sundays, a quiet gangling man she knew by sight, told her that a bundle of John Blair's possessions had been delivered to him.

He said: 'They apparently came here because he was working

for me at the time. What do you reckon I should do with them, Rose?'

'Er . . .' She rapidly ruled out directing them to the ex-wife, Christina, who was probably the best person to decide their correct resting place as she had made all other arrangements. 'I'll take them, Ray,' she heard herself say.

'It's not much.' He sounded uncomfortable, it was a distasteful task. 'I'll put them in a taxi and send them over.'

'Fine.'

He saved her questions by saying he had been in the Middle East for a few weeks and had not heard about the shooting. Neither had he bothered to tell any of his colleagues he had commissioned Blair to research a story.

'Then this morning a parcel came for me from Malaga. Our stringer down there was handed the stuff and couldn't think what to do with it except send it here.'

She said he had solved a puzzle: no one else seemed to know who John was working for or why he was in Spain.

'Rose, I can't explain Spain. I understood he was going to France. Either he hopped off for a weekend in the sun or else he was following a lead that took him over the border.'

Not holiday, she was sure. She knew from experience, from the abandoned plans and the impossibility of making a life with the man. He played hard in between stories but when he was working there was no room for anything else.

Ray tried to lighten his own, shocked mood with a joke. 'The betting around here is that he was in pursuit of a *señorita*.'

She matched his tone. 'A particular *señorita* or would anyone do?'

'We had a joke before he went away on the story . . .'

'Was this the Devereux story?'

'That's right.' His voice betrayed that he wished she did not know. 'He said the only other thing on his mind was chasing a woman.'

She recycled the quip. 'Any particular woman?'

'Oh, I suppose it was some bitch playing hard to get. I wished him luck when he went to *cherchez la femme*. That's the last conversation we had.'

She waited for the taxi, dreading its arrival and yet at the same time eager. The bundle might provide answers to the whirling questions. If she was lucky, it could reveal what he discovered about the Devereux family, why he went to Spain and who the woman was. Unless it proved otherwise, she was afraid she was the woman. She had ignored messages, she had been determined to shake herself free of him.

'I can't have a messy half-way thing,' she had told him. 'I can't be free in the way you can. Either we're together or we're not. The worst possible option is the occasional bout of love-making when you happen to fetch up in London with nowhere more comfortable to sleep and no one more interesting to sleep with.'

He argued that he was not proposing that at all. No doubt he said more but she could not exactly remember. At the time she was angry, hurt and humiliated, and she was not prepared to listen. Right then it suited her to have him out of her life, out of her way. She was ruthless in believing that for each placating word he spoke, there were contrary words unsaid. Neither could she recall how it ended, except that the whole affair ended with her dodging his phone calls and hoping she would not run into him somewhere by accident. And this phase ended with the horrifying news that she need not dodge any longer, that he was gone.

The taxi came. Rose dropped the bundle on the floor of her sitting room and hesitated, consciously weighing her reluctance and her inquisitiveness. Someone had found a stout mailbag, pushed the travel bag into it for its unattended journey across Europe. She pictured the stringer, probably an ambitious young Spaniard proud to be working for a major British newspaper but aghast at having the effects of a major British journalist dumped on him.

She recognized the travel bag. She was sure there ought to be other things too. A slim lap-top computer, for instance. Instead there were clothes, a much-used passport and international driving documents, a cheque book, a folder containing papers, a notebook and a Filofax. She began with the Filofax but there were no entries in the diary section for the week before his death and few in the weeks before that. This was hardly surprising as his inquiries were not the kind that began with formal appointments. He was likelier to have arrived somewhere, turned on the charm and talked his way in.

She set the Filofax aside and opened the notebook. His shorthand was idiosyncratic but she was familiar with it. Not as easy as reading an item from a newspaper but it was not impossible for her either. Rose skimmed, beginning with the final jottings.

He had written three names, each followed by a query. The middle one was the name of the place where he died.

Before the three names were notes in a mish-mash of shorthand and scribbled longhand. 'Check out Gib link.' 'D says . . .' The word says was underlined, indicating that whoever D might be he was not necessarily to be believed. On the previous pages the key words were 'snow', 'cover up' and 'Ramírez'. The capital D featured frequently.

John Blair had written August on the cover of the notebook; she could assume everything inside the covers to have been written since the first of that month. There were no other dates, unless figures half-way through the notes referred to days and months of the year. The context did not help her.

Much was indecipherable, much else inconclusive and yet a picture was emerging. Someone called D had been telephoned and the strands of that conversation were followed up by various inquiries including telephone calls (suggested by the fluency of verbatim reporting of speech) and face-to-face encounters (suggested by encapsulating notes broken up by occasional sentences or phrases within quotation marks). The story? Even with the knowledge that it concerned the Devereux family, it was possible to make all kinds of guesses.

Rose telephoned Ray, who had sent her the bag. 'Did you remove anything from it?'

His pause was enough.

'Ray, what was it?'

'There was film in the camera. We're developing it.'

'Then I want to see it. How soon can I come over?'

She stood in his little cupboard of an office. He stooped over the desk, dealing out the prints and looking like Gary Cooper in a Western poker game that could only end in trouble. He dealt them in the order in which they were taken. Ten prints, the rest of the reel was unused. Black and white prints: a picture of a document that would have to be blown up to be read; snatch pictures of an old man emerging from a car; a shot of a naked young woman on a sandy beach; a study of two sun-creased old men drinking beer at a pavement café; and a tilted, blurred sweep of tall building and sky.

Ray held out a magnifying glass. 'It's in French. Seems to be a newspaper cutting.'

She squinted at the fuzzy magnified image of the document.

He said: 'A pity it doesn't say which paper it's from.'

'Or why he had to photograph it. If he'd read the item in a library surely he'd have been able to photocopy it?'

A man poked his head around the door with a query. Ray answered that he would be along in a minute. He bowed over the desk to gather up the other photographs and offer them to Rose.

'We have another set. And you'd better put this with Blair's stuff too.' He swooped on a drawer and produced a camera.

The camera was scuffed on one end and along the back although it was not very old. Rose had given it to John on his birthday.

She asked: 'Ray, are you picking up this story where he left off?'

Ray folded his arms, leaned against the wall behind him. 'Who's to say where he left off? He had an idea he wanted to explore, about the reasons for the declining fortunes of the House of Devereux. I said OK, come back when you've done it.

That was it. I looked through the notebook but couldn't make head nor tail of it. Did you do any better, Rose?'

'Not much.'

'Well, I haven't the resources these days to send anyone down the trail again, especially someone without a clue what they'd be looking for. So it's yours if you want it, Rose.'

'Me? I have a Euromag to get off the ground. Remember?'

'All this is idle curiosity then?'

'I wish I knew what it was.'

She turned the camera over in her hands. The scratches on the back were deep, scored in the same direction. It had hit a hard surface and slid. In her mind's eye she saw a man focusing, then being jostled so that the lens rose and took a soaring shot of a building and an empty sky, and then the camera dropping to the ground where it was kicked aside. Accidentally, perhaps deliberately, he had been prevented from taking the photograph he had wanted. It had happened when he was shot.

She said: 'Your stringer in Malaga, Ray. I'd like his name and phone number, please.'

'He wasn't there, you know.'

'That doesn't matter.'

He recited the name and number from memory. 'Francisco Ramírez. Paco to his friends.'

They went out into the passage, Ray on his way to a news conference. Cheerful since shunting the responsibility on to her, he said: 'Me, I wouldn't be bothering with Señor Ramírez, I'd be chasing the lounging lovely who'd forgotten her bathing costume.'

'I bet,' said Rose and left.

Ramírez denied being handed a computer along with John Blair's possessions. He denied having inspected the contents of the travel bag and he denied knowing anything about Blair's reasons for being in Spain. 'He was, you know, independent.'

She said she did know.

He described events on the day of the shooting, stressing he was not present himself but the story was well known. A

59

demonstration by strikers turned nasty, the authorities over-reacted, shots were fired. No one else was killed, no one was injured. The police claimed they fired into the air.

'When John spoke to you . . .'

'No, that's wrong.'

'But . . . I don't mean that day, I mean any time in the weeks before he died.'

'He didn't. You know, until he died I didn't know he was in Spain. If somebody has told you this, they are wrong.'

She came off the line with the firm impression that Francisco Ramírez, Paco to his friends, was lying. There it was among the last pages of John's notes: Paco Ramírez. And the name was followed by disjointed notes. Not a telephone call, it read more like rapid note-taking immediately after a meeting.

She returned to Paris.

'Rose, this is like a detective story,' said Joelle, everybody's helper. She enjoyed a good *policier* but other sorts would do.

'Your turn to play Maigret, Joelle.' Rose gave her a list of jobs. Identify the publication in the photograph. Round up recent press cuttings about the Devereux family. Get photographs of the family.

Joelle loved it. 'But you, Rose. What will you be doing?'

'Leaving you to get on with it. I have real work to do.' Hours later she was flying to Rome and on her way to an interview at the Vatican.

Joelle was right, she thought, the Devereux story was a teaser. But her soft-spoken Paris colleague, Steve, who had broken the news of the shooting to her, was also right when he remarked: 'I guess John Blair gave up and went to sun himself in Spain, it was a good idea that didn't work out.' And Larry, her brash bulldog colleague? All he added was: 'For God's sake, Rosie, where's this bloody spy I'm waiting for?'

'In Prague, Larry. Don't fret, he'll keep. When he's ready to talk I'll know.'

If the contacts she had made in Prague bothered to let her know, she would. Maybe she should go back there, check for herself. She could justify the trip on several counts, not least that there was a worrying silence from the woman she had engaged to work for her. Was she ill? Incapable? Absconded with a lover instead of working? Could be anything.

After the Vatican interview, Rose had supper with a couple of men from her Rome office. She reached her hotel late, rather wearied. The company had been good, the restaurant famous and the fish wonderful but her day had been long and complicated. She craved solitude and a soft bed. Instead she got an urgent message to ring Joelle.

'Sorry it's so late, Joelle. I've been out all evening.'

'Doesn't matter, I'm sitting up in bed watching a video. Rose, an urgent fax came for you today from Frankfurt. It said: "The unholy grail is in sight." And it was signed: "Your partner Willi." Does any of that make sense?'

'All of it,' said Rose. 'It means I won't be coming back to Paris. I'm going to Prague.'

The taxi dropped her at the foot of a street rising up to the castle. She let herself in through a high wooden door in a coach arch, paused in a tunnel of gloom and made out the iron grille of a security gate. The faintest of light bulbs glimmered overhead, insufficient to illuminate the names on the tabs beside the vertical row of bells. She ran a hand over the row, guessed they were numbered from the bottom and pressed the second one up.

Then the light went out.

Rose shivered. The archway was dank. She was caught in a limbo between the street of honey-coloured eighteenth-century buildings and a greyish courtyard whose lines were broken up by the slanting shapes of stout wooden scaffolding.

A voice called down, making her jump. '*Jste Angličan?*'

She said yes. Above, to her right, another ghostly lamp came on. She heard running feet and a child, a boy of about ten, appeared round the curve of steep steps.

Gravely he asked: 'Rose?' And when she said yes again he added very carefully: 'Good evening.'

It was not evening. He opened the gate and led her to a door under the arch. Without his help she would have missed it. He ushered her in. A tiled entrance hall, a bathroom, a kitchen, a big vaulted sitting room and beyond it a bedroom. She had a flat in Prague for as long as she wanted it. The boy was anxious for her approval.

She told him she liked it. '*Je hezký.*'

He nodded, too shy to smile back at her. She asked his name. 'Karel.'

'Well, thank you, Karel. *Děkuji.*'

She got the smile. He offered up two keys, one for the gate and one for the door to the flat. With dumbshow he explained their separate uses. Then he wished her: 'Good evening,' and ran back upstairs.

Heat in the flat was overwhelming. She searched for a thermostat to turn down the central heating and, when the hunt ended in failure, resorted to switching off radiators individually. Unpacking took very few minutes, then she left the flat and walked downhill, past shop windows full of flattened sausages and long cylindrical dumplings, past a queue outside a butcher's shop and another at a tram stop, past a window of bread rolls and loaves gleaming with salt-glaze, past medieval arcades and shops tucked into baroque buildings, and on over pavements whose cobbles were working loose, down towards the towers and the arch between them that led her on to the Charles Bridge.

Willi had waited for her near the steps leading to Kampa Island. Dark overcoat, fair hair, he was leaning on the parapet and looking down. He did not hear her approach until the last moment, when he looked up with a delighted 'Ah, Rose!' and greeted her with an affectionate squeeze.

In the square below a chain of ponies was trudging nose to tail, round and round and round within a canopied cage. Dulled children rode on their backs. Close by, a film unit had parked its high grey van and a man dressed as Joseph K. was lounging outside it drinking coffee from a thick china mug.

'Those animals,' said Willi, 'have the dreariest job in all Prague.'

'Worse than hanging around the bridge for a guide who never turns up?'

'This time he'll come, I can almost promise it.'

They sauntered a few yards along the bridge. Makeshift stalls displayed bits of Bohemian porcelain, Russian army hats with the cosy furry ear-flaps, ear-rings, and paintings of Prague. Several people were singing folk songs, including the girl in shimmering tights who strummed her guitar beneath a lantern. The gull catcher flicked a handful of crumbs into the air and birds dived and veered.

A dozen German tourists came to a stop near him while their guide shouted at them about the saints and the kings, especially St John of Nepomuk who was pledged to save anyone who fell into the Vltava. 'And does he?' someone asked. The guide had a ready quip to deal with a predictable question, and hurried on to recite facts and fables about the building of the bridge, the castle crowning the hill, St Vitus and his cathedral.

Other tourists came singly or in couples and lingered to watch the frothing weir or the scudding sky reflecting sombre colour in water. Willi and Rose posed as tourists, talking idly but each keeping watch along the bridge. A party of wealthy Russians, the women in couture clothes and sable, took up the place vacated by the Germans and heard a different version of the facts and the fables. As they too moved away a man came purposefully towards Rose and she felt her stomach tighten. So this was the messenger?

But he went by, spoke to the gull catcher, helped him secure his bags and carry them away. A keen wind was blowing downriver and it lifted the men's hair on end as they went.

Colours faded from the day. Sellers wrapped their goods with care, folded their tables and counted the day's takings. Tourists melted, the girl stopped singing and pocketed the change that had been thrown into her guitar case. Suddenly there was no sound but the wind-whipped water and the rhythm of footsteps over stone.

'You will come with me, please.'

The girl's voice was soft and clear like her singing. Willi stared disbelieving but Rose demanded: 'Why did you keep us waiting?'

The girl ignored criticism. 'Come.'

The wind tugged at them. Rose battled to tame her scarf and felt her cheeks stung to colour but the girl in the home-made mini-skirt seemed unaware of the worsening weather. She took them to the traffic lights beneath the Bridge Tower, motioned them to wait before crossing although there was a useful gap in the traffic, steered them through short cuts and brought them ultimately to a high thin house in the Old Town. They exchanged not a word along the way.

She rang the bell. When the door opened they were beckoned inside by a stooped man coiled in cigarette smoke. The door shut behind them. The girl had not followed. With a gesture of his cigarette, the man motioned them into a rear room, bare except for a table, an ashtray and a chair.

Willi did not conceal his disappointment. 'Where's Krieger? And who are you?'

'My name is not important. Before you meet Krieger we must speak of other matters.'

Willi's exasperation increased. 'What other matters? We've been speaking for many weeks now and there's still no sign of Krieger. Why are you doing this?'

The man drew on his cigarette, unperturbed by Willi's impatience. 'He has been here. Yes, perhaps he will speak to you.'

Rose intervened, afraid Willi might spoil what they had achieved. 'Please would you explain why Krieger isn't here today and when we can actually meet him.'

'He wishes me to ask you some questions. You must understand he is not a man who meets just anybody.'

She murmured the wry comment that she had in fact gathered that much. Then: 'We both wish to discuss business with Krieger. They aren't matters others can decide for him. And there's really no possibility of progress until we talk directly to him.'

Willi enlarged but the man was implacable. He lit a new cigarette from the butt of the first and let them talk. He was the man Rose had spoken to on the telephone several times, he did not deny it. He sat on the broken chair and created a pall of tobacco smoke and obfuscation.

The fug was making her feel sick. She pushed things to a head. 'Look, is this an elaborate way of saying Krieger doesn't want to see either of us at all?'

An expression of innocence. 'No, no, I haven't said that.'

'Good,' she said briskly. 'Then are you saying – is *he* saying – that he will?'

'Perhaps.'

She bridled. 'If you'd simply explain what all this is about!'

He balanced the cigarette on the rim of the tin ashtray. 'Things are not simple. Because there are no longer border guards you people think all things are easy. I say to you, they are not.'

Back in the street again Willi burst out: 'They're making fools of us, Krieger and this man, and that girl with the guitar and heaven knows who else. Rose, I think Krieger's lost his chance with me. Let another publisher chase after him and cajole him. Think of it: if I meet him and he agrees to a contract, can I trust him to keep his word? A man who can't keep an appointment?'

'We need a soothing experience,' she said and headed for the bar of a plush and refurbished hotel. When the drinks were brought she told him: 'Not partners then, after all, Willi. But I don't blame you for giving in. He's cost us time and money.'

'When you think of all the people who clamour to be published, or all those who made money by telling Krieger's story at second-hand . . . He needs a new start, his book could finance that. I don't understand what's holding the man back.'

'Except caution about breaking cover,' she suggested. 'That infuriating man back there was right. Boundaries have come down but history isn't wiped out. Many people hate Krieger. He ruined lives.'

Willi snorted and drained his glass. 'I think, Rose, you're dreaming up excuses for Krieger. Well, you may do so, but I don't accept excuses for him and I've been refused explanations. No, I don't wish to spend any more energy on him. Tomorrow I shall go home to Frankfurt and run my business and that will be an end of him.'

She gave him a sly look. 'So if I find him I'd better say you're no longer interested?'

He wriggled with irritation. 'You won't find him, Rose.'

'But if?'

'What use is if? You think I'm weak to cast him aside.'

'No, Willi. I think you're demonstrating the difference between a publisher and a journalist. You have the luxury of making that decision and I don't. I have to go on.'

He snorted again and then asked her where she would like to go for dinner.

The following morning Rose woke to the ringing of a telephone. Disorientated, it took a moment for her to remember where she was and why. An excited Joelle was on the line from Paris.

'I have the information about the Devereux family, Rose. Shall I send it to you?'

'Yes, please.'

'And how is the flat?' Joelle was alarmed at Rose renting a flat through friends of friends instead of using an hotel.

'Interesting,' said Rose. And glowered at the big Calex fridge that had gurgled through the night.

The fridge was empty except for milk donated by the parents of Karel, the boy who let her in. Rose located a bag of coffee and some cups in the metal wall cupboards whose screeching hinges set her teeth on edge. She found a jug, made coffee and tried to assemble her wits.

Consoling Willi for his disappointment over Krieger had taken longer than might be expected. After dinner they spent an hour in one of the smarter and less smoky bars. By then it was raining but the longed-for taxi did not materialize. They splashed back across the bridge.

Wincing, she remembered a ridiculous fumbling for her keys – security gate and front door, and don't get them mixed up – in the near-dark of the archway. And had there not been a perfunctory kiss before the gate slipped and slammed between them? Would it have been less perfunctory if her grasp on the gate had been surer? Besides, what did the kiss signify? Farewell, because he was off to Frankfurt today and they did not know when, if ever, they would meet again? Or did it signal a quantum leap in their relationship, a minute but significant shift from flirting friendliness to a tenderer emotion? Or was it entirely attributable to an overdose of alcohol and consolation? God, she wished she knew.

She discovered the shower was dangerously hot, the extractor fan did not extract and the entire flat became enveloped in steam. Flakes of plaster floated down and clung damply to her skin.

Rose thought a new home, however temporary, was like a new love affair. One had to get to know its quirks, what it allowed one to get away with and what treatment it would *not* tolerate. She suspected the relationship with the Prague flat would prove a testing one. The fridge was harassing her and the shower had launched an all-out attack. But at least she gained the upper hand over the central heating when she turned off half the radiators. She was not ready yet to admit Joelle might be right and to head for a hotel. First, she meant to tame the fridge and give it more to guard than a polythene sachet of milk.

The local self-service food shop was an adventure. Small, it was kitted out with miniature trolleys. Before venturing in, shoppers queued for empty trolleys to be passed over, baton-like, by customers whose own tours of the shelves were over. Plain packaging, choice limited to one brand of any line, made shopping uncomplicated and fast. No hanging around, eyes glazing at the impossibility of choosing between the rival claims of manufacturers of competitively priced goods.

Rose was soon back at the flat and telephoning. She fixed a meeting with the woman who was to be her Prague staff, then spoke to a photographer in Rome and sorted out a series of minor problems. Eventually, she was free to return to the house in the Old Town. It was on the edge of Josefov, the Jewish area with the oldest synagogue in Europe and the cemetery where memorials are flung together like stones on a storm beach. A party of Hassidic men in yarmulkas walked ahead of her, a handful among the thousands of Jews from all over the world drawn to Josefov for its monuments and, paradoxically, the museum the Nazis established, the Exotic Museum of an Extinct Race.

The Hassids turned left and her way was clear. But there was no answer when she rang the bell at the house. She was patient, tried again. No one came. Rose wandered off to a *kavárna*, spent a pittance and a lot of time, dawdled back and pushed the bell. No one answered her.

She wanted very much to be able to tell the bulldog Larry in Paris that she had tied up Krieger but she feared she had lost her contact as well. Although she tried asking at adjoining properties whether anyone knew what had become of the stooped man who was at the house the previous day, the language barrier was insurmountable. Rose went to fetch an interpreter.

At the flat that served as the magazine's office, the bright young woman who was her new colleague distracted her by handing over a wodge of paper. Joelle had faxed the Devereux information.

'Rose, it is a wonderful invention, the fax machine,' the woman said, gazing nervously at the miracle. 'But, you know, it makes me think how much more wonderful it would be if I could slide in there and fax myself to New York, or to London, or anywhere.'

'That comes next. They're working on it.'

Rose riffled the papers. They were not in date order, they needed to be rearranged before reading. But what was the hurry? She had a free evening unless she could catch Krieger or the stooping man.

Rose explained about the man with the stoop, about the need to question the neighbours.

Her new colleague rearranged the combs in her hair. 'Tomorrow. Today I'm busy.'

Rose did not argue. 'I'll be here around ten, we'll go over then.'

'Make that eleven.'

They agreed on eleven. Rose left, amusement breaking through in a smile as she reached the cold air sweeping across the square. She wondered what the Czech word for 'urgent' was and how long it was since anybody had used it.

She ate a long lunch with a man involved with measures to privatize businesses who provided fascinating insights into the obstacles created by forty years of state ownership. Then she took tea with the president's wife who was creating a national charity to fill the gaps in social care that the Communist state had refused to plug and denied anyone else the chance to. It was mid-evening before she shuffled the sheets into chronological order and sat down to read what Joelle dubbed The Devereux File.

In 1965, while the Beatles were at Buckingham Palace collecting MBEs, Claude Devereux, an heir to the perfume business, was marrying his sweetheart, Andrée, who sacrificed her career as an opera singer for love. The bride wore a gown of wild silk designed for her by Dior. Two thousand rich and glamorous people attended the reception, including heads of state, European royalty and American rock stars. Claude and Andrée spent their honeymoon on the family yacht, cruising around the Canary Isles.

The next year a perfume called Diva was launched with a lavish presentation to the fashion press and an advertising promotion that ensured the name became familiar around the world, although the tiniest fraction of those who knew it would ever feel bold enough to spend so extravagant a sum on so mean a splash of fragrance.

A year on, the head of the family, Maurice Devereux, purchased a Picasso painting called Diva. The perfume and the painting were taken to be references to his daughter-in-law although the sharper-tongued gossip columnists relished pointing out that she had not achieved anything like the status of a diva and lacked the talent to do so. Kinder journalists ran stories about her modesty in declining to have her own name used for the perfume and her admiring father-in-law's compromise.

In 1967 the baby, Nicole, was born, an event followed by a christening ceremony featuring an antique gown of handmade lace for the child and a spectacular outfit from Courrèges for the mother. And then the sun that beamed down on the House of Devereux was clouded. Illness, first. Andrée was rushed to hospital, flown from the yacht during a cruise of the Cyclades and rumoured to be dying. Days later the hospital leaked that she would live but bear no more children. Glittering opera star became, in the gossip columnists' parlance, Tragic Andrée.

Another year, and tragedy was confirmed when her baby vanished from its bed at the château.

When Judge Georges Laroche, in his stumbling fashion, gave Philippe Devereux the news of the discovery of his niece's body, it put an end to two months of agonizing uncertainty.

Philippe said: 'Dead? We wanted to believe in kidnap.'

'P-perhaps something went . . . went wrong?' said Laroche, with a hint of inquiry in his voice.

Philippe came away from the telephone silent, holding the information to himself. His brother, the child's father, was travelling from Geneva to Paris and not to be reached. Andrée was upstairs, seeking consolation in music. The old couple were out, his mother down in the vineyard fussing over vines she suspected were none too healthy, which was unsurprising given the heat of the summer and the ferocity of the storms. And his father was keeping a promise to meet an old friend for lunch in the town.

He dismissed the idea of telling Andrée. Her scream rang in his head the moment he thought of it. On the night of the abduction, he fought her, stopped her racing down the stairs risking injury or death. He had slapped her and quietened her, and he recoiled from a second scene like that. So Philippe sat down again at his desk and awaited a better time to relay the news.

Anna, his assistant, came into the room, her ankle-length cotton skirt swishing, light glancing off long loose brown hair. She was wearing a touch of 'Escapade', his favourite, flattering him.

71

'Something the matter, Philippe?'

They were very close, the professional relationship long overlaid with intimacy. Sometimes she wondered whether she was foolish about that, whether he would ever want to marry her and whether she wanted him to. She did not know about his other woman, Margot, in Paris.

He ran a finger over the silken surface of his desk. The maid had polished it, it exuded lavender. 'Anna, it's something I ought to say to the family first.'

'But?' There had not been a but, she invented it.

'I had a call.'

'I heard the telephone as I was coming down the passage. Who was it?'

'Laroche.'

Her kohl-dark eyes widened with interest, a facial gesture he found endearing. He went on: 'Yes, Laroche. They've found a child's body.'

She pressed her fingers to her lips, unable to trust herself to speak.

He said: 'Andrée's here alone, I can't tell her. I *can't*.'

Anna nodded vigorously, regained her voice. 'I understand, Philippe. But is Laroche sure it's Nicole?'

'If he isn't sure, he wouldn't have telephoned. There wouldn't be any point.'

Maurice Devereux was first home, pale and agitated. He bustled into Philippe's office, saying: 'They've found a body near the bridge. Police everywhere and Laroche stamping around in the middle of it all, stuttering and full of self-importance. I stopped and asked. It's Nicole, they're convinced of it.'

Philippe said: 'I know, Father. Laroche telephone me half an hour ago.'

'Ah. How's Andrée taken it?'

'She doesn't know. I haven't told her.'

'And Claude?'

'Driving between Geneva and Paris. I've told no one except Anna, I was waiting for you or Mother to get back.'

His father shouldered the burden. 'Very well. I'll tell her myself.'

Anna said: 'Suppose they're wrong and it's not Nicole? It would be wretched for Andrée if she were told they'd found Nicole and they hadn't.'

Philippe said: 'Someone will have to identify the body.'

His father looked from him to Anna and back. 'You don't understand, either of you. This isn't the sort of body you can look at and recognize, this is one that's been lying unburied in long vegetation during a hot damp summer. How much do you think is left? Hair, bones, rags – that's what we're discussing.'

'Father, you didn't . . . ?'

'See it? No, I didn't do that. But I talked to some of the men who had. It was a child of about two and there are the remnants of a whitish garment. Now, if you will excuse me, I must go and speak to Andrée.'

Over the next days tests confirmed that fibres from the rags tallied with those from a nightdress similar to the one Nicole was wearing when she was snatched. Laroche went to the press with a statement that the body was Nicole's, and the headlines blazoned the news.

Journalists outnumbered mourners at the funeral and the occasion prompted speculative articles about the troubles that beset the Devereux family. Savage deaths and shady dealings in two world wars; a disaffected chemist claimed, aptly and literally, that his research was stolen from beneath his nose, another pursued the founder of the company, the late Raoul Devereux, through the courts until his money ran out and a war intervened; fire consumed antiques and paintings at one of the family's homes; a famous actor died of a heart attack during a party on board the yacht; Andrée almost died and was left unable to mother further children; and Nicole was murdered. The Curse of the Devereux leaped into print for the first time and was to prowl the gossip columns ever after.

Little Nicole's killer was not found. Local people murmured about gypsies camping in the valley earlier in the summer, but they were not referred to until after the discovery of the body. People who did the murmuring clammed up when an exasperated Laroche sought to get to the root of the story. Sultry summer burned into autumn, and as colours faded to winter so the Devereux story dropped out of the news. Violence had broken out again between Catholic and Protestant factions in Northern Ireland. The world was waiting to see whether President Nixon, who took office that year, actually would withdraw United States troops from Vietnam. Churchgoers mulled over the introduction of the vernacular mass. And gossipmongers said the Beatles were splitting up.

Once in a while Laroche went to the château. He refused to admit publicly that he had failed, given up, closed the case. But the city police finished their inquiries and retreated, and the only suggestion of an investigation proceeding was the sight of Laroche driving up the valley. People turned their heads as his car rushed by and said to each other: 'Ah, he never gives up, that one.' But in effect he had, he had been obliged to.

Then he had an inspiration. On the anniversary of the child's disappearance, he demanded a reconstruction. He wanted Andrée to shout for the nanny, the pair of women to re-enact what they had re-enacted for him when the case was fresh. But this time, once family and servants converged on the nursery, he wanted Andrée to repeat the scream.

She never did. Laroche discussed the plan with her father-in-law who ruled it out as callous and unprofitable.

Maurice Devereux was adamant. 'Nicole has gone, Laroche. We have our lives to lead. We can't be dragged back. Andrée is rebuilding her life and I'll agree to nothing that interferes with that.'

But she was not rebuilding, not really. She was neurotic and moody, she clung to the house in the Bois de Boulogne and feared the château. She tried vacations on the yacht or shopping in Milan and London but she was inconsolable. She still enjoyed driving fast and singing, but that was about all she enjoyed. Gossip columnists looked for cracks in her marriage and found them. Then she was in hospital again, a clinic that was circumspect about what it revealed. Rumours were various, favouring either the nervous breakdown or the suicide bid. Whichever it was, Tragic Andrée was living up to the soubriquet the press had given her.

EIGHT

Ellie's first sight of the countryside was vague, she might have been peering through sediment in the bottom of a glass. Then wisps of cloud thickened to white haze. Yet she did not stop staring down, craving the next glimpse but fearful of it too. When it came there were gingery forests, roads thin as twine thrown on the ground, and soon the unmistakable outline of Hradčany Castle measuring its length along a hilltop. Ellie had come home.

Ellie had come home through a series of accidents and encounters, not through any desire to visit the city of her birth. Her mind was concentrated on tracing a Frans Hals woman; she was taken aback when she realized where the trail was leading.

The helpful balding man at the Rijksmuseum had smiled broadly. 'It's a good time to go to Prague.' He thought she was English.

She had come out of the gallery and walked for a while, thinking. Hals was a digression, she was supposed to be writing her book on neglected women artists; how much further was she prepared to go on this jaunt? But having come as far as airy, watery Amsterdam, then Prague was close. The missing wife of the Washington man teased her. Not to go to Prague would be like abandoning an engrossing detective story with one more chapter to go. On the other hand, she thought, that might not be true at all: Prague could be a dead end or it could point her across Europe. One day she would have to draw the line. The actual question was whether she could bear to go to Prague at all.

She went into a brown bar near the Museumbrug. Trees hung over the canal beside it and racks of bicycles reared up as though they were prancing into the water. Ellie loosened her coat in the steamy warmth and took in her surroundings: tables covered with rugs woven in Oriental designs; vases of flowers on each table, each shelf, in each window, along the bar; men balancing on stools whose footrests were scuffed clear of varnish by all those other men who had balanced there before them.

Frans Hals had not enjoyed Amsterdam. He avoided it and anyway found enough to do at home in Haarlem painting the elite who controlled the civic and military life of the place, worthy citizens in chessboard colours. The time he was tempted to work in Amsterdam it ended badly. His militia group portrait, *The Meagre Company*, was begun there in 1633, broken off three years later when he fell out with his patrons, and after much argument completed by Pieter Codde, apparently in 1637.

Hals tried everything to wriggle out of painting the picture in Amsterdam. For a start, he claimed it was agreed he should do the heads of some militiamen there but finish the remainder in Haarlem. Then he rejected a payment of an extra six guilders per sitter to return to Amsterdam. His counter offer was to roll up the massive one-piece linen canvas and transport it to his studio where he would complete the partly painted figures, and where the rest of the Dad's Army outfit could go and sit for him. Stalemate. Enter one Pieter Codde, minor painter but known to members of the Meagre Company, possibly himself a member of it, and a chap who could be trusted to finish the job.

The big Hals commissions were safe, in public or semi-public settings. Smaller portraits were scattered. Pictures were inherited, or sold off or discarded when black and white Calvinist solidity became too depressing to hang on the sitting-room wall. And with them, in the long, long years when Frans Hals was regarded as any old painter, went the Washington woman. Or so Ellie was convincing herself.

Her adventure, as she thought of it, was disturbing her life. The book was not being worked on, Sam and New York barely impinged. Her head was crammed with seventeenth-century Dutch manuscripts, with exhibition catalogues and dull documents from which she plucked tantalizing details.

The key was the sad, loveless man in Washington who cried out for a companion piece that appeared created to hang beside him and not one carelessly attached. Predictably, the Witt library failed to offer a match but she was seduced into exploring the history of the male figure. She started from basics, reading everything easily available, from the Hals entry in the Oxford *Companion to Art* to catalogues of exhibitions at the Royal Academy in London at which he was shown in 1894 and 1910. She dipped into the half-dozen books that referred to him. Every reference was checked back to its earliest source, nobody's word taken as gospel because that was never good enough and, although this was a mere sideshow to her proper research, she refused to be less thorough.

Studying the paintings at the Halsmuseum in Haarlem, in one of the almshouses whose regents he famously painted, did not add to her store of knowledge. She was encouraged, though, by a Judith Leyster portrait. Judith was already a paragraph in Ellie's book: a Hals pupil whose work the experts long accepted as being by Hals – despite the canvas being initialled JL. Experts could miss the obvious.

Walking the old streets, alongside the canals, of Frans Hals's home town, she erased the additions of the centuries. Bicycles and cars vanished and canals filled with boats; streets were peopled with figures in black stuff and white cambric; and she expected a flurry of regentesses to burst from an almshouse doorway at any moment, or men of the guard to round a corner.

'Running away,' she thought. 'That's what it means, I'm running away.'

She took a lane leading to the railway station and caught a fast train the few miles over the flatness to Amsterdam. Indonesian drumming filled Dam Square. A black cloth shape lay on the ground, quivered, became bat-like, ghost-shaped, a concealed human dancing, and at the final drum roll the black peeled back to reveal a young woman.

Ellie walked part of the way, detouring to the scented splendours of the floating flower market on the Singel canal, and past skinny waterside houses where Amsterdammers climb steeply to front doors and then hide behind lace panels. Cats, catching the best of the thin sun, looked out at her from cosy niches between lace and window pane.

Haarlem had been enjoyable, but genuine help came from the man at the Rijksmuseum. In the middle of the last century, he said, some paintings by Hals were sold through a dealer in Amsterdam. A description of one of them was similar to that of the man whose missing companion interested Ellie. He tantalized her by repeatedly reading through to himself the passage in the reference book.

Tentatively she said: 'But we do know where my man was from 1820. He's believed to have been in Kent, part of Lord Frederick Campbell's bequest.'

'Yes. What's interesting about this Amsterdam sale is that the paintings were unfamiliar. Two disappeared during the previous century and another was never recorded.'

He started to remind her how Hals was disregarded until a French critic, Burger-Thore, published an enthusiastic article after encountering his work in 1857.

Ellie curtailed the lecture by chipping in: 'At the Manchester Art Treasures Exhibition.'

'Yes. And then Manet enthused, and van Gogh also, and within ten years Hals was famous and in demand.' He was distinctly ironic as he added: 'Being credited with influencing the Impressionists has done his reputation no harm at all.'

She gestured at the book on the table in front of him. 'But were those paintings genuine?'

'They were accepted as such and still are. By most authorities – you know how paintings fall in and out of favour with the experts. A little poking around with the overpaint, a spot of radiography and opinions change.'

Ellie asked whether the dealer's business still existed. She was out of luck.

'Until the war,' he said.

Not bombed out, then. Hitler did not bomb Amsterdam, he

flattened Rotterdam instead and showed how it would be. The Rijksmuseum man did not amplify, except to tell Ellie: 'No records for you there. However, this document states that the three paintings were sold along with work by a variety of artists.'

'All Dutch?'

'No. A few Rembrandt drawings, a modest Canaletto, a Vermeer and a Titian.'

'An odd mix.'

'But offered to the dealer by the same person. A German name. Herr Abetz inherited these paintings and drawings and sold them. Now what might be significant to you is his explanation to the dealer that they were his share of a family collection. If that was true, then one is entitled to wonder who inherited the rest and what was among them.'

'And for that, I suppose, I must go to Germany.'

'Herr Abetz lived in Prague.'

And that is when he smiled and remarked that it was a good time to go to Prague.

Ellie ordered a second cup of coffee in the Amsterdam bar and steeled herself to make the decision to fly on to Czechoslovakia. It was a desperately lonely decision with nobody else's encouragement or caution to sway her. Years ago when she was seventeen, in London for a year to learn English, and the BBC announced the crushing of the Prague Spring beneath Russian tanks, her decision was swift and public.

John Blair's cousin, in whose house she was living, whose child she was caring for, broke the news and, before Ellie absorbed it, was telling her: 'You must stay, Ellie. If that's what you want, then you must stay here. We'll help you, of course we will. Oh God, Ellie, your family – if only we could get them out too. What will you do? You can't possibly want to go back, can you?'

Ellie made up her mind there and then but delayed telling anyone for a day or two. It was a positive, determined act, a promise to herself that her life would be as free as she could happily make it. The first step had been the *au pair* job, a toe dipped in the waters of the West. If she had hated it, she could have gone home and added her iota of experience to that of all the others of her generation whose youthful flowering coincided with her country's reawakening.

The months in London had been up and down, sometimes wonderful, sometimes depressingly difficult. They were nearly over. She was lucky in her employers, an outgoing architect and his wife, and made to feel welcome without being smothered. London was perfect. It was the era of youth, the whole world wanted to be seventeen and in Swinging London and, against odds, Ellie was.

John Blair, a student then, ensured she was invited to parties and met people of her own age. Her English was limited but they spoke German together. John had a spectacularly beautiful girlfriend, the leggy Scandinavian type fashionable then, but Ellie was not jealous. She was content John was like an older brother, except that her own brother had never been good to her.

After the news from Czechoslovakia John called. They were all in the kitchen, a cavernous room brightened with red and white gingham curtains and table-cloth. His cousin was repeating her opinions about the awfulness of the invasion and her reassurance that Ellie need not leave England. Ellie was doing something with the boy. He was not a bad child but he was wild, always leaping about when she needed him static, always shouting when she wanted to speak, always battering her with demands when she needed to think.

John asked her: 'Are your family all right, Ellie?'

She looked round to answer him. The child struck out and snatched a fistful of her silvery blonde hair. Ellie was forced to give him her attention.

'Hey, no. Be good. Please.'

The child shrieked with laughter, bouncing in his chair and flinging his arms and legs about. A foot connected with Ellie's shoulder. She caught it and held it down, talking to the child, trying to calm him.

John said to his cousin: 'Can't you look after him for a few minutes? We want to talk.'

The mother seemed about to object but instead said: 'I should leave him, if I were you, Ellie. He'll be fine if you stop fussing around him.'

Ellie moved away quickly towards John.

He said: 'Let's go outside.'

The garden was given over to scattered playthings but on a paved area at the end was a weathered wooden bench beneath a plane tree. Ellie and John went down there, the child's whoops receding but never dying away.

'Kids! I don't know how you stand them, Ellie.'

'I like them.'

'But not that one, you can't. He's a shocker.'

'Perhaps he'll learn to be sensible like everyone else and it will be boring.'

'Bet you didn't know what you were letting yourself in for or you'd never have come.'

'I admit it, he was a surprise.'

He laughed. 'An enormous one.'

They reached the bench and she sat. He stood over her, a foot on the seat balancing his weight. They looked at each other, seriously.

'How are your family?'

She shook her head. 'I don't know. No, I'm sure they'll be all right. They don't have a telephone but there's someone else I've been trying to ring. The number isn't answered.'

'Are you thinking of going back as planned next month? Or staying on until the position becomes clear.'

'It's clear, John. I don't have any doubts. Things won't be allowed to continue as they were. Good things were growing and now they will die.'

Hoping to comfort he said: 'It mightn't be so bad. Perhaps . . .'

'Perhaps what? Perhaps we should be used to it, to having our country occupied? You don't know what it means. Who's ever come here and changed the way everything must be done and made you all prisoners?'

'William the Conquerer. But it *was* some while ago.'

'You see?' She put out a placating hand but did not quite touch his arm. 'I'm sorry, I mustn't be angry with you, John. I'm angry with them, with my people, for letting this happen to them. And we do, you know, over and over. We're told we must belong to the Austro-Hungarian Empire, then we're told to become Czechoslovakia, and then the Nazis seize our country and after that, while we're fighting for Prague, the Russians march in and say we're in the Soviet bloc. History never lets us decide.'

'Geography,' he corrected her.

There was a pause. A pigeon flapped amongst foliage overhead and a blue-grey feather floated down. John stretched a lazy hand for it before it settled on her hair.

He said: 'It sounds as though you've decided to stay.'

'Yes, I shall stay.'

'Won't it be very hard, not to see your family?'

She did not reply.

He had noticed she very rarely mentioned them, just sufficient to give a polite reply to a polite inquiry. He asked: 'Will they try to get out, do you think?'

She looked up into his face, her hair falling back to emphasize the high cheekbones and the almond-shaped grey eyes. 'No. They wouldn't wish to live somewhere that wasn't a Communist country. They're better than I am at believing what they're told.'

Usually John and Ellie talked about light things, he did not probe or treat her as a curiosity. She liked him for it. And when there were more solemn things to be considered, she was confident she could trust him with them. She saw that he understood.

Another hiatus before, in the manner of someone giving a

83

pep talk, he said: 'If you're going to stay, Ellie, you have other decisions to make. You can't drift, you know, looking after other people's children. Oh, they'd let you. Either my family or other families would. Girls who're reliable with kids are at a premium but if you want anything better you'll have to fight for it.'

They talked practicalities for a while, John revealing possibilities she had been too busy and too preoccupied to consider. They would have talked longer if the boy had not been released from the house to come tearing after her, claiming her time.

The passengers on the aeroplane to Prague were a jumble of proselytizing Western businessmen, home-going Czechs and tourists. There were not many of the tourists. They gave themselves away with their suppressed excitement, trying to look worldly while marvelling at their own mischievousness in opting for a few days on the other side of the Iron Curtain. That the curtain had been rent and then fallen a year before did not defuse the emotion: good heavens, if it had *not* they would have been in sunny southern Europe with their friends.

Ellie pursued a party of four Britons along the corridors and through the checks. Their eyes were avid for any detail that was different and therefore interesting, although, an airport being an airport, these were sparse. The stares from the officials were blanker, perhaps, and there were no Asian men and women performing menial tasks in the concourse as there were at Heathrow. Neither did the exit doors slide open automatically on approach, something the quartet discovered when they crashed a luggage trolley into the glass. Ellie last saw them looking round nervously, giggling, and taking their first steps out into the once-dangerous unknown.

She hired a taxi and gave directions for her hotel. The journey was flat and featureless with the disappointing preamble of run-down blocks of 1960s flats before the older more handsome houses began and there, drawing her on, was the hill topped by the castle and St Vitus's Cathedral.

There was none of the gaudy in Prague. That was what was

missing. One or two advertisements had ventured on to the flanks of buses (Fly British Airways, Use So-and-so's computers) and there was a sprinkling of fast-photo businesses obviously hoping for custom from tourists because their details were in a range of languages. Otherwise, nothing.

Traffic on the roads was light and slow. She had forgotten the volume of pedestrians, criss-crossing the city. But this was new: the Metro the Russians built in the 1970s. She realized there was an extra bridge over the river too, that alongside all the subtle changes those two engineering achievements stood out as symbols of the way her city had changed and made of her a stranger.

She checked into the Hotel Ambassador in Wenceslas Square, a hundred yards downhill from the publishing house where Václav Havel and Dubček stepped on to the balcony of *Svobodné Slovo*, the free word, together, during the days the rest of the world calls the Velvet Revolution and Czechs call the November Days. In London she had scanned faces on her television screen without spotting one she recognized. What became of them, those boys and girls she grew up with, the ones who wanted to make music, or make a new world, or simply make something of their lives? She had wondered as she hunched in front of the set, and wondered again as faces flowed past on her way up the square to raised beds of municipal pansies, an avenue to the Jan Palach memorial.

When Ellie was last in Prague this was a flower bed too, a circle of blossom in front of the most celebrated of Prague's hundreds of statues: St Wenceslas, patron saint and king of Bohemia, riding forth, banner aloft. Returning, she saw for the first time the clustered photographs of modern martyrs, held within the protective border formed by the dribblings of thousands upon thousands of candles. Several people moved with ceremonial reverence around the memorial, some bending forward to see more clearly. Six candles were burning, the tiny promises of their yellow flames tremulous in the breeze. A girl arrived and with practised haste lit a fresh candle, planted it in the cup of a dying one, crouched a few contemplative seconds and then was gone.

To have been away in 1968 was both a saving and a misery. Ellie had won a life of her choosing but she felt cheated. In London, or in New York with Sam, acquaintances asked her whether she ever doubted her decision and she lied and told them no. Her emotions were too conflicting and confused for her to unravel them for strangers who had no comparable experience and no means of imagining. The crass assumed she felt rather like someone on holiday in a wonderful resort who discovers that staying on is not a crazy dream but a necessity.

As a woman said to her at a party in the Hamptons: 'It's the ones that went back that I could never understand. I mean, what *for*?'

Rhetorical, no answer required. Ellie acknowledged the woman's bewilderment with a smile to be interpreted anyhow. And she cast the subject aside with a reference to one of Sam's better-known pieces, *Exile*. This was a provocative assemblage of paper-clips with a drawing pin or two and other bits of desk-drawer detritus. There were those who had been large in its praise, writing about the splendid effect of those paper-clips, making as they did a chain. As everybody knew without telling, a chain was a restraint, a boundary, a toy of the S and M brigade or, if knowledge stretched thus far, an old-fashioned measurement surviving in the usage of railwaymen.

Having got to know Sam, who was more inclined to mutter that his work spoke for itself than elucidate, Ellie came to believe that *Exile* had more to do with Sam's own alienation from the nine-to-five office life than with the deeper themes critics discovered. She kept that view to herself. Sam was tricky in interviews, it had to be said. He glowered and pondered and cut short intricate theories with the declaration that he was not a maker of words, the interviewer would have to find his own. So long as they did, and went on doing it, he would be all right.

There was a balance to be struck between chucking the theorizing back to the journalists and being so uninformative that word went round that he was a hopeless interviewee and best avoided. Sam teetered on a tightrope. Or so Ellie thought.

She had, by arrangement, interrupted one of the interviews he gave in London. They cooked up some nonsense about a problem at the cold store where his ice sculptures were held.

'Ellie, I won't be able to take more that twenty minutes of this guy. Could you give him that long and then break in on us?'

'Twenty minutes? But, Sam, he's travelled up from Cornwall.'

'Then he'll be in plenty of time for the ride home.'

'Oh, Sam. Couldn't you . . .'

'Twenty minutes, I can't see me lasting two seconds over. You haven't met him, he's a pain. Wants to put me into some historical context he's always on about. Well, I don't want to be put anywhere. All I require him to say is the name of the gallery and that it's a great show and everybody better get right over there.'

Her interruption was Oscar-worthy. The interviewer left believing that Sam's *Harley Davidson Remembered* no longer resembled a collector's motorcycle as much as a well-licked lolly. When he had gone Sam was edgy until he telephoned the cold store for confirmation that nothing was melting.

'Sam, you're a disgrace,' Ellie said through conspiratorial laughter.

'Oh, come on. You should have heard him: "Would you say your work has moved away from sexual imagery to the purely political?" I said I'd expected him to perceive a connection between ice-sculpture and frigidity.'

'You didn't!'

'Sure. You see what happens? They come along with their complex analyses and they get me thinking that way too.'

'But he'll print it. It'll become part of the myth.'

'It could even be true. How do I know? Who's to say what goes on at a subliminal level?'

'It isn't much, you're always saying so.'

'Ellie, that's private. Public opinions aren't the same. Well, mine aren't. Anyway, thanks for kicking him out.'

She bowed. 'How did the rest of it go?'

'Not one of my great performances, I guess. I backtracked from the frigidity situation and took the usual line that the work speaks for itself. And he said: "But that doesn't quite tally with your statement a couple of years ago when you were being asked to justify the price tag of your collection of curtain poles, that 'There isn't any Art until someone points it out.' " Then he invited me to "amplify my message" in the ice pieces.'

'And?'

'And then you waltzed in with your Katharine Hepburn number and between us we made damn sure he bolted.'

'Was that all? What were you two doing the rest of the twenty minutes?'

'Trying to get the window open. Did you know it got stuck when you redecorated?'

Being a resourceful kind of fellow, the interviewer contrived to fill his fifteen-hundred-word slot in *The Times* in spite of the interview being curtailed to three and a half minutes. He wrote about the jammed window and about the panic at the unfreezing cold store. He described what Ellie was wearing (cream suede trousers, a coffee-coloured silk blouse and cream and brown pumps, if he was to be believed); he attributed next door's cat to the Sam and Ellie ménage and misspelled its French name; and he theorized about Sam's work. He contributed generously to the myth. Sam, readers learned, shied away from committing himself to a full statement of his intentions with *Harley Davidson Remembered*, *Pitchfork Rebellion* and the rest of the series but by employing the word frigidity he confirmed that sexual images continued to dominate. And so forth.

Sam was entirely satisfied.

When she first got to know him and was warmed by the glow of his fame, Ellie assumed Sam feared, as many creative people fear, being found out, being revealed as not half as much as the critics cracked him up to be. She supposed he was nervous that one day he would open a magazine and read that someone was saying: 'Hey, you know that Sam Whatshisname? Well, he isn't any good after all.' And that would be It.

She was wrong. Sam did not think that way. He despised people who could create nothing of their own and went talent-spotting among those who could, boosting reputations but particularly their own, and complicating books, paintings or sculptures by concealing them behind fanciful ideas whereas, uncomplicated, they communicated better with more people. If all that were debunked, Sam's response would be: 'I told you so.' Like many creative people Sam was disdainful of critics but could not live without them.

The revelations about him, the truth, came as a series of jolts to Ellie. On the inside of his life, she readjusted all her notions about the man and his work. Adaptable, she adapted to saying nothing about him and became a disappointment to the people who relied on her for insight. His three wives had frozen out the inquirers and so did she.

Frozen. Ice sculptures. There was a sense in which Sam was dedicated to reining things in, fixing them. To Ellie this seemed a reversal of what artists were supposed to do but as no one else noticed she kept the thought to herself. It came to her, as one of those jolts, the day he begged her to get over to the former food factory, where he was working, with a new chisel mislaid at her flat. His old one was blunt.

He had a chunk of ice, a 500lb crystal block delivered that morning by an ice dealer, and he dared not leave it. Ellie gave him the chisel and watched, fascinated. The chisel was extremely sharp and made a scraping sound as it cut into the ice.

He stood back and ran a hand through his thick hair. He was in shirt sleeves, the place at normal room temperature because ice is brittle if worked when very cold and then it shatters.

Sam grunted. 'The first block was better than this. Look at the number of strains.'

She went closer to examine the breaks and fractures. 'That's going to make it hard to work. Won't it break?'

'Oh, if it comes apart I can stick it back together with a drop of water. But I wanted a clearer texture.'

He began to carve again, following the line of a thread-like grain. She asked a question about that. He explained that ice freezes from the outside to the centre and this process forms the grain. 'If it's frozen at the correct temperature, minus fifteen degrees, you get rid of the air and minerals and the result is a clear block. Well, this isn't perfect but it will do. I can disguise most of the flaws and I'll have to make a virtue of the rest.'

The chisel scored again. Ellie put her jacket on. 'I'd better get back home. What time do you expect to be finished here, Sam?'

'I'll work until around seven, then slide this into the refrigeration room. We could eat at that Japanese place if you like. Around eight?'

She travelled home on the Underground, thinking. As she understood it, and she knew a number of artists, sculptors thought in terms of releasing forms from the hunks of material they started with. Sam, she was convinced, was releasing nothing. He was imposing a form on his material, forcing it to accept and hold a shape. Of course, the outside view was necessarily that this was so. Anyone who watches an artist chiselling away sees a man making one form into another. The difference was on the inside, on how Sam felt about it. His occasional remarks about his progress on pieces, his vocabulary, suggested to her that Sam's nature was not one to free anything. He liked to contain and twist and, ultimately, to control.

That evening, over a bowl of *wakame no suimono*, he asked her to live with him.

She was not at all certain she was in love with him but she was enthralled and their sex was especially good, the quilt thrown over the carpet, the hours of pleasing and being pleased. Her original, fatal, impression that he was an old friend, someone she knew way back in an unnameable time, was overlaid with mysteries. She enjoyed mysteries.

That initial impression was a false one, based on who knew what mix of chemistry? In reality, Sam was unlike anyone she had ever experienced, although the photographs she was to see among the newspaper cuttings showed she bore more than a passing resemblance to his second wife. The same fair shiny hair and high cheekbones although wife number two lacked the almond-shaped eyes.

Living with him had, in practice, meant him living with her. Moving into her flat, altering everything. Intrigued, she studied herself giving way. This was not like her. No other lovers had been allowed to move in. Her privacy, her autonomy, were precious. Sam had small but powerful reasons, as he did for all the things he attained. The flat was a good example. Sam was borrowing a friend's place in London but it was needed so he had to shift himself anyway. But the other examples? Agape, she saw her independent self being usurped by this man who had no idea what he was doing.

In her diary she wrote: 'It's his life that's being lived. I fit into it or I refuse to and then that puts me out of his life. I don't want that. Or I don't think I do. Not yet. Sam doesn't ever fade into the wallpaper and let me live my own life. His presence is always there even if he happens to be away at the studio or somewhere else. I either have to accept all this or put an end to it. I know this is absurd but I can't see how to handle it.'

What tipped the scale in favour of letting Sam be was Ellie's knowledge that he needed her. She knew what it was like to be adrift in a foreign country and she also knew that without her, or wives one to three, he would give himself a hard time. His very helplessness played on her. If it was not love, or not the passionate kind she had known, then it grew near to it.

And then he took her to New York. And in New York he changed, their relationship adjusted and became more equal. Eventually, when he was struggling to contain the *Icons of the Twentieth Century* in a plastic bubble-pack, she felt able to take the decision to return to London. There was no sense of abandoning an incompetent child who would not know how to get through the day without her.

London. Amsterdam. Prague. On her second day in Prague she met Rose Darrow.

NINE

They had coffee and cakes amid the art nouveau flourishes of the Pariz Hotel, a touristy thing to do.

Rose said: 'It's idiotic, you staying in a hotel in Wenceslas Square and me in a borrowed flat.'

'My family don't know I'm here. To be honest, I don't know for certain whether they are either. It would be a shock to bump into any of them in the street the way I bumped into you.'

The matter-of-fact words masked confusion. She had realized things would be different but the physical changes, like the Metro and the new bridge, were easy to come to terms with. What she had not expected was to be cast adrift, more the outsider in Prague than in London. Meeting Rose highlighted this. Ellie had encountered her with joy. A friend. Someone she could really talk to. A fellow stranger on the surface of the city.

Yet her link with Rose Darrow was tenuous. They were not confidingly close and there was a gulf of ten years between them. For Rose, 1968 was a piece of turbulent history of no special significance. Tempted to share her feelings with a sympathetic listener, Ellie was cautious of Rose's reputation as a questioner. She could not decide, she was not in control.

Rose left a pause, hoping Ellie would go on. When she did not, Rose coaxed her with: 'Being here must be churning your memories.'

'Ah, yes, Rose. Remember Coleridge's recollections that "sometimes leap/from hiding places ten years deep"? Well, mine are buried deeper. Twenty years deep. I walk into Old Town Square and suddenly I'm a teenager on my way to hear once-forbidden music. Or I hurry towards the bridge and I'm a girl in love with a dark-eyed young art lover from Malá Strana.'

'An art lover?'

'Oh, yes. I was always a sucker, you see, for people who knew about such things.' She hesitated, then did not speak his name after all. 'He taught me the first things I knew, really understood, about paintings. We used to walk up the hill to the galleries.'

'Have you been up there this week?'

'No. Tomorrow. Although yesterday I meant it to be today. But I must go tomorrow. There's a Hals painting I'll enjoy seeing but more pertinently there's a woman who may be able to tell me what became of the remainder of the collection that was partially sold off in Amsterdam.'

Rose signalled the waitress for refills. Ellie protested. 'I'm not sure I'm ready for more.'

'Don't worry, you will be by the time it comes.'

Laughter, then: 'That's true. I remember *that* kind of thing, the dumb resistance. I wonder, do I carry that around with me?'

The waitress spoiled their jokes by being quick. Then Rose decided it was time to ask a favour. 'When we met I teased you that you were exactly what I was looking for, an interpreter. Well, although it sounded general there's a specific problem. I prefer not to discuss it with the people who are going to work for the magazine.'

'You don't trust them?'

'I don't know how discreet they are. And it's delicate, Ellie. I believe Krieger is here. In fact, I know he is and I want to interview him.'

She recited details of the abortive attempts to meet him and her failure to find the contact, the stooping man, at the house in the Old Town. 'Will you come to the house with me?'

'Of course.' Then: 'But tell me, Rose. Are you planning to pay Krieger a lot of money for his story?'

'You think that would be immoral?' The question was superfluous.

'He's not a good man, does he deserve to be rewarded for the dreadful things he did? But I suppose that's the way journalists work.'

'Not if they can get anything for free, they don't. I'm prepared for him to ask for money and I'm prepared to pay. If I don't, someone else will. An exclusive interview with him in the first issue of the magazine would be a real prize. It would show the doubters we're serious.'

Quietly Ellie reminded her: 'Krieger was serious. He deceived and betrayed, then he got away. Escaped into East Germany leaving wrecked lives and, if the rumours are true, several dead bodies. How many others will your serious magazine pay to chat about their sins, Rose?'

Rose refused to be needled. 'He's the important one, the famous one. I'll take him if I can catch him, the others I'll have to see about.'

Ellie reached forward and touched her hand. 'Take no notice, I'm being too hard. Things are . . . difficult for me.'

Rose forgave her with a smile. She was not foolish enough to claim she understood. *There is no life without memory,* she murmured, and added brightly: 'Gabriel García Márquez. Not as classy as Coleridge, I dare say, but doesn't the name trip off the tongue?'

They went to the house in the Old Town. No answer but Ellie spoke to the neighbours and learned that the house was currently unoccupied.

She persisted. 'There was a man, a thin man with a stoop, always smoking. He had brown hair. He was there a few days ago, late in the afternoon. Who was he?'

But the neighbours did not help.

When they parted in the falling darkness, Rose for the flat to make telephone calls to Paris and Ellie to return to the hotel, a cold wind was cutting across the squares. Ellie stood in a shadowy doorway, let Rose move out of sight, and then set off very slowly the way the younger woman had gone.

She was observing every facet of her city. Warm honey colour of stonework; exact shades of pinks and blues on painted façades; a richness of statuary and ironwork; precise angles of cobbles that broke free from badly maintained pavements as pedestrians walked over them; the blight of scaffolding and apparent dearth of workmen; buildings of sentimental interest, like the Týn Church, closed for a restoration that was plainly not taking place.

She noted knots of young people gathered around those who played their old-fashioned guitars and sang their unamplified songs beneath arcading. Then there was the male clubbiness of the *pivárnas* tainting the street air with the bitter scent of tobacco smoke and beer, and the competing sourness of soft brown coal burning in the city's fireplaces. The sounds, the totally human sounds, were the brushing of shoe leather over stone and the mumble of not very loud voices in a musical language.

Ellie reached the medieval bridge. There was a pain in her heart, an ache of melancholy, regret for the years she had not been there and bitterness for the reasons that kept her away. Public reasons and private ones. Sam had his private opinions as well as his public ones, and so did she. Ellie started over the bridge, down the proud avenue of saints. Lamps threw light enough for her to see the black rushing river but she did not pause until she reached the centre and St John of Nepomuk. Bronze among the stone, light glinted from his angularity. He seemed wasted, shrunken after his drowning for, variously, opposing a king or keeping a queen's secrets.

Hands on the parapet, she raised her face to the castle with its rows of lighted windows, to the floodlit dome of baroque St Nicholas's Church below it. And then, looking back the way she had come, she saw the theatre and the lighted towers in the Old Town. She could not remember floodlights from her youth but perhaps it was the same then. Her memories were sharp, jagged, but she was discovering they were not always accurate. She did not like to ask about the floodlights. Prague people and a scattering of tourists were passing back and forth but she spoke to nobody. Her heart was bursting.

Every corner, every step she took in the city, was rich in remembered happenings. *That* is where she walked with her friend, Misha. *That* is where Nina said she was going to England to work as an *au pair* and would Ellie like to come too? Ellie went, and Nina did not. *That* is where she came to meet the boy her parents did not know she was seeing, and *this* is . . .

Here, half-way along the bridge, near St John of Nepomuk burdened with his cross and his vow to save those who fell, he had come for her. He trailed her, unhurriedly, knowing she had nowhere to go, that sooner or later she must falter and turn around. And he followed her beneath the tower, on to the bridge, and waited, waited, until she dragged her thoughts to the impracticability of any other course and turned back.

Until now she had forgotten the exact details of that moment, the degree of her revulsion as she saw him and knew he had pursued her and he understood. Everything. He understood everything and he did not care.

She clapped a hand over her mouth. She felt sick, faint, a flush of fear weakened her. Just as it had been so long ago. She jerked away, as she had done then.

Her mind rattled instructions to her. 'Don't be a fool, there's no one there. Walk on, you don't have to go back. For heaven's sake, pull yourself together.'

And with an effort of will she walked over the bridge towards the castle. She fought down her panic and dealt with the ᵕirrational fear that a hand would grab her shoulder, wheel her round, force her where she would not go.

Gradually it became all right. She passed the steps leading down to Kampa, she went through the archway and climbed he sloping road up to the square in front of St Nicholas's Church. Her pulse was no longer a throbbing in her ears but her breathing was painful, unreliable, and she was conscious of the clamminess of her skin. She ordered herself to believe it was over, the fright could never happen to her again.

But what else might? What else might reduce her to girlish feebleness? She knew De Quincey as well as Coleridge, could quote him on the recollections that 'bring into collision the present with some long-forgotten past, in a form too trying and too painful for endurance'.

There was a cab rank below the church. She rode back to her hotel.

Next morning she went up to the castle and confronted Jasper Schade. He was younger, more arrogant and dandified than Frans Hals's Washington man. She lingered with him, admiring the splendour of attire, the cunning verticality of the portraiture that made him both a haughty figure and a fellow never to be trusted. She had known fellows like that in her own life. Then, dutiful, she looked at the Skretas, the home-grown artist who had occasionally painted similar subjects. She would be very disappointed if she had been sent by mistake *en route* to a Skreta.

At the offices she asked for Milena Hobzek. There had been a telephone call, the woman was expecting her.

'But I've found very little for you,' she apologized when Ellie was seated across the desk from her. 'Now if you wanted to know about Karel Skreta, for instance, I'd have everything at my fingertips.' Her smile was wintry.

There was a notebook on the desk. Milena Hobzek turned the pages with a manicured hand. Everything about her was precise, cared for. The collar of her blouse was raised exactly so above the neckline of her beige suit, no hair dared to float free of the perfect pleat, the stone in the ring on her finger was a match for the one in the brooch on her lapel. Ellie watched her turn the pages.

Milena Hobzek said: 'I made inquiries among colleagues but no one knows of Abetz. I feel sure that if a family of that name had owned a substantial collection we'd be aware of it.'

'I don't know how substantial it was. If the story is true, it was broken up in the first half of the nineteenth century. And we don't know how many people received a share of it. All I have to go on is the name.'

'We have no record of anyone of that name being the owner of a collection at any period. But what I've done for you is this.' To Ellie's surprise she ripped a page out of the notebook and passed it to her. 'Those are the names of people known to have owned important collections during the period when Abetz claimed to have inherited. This information was gathered during someone's research. It could prove very lucky for you. Although, naturally, it may prove of no use whatsoever.'

Ellie ran her eye down the list. Each name was accompanied by an approximate address, a town or a district.

Milena Hobzek said: 'For all we know, your Herr Abetz was a thief or a liar although it's possible he had a legitimate means of acquiring those paintings that surfaced in Amsterdam. If one knew why it was Amsterdam it would be easier to gauge the truth of his story.'

Ellie hoped for more. 'I'd like to follow up by speaking to the person who carried out this research.'

'Unfortunately that won't be possible. He's very busy and he has to go away.'

'But I'd only want a few moments of his time and . . .'

'He has no spare moments. He has to deliver the manuscript of a book to a publisher and then he goes away.'

Ellie suspected she was being encouraged into a blind alley. She masked it, knowing that persistence would be met with implacability. It was usually more profitable to pretend to be unaware and shift to other ground. She put the sheet of paper in her pocket but did not get up to go although Milena Hobzek anticipated her doing so and was rising herself.

'Tell me,' Ellie said, 'if a painting by Frans Hals was known to be somewhere in the country, would the national gallery have made any effort to acquire it?'

The woman raised an eyebrow. 'Hals? It would have to be very inexpensive or very wonderful. We have one that's very wonderful, Jasper Schade. I should personally be very surprised if a genuine Hals came to light in Czechoslovakia. Is this what you're hoping for? A Hals that your Herr Abetz held on to and did *not* sell in Amsterdam?'

Ellie rose. 'Possibly. But first I must trace Abetz.'

The glossy fingernails flashed through the pages of the notebook again. Another page was torn out. 'Just a minute. There's this too. If you go to see this man he might be able to help you with Abetz. When he lived and died, that sort of thing. Other than that, I can't help.'

'You've been very kind. I appreciate it.'

Milena Hobzek came round the desk. 'Not at all. It's little enough. And, who knows, you may return with some interesting information for me.'

There it was again. That sensation that beneath the words were unspoken thoughts, a parallel discourse in which there was no trust and no confidence and no intention of providing either.

Ellie made the promise that was required of her. 'Of course.'

'Distrust,' Ellie murmured to herself as she went down the corridor. There was an inbuilt scepticism about what the other human being was actually up to. She remembered it well. Schoolteachers whose vigilance wobbled now and then to reveal they did not trust in the wisdom they were obliged to impart. Adult conversations that dealt in obliquity because that left room for denial if denial became necessary. Hints so wrapped up they would have been missed if the listeners were not skilled in hearing them. Answers ducked and direct questions dodged because it was practicable to let the truth seep through the gaps between words and it was wiser that way.

She went along passages and corridors at another building soon after, each step into the labyrinth seeming to deny her the chance to retreat. She might have been sinking into the past. The elderly sinecure holders were still in place, literally, gossiping together so that two pairs of miss-nothing eyes made her self-conscious. The dragon was dead but these people had been its guardians and they were too ancient to learn new ways.

From that building she was directed to another one. More eyes oppressed her. 'Boredom,' she assured herself. 'That's all, boredom. They have nothing to do, even less than before. At least their curiosity used to be official, now they're valueless.'

But it was hard to believe in their uselessness. They watched her go by and they watched her come back. The same at the third building. By then she was used to it, not able to ignore them but reacquainted with existence in a country where there was no freedom to move unobserved. She found her chest tightening, the clutch of asthma.

Elsewhere she would have stopped, relaxed and chased the tensions away. But she refused to give these watchers the satisfaction of anything worth watching. Snatching at her breath she strode on, her pace unfaltering.

She identified a special fear, a particularly foolish one and despite discomfort she smiled. She had an uncle who was one of the watchers in corners. As he was a good Party member who lost a leg in the war, a grateful nation allowed him to sit all day on a chair and pretend to be working. But he was prone to doze and when he dozed he had nightmares and screamed. The remedy was to set another war cripple beside him. Usually one or other of them was awake. Her fear was that she would round a corner and come across him. Nonsense, he died long ago, within a year or two of her leaving the country, back in the days when she wrote and received letters.

Finally she was free of the buildings. Her breathing calmed. She watched the river gnawing at stone, swirling under its garland of bridges, creaming round bends and running away until it changed its name and flowed through Germany to surge into the sea. This is where she used to stroll and marvel at the ease of its escape and the unlikelihood of her own. But that was when she was a child, before the years of dreaming and the days of desperate plotting.

She came to a bench and sat, mulling over all she had learned in the labyrinth that day. An Abetz had lived at a house in the New Town. She had the address. He was born in Prague in 1791, the year of Mozart's death, and he died there in 1841, the year Dvořák was born. He lived to see the opening of the railway line linking Prague to Vienna but died before tensions between Czechs and Germans culminated in bloody uprising. She knew where he was buried. But she did not know whether he might lead her to a companion for the Washington man.

Besides, it was supposition that this Abetz was the one whose name had crept into the records in Amsterdam.

Her inclination was to go straight to the cemetery and seek him out but she had first to meet Rose Darrow and try once more to get an answer at the house where Rose saw the stooping man.

They met in Old Town Square, a couple of minutes before the five-hundred-year-old clock went through its hourly routine. The newest party of German tourists was grouped, faces upturned so no sight should escape them, being lectured by a man in a green hat. Rose stood to one side of them, ready for Death to ring the funeral bell, for Christ and the parading apostles, and the crowing, wing-flapping cock. Meanwhile her glance took in the scaffolded Týn Church where Jan Huys had preached against the authority of the Pope and started a movement that led to religious reform and its inevitable concomitant, war. But her attention was distracted by the passage of people, drably dressed older people and the younger women with their home-made approximations of the Western fashions flaunted by tourists.

For several minutes Rose did not notice Ellie's approach and Ellie herself became a watcher. Rose stood out, obviously not one of the intent Germans although just as clearly a visitor. Clothes, hair, self-confidence prevented her from passing as one of the crowd. Ellie caught sight of her own reflection in a window, a woman of around forty striding by in her expensive boots and leather coat to keep an appointment. A woman whose appearance gave her away as an outsider.

Gypsy children surrounded Rose, pestering for change she did not have. They dispersed when Ellie spoke harshly to them.

Rose said: 'I suppose that was Czech for clear off.'

'They don't speak Czech. This is a city of refugees now, they're Romanian. But clear off is a direct message in any language. Do you want to see the clock again?'

It was girding itself up for the feat. Tourists pressed closer together, adjusted positions as heads blocked views. Their guide dried up.

'No,' said Rose. They went to the house straightaway.

The girl who played her guitar on the bridge appeared. Rose touched Ellie's arm. 'She's the one who guided me here.'

Ellie questioned the girl. There was an anxious moment when the girl tried to get away only to find Rose obstructing her. The moment passed. Ellie and the girl talked some more. Then Ellie released her.

'Well?'

'Rose, she argued she knew nothing about it, says all she did was agree to collect you and your friend Willi from the bridge and deliver you here. But in the end she conceded that the ground-floor rooms of this house are used sometimes by the son of the tenant. The tenant herself is in hospital. She's a Mrs Zak, a very old woman. The girl claims not to know where the son is when he's not here but I think she's lying.'

'You didn't mention Krieger to her, I hope.'

There was a flicker of indignation before Ellie said: 'No. Anyway, if she'd known his whereabouts there's no chance she'd have told me.'

Rose groaned. Then: 'Thanks, Ellie.'

'What next?'

'Try the door bell yet again and visit the hospital.'

The bell went unanswered. At the hospital Ellie talked her way in and they saw Mrs Zak. She was a thin husk of a woman, so light her head appeared not to dent the pillow. Her face was papery and blotched with the dark patches people call grave marks. A nurse stood guard throughout.

The patient's black eyes flickered from Rose to Ellie as Ellie pumped out questions rehearsed on the way. Mrs Zak was not ga-ga but she was wary. Ellie recognized the signs even if Rose could not be expected to.

In slang, hoping the nurse who might be concealing a little English would be unable to follow, Ellie suggested Rose get the nurse out of the room because the old woman was extremely unlikely to say anything in her presence. A few minutes later Rose managed it.

She kept the nurse in the passage, out of earshot. In German she and the nurse discussed directions to the toilets while in the background she heard the melody of Czech as Ellie coaxed the patient.

Returning to the room a few minutes later, Rose saw the nurse at the bedside concentrating on Ellie, who was addressing the taciturn old woman. The husk seemed emptier than before. The nurse said: 'That is enough now. Mrs Zak isn't strong.'

Ellie pushed the chair back where she found it. By the time she looked round to say goodbye the old woman had been claimed by sleep.

'Air,' Rose muttered, hurrying out. 'I must have air. I can't stand those places. They're so final.'

Ellie laughed at her. 'It's all right, Rose, you're free to run off. But before you go, don't you want to hear what Mrs Zak had to tell me?'

'Oh. I thought the whole episode was a flop. You got her to speak?'

'Come. This way.' Ellie led her down a short cut through a slit of an alley linking one street with the next. As they emerged she said: 'She agreed her son uses the house. Lives there while she's away, to look after it, she said. And she told me he normally lives at Budj.'

'Another town?'

'No, a suburb of Prague. I haven't been on the Metro yet, this looks like my chance to try it out.'

Rose admitted that Zak, the man with the stoop, spoke German and a certain amount of English. 'I could manage alone if you have other things you'd rather do.'

'I'm coming with you. I wouldn't miss my ride on the Metro.'

Rose said the Metro was wonderful. 'Clean, uncluttered and the trains look new and run on time. After poor old London Transport it's a joy. Oh, and it costs a fraction of nothing.'

And so Ellie let Rose treat her as a tourist and introduce her to the simple Underground system with its three colour-coded lines, its easy interchanges, its pristine platforms and escalators innocent of advertising.

At Budj they came up out of the ground into early evening fog. Apart from the condom machines at the station entrance (Men's Shop Anti-Aids, written in English) it was like stepping back in time to Britain in the 1960s, to a council estate with blocks of flats, mostly low rise but a few thrusting up to ten storeys high. There were narrow streets, not many cars and scant parking space anyway. Ellie asked directions to the address she had squeezed out of Mrs Zak.

They took a walkway between a couple of blocks of flats whose concrete was stained with damp, whose windows showed signs of repeated repairs in the struggle to make them weatherproof. Fog and a scattering of trees and shrubs softened the scene.

'Here,' said Ellie. 'This one.'

They looked up at the grey cracked slab with its five tiers of windows. 'After you,' said Rose, doubtfully.

On the fourth floor Ellie knocked on a door. It was opened by a stooping figure with a cigarette in his hand.

Rose stepped forward. 'Well, hello, Mr Zak. I called at the house in the Old Town but you always seemed to be out.'

He scowled. 'Who sent you here?'

She shook her head, denying him the answer. 'Please, we must speak about Krieger.'

His hand was on the door, intending to shut it but she had years of practice at talking her way into places. Her boot was already over the threshold.

She said: 'Wouldn't you prefer to talk about it inside? Anyone might hear us out here.'

With no choice, he let the two women walk past him. The flat was messy and cramped. In the centre of the room stood a table and on it a couple of glasses and Pilsner bottles, a brimming packet of bitter Czech cigarettes. He offered it, an automatic courtesy. Rose and Ellie murmured no thanks. Then the pungent smell of his tobacco smoke blended with the staleness that pervaded the dingy room.

He addressed Rose, relegating Ellie to the role of a hanger-on he need not bother with, a colleague on Rose's magazine, something like that. Ellie kept her mouth shut.

'You have wasted your time coming here. Krieger is not here.'

'The other evening,' Rose began, 'you were going to explain the difficulties that prevent Krieger seeing me. You said I must understand that things aren't that simple. Well, for me they are very simple. I would like to meet Krieger and discuss an interview.'

'You could pay?'

'You know I could, I said so on the telephone. But this is a matter to discuss with him. I won't be ungenerous but neither will I be a fool.'

He sucked at the cigarette, breathed smoke out towards her. She was unflinching, hating the room, the stink, his stubbornness that had her going round and round the same course. All at once he ducked forward, perched the cigarette on the rim of the ashtray and pulled out one of the chairs from the table. 'Sit down.'

She took the chair nearest to her instead. Progress of a sort. Behind her she heard the scrape as Ellie helped herself to a chair.

'OK,' said Rose, and folded her arms on the table top and waited for what he had decided to say.

'If Rose Darrow and her Euromagazine are prepared to chase to and from Prague looking for him, then Krieger is worth a lot of money. If she is as keen as that, plenty of other journalists are too. And publishers, remember. There was that man from Frankfurt.'

'Willi Frankel.'

'There is an enormous amount of money to be made from a book.'

'Agreed. Although, as you see, Willi isn't here this evening. He's home in Frankfurt, not chasing Krieger.'

'But he is your friend, perhaps you will act as his agent.'

With the slightest frown she discouraged that line of thought.

He said: 'But no matter. If one publisher is interested, then others will be. Krieger's story is a valuable commodity, we understand that and we will not be undersold.'

Rose drew a shape with her fingertip in the dust on the table. 'Well, now. You're making it sound as though you intend to conduct an auction. But let me warn you that until Krieger appears in person and convinces people he's ready and willing to provide the story, nobody is going to be bidding. What would be the point? There have been other books about him, a pile of magazine articles as high as this block of flats. The only possible interest is in being able to publish his story in his own words. Either he can write it himself, which is unlikely, or he needs to sit down with a journalist who'll shape the story. Before I make any sort of offer, I must know what I'm dealing with.'

He took up the cigarette and leaned his chair back on two legs, looking at her through the smudge of smoke. 'Miss Darrow, you are dealing with me.'

She mocked with a smile. 'Not good enough, Mr Zak. What proof is there that Krieger's in Prague or that you've ever met him? You've told me various things but there's been nothing to substantiate them.'

Her gaze was unwavering. But eventually she was the one who looked away. The hand that had sketched a question mark in the dust reached in a lazy movement for the almost-empty beer glass on her side of the table. She lifted it, jiggled it to set the inch of brown swilling around and cast him a sidelong look.

She said: 'Why don't we settle all this now?'

He drew on the cigarette a couple of times, agitated. But he pretended not to understand her, saying: 'What kind of proof would satisfy you?'

'Invite your companion to join us.'

His eyes slewed to the door on the left of the room. Without warning Rose was on her feet, moving left. Zak bounded up, chair crashing back against the stove. His arm dropped hard across her forearm, spoiling her grip on the door handle. They stood, pressed close, his fist tight around the handle.

'Open it,' she demanded. She gritted her teeth against the pain in her arm, ignored the longing to hold the arm, cuddle it to her, soothe it.

His voice was vicious. 'You must go.'

'That's not what you want.' Pain was flowing up towards her shoulder. Despite herself she realized she was curving the injured limb, folding it against her body for protection against further attack.

And then the door was wrenched inwards. Zak attempted to resist but the gesture was a token. He let go and the door gaped.

A middle-aged man stood there. Short, thick-set, dark hair receding and sprinkled with grey, intelligent brown eyes. There had been no published photographs of him for fifteen years, and those years had marked him. Yet, at a second glance, she would have recognized him.

'Krieger,' Rose said.

He spoke to her in German. 'You have your wish. We're to meet this evening.'

He looked over at Ellie, seated at a table. Rose said: 'Ellie's a friend from London. Her German's better than mine.'

Krieger accepted the explanation. He stepped out into the room and spoke to Zak.

'A cigarette.'

Zak tossed him the packet and Krieger lit up before throwing the packet down beside one of the empty bottles. Rose wished there was a way of not breathing, the fug was making her eyes smart.

'God,' she thought, 'if ever I do interview this man it's going to be upwind in a park with a stiff breeze blowing.'

Zak, stooping to recover his cigarette packet, muttered a few words in Czech. Krieger replied briefly. Zak appealed again but Krieger chopped the words off with a wave of his hand and then spoke to Rose.

'I can tell you about the time I was in France, about my work in West Germany and the events leading up to my departure for the East. There are events that have never been described and reasons that have never been given. All that, I'm prepared to speak about. But you must appreciate my need for caution. I'm not a free man. I never will be. Governments may officially draw a line between past and present because it's expedient, too time-consuming and unconstructive to pursue former enemies. But individuals with grievances see no virtue in drawing lines.'

'I understand.'

'Then perhaps you also understand that while governments may declare their policies, ministers of those governments may sanction activities which run counter to them.'

She said: 'You'll want safeguards but I don't anticipate difficulties about agreeing to them.'

'And making those agreements stick?'

'I don't deal in the other kind.'

'We have an hour, Miss Darrow. Then you must leave.'

Zak interrupted but Krieger argued and he lost. Zak angrily stubbed out his cigarette and prowled into the next room and back. Rose sat at the table again, facing her quarry, Krieger.

He did not discuss money or safeguards, he talked about the early years, in France, galvanizing student unrest that culminated in the disturbances of 1968. When he broke off it was to ask Zak to pass him a bottle of beer.

Sometimes, when Rose flagged, Ellie contributed a neat translation from German to English. Otherwise, Ellie was quiet and kept an eye on the tape recorder Rose had asked her to carry.

As the hour drew to an end Zak became restless, the prowling resumed. He had been sitting in the bedroom, visible through the open door, but now he was hovering over the table, demanding and finally getting Krieger's attention.

Krieger let him have his way, saying to Rose: 'There's no more time. Tomorrow you may come again, after dark. We'll talk for longer.'

With reluctance Rose prepared to leave. Zak, by the front door, urged her: 'Hurry up.'

Rose put him out of his misery. She and Ellie left. They were away from the flat, down the walkway and facing the tramp through fog to the Metro station before Ellie confirmed Rose's suspicions.

'You have a problem, Rose. Krieger promised Zak he'd give you an hour tonight and get rid of you. They'll be making arrangements right now to move him to a better hiding place.'

'I thought so. That stuff he told me this evening, none of it was new. He gave away nothing and he didn't want to negotiate money.'

Their footsteps echoed on damp pavement, trees and buildings were ghostly. Ellie said: 'Are you thinking we ought to be hanging around near the flat to follow when they leave?'

Amused, Rose replied: 'I was thinking there's nothing I fancy less than dodging after them in the fog. We don't even have a car.'

'Well, at least you've seen him with your own eyes and can assure your office he's in Prague.'

'I've been doing that for weeks,' she said drily. And added: 'Do you know, I don't think I've ever been face to face with a fugitive spy before.'

Tart, Ellie responded: 'He didn't look well on it but he doesn't deserve to.'

Fine rain was glistening on stone. Ellie began at one corner of the graveyard and systematically read the inscriptions.

The place was reminiscent of Highgate Cemetery and Poets' Corner in Westminster Abbey: a culture corral where the arts were laid to rest. She was stern with herself, curtailing browsing or musing on ambiguities, intentional or otherwise, of the wording. Wind caught at leaves and sent brown shapes flapping along the paths. Ellie wrapped her scarf closer about her head and moved more quickly.

When the shower grew heavy she broke off and sought cover, leaning against a pillar and watching slanting rain linking stone and sky in a grey miasma. A sheltering sparrow hopped away from her and found a hiding place behind a memorial. Beyond the glossy stones, a fringe of trees was reduced to a blur.

Delay was frustrating. She fixed her thoughts on what to do after she discovered Abetz. There was no longer only her own quest, she had let herself be hooked into helping Rose Darrow chase after Krieger. Ellie was cross with herself about this. If a man declined to help, on the grounds that his own interests were far too interesting to be set aside, he would not be obliged to dream up an excuse. Guilt or disloyalty did not enter into it. But women were a helpful breed, willing to shape their lives to accommodate other people's needs. And if Rose begged a busy male acquaintance to be her translator, she would be prepared for refusal and not offended by it.

Selfishly, Ellie was happy that Krieger was spirited away because it curtailed her involvement. She had, though, promised Rose she would return to Budj with her that evening to glean information from the neighbours and, if he were there, to tackle Zak again. Ellie thought it must be dreadful to be a journalist always hanging around trying to squeeze information from people who had no wish to impart it.

The rain eased and she ventured out again. Her eye fell on the name of Abetz.

BENEDIKT ABETZ
1791–1841

JULIANA STEHLIK
1797–1843

The dates were right. He was her Abetz. Ellie recognized the name Stehlik, a rich family who had owned estates in Bohemia. Better, it was one of the names on the list Milena Hobzek gave her at the art gallery. The link was made.

She splashed through the cemetery, down empty streets awash and jumped aboard a tram. Ripping off her scarf, she wrung it out. Passengers looked at her with disapproval, she was grinning with a glee their curiosity could not curb. *The link was made*.

She imagined Abetz orchestrating the sale of the paintings, and possibly other property, that his wife had inherited. She saw the removal of the pictures to a distant dealer who guaranteed higher prices and greater discretion. Ellie's eager imagination recreated it all, until the central question reared up: did this take her nearer a missing companion piece?

She left the tram a short distance from Wenceslas Square. The lack of traffic surprised her: so near the heart and so empty. Few cars, no motorcycles, and cobbles plus hills made cycling unattractive. Rain was slackening and clumps of people stood in docile resignation waiting to be allowed inside stores. She adapted an old joke: 'When three Englishmen meet they form a club, when three Czechs meet they form a queue.' A few people hugged the window of an electrical goods shop displaying a television satellite dish. A saturnine man was sloping up to tourists and offering crowns at blackmarket rates. Ellie ran past them all, through the uninspiring foyer of the hotel, up to her room to rub her hair and change into dry clothes. There was a message for her, from Rose.

With the towel in one hand and dabbing at her pale hair, Ellie returned the call. If she was lucky, Rose was going to cancel their evening in Budj.

Rose said: 'I thought you might be there, in this weather.'

'I wasn't. I was in a cemetery.'

'Abetz?'

'I've found him.'

'Then we're both having a good day. I went to Budj this morning and, just as we expected, the bird has flown. The next-door neighbours spoke German so I managed.'

Ellie hoped her relief at being excused a second trip to Budj was not glaring. 'Did you learn anything useful?'

'The woman said Zak's often away. Of course, it might just mean he stays at his mother's house in the Old Town. She didn't know anything about a man of Krieger's description but says various people stay there from time to time.'

'I'm surprised she was talkative.'

'I think it was because I'm a foreigner, which is to say totally unimportant.'

The explanation was credible. 'Very perceptive. If I'd used Czech on her I'd probably have got nothing.'

'There's something else, Ellie. I want to ask you something completely different, about John Blair. Do you remember we talked about him hoping to go to New York on a story? Well, do you think it had anything to do with the Devereux family?'

'Everything to do with it,' she said.

'If you and Sam have a spare bed – or even if you haven't – I'll be moving in on you soon,' said John Blair.

Ellie was delighted. 'New York's full of new friends but I'd love to see an old one. How soon?'

The connection was excellent, he might have been in the next flat. Difficult to picture a whole Atlantic Ocean swishing between them.

He said: 'I love your impatience, Ellie. It does my soul good. How many people can I ring and be sure of such enthusiasm?'

'Plenty,' she said truthfully. 'How soon?'

'Depends. I have to convince a news editor he's serious about shelling out part of his budget on the trip.'

'And he's being sticky?'

'Alas, it's not like it was in the good old days. They count pennies now. But pencil me in for three weeks' time. If my powers of persuasion are up to scratch, I should have won him over by then.'

'You tell him from me, we need you here.'

'How's Sam?'

'He's being very Sam-like. Eyes glazed, concentration impenetrable, a major new work in gestation. Or let's hope so. Ice sculpture was all very well but it's a good way to see one's reputation trickle away. The next series will be timeless.'

'You mean it won't rot or melt?'

'I mean – or, rather, *he* means – it will have an historical perspective.'

There was a mischievous irony when Blair remarked that he could not wait. Then: 'I shall be blundering into the art world myself, Ellie. Besides providing me with a bed and saving huge hotel bills, you'll be having your brains picked. You and Sam. Consider yourselves warned.'

'What's the story?'

'You know the Devereux family?'

'The perfume people?'

'Yes. You know they're collectors?'

'The old man, Maurice Devereux, started the collection back in the 1970s.'

'Well, he doesn't dip a hand into his hip pocket, he established an art fund that operates as a charity. Presumably that was an accountant's move. Anyway, it's all gone into reverse. These days they're selling.'

This surprised Ellie. He explained that the selling was going on discreetly. 'Mostly it takes place in New York. I need to know why they're selling.'

She suggested the good times were over in the sale rooms as well as the newspaper offices. Art was no longer a buoyant market. He agreed, adding that the further he investigated the Devereux finances the more puzzled he became.

'I think some of the answers will be found in New York.'

Ellie offered, without him needing to hint: 'I'll keep my ears open. I might pick something up. Oh, and I won't breathe a word, not even to Sam. He's so vague at this stage, he wouldn't be able to cope with the concept of confidentiality.'

'I'll ring you in a few days. And thanks, Ellie.'

The few days became a fortnight. Another month went by. John Blair never did reach New York.

After she dried her hair and revived herself with a hot drink, she tackled the problem of finding the compiler of the list Milena Hobzek gave her. Thinking back over their conversation, Ellie spotted a potential clue. The woman mentioned the man had to deliver the manuscript of a book to a publisher that week.

Ellie went to a bookshop and noted the names of Czech publishers who handled books about art. This took a long time because she had to rely on an assistant to fetch titles for her. The books were not available to browsers, they were in the window or displayed on shelves behind counters. The assistant was initially obtuse and then irritated. Other customers came and went and Ellie was still requesting books, writing down details from their covers and passing the books back to him. Finally, she asked to buy a couple and became a player in a remarkable game designed to delay possession and to involve as many people as possible.

Once she handed him the books, the assistant who had been her reluctant helper issued her with a numbered docket, passed its carbon copy to the colleague at his right elbow who passed it on to an assistant at *his* right elbow whose job it was to work the till. The one in the middle wrapped the books, handed the carbon to the one on the till who took Ellie's copy, compared it with the carbon, and accepted her cash. Then the one in the middle gave her the parcel.

She had forgotten how relentlessly time-wasting, how people-consuming, how pointless the procedures were. They would go, of course, now that the politics had changed. People would gradually shake off their conditioning to collude with the absurd. They would no longer be prepared to stand in the rain outside a half-empty shop and wait their turn to accept a basket and enter, all because someone decreed the shop might issue only x number of baskets and therefore accommodate only x number of customers at a time.

Streamlining her story about seeking the author of a new manuscript concerning Bohemian art, she set off on a tour of the city's publishing houses. She was lucky straight away. Without quizzing her very deeply, a young woman at the first house said: 'If it's that sort of book, then I think I can suggest where you might try.'

Within the hour Ellie persuaded a threadbare man at a publishing house to divulge the author's name. The man left her for a few minutes while he checked an address, then presented her with a sheet of paper with everything written down. She survived the brief interview with half-truths and made her escape before he probed.

Outside the building, with a tourist guide addressing his troops in the background, she unfolded the paper. Her heart lurched. The name printed in ballpoint capitals unfurled memories of her teenage years.

She was a girl again, strutting through the streets with newly washed hair and a skirt she had put the final stitches in that morning. Across the square, down alleyways, pause at the busy road before the tower and then safely over, jostled by the other pedestrians, and on to the bridge. In the past there was a tradition that people took the right side when they crossed the bridge, upriver on their way to the Old Town and downriver going towards the castle. The tradition died away. Ellie zig-zagged between them putting in little skips and runs to avoid collision.

The saints went by, the kings went by, down below the water went by. Everything around her was a delicious blur. The bridge was not straight, it veered over the water as though it had been paced out by a drunkard repeatedly correcting his line. Ellie took the first angle, near the Virgin and her two companions, St Dominic and St Thomas Aquinas, and her view opened up as far as St Wenceslas on the seventh of the fifteen piers.

She was most of the way across before she saw his figure, near the end where he always met her. Elbows on the parapet, he looked upriver, towards islands and a frothing weir. He flicked away the hair the wind blew into his eyes and in the same movement saw her. There was a smile in the thin line of his mouth, warmth in the eyes beneath the long dark lashes. When she came close he squeezed her hand and said a few words, nothing special, a sentence to show he was pleased to see her. And then they walked through the arches and began the long trudge up the hill to the galleries.

He had introduced her to art. There was plenty to be seen but he knew what was worth looking at. They would walk into a gallery and he would interest her in the best that was there, stir her curiosity into appreciation.

'Look at the way he's caught the play of light on the fabric of the garments.' Or: 'The composition of this is perfect, look at . . .' Or: 'Yes, it's pretty but I prefer the other one. More subtlety, a lighter touch. Do you see how . . .'

He was destined to be an artist, there was no question. Impressed, she listened and learned, let him open windows in her mind. She had never known anyone like him and she was hungry for more of him.

When he told her who were the good painters and who were not, she believed him. When he lent her books, she read them, twice, and embarked on discussions during which she tested her conclusions against his. She began to look at life with his special eye, seeing the beauty of their city and the bungling of its modern rulers. Ellie nurtured her own version of his irony at the restrictions under which they were expected to thrive. Only artists, he explained, could be truly free because they did not deal with the currency of day-to-day. Theirs was the currency of the spirit, of emotions, of beauty and truth. She loved it. She loved him.

She loved him with hesitancy. He shone, she stood in the shadow, doubting her worthiness to be there. Her friends chided her for the way she was altering. In fact, they chided her for switching from their kind of thinking to his. Her friends seemed childish and ill informed. She did not blame them for being blinkered but she was grateful to have met someone who was leading her towards light.

Her closest friend, Nina, whose horizon stretched to an *au pair*'s job and English classes in London, became especially tiresome, warning Ellie not to get too involved, that he was too old for her, that he would lose interest and Ellie should guard against getting hurt. Ellie was annoyed, suspected Nina of jealousy and continued to let him open her eyes to beauty and to truth.

As summer passed into autumn she noticed her relationship with him adapting. They became more sure of each other, more settled, more equal. She no longer regarded herself as privileged to be allowed a glimpse of his life, she had become an integral part of it.

Constraints were loosening. She saw the way ahead. Perhaps with him, but certainly with the good things he bestowed on her, she looked to her future. Glad, confident morning.

Nina never understood. It was not his body or his promise to stay with her for ever that he gave Ellie, it was a dimension to her life. Wherever she went, whatever she did, whoever she spent her time with, she would carry within her his gifts. Ellie was certain about her future, and in the meantime she loved him.

She had come to expect life to be good, to get better and go on improving. That summer and through the autumn she loved him. And she had spent her life trying to replace him.

The harsh voice of the tour guide alerted her. She grew aware of a mass of people bearing down on her. A split second later she realized they were uninterested in her. Their faces were obediently uplifted to study a sculptured serpent on the wall over her head.

'Prominte.' She mumbled apologies and eased her way through them. Going where? To his address? The *address*. That was another blow. It was the street where she grew up, where her family might still be living.

Without conscious decision she was speeding towards Wenceslas Square and the sanctuary of the hotel. All she wanted to do was get behind a door she could lock. No, more. She wanted to pack and fly away. She was a fool to come to Prague, to pick at memories as a child picks at a scab on its knee. Coming here was wrong, it could make nothing better and everything worse. All her adult life she had refused to be the Czech woman she ought to be. She was a convincing Londoner, a temporary New Yorker. What had she to do with Prague? Even Rose Darrow had contacts to provide her with a flat, while she, whose home town it used to be, was consigned to a tourist hotel. John Blair had known this city, too. Known it when the CLOSED sign was up and she refused to go there.

'I'm looking for something,' she had said to him, over her shoulder, delving in a cupboard.

'I know, Ellie.' And he teased her with his mock profundity. 'We all are. What have we lost? Ourselves, of course.'

Her chest was tightening, she slowed her pace, fought to keep a sensible perspective. It was possible no one she used to know was in the city. Twenty years was a long time and people had not been allowed to live or work where they chose. Secondly, she need go nowhere near that street or that man. He was a short cut for information about the family of Abetz's wife but he was not the one and only route. The Stehlik family had been well known and were far easier to trace than Abetz himself. She could take a fresh line of inquiry next day and avoid unnecessary anguish.

And yet it was too late. Her secrets were stirred. They crowded in on her all evening. She met Rose at a restaurant for supper. The subject that dominated the conversation was not Frans Hals or Abetz, not Krieger. It was the House of Devereux.

'Joelle – that's our wonderful dogsbody in the Paris office. She looks like a black-eyed pixie, you'd love her – well, she's sent me a file of information about the Devereux family. It makes amazing reading, Ellie.'

'No doubt the Curse of the Devereux features prominently.'

'Very prominently indeed. It's the sort of stuff the tabloids love: the family that has everything and yet loses all the time. The baby stolen from its bed and murdered, the beautiful mother crazy with grief . . .'

Ellie said: 'But have you discovered why they're selling off the art collection?'

'Not yet but I'm getting an idea or two. The obvious explanation is they're running out of money although when you look more closely into the finances of the business that seems not to be true. Profits are lower than they were in the boom years of the eighties, as you'd expect. But it would be a very long economic decline that left them short. They're not like those super rich people who played around with money. The Devereux folk own things outright, they weren't borrowers and therefore they aren't going to be hurt by soaring interest rates or unkind banks. They have an exclusive, very expensive product and they know how to protect it. Old-fashioned, if you like, but it's the way old money was made – and kept.'

'But the art sales, Rose?'

She hunched her shoulders. 'A mystery. I can see why John Blair wanted to ask around in New York but I'm not convinced he'd have picked up more than auction house guesswork.'

'And?' prompted Ellie.

Rose looked inquiring.

Ellie said: 'Come on, Rose, you're playing with me. You know more than you've admitted. You didn't spend all day reading that file and scratching your head in bewilderment.'

Rose raised her hands in surrender. 'Gosh, you're tough, Ellie. I confess. But this is purely theory, a guess, that's all. John's notes, coupled with information in the cuttings and also the material I gathered from contacts in London and Paris . . . Everything points to a drugs connection.'

'Drugs?'

Heads swivelled.

'Shhh!' said Rose. 'I told you, it's nothing more than a guess.'

'A crazy one. Why on earth would the Devereux family tangle with illegal drugs? You've just demonstrated, they have so much legitimate cash there's no incentive.'

But Rose had seen John Blair's notes about 'snow' and the 'Gib connection'. A lot of money that had been washing around in the Devereux art fund had vanished. She said: 'Perhaps I'm being simplistic but it would explain why John went to Spain.'

Ellie dismissed it. 'I'd take a lot of convincing. Granted, art isn't the investment it was a few years ago but the Devereux presence in the market wasn't about buying and selling and making a few francs on the way. It was serious collecting and that's about possession. Showing off, if you want to be heartless.'

Rose detailed the factors that directed her towards the drugs theory. Ellie cupped her chin in her hand, leaned on the table. 'You think that's the conclusion John drew.'

Ellie noticed the younger woman's eyes slide away for a fraction of a second. Then there was a touch of colour in Rose's cheeks as she met Ellie's gaze again and told her: 'There's a rumour in London that he was shot deliberately. If that's true, Ellie, and if I'm right about all this, then I know why he was killed.'

ELEVEN

Sam sounded plaintive.

'The fridge is bust. Can you believe this? The USA in the 1990s and the damn fridge won't work.'

'How are the icons coming along?' Trans-Atlantic and he was telling her about a fridge.

'The what?' It was a poor line too.

'*Icons of the Twentieth Century*. The bubble-pack.'

'Ellie, I've spent two days trying to buy a new fridge.'

She tried a joke. 'You know, Sam, a broken fridge might qualify as one of the symbols of the century.'

'An illustration of built-in obsolescence, you mean? Ellie, you could be on to something there.'

She winced. 'No, no, Sam. It would be too big. You couldn't fit a fridge into one of those bubbles.'

'Well, no, but the concept is one to consider. Maybe a fridge isn't exactly the thing to use but the twentieth century is the era of obsolescence. It would make sense to include an example.'

'How would it sit, though, alongside Monroe, Che Guevara, a hammer and sickle . . . ?'

'No, Guevara's out. I junked Guevara, remember?'

'Oh, yes, along with Mickey Mouse. But you kept the Dali soft watch and er . . .'

'A computer. You see? A broken fridge or its equivalent would look fine. It'll help swing the emphasis away from personalities.'

She conceded. So it would.

'Sam, I may have to take a trip up into Bohemia.'

'Is that far from Czechoslovakia?'

She rolled her eyes skywards. He was not joking. 'No distance at all, Sam.'

She must remember to tell him he was in good company in his ignorance: Shakespeare, turning Robert Greene's novel, *Pandosto: The Triumph of Time*, into *The Winter's Tale*, copied the mistake of making Bohemia a desert country with a coastline.

Sam said: 'This woman you're looking for, the Frans Hals painting. I don't see what she has to do with your book.'

He made her feel guilty. 'I know, Sam. It's peripheral, the Hals woman will only make a footnote, but I want to go on with this a bit longer. Not much, just a bit longer.'

'Well, don't stretch it out. My exhibition opens in February, you took a solemn vow to be here for that.'

'That's months away. And I'll be there. I'll finish the book in London and fly to New York immediately.'

They quibbled about whether she was being self-indulgent, about whether he worked better when she was around or when she wasn't there to interrupt.

'Ellie, I miss you.'

'And I miss you, Sam. And I'll be back as soon as possible.'

The conversation was running down when he said: 'Hey, I nearly forgot. I heard the other day that *Exile's* coming on the market.'

'*Really?*'

'Dunstan tipped me off about it. Thought I might hear it some other place and it was a good agent's duty to warn me.'

Exile, his assemblage of paper-clips and other office paraphernalia, was on permanent exhibition with a number of his pieces at a West Coast gallery. His most famous sculpture, it was the corner-stone of the exhibition.

Ellie said: 'If the gallery has to dispose of something, why *Exile*?'

'They don't own it. It's on long-term loan to them, that's all. Dunstan says there's no way they can afford to buy it although they'd love to. The owner gave them time to make an offer but short of a miracle they won't be able to meet the price. It will probably be put up at auction in the next two or three months.'

She detected his anxiety and made an effort to reduce it by

treating the matter lightly. 'So then you find out how high your reputation really stands?' The words came out wrong. The humour that would have been there if she and Sam were face to face was lost, the remark sounded like a bald challenge.

'Ellie, the market's a mess. Nobody has any money. For me the key issue isn't going to be whether bids top an outrageously high reserve but how classy the bidders are. If the important people rate my work enough to bid, then I'll be satisfied with that.'

Hearing Sam so phlegmatic, Ellie mentally congratulated his agent for doing a thorough job to prepare Sam for sale-room disaster. Sam did not have a direct financial interest in the outcome but it would influence the prices his new work commanded.

Sam was not a lavish man, nor was he a miser. He did not fuss over cash and never needed to. Whatever happened in the art world, he had done very nicely over the years and money silted up around him. The agent put it in safe places, so that even if he continued to marry and divorce greedy women Sam would not slide into penurious old age. But if his reputation suffered, if the bubble burst, there was nothing agents or friends could do to spare Sam's frustration. He would not be free to point out he always knew it was empty nonsense. His public opinions had connived at the myths.

Ellie trotted out her familiar encouraging remarks, the nub being that so many people had an interest in shoring up his reputation as a leading artist of the period that no one was going to prick any bubbles.

'You didn't,' she added, 'say who, in fact, owns *Exile*.'

'The Devereux family,' he said.

She tried to telephone Rose Darrow, to let her know about the potential sale of *Exile*, although she was doubtful the news was much use, but she did not get through. Left with no other diversion, she faced a decision about determining the provenance of Abetz's Hals paintings. Set out on a fresh line of inquiry to unravel the history of the wife's family, the Stehliks? Or take the short cut that led her to the street where she grew up?

Out in the square, she bent into a lashing wind. A piece of wrapping paper, one of the rare examples of litter in the city, went skittering away from her.

There had been good times, she had to cling to that. To be honest, they were almost entirely good times. Frustrations, but no worse than the frustrations of growing up elsewhere. All restrictions seem impositions to children, adults are the ones who make rational decisions about liberty.

Families turned inward, relying for social life and freedom on the comfortable context of the family. Her parents were not resisters, not to any degree that became apparent to her. If there were grumbles about burdensome bureaucracy, if they were weary of being refused the means to express themselves, then they did not express that to her either.

Tactless, she had accused her mother, 'Why don't you say what you're thinking? I know what you're thinking, but you don't say it.'

'I've seen things, Ellie. There's been too much suffering.'

'But that's the past.'

'Is it?'

Her mother looked older than her years. Ellie did not know that, not for a long time. Not until she was mixing with women who turned out to be her mother's age and whom Ellie took for younger. But that was later, in another country.

Ellie's mother taught her to sew, showing her how to make neat running stitches and secure the seams with a backstitch every inch for strength. She taught her how to unpick clothes that were outgrown. A faded dress of her mother's was undone that way. When its panels were separated, Ellie ironed them. Each was edged with the vivid green and clear white of fabric that had been tucked away inside the seams.

'Be careful, Elena. You'll scorch it.' She was always Elena when her mother disapproved.

Her mother took the biggest piece, that made up half the

skirt, and spread it on the kitchen table. On it she pinned a shape cut from newspaper. Then she butted another shape up to the first, the curves interlocking. When the cloth was covered with newspaper shapes, she began to cut very carefully around them.

It was Ellie's job to unpin the precious home-made pattern and fold it away. She guarded the steel pins from rolling off the table and stuck them into a pin cushion. Her mother sat many evenings, needle glinting beneath the light bulb, until her old green dress was transformed into Ellie's smaller one.

Ellie saw in the houses and flats around her the differences in the lives of those who managed in deprivation and those who could not. A talent for carefulness needed to be nurtured. It did not occur to her that her parents' life, her mother's in particular, was a mean and dispiriting existence. Her father had his work to go to, the company of men, tasks to perform and money to bring home. For her mother, the walls were a cage. Stepping outside meant spending money and money was never to be spent when not necessary. Food had to be bought wisely but the buying of it was a chore. Ellie remembered no occasion when her mother had shopped for pleasure or for comfort or for anything but sheer necessity.

If there had not been a younger child too, her mother would have been less walled up. Ellie was the middle of three. For a few years there were four but the brother a couple of years older than Ellie died of an infection following injury. Her surviving brothers were five years older and three years younger than her. If she met the younger one in the street now she would not know him, she left Prague when he was fourteen.

She entered a broad street with cars passing, a black Tatra limousine followed by three brown Opels. She crossed over, whisking a glance at shop frontages and modern buildings, all new since her time. On the far side, she dived down a meagre street where builders' materials hogged half the width. In a square at the end of it a recorded baritone serenaded her from a window: *'Naught but your love has made the miracle happen, naught*

126

but your love.' Josef Suk, worrying at the meaning of life. Suk, ill, Professor of Composition at Prague Conservatoire, struggling from *Asrael* to *Epilogue*, with existence, with things lived and dreamed.

The square was altered. An archway was closed with an iron gate. She walked around the perimeter of the square seeking an alternative route. A man appeared and she asked directions. How odd it was to speak the name of the street again.

She retraced her steps, used an arch she had dismissed as leading to a dead end and came to the street where she grew up. Its name had been changed several times. It had borne the names of saints and politicians, and had been rendered in German, Czech or Russian. Not an attractive street, it was a crush of houses on which no one lavished attention because when things belong to everybody they belong to nobody.

A stranger would look and move on, ready for prettier places near by. Prague was full of prettier places. The stranger's step would slow where a vaulted arch revealed a flowery courtyard, but nothing else was worth a pause.

Ellie went slowly, the dullness of the present contrasting with the vividness of remembered days. A little girl, she skipped out of a door and on to the paving, waited for her mother to join her towing the younger brother. Or she ran home from school, hair streaming, racing an imaginary companion to the door knocker.

She could not quell the later memories. They followed as naturally as the days had been lived, those scenes she had striven to forget. Sweat broke on her forehead as, sixteen again, she fled from the house, praying she would meet no one she knew, that no one would ask why she was crying.

Her breathing was becoming troublesome but she had come this far, she must go on. Her uneasy calm was threatened with the despair of another time, the evening she told a lie and left the house never to return.

She had *wished* never to return. Standing on the bridge, desolate, she gave in to the knowledge that there was nowhere to go but home. And then she turned and saw him, felt the weight of the proprietorial hand on her shoulder and let him lead her back to this street. Her legs leaden with cold and with misery, she had stumbled, putting out a hand to steady herself and grazing knuckles on the wall. He flung out an arm to save her, kept a grip on her until she was inside the house. There was a hall, a light. Ellie glared at him, her colour high. And he smiled at her, a spurious smile of triumph.

Ellie walked past the house where these things had happened to her. Innocuous, plain, it rested between its neighbours with nothing to distinguish it but a roughened patch of pavement where cobbles drifted loose. They shifted beneath her boots as she went by the front door, the old scarred door where her child's fingers had needed both hands to twist the knob. She struggled for calming thoughts, but could not fool herself. In a few yards she would be in front of that other house, the one where the man who had been her young art lover now lived. Memories of him would rush her back to the horrifying ones.

There were metal numbers on the buildings. She reached number seven. Instead of going in she went to the end of the street, turned the corner, persuaded herself she would be all right in a minute.

A passing woman looked at her solicitously but Ellie swerved away. She kept going until she found a *kavárna*, then hesitated. She was bullying herself to return to the street, to put her questions about the Stehlik family, Abetz and the Frans Hals portraits.

With an effort of will she walked back. The opening remarks she planned seemed inappropriate, she worked on other ways of reopening a conversation broken off twenty-two years earlier. None of them was easy.

'He won't hear the words, anyway,' she reasoned. 'He'll be astonished, all he'll register is his own astonishment.'

Without giving herself time to weaken, she opened the door of number seven. There was a passageway, much like the one she had been used to several doors along. Beside a weak wall light there were bells for the flats. Her eye went immediately to his name. But her outstretched hand dithered an inch from contact with the bell.

Somebody ran down a stairway, a man came dashing towards her on his way out. He shot by but then slewed to a stop. 'Are you looking for someone? Can I help?'

'It's all right.' She spoke quickly. Her thank you was an afterthought. She averted her face and heard the front door thud behind him as he went out.

She would have known him anywhere.

The voice was the same, the eagerness, the light in the eye. He had not changed as some men change. The face was the one she conjured when she shut her eyes and made love to other men. For the first time since she realized she had to seek him out, Ellie wondered what his life had been. He could hardly be a painter at this address. If he was lucky he might have a studio somewhere. And if not?

All down the years she had assumed him to be a painter, to be pursuing truth and beauty, to be taking that route to that particular freedom. What if she were wrong? Unconsciously, she had been shielding herself from the questions and now they were unavoidable.

The street door creaked open. She gave a nervous start. A man stood in the doorway, a silhouette against the light.

'Excuse me,' he said softly. 'You remind me of a girl I used to know.' There was a question in there, tucked away between the words.

'Yes,' she said, answering it.

He came forward until she could see his face in the glow of the wall light. His expression was a confusion of pleasure and amazement.

'Ellie? It really is Ellie!'

He ran out of words but she reached for his hand in a contact that was not quite a formal handshake and not quite an affectionate squeeze.

When she tried to speak her voice was thick. She cleared her throat, said: 'If you have time, I'd like to talk to you.'

Her phrasing was stilted, awkward. Not any of the things she rehearsed but then neither was the abrupt encounter.

'Time?' He echoed, equally at a loss. 'Of course. Come up.'

The stairs were badly lit, the flat poky and dark. There was evidence of a wife, a woman anyway. A pinkish blouse airing on a hanger, a handbag on a chair.

'Please, sit down.' He meant a grey moquette chair, the only soft one in the room, but she pulled out one of the wooden ones by the table. She wished she could drum up something to say. But every thought was banal and every topic absurd after a pause of decades.

He said: 'There was wine but they drank it. They've left us these, though.'

She had no clue who 'they' were. He took a couple of bottles of Urquel from the fridge. Hinges of an enamel cupboard screeched as he fetched glasses.

He sat opposite her. They opened the bottles. He said: 'Well, then. Tell me what on earth you're doing here.'

That was the simple part. He let her begin where it was least painful to begin. She was grateful, wondered whether he guessed this was her reaction.

'Hunting for a female portrait by Frans Hals,' she said by way of introduction to a tortuous tale. Once she had said enough for him to get the drift, she mentioned her reasons for calling on him.

'I'm hoping to use you as a short cut because you already know who owned what, where and when.'

'I wish Milena Hobzek had explained better. She didn't mention Hals and she didn't mention you. She made it sound like a general inquiry for reasons of her own. But yes, I can help you with the Stehlik collection. Let me get my notes.'

He went into an adjoining room and drawers were slid jerkily to and fro. Ellie looked around, at the ugly room with its worn furnishings. There was no evidence that anyone painted here, no tell-tale whiff of paint or spirit, no brushes drying, and in any case no space.

He brought a folder of loose sheets and flicked through them until he found what he wanted. The Stehlik family, he said, were patrons of the arts in the eighteenth century. Their special love was music but they encouraged new painters and put together a good collection of both old and new work.

'Now, what will interest you is that early in the following century the paintings were bequeathed to five children, including the youngest daughter, Juliana, who was married to a man called Abetz.'

Ellie said this virtually tallied with what she learned in Amsterdam: Abetz told the dealer he inherited the paintings.

He dropped the sheet of paper back on top of the others, rested his hands on them and laced his fingers in a didactic pose. 'The Stehlik papers itemize the paintings that went to Juliana. There was a male portrait by Hals but no companion piece. Among the paintings owned by the family there had been three Hals portraits in all.'

Ellie gave an exaggerated sigh. 'Tell me the worst then. No, let me guess. The four other inheritors also sold everything and the entire collection is scattered to the four winds.'

He refilled his glass. 'Not exactly. The eldest son wanted to keep the collection intact and did his utmost to acquire the paintings from his brothers and sisters. There's a heap of correspondence about all that. He was largely unsuccessful. He swapped farms and forest and heaven knows what. I'm convinced the others thought he was crazy and he possibly was. Anyway, the collection survived until the twentieth century with only the Juliana pictures and a handful of others disappearing.'

It felt strange to be in a private room with him, unfamiliar. Theirs had been an outdoor love, a secret, public affair. She remembered his face in sunshine, between candle flames, in the mysterious glow of street lanterns and dappled by the leaves of trees in blossom.

Ellie was uncomfortable under his gaze. The occasional smile was the one he used to warm her with when they met on the bridge, but between smiles the eyes were guarded, inquisitive.

For a second she saw herself as he must see her: a woman of thirty-eight, the natural silvery blondeness of her hair disguising the grey that had crept into it. A neat sleek haircut that cost a fortune in Knightsbridge every couple of months. A stylish, expensive leather coat flung over the chair beside her. Clothes in fine fabrics and flattering colours making her skin glow. And her skin was good. She took care of herself, exercising to trim her figure and eating fruit and raw vegetables to keep her skin elastic and youthful. Compared to the average woman in the city's streets, compared to the woman she might have developed into had she stayed, Ellie exuded glossy healthiness.

She dragged her mind away from self-examination and listened to what he was telling her.

'Unfortunately, the record doesn't give details of the other two Hals pictures. I can't say whether either of them could be the companion piece you believe exists. One of them, though, was a painting of a woman, that much is clear. And you already know the male portrait was similar to the one in Washington.'

He waited for her question. 'What happened to the collection after the bulk of it was kept intact?'

'A war or two, some selling, possibly some thieving. If it had survived up to the present day it would be an important collection. But, as you'll appreciate, it would also be a miracle.'

She wondered whether he knew what happened to either of the Hals pictures. He said not.

'My mind was on more important paintings. It would be good to know what became of a Leonardo, for instance. There *was* one, definitely, until the turn of the century when it vanished without explanation. Some of the Stehlik treasures are known to have been scooped up by the Nazis, several others are in Russia and a number in the national collection here.'

Ellie doubted the Nazis cared about Hals. 'Goering went for acres of nubile female flesh, Hals would have bored him.'

The beer bottle tilted over his glass again. 'If the *Laughing Cavalier* had been here instead of safely in the Wallace Collection in London, he'd have grabbed it. None of the other Hals paintings had enough cachet.'

'So?' She was neglecting her beer, she raised her glass to drink another inch.

'There's a chance the Hals portraits the Stehliks acquired in the eighteenth century are still in the castle.'

It could not be that easy. She hunted for a flaw. He saw her chasing after objections. He laughed at her.

'Honestly, Ellie. They might well be. I wish I'd looked.'

'*I'll* have to,' she said. And she was both excited and alarmed.

'As a matter of fact, a Stehlik lives there to this day.'

'In spite of . . .'

But Marxist-Leninist theory had not resolved whether private collections were damaging to society. Were paintings property for confiscation, or furnishings to be left alone? Cautious owners had unfastened canvases from stretchers and rolled them up, as Hals had once offered to roll up *The Meagre Company*, and hidden them. But only major treasures were moved, the rest recorded because how could the public collections cope if everything worthwhile descended on them? Even then, the system was inefficient.

He said: 'In spite of every kind of social upheaval, yes. Some people are survivors.'

She shook her head, trying to clear her confusion. 'I must keep reminding myself that even if the paintings are there, the chance of either of them having anything to do with my fanciful quest for a companion piece to the Washington man is extremely remote.'

'Extremely.'

'But I'm finding it tough to believe that. How do I get myself into this castle?'

'It's not impossible, I managed it. It took several months of badgering and string-pulling but in the end Stehlik let me in. Of course, I was able to convince him I had a scholarly purpose and wasn't there to spy for the authorities and tell them what was worth looting. How you dress up your curiosity into something impressive, I don't know.'

'Me neither.' A minute ago it seemed simple, but now more like a long haul starting with wheedling letters and probably ending in refusal.

He looked at his wrist watch. Then he closed the folder.

Ellie wriggled her arms into her coat. 'I'm sorry, I'm holding you up.'

He took the folder into the next room and returned, saying: 'I'm going to a place off Engels Embankment.' He pulled himself up with a short laugh. 'I mean *Wilson*, of course. Old names keep slipping out. If you don't mind a walk, we could talk on the way.' He pulled aside a curtain and peered down into the street. 'It doesn't look good but it's not actually raining.'

They walked past the house where she used to live. He said: 'When I got the flat, around ten years ago. I thought of you each time I came along here.'

'You must have wondered.'

He gave her a sidelong look rich in irony. 'You could say that.'

'I'm sorry. I was sorry then and I'm sorry still. A situation arose and I wasn't equal to it. I just . . . went.'

'Yes.'

'Please, it's important you should understand I didn't mean to hurt you.'

'Well, as you see, I'm still here. I didn't throw myself off the bridge or anything.'

They reached a square. A horse and cart were running over the cobbles towards them, the noise magnified. An old man stood in the cart, a ragged cape thrown over his jacket. The cart was empty except for a sack by the man's feet.

'All sound and fury,' she said as the cart receded.

He prevented her changing the subject. 'But I've always been puzzled. Today, I think, is the day I find out the truth.'

She looked away, to where pigeons were stabbing at titbits between the stones, to where an impoverished young man was slouching by with the head of a dead cockerel sticking out of his shopping bag, to a soldier licking the ice-cream his sweetheart held out to him.

'No,' she said at last. 'Only the fragment of the truth that reassures you my reasons had nothing to do with anything that happened between us.'

'I didn't see how they could have. That's what made it so startling and mysterious. Come on, Ellie. After twenty-something years it can't be a secret worth keeping.'

But it could and with a heavy heart she said so.

They went some way in silence. She was annoyed with herself for not being more adept at manoeuvring the conversation. Her refusal made her seem heartless, as though her regret for the youthful rebuff counted for nothing because here she was refusing to make the slightest amends.

She broke the silence. 'You heard I went to London?'

His words were clipped. 'And stayed there. Yes.'

She tried once more. 'It was supposed to be for a year, looking after a frightful small boy and learning English. Most of my English was in the imperative: don't do this and don't do that, put that down. My English conversation was nil but I was awfully good at giving orders.'

She earned a smile. 'I don't remember you as the type to issue orders. You were malleable, more likely to be following someone else's lead. It was rather charming.'

'Oh dear. I do rather suspect charm, don't you?'

'Not at all! Especially in the young.'

She protested. 'You used to criticize it in paintings. "Oh, yes," you'd say, "it has *charm*." And the way you said it, so dismissive, made it absolutely clear that charm was a quality to be avoided.'

He burst out laughing. 'I don't remember that.'

'I remember everything. No one else had attempted to reveal visual things to me, to treat me as though I had eyes that might be educated to see.'

He was still laughing. 'Heaven knows what I told you. Heaven knows what I knew myself.'

She was rattled. 'That's not the point. What matters is you opened up the world for me. Because of you I lead the life I now live.'

He was laughing too much to speak. Passers-by looked from her flush-faced anger to his mirth and exchanged glances. He took her arm, steered her towards a *kavárna*.

'Never mind if I'm late, Ellie, I want to hear about this life I've led you into.'

Over coffee she told him, roughly, the course of her last twenty years. She did it quickly, trying not to make her art school years too exciting, nor her books about women painters too satisfying, nor her life with Sam and, earlier, other artists, too glamorous. It was a tricky balancing act and she failed. But she had skimmed, knowing that in return, if indeed he offered her anything in return, she would not hear a happy tale.

'Patchy,' he said. 'Not a smooth run. University but there were problems and they made me leave. After a while I was able to take another course. Gradually things worked out. And as you know, I've been researching various aspects of Bohemian art.'

But what she had heard seemed more like tedious cataloguing rather than the kind of research she herself indulged in, following instinct and imagination, plucking out the disregarded information that would in future shape people's attitudes to her subjects.

'No painting?' she asked.

'A little, now. Perhaps I'll get to it after all. But not seriously, of course, you need youth and idealism to put everything into it. Those days have gone, if they ever existed.'

She asked where he painted, the flat being too cramped. He said there was a space he shared, now that it was no one else's business who was using it.

'I could take you to a place,' he said, 'where you'd see the art that's being produced at present but it's not truly the product of these times. It's the effect of those forty years. Oh, yes, there's talent, although you'd say it's stunted, crippled talent. Good things will come but there has to be this interim, this period of recovery.'

A country waking from the nightmare of its history. They no longer had 'to live within the lie'. Ellie shivered, guilty at having run away and missed the worst, proud she had the wit to do so. She had never come to terms with this contradiction and believed she never would. Questions hovered but she left them unvoiced. None of her business how he had managed or what he had suffered. She had no right to satisfy her curiosity about how far he resisted or acquiesced, even colluded. People had coped the way they knew best. In all their lives truth and beauty had been the victims.

He brought up one of the subjects she was skirting. 'Did your family know you were coming?'

'They still don't.'

He arched an eyebrow. 'You'll see them, won't you?'

'No, I don't think so. Too difficult. They gave up writing.'

'Maybe there were problems.'

'No, it wasn't that. There was nothing to say. I stopped being the person they knew. It's what happens.'

She looked at his hands, fingers linked, resting on the table top. Slender, smooth hands, the kind that shuffled paper for a living. On the left thumb was a blue scar she did not remember. Suddenly the hands moved, he pushed his sleeve back and read the watch.

Ellie apologized. 'I'm making you late.'

'I can catch a tram the rest of the way.' He checked his pocket for a ticket.

She probed for information she had determined, until then, not to seek. 'Do you ever see any of my family?'

He put the ticket away. 'No.' He gave her a searching look. 'They were moved out to Braník.'

Braník used to be a small place, to the south of Prague, until the big housing estate was built in the 1960s and it became a suburb. The news that her family were there eased her fear of bumping into them by accident.

Then he qualified it. 'All except your brother, of course.'

She felt the tingle along her spine, the wateriness inside. But all she said was: 'I have two.'

'I meant Pavel.'

'You remember his name? I didn't think you'd ever met him.'

She was positive they had not met. She had been exceptionally careful, protecting that summer's friendship from Pavel's scrutiny and interference.

He pushed back his chair, said savagely: 'Oh, yes, we met, Ellie.'

And then he was gone, leaving her to get herself out of the café alone. She sought a glimpse of him but he had been too fast. People straggled over the road, went in or out of shops, tramped the length of the pavements but his hurrying figure was not among them.

Ellie groaned, blaming an unforgiving heaven. 'Oh, *no*.'

She had disturbed the pool of her own secrets, the ripples would trouble other people and she was powerless to stop them. But what did he mean about her brother, Pavel?

Ellie moved on, not certain where she was heading or where she wanted to go, not in any sense. Her search for the missing Frans Hals woman seemed a cruel parody while she was adrift herself.

'I must,' she thought, 'visit the Stehlik castle. If I'm incredibly lucky that will be the end of the hunt. I'll fly home vindicated for spending time and money on a footnote to my book. And yet . . . and yet I don't think that ending will be neat enough. For everyone else, perhaps, but not for me.'

A few stops on the Metro, a bus ride, would bind up the wounds but she baulked at going to see her family. She doubted her courage. Knowing that Pavel was not there changed the emphasis but that was all.

Since she arrived in Prague she had been fascinated by what her feelings would be if she met them. Her mother she imagined to have become like her grandmother, faded and thin-haired with cheekbones shiny through blotched skin. Her father she pictured more or less unchanged although inheriting his family's tendency to baldness. She assumed that their wariness in speaking up or speaking out had reduced them by now to taciturnity, the sullen reticence of people who have been too long together and are stuck with it. Her younger brother she regarded with affection, supposing his face similar to her own, as they were alike in childhood. She was less nervous of meeting him than the others. Pavel she hated. If he were there, if she travelled out to Braník and by an unfortunate conjunction of the stars he were there, she would not be able to disguise that loathing.

Rain began to fall. She went into the Metro, planning to travel the few stops to her hotel and telephone Rose Darrow to invite her to make the trip into Bohemia with her. Instead, she caught a train in the direction of Braník.

TWELVE

Philippe Devereux sat at a Louis XV *bureau-plat* across an acreage of flower-garlanded Savonnerie carpet and faced a high window. Four small glass bottles stood on a tray in front of him. Seated, with his back to the window, was a tense young man in an expensive suit.

Philippe stretched a hand towards the bottle on the left of the row. He uncapped it, holding it away from him, and then took one of four white cloths from the tray and sprinkled some of the contents on the fabric. He set the bottle down on the exact spot from which he had lifted it, shook the cloth to dispel the alcohol and then brought it close to his face, shutting his eyes as he did so. Philippe sniffed, audibly, several times, snorting the scent as if it were cocaine or, in an earlier era, a pinch of snuff. Sniffing, exhaling luxuriously, he dissected the scent, approved the balance of oils and spices. It was good, naturally he expected no less. But to enjoy a pleasant olfactory sensation was not enough. He was seeking the smell of money.

The younger man stirred, adjusting his green-framed spectacles. Philippe said nothing. His eyes opened but he stared straight ahead, pretending to be unaware of his companion's presence. Then he lay the cloth down in front of the bottle. He took up the next, opened that with the same care not to gulp the concentrated perfume. A second cloth was raised, he closed his eyes, sniffed, set the bottle and the cloth down in their place in the row.

By the time he finished with the fourth bottle, non-committal, the other man was restless: a forefinger jerked the glasses up on to the bridge of the nose again, a surreptitious finger eased the tightness of the shirt collar. Philippe looked right past him, out through the window. His fingers played along the brass trim of the ebony desk top. Since childhood he had understood the perfumer's arts – distillation, maceration, enfleurage – that enticed flowers to surrender their fragrance. But he still found it magical that the spirit of a summer's roses and jasmine, orange blossom and violets, any flower that tempted the perfumer, could be captured in a glass phial.

The other man cleared his throat. 'Well?' His voice was soft, low, he might heave been addressing a woman he loved and desired. Dealing with Devereux was tricky, delicacy was required. There was no inquiry, no urging, only a reminder that a response was awaited.

Philippe turned to him. 'A shade . . . tart? The second one's best. The deeper notes are good, it's mellower. But not the last one, much too astringent.'

'Oh . . . er.' He was at a loss: this was counter to what his colleagues had decided.

Philippe took up the cloth moistened with the second perfume. He inhaled again. 'This isn't one of those occasions when I can promise we've come up with a great new fragrance.' He allowed a glimmer of humour. 'Of course, those occasions are rare.'

The green glasses needed resettling once more. Then: 'If I may be frank, m'sieu . . . Well, the truth is that the second one's the least popular.'

'Really?' He made a moue. 'Then I'm afraid I must differ. But tell me, which is the one they favour?'

'Well . . .'

'Ah! So it's this one?' He tapped the last bottle.

'Yes, it is.'

'And is this also your own opinion?'

In great discomfort the man told him that, actually no, his personal choice was the first one.

'This one?' Philippe lifted the first cloth and, pulling a disparaging expression as he did so, passed it in front of his nose. 'You know, I find this almost metallic.'

He rejected the tray with a gesture. 'There's a better way of

141

testing this.' He pressed a bell on the wall near the desk. Then he looked out of the window and waited for Yvette to come.

Some of the panes of glass were very old, imperfections made the scene wiggle. He could see the distorted image of an elderly man walking down a path through a vineyard. The man wore a battered hat with a turned-down brim, an item that sat oddly with his good-quality clothes. In his hand he carried something. Philippe was too far away to be sure what it was, but it was narrow enough to be grasped in a hand and held down negligently by the walker's side, swinging to and fro as he went.

The door opened and a girl of around seventeen years entered. 'Yes, *m'sieu?*'

'Come here, Yvette. M. Marais and I wish to borrow your arm.'

'Yes, *m'sieu.*' She rolled up her sleeve without demur. She had been called on before. Whether it actually made any difference to test perfume on the skin of a young woman she did not know and chose not to ask. She liked working at the château, why spoil it?

In a few moments she was called on to name her choice and she told Philippe: 'This one, the second.'

Philippe inclined his head, deferring to her opinion. 'So. The second it shall be then.' He ignored the agonized, wordless protest of the other man and asked Yvette: 'What is it you so like about this particular fragrance, Yvette? Compared to the other three, I mean?'

'Well, *m'sieu*, I think it has more character.'

The young man winced but Philippe encouraged her with: 'Anything else, Yvette?'

'It's smoother, more feminine. Well, I don't wish to offend, of course, *m'sieu*, but some of the others are really sharp, what you'd expect in a man's aftershave.' She looked from one man to the other. Then, dropping her eyes and rubbing at her forearm: 'Of course, it's not as though I really know anything about it.'

Philippe dismissed her with a 'Thank you, Yvette.' She went out, unrolling her sleeve.

'So,' said Philippe. 'We now have the view of the Ordinary Young Woman.'

The man decided to treat this as a joke. 'Quite so, but is the Ordinary Young Woman a customer of the House of Devereux? No, and she can't be, not at our end of the market. Or should I say, our pinnacle of the market?'

Philippe smiled, a genuine, comfortable smile. 'Nicely put, Marais. No, the Yvettes of this world will never afford our perfumes, but I don't believe we're free to assume their noses or their aspirations are any different. Take these away, play around with them. We aren't ready, are we? We can afford to wait – our customers *must* wait – until we're certain the next fragrance we launch into the world will be the same unbridled success as our best.'

The man leaned forward, gathered the bottles and tucked them into a case by his feet.

Philippe told him: 'Don't be too disappointed. We'll get it right rather than take a risk.'

The man grunted what might have been an assent; he was bending down to fasten the case.

'By the way,' said Philippe, 'what name is chosen for the new one?'

He bobbed back up into view. '*Risque*,' he said.

When the young man had made his farewells, to begin the long drive back to the laboratory with the dispiriting news, Philippe Devereux went to the window. He positioned himself by one of the newer, truer, panes of glass, watching the falling leaves and a cloudy sky. The old fellow in the broad-brimmed hat was no longer visible. He had disappeared to the right once he was beyond the vineyard.

Philippe guessed where he was going, and expected to see him again when the old man reached a gap in the trees that bordered the lane. He might have missed him, while the new director of the laboratory was toying with his samples, but he thought not. Philippe allowed a few minutes for the old man to cross his view.

The director was a mistake, he thought, appointed for the wrong reasons. That he was connected to a social acquaintance of Philippe's father was not a good enough reason to entrust the running of the laboratory to him. Doubtless he was a highly qualified and intelligent young man and no doubt he possessed a reasonably good nose, but he was not right for the job that Maurice had, effectively, given him. And David, Philippe's own son, connived at the appointment. Philippe's jaw tightened as he remembered how his father and his son had joined forces to push the appointment through, bypassing him and his misgivings.

Philippe had offered his own suggestions about a successor for the retiring director. He was set on having a certain perfume consultant, now working independently after leaving a rival perfume house. He expected the man to be costly, the job would have been redefined for him. But he had one of the best noses in France. There were only half a dozen to rival him, perhaps only five if it was conceded that Maurice Devereux, due to age and failing health, no longer counted as a *Nez*. But before Philippe could talk them round, before he could approach the *Nez*, his father and his son settled on Marais.

In the distance a slow figure in a distinctive hat moved from the cover of a stand of poplars and passed towards the left, clear for a minute until the next trees hid him. Pure Corot. Philippe's sigh interrupted the peace of the room and the first raindrops splashed against the glass.

He pressed the bell, sent for his secretary, a chic woman of mature charm if not genuine good looks.

'Lise, have we heard from David today?'

'No, nothing since he telephoned on Tuesday to say he was in Milan. Would you like me to try and make contact with him?'

A hesitation. 'No, but let me know if he calls here.'

He might have fleshed this out but it was embarrassing to explain to his secretary that he had no knowledge what his son was doing in Milan. Besides, he suspected the shrewd Lise appreciated the situation.

He asked instead: 'What time is that writer coming?'

'Three.' She gave a wry smile. 'Assuming she can find us by three.'

'Yes, it isn't easy. Anyway, that's her problem. I'd better refresh my memory with a few facts and figures before she arrives.'

'The file's ready. I'll bring it.'

They both started nervously as a squall whipped the rain against the window. She said: 'They forecast severe showers, and it looks as though they were accurate for once.'

'Is Georges here?'

'No, he went into town. Your father sent him on an errand.'

Philippe looked resigned. 'Very well, I'll go out myself.'

She glanced towards the window, understanding. 'Then I'll leave the file on your desk for you.'

'Thank you, Lise.'

They left the room together, she a couple of steps ahead, Philippe Devereux admiring the shape of her calves as she crossed the hall to her office.

With the chauffeur out, Philippe had to dash through the rain to the garage in the old stable block. His grey jacket was spotted with dark splodges, he needed to dry his face with a handkerchief before getting into the car. 'Of all the times!' he muttered. But he was not truly baffled by the timing.

He drew out into the courtyard, pulled on the handbrake but, with his hand on the door handle, changed his mind and moved off leaving the garage open and rain blowing inside. He was already wet and expected to get wetter before long.

The road ran in a different direction from the footpath. It circled the vineyard, a family sideline that allowed them a few bottles off their own land each year. Then Philippe joined the road to the remnant of the village for several hundred yards before veering left down a lane leading to the church. Outside the church was a space where the lane was broadened years ago, walls being knocked down and set back, to make room for cars to swing. Philippe parked close to the churchyard wall, foliage dripping over the roof of the car.

He hunted for an umbrella, under the passenger seat, in the door pockets. There was not one. He was going to be drenched. He sat, delaying the moment. Water filmed the windscreen, scraps of leaves floated down it and wedged behind the resting wipers. The ticking of the engine ceased and he heard only the melodies of water.

Philippe Devereux shut his eyes and sighed.

Andrée had given up crying but she was brittle.

She would not go to Paris to be with her husband. She clung to the château, begging the gods to send her baby back to her.

The summer of 1969 was hot. Jets scored a pale sky, the mountain above the house was yellowing and tired. Where a stream usually ran, plants were shrivelling. The earth was hard, its surface powdery. As Andrée stood on the terrace, she could hear the knock, knock, knock of spades against resisting earth, of men labouring to dig the grave.

On the morning of the funeral she rose early. Her black linen dress was hanging ready, a black ribbon for her hair was draped on the mirror of her dressing table. She bathed and dressed with trance-like method. The house was asleep.

She carried her shoes in one hand, the other skimmed the banister of the grand staircase. On the ground floor she slipped her shoes on but then tip-toed across the hall and turned a door knob.

The scent was overwhelming. Flowers had been arriving for two days, some for the funeral, some to comfort her, many from people she knew and many from people who read about her in the newspapers or saw her gaunt face on their television screens.

The family had not known what to do with the flowers, especially in the heat. But this was one of the cooler rooms, and until the funeral its shutters would be kept closed. Andrée touched a switch on the wall, a lamp flicked on. The room was an orchard of white blossom.

She swayed. Glowing whiteness of a million petals, creamy light beneath the lamp, hot-white bands of daylight slinking between the louvres, the bleached casket in the centre of the table . . . She pressed her fingers to her pale lips.

The casket was small, so pathetically small.

Andrée glided forward, her eyes on the clean blond surface of the wood. She craved a sign, an indication, a connection. But she sensed nothing to persuade her of what she had been told.

With an abrupt movement she lifted aside two of the bouquets impeding her and stepped right up to the table. She moved out of her way the sprays arranged around the coffin. From the pocket of her dress she took the chisel.

She prised ineffectively, the chisel was not an appropriate size but she had no time to go in search of a stouter one. Shoving more flowers aside, she sent a bouquet over the edge of the table, where it dislodged others, settling with a noisy rustling and releasing intense waves of fragrance. She gained access to another section of the lid and set to work. In a minute or two she was rewarded with the sharp splintering of wood.

Andrée lay the chisel down and tried to rip open the lid with her fingers. The lid held. She forced the chisel beneath it at another point and again the wood gave way to her pressure.

And then her arm was dragged back. She flung down the chisel, sending it clattering after the fallen flowers. 'No! *No!* Leave me alone.'

The man was hauling her away. Her legs kicked against the heaped wreaths as she fought him. 'Please, leave me. Don't you understand? I must do this, *please*.'

But all the while she cried out, the casket was receding from her. The man spun her round, kept an arm tight against her waist and a hand firmly on the fist she was using to batter him.

'Andrée you must *not* do this. Of course we understand, but you must leave the child in peace.'

147

'Peace? What about *my* peace? What do you know about that? Take your hands off me, Philippe.'

'Hush! You'll wake people.'

He battled to get her out of the room, locked the door while she stood sobbing against the wall beside it. Then he said: 'Come now. You're to keep away from that room.'

With his fingers gouging into her elbow, she went where he led her.

The servant he summoned to the breakfast room was asked to bring *café au lait* and food. Andrée sat, head bowed, ignoring the inquisitive eyes and Philippe's bullying control.

They had to wait for the breakfast, the family seldom demanded anything so early and nothing was ready. Andrée looked down at her fingers plucking the linen of her dress. She squeezed an inch of linen between forefinger and thumb, noticing the liveliness of the fabric: the raised part shone, the woven strands were distinct from each other. Sometimes she looked at leaves or petals in this intricate way. Since the tragedy, involving herself with basic natural things helped persuade her of the need to go on living.

When the breakfast arrived, Philippe told her to eat. She had been unwilling or forgetful if food was not urged on her. The servant poured her coffee but Andrée pushed the bowl away.

Philippe said: 'Andrée, you have a difficult day ahead.'

She gave him a pitying look. His attempts to be solicitous were invariably bungled. He was not a naturally empathetic personality. What could he know about her 'difficulties'?

He heard footsteps and went out of the room, keen to hand over the key to the locked room and instruct someone to tidy the disarray. If necessary, to arrange repair of the casket.

When he returned she was smoking. She looked defiantly at him. 'It's natural for me to want to see her, Philippe. What are you telling people? That I went crazy?' She blew smoke towards him.

'You don't need to see in that box. And you don't need me to explain why.'

'Because Claude identified her? If her father has the right to see her then so do I.'

But he did not mean only that. He meant that the child's body was decomposed beyond recognition. It lay in a summery field for two months and nature had done its damage. His brother had faced the appalling task of looking at a hank of hair and the rags of flesh and garment. No one would wish that agony on the child's mother.

Philippe said: 'Face the facts, Andrée. If it was appropriate then several other people would have seen her. Her grandmother, for one. You'll have to accept it sometime, and better today than later. Nicole's gone, she isn't coming home.'

'But how can I believe she's in that box if no one will let me look? If you hadn't come interfering, I'd have seen for myself. Then I'd have believed.'

'Would you?' He betrayed the deepest scepticism. Andrée mystified him. Beautiful, brilliant, gifted but with an irritating trait of sliding away from reality.

'Yes,' she shouted, leaping to her feet. '*Yes*. How else am I to be convinced?'

'Sit down!' He did not want her rampaging through the house. She was not the only one upset. His mother was coping wonderfully but if Andrée lost control it would be wretched for her.

Andrée sank down. 'How else?' she repeated more quietly.

'You must trust Claude . . .'

'I don't. Suppose he was wrong. Do you know, when he came back from seeing her he shut himself away and wouldn't tell me about it? I asked him: did she look as though she suffered? He refused to answer, he turned his back on me.'

Philippe carried on as though she had not spoken. 'And you must trust the police and the pathologists and the examining magistrate.'

She snorted. 'The examining magistrate? And aren't you the one who complained to the press that he was making a mess of the case, and you wanted the city police and Laroche to withdraw?'

'No, I didn't say all that. They exaggerated. I wanted to get rid of the press, that was it.'

'Huh! Well, the police found her. They didn't make such a mess, did they?'

Her logic eluded him. Either she knew her baby's body lay in the casket in the room along the hall, in which case she trusted in the police, the magistrate and her husband; or she refused to know what was in the box and did not trust them. Philippe could not see how to handle her perversity. He willed Claude to appear, or one of the others.

Philippe had not seen any of the family for over a week. He had been in Paris, working, knowing that the funeral would cause considerable disruption. He did not dream of avoiding it, but the timing was unfortunate as the company was very busy and important meetings were being held that week. He stayed in Paris and crammed several days' work into half their number. And he left Paris before dawn to reach the château in time for breakfast. The roads were empty, the journey fast and uneventful. When he arrived, only the servants were stirring. For a time he rested in his room, but then a premonition, or maybe a half-heard sound, sent him downstairs in search of Andrée. He did not know about the casket in the flower-filled room. A scraping sound had drawn him to it.

As he sat across the breakfast table from her, praying for somebody to relieve him, he thought of Margot abandoned in his bed in Paris, of the work he might be doing in his office at the château. Instead, in spite of his efforts to make the best use of the time, he was obliged to waste it playing nurse to a difficult woman made irrational by grief. God, where was Claude? She was his wife, why didn't he come and take care of her?

It was the English girl who crept into the room and saved him. Her mousy hair clipped back and her skinny figure wrapped in a dull grey dress suitable for a funeral, she looked every millimetre the caricature of the English nanny. If circumstances had been different, he would have laughed. It was obvious she had made a deliberate decision about her clothes: the long boring dress, the black stockings and flat black shoes. He had never seen her so frumpish. Not that she was ever attractive, no more than average, and she had one of those puddingy English faces that marked her out from the family and staff at the house. Yet Andrée was fond of her, found her helpful. Philippe welcomed the girl in an unusually vigorous manner, verging on the exuberant. She grasped that something was wrong.

Philippe escaped from the room and went in search of Claude. 'Look,' he told his brother, trying to hint rather than horrify. 'Andrée's in a hell of a state. I found her in the room with the coffin.'

'Well, it won't be there much longer.'

'I'm telling you she ought not to be left alone.'

'And what am I to do? Keep her on a lead? Honestly, Philippe. The woman does what she wants, I can't be watching her every minute.'

Philippe refused to be brushed off. 'Well, you should make damn sure somebody is. Just until the funeral is over.'

Intensity achieved what his hints failed to do. Claude groaned: 'Oh, no. What did she do?'

'She hasn't had much practice with a chisel, she didn't get very far.'

'Christ!' Claude touched his younger brother's shoulder. 'I'll make sure she's never out of sight.'

'She's in the breakfast room.'

Claude headed that way. Philippe went into the salon, the most elegant room in the château, with its Empire furniture, all white and gold wood with rich pink fabrics. Arguably, too, the least comfortable room. He knew no one would be there. From the window he looked out over the parterre, over the flowery garden beyond it, down over the luxuriant vineyard, his eye drawn to a remote gateway seen through an avenue of old poplars. Someone, Judge Georges Laroche insisted, had kept watch on the house from that gateway, steadied powerful glasses on an horizontal bar of the gates and awaited his opportunity to snatch the baby.

Laroche had said to Philippe: 'There's a direct view, m'sieu. The man needn't have hung around the house. He could study it from afar and watch the lights go out and calculate his b-best chance.'

'Judge Laroche, I don't wish to belittle your efforts but has anyone in the village confirmed that a man ever did that?'

'Ah, no, b-but you know how things are in villages. People are not always free to speak.'

Philippe's hackles rose. He hoped he was aiming his glare at Laroche's good eye. 'We aren't feudal lords! We live in a big house, that's all. People in the cottages work at the house or on the estate, or else they live in the city and turn up at weekends to amuse the others with their townie antics. You won't find any evidence that people are fearful of speaking out and describing anything they saw. They're shocked the child's been taken, they'd offer any help they could.'

But the examining magistrate smiled mysteriously and Philippe was left with the impression that one or other of them was guilty of misinterpretation.

Philippe Devereux raised the window of the salon and stepped out on to the terrace. He ought to have gone into his office and read through the mail that came for him while he was in Paris, but after the scene with Andrée he lacked the heart for it. He wished Margot was with him.

Margot was capable, serene, the perfect antidote to the tensions at the château. She offered to drive down with him and attend the funeral, but he dissuaded her. However well the bereaved family behaved, the event was certain to be a public spectacle and he had no wish to subject Margot to that. Besides, he was not purely protecting her from a nerve-racking experience. The press would be there and Margot was well known as another man's wife. Philippe encouraged her to stay in Paris while he drove to the mountains.

He walked down the steps to the parterre. The day was holding its breath but it was not a restful stillness, it was more like the moment between collision and pain. Pain. If the day brought nothing else it was sure to bring that. He turned abruptly and went indoors.

Someone, he thought as he closed the window, let himself into this house, climbed to the top floor and took away and killed a small girl. It happened when the house was full of people, any one of whom might have heard a sound and investigated. Whoever entered the house showed courage, albeit in a despicable act. Not for the first time, Philippe marvelled at the nature of the abductor. He could not conceive similar courage in himself. And that, he thought, was the extraordinary thing: criminals had access to a cunning and a daring denied ordinary mortals. Or was it, rather, a lack, he wondered? A lack of one of the elements of self-preservation that prevented them from appreciating the potential consequences of their actions?

Going from the salon into the hall he met his mother, who had breakfasted in her room. Mme Devereux had never looked young, Philippe took after her in that. Photographs proved that at a mere nineteen years she had appeared mature, ten years older. In a woman less wealthy that might have been a disadvantage. At fifty her hair was steely grey and her figure puffed-up. But her features were good, her expensive clothes disguised figure faults, she was a woman to be looked at twice. Unfortunately, at fifty she was regularly taken for sixty.

'Good morning, Mother.' Philippe waited for her at the foot of the stairs.

'You've made it in good time, Philippe. I wondered whether you might be late.'

'The roads were clear.' He held out a hand, seeming to offer to help her down the last stairs as he might help an old woman. She squeezed his hand.

'I'm glad you came.'

This surprised him. 'Did you think I'd avoid it?'

'No-o.' But it sounded like yes.

He gave a half-laugh. 'It's the last thing one wants to do, but of course one wouldn't miss it. *Couldn't.*'

'How is that poor girl this morning? Is she down yet?'

He edited out the episode with the chisel. 'She's being looked after. Claude's seeing she isn't left alone.'

His mother smiled at the name of her elder son. 'Poor Claude, he's so good to her. People forget it's as much his tragedy as hers. I think he's behaving impeccably, Philippe, I really do.'

He was walking beside her on the way to the breakfast room for her to say her good-mornings to the rest of the family. Habit helped him agree with her praise of Claude. As it was what she wanted to hear, he said it, knowing it fell short of the truth. But it had always been the same: Claude was his parents' favourite and it was unchangeable. Claude's talents and virtues were inflated by them, his misdeeds laughed away. When they were boys he . . . But what did that matter? Some parents were blind when it came to observing their own children.

According to Maurice Devereux and his wife, their elder son was cleverer, kinder, more handsome and an unqualified social success. He made a brilliant marriage to an opera singer and provided them with a grandchild. Not, unfortunately, a grand-*son*, which is what they hankered for so the business could continue in competent hands. Women, in Devereux eyes, were to be beautiful and add sparkle to the social scene. They were not to grapple with marketing targets or balance sheets, neither were they to trouble their heads about the scientific juggling and leaps of artistry that created new fragrances and sustained a perfume-making empire. When Claude's daughter was born, the grandparents' pleasure was tinged with jokes about making sure of a boy next time. And when Andrée's illness ensured there was to be no next time, their disappointment was undisguisable.

This annoyed Philippe on several counts. He had said to his mother, camouflaging his attitude with irony: 'We're a family business, you know, not a royal family. All is not lost if there's no male heir.'

She joined in the joke, mocking herself for her old-fashioned views and then excusing herself on the grounds that, with several brothers vying to take over the reins, she had never been bold enough to consider playing a role in her own family's concerns. 'Women are different these days, I know that. Maybe Claude's daughter will want to become head of the company and it might be a very good thing if she did. We shall wait and see, Philippe.'

'Yes,' Philippe said. 'That would be best.'

Only after the murder did the grandmother ask herself whether it might not, after all, be stolid, unadventurous Philippe who guaranteed the future of the family tree and with it the House of Devereux.

The day of the funeral was a torment. Staff and villagers were in the church by the time the family and friends arrived. But outside, slotting themselves in between gravestones and perching along the walls around the churchyard, were sightseers and press. The photographers craved two shots in particular: devastation on Andrée's face, and the coffin.

Because of the crush, Andrée could not be hustled into the church as fast as Claude, who held her arm, had hoped. During the mêlée, the pair found themselves on the wrong side of the hearse, shielding their faces from the cameras and unable to get to the door. The bearers, about to carry the coffin into the church, were called back because the chief mourners were not in place. Claude pushed a journalist sprawling and pulled Andrée through the gap to reach the porch. This brought them up against the party with the coffin. Andrée stretched out a hand to touch the box but Claude was drawing her on. A photographer from an agency snapped the instant when she appeared to be tearing herself away from her husband and lunging at the casket. The incident was not at all like that, almost the opposite, but it made a dramatic photograph and it made thousands of francs.

The heat of hundreds of people crammed into the church on a baking day was insufferable. The few at the ends of rows were able to slip outside and gasp air but the rest, trapped, were obliged to sit it out. Handkerchiefs dabbed at faces, making mourners who were peripheral to the tragedy seem overcome with sentiment. The priest was rapid, which showed great consideration for the living, who needed to leave as fast as might be, but resulted in a display of indifference towards the dead. One or two journalists were to report on the 'gabbled' and 'insensitive' service.

Emerging into the glare of the morning, Philippe saw photographers standing on tombstones close by the open grave, cameras aimed. Moments later, harassed, jostled, utterly ruined, Andrée slid forward, her knees jelly, all light and activity blacking out. Claude had hold of her. Philippe yanked her up by her other arm.

The priest's words scurried on. Mme Devereux clenched fingers into Maurice's arm, fighting a pain that was slicing her left arm. Maurice stood impassive, maintaining dignity in the face of chaos.

Then the coffin was down. A foot caught a discarded film packet and involuntarily kicked it into the grave. A handful of dusty earth marred the whiteness of the coffin lid. It was virtually over. Then Andrée pitched forward. Her movement was too fast for her husband but Philippe clung on to her lower arm. He braced himself to hold her, although she dived with a strength that sent him stumbling after her, unable to prevent her reaching the hole. Other hands were straining for her. But Andrée was over the edge, one leg in the air and her other knee on the graveside earth. Philippe could not hold her. She was twisting and his arm might break. Desperate as he was to prevent it, his fingers uncurled and he let her fall.

He saw dust on the black linen dress, holes in the dark stockings. Andrée was crouching on the coffin, her muddied fingers plucking at the lid. And all the while she was moaning.

Hands reached past him. He helped them gather her up. Claude folded her into his arms. A path was cleared, she was carried through, pushed into the back of a car. Men swatted at the journalists and the onlookers to make a way for the car to escape. Faces and lenses pressed against its windows. Andrée huddled, face down on the seat, shuddering with sobs.

Philippe was sickened. He travelled back to the house in another car, in horrified silence. 'The stuff that nightmares are made of,' he thought.

'Thank God Margot didn't come. I was right. I knew it would be hell.'

At the house he met his mother sitting in a cool corner, shutters drawn, a fan in her hand. 'Oh, it's you, Philippe.'

'Yes, Mother. Can I get you anything?'

'I've sent for a cold drink. The heat, you know.' She did not confess to the pain in her upper arm. In any case, it was passing. If she could lie down, if she could just lie down.

He said: 'Thank God that's over.' He sat on a stuffed chair near her.

The fan stirred the air between them a few times. Then she said: 'Do you really think it is?'

He did not answer. Murder was never over, especially not unsolved murder where there was no culprit to blame. Without a guilty party, they were all guilty. Guilty of negligence in not noticing footsteps up a marble staircase; of not hearing a child cry in the night; of not imagining it could happen to one of theirs; guilty, over and over again, of blaming themselves.

She leaned back, rested her head, lowered the folded fan to her lap. 'She thought too much of that baby. She spoiled her. It was an unhealthy devotion. What has she now? What will she ever have?'

Philippe cleared his throat and murmured that it was not possible to control the degree of one's love. 'Andrée's a passionate woman.'

He wondered why he said that. He thought of her as unreasonable and volatile. But, yes, she was passionate. Not like Margot with her cool appraisals and self-regulation. Andrée was all will and emotion.

His mother's eyes closed. By now he was used to the dimness

and saw her better. Tiredness disfigured her face and her colour was poor.

'Mother, why don't you lie down for a while?'

She opened an eye. 'Hmm. Good idea. And how often have you heard me tell your father I'd like a lift installed in this house?'

'Come on, I'll walk up with you if you're exhausted.'

She let him guide her, holding on to his arm as they mounted the stairs. When her bedroom door closed between them, he started along the passage to his own room. Downstairs there were people to see, politenesses to be observed, excuses and apologies to be made. But for now he wanted a few minutes' solitude.

His room was masculine and austere, very much the bachelor's base. None of it was of his choosing, the heavy mahogany pieces had been there since he was a youngster. But it was a room that made him feel easy, an undemanding place. Unlike the Paris flat for which he hired an interior designer and which, while magnificent in its way, did not look like anywhere he would choose to live.

He took off his jacket and tossed it over the back of a chair. He loosened his tie, hesitated before removing it and stripping off his shirt. The messy emotional morning made him feel unclean. He decided to steal a few more minutes and shower.

The water was practically cold but that was all to the good. Refreshed, he changed his shirt and underwear and put on again the dark suit and tie. The clock by the bed reminded him he had spent too long over all this, people would be wondering why he was not with the rest of the family offering wine and accepting condolences. His father had a phrase about 'observing the rites' that in practice meant doing what other people expected of one whether it made sense or not. Who, among those the family invited back to the house, was silly enough to believe the Devereux wanted to see anyone after the frightful scenes at the church? Families needed to close in on themselves, lick wounds, before they were fit to face outsiders after an onslaught. But what must be done must be done. Philippe combed his hair and went downstairs to observe the rites.

He touched the hands of damp-eyed women who were 'so sorry'; he gave gruff thanks to the men who were enduring the day; he avoided outright condemnation of the press, the gawpers, the examining magistrate who was failing to solve the case and the police who, along with Laroche, were present at the funeral but did nothing to curb the excesses.

Claude was not there. Nor, of course, was Andrée. Philippe caught his father's eye across the room and tried to convey that his mother would join them any moment. The guests were avoiding asking after the absent members of the family, but as time ran on the absences grew mysterious. Philippe had the absurd idea that he and his father would be trapped, forever circling among these unhelpful and inquisitive people, until all the unposed questions were resolved. A life of unrelieved socializing was his worst fear.

Eventually his mother came, preceding Claude. They looked as though they had enjoyed a long and comforting talk, their mutual support system was at work. Philippe had noticed it in the past, at other times of family stress. Those two turned to each other. He and his father did not.

Mme Devereux had switched on her smile before entering and she located a friend and hurried forward, hand outstretched, cheek ready to be kissed. Philippe thought: 'Good old Mother, another excellent performance coming up.' The faded woman he had helped up the stairs to her bed was replaced by one with vigour and a willingness to show gratitude to her friends for gathering to sustain her. She plunged in, and people who were awkward or withdrawn when Philippe spoke to them blossomed at his mother's approach.

Claude moved easily among them too, combining sadness with sympathetic interest. There was a buffet lunch during which visitors were reluctant to eat for fear of seeming too healthy in the midst of death. Andrée did not appear, although the nanny, who stayed with her while Claude did his duty, looked in. Still the boring grey dress and flat shoes but she had removed the clips and her hair framed her pudgy face. One of the younger male guests was taking considerable interest in her. Her French was coming on wonderfully, she locked him in conversation. God, Philippe wished Margot were there.

As soon as he decently could, he broke away and went to his office. Cars were starting up as guests made their getaway. He could practically hear the sighs of relief as they found themselves free of the miserable atmosphere. Philippe opened his shutters, the sun had moved round from this side of the house. He loosened his tie, threw his jacket on a chair and started on the pile of mail. The previous day his secretary had told him on the telephone what there was: a report on a proposed marketing strategy to be studied; a handful of replies to letters; an inquiry from a manufacturer who hoped to use the name of a classic Devereux perfume for a range of make-up; another manufacturer keen to discuss a franchising idea. She had left two envelopes unopened, one from his solicitor and a smaller envelope marked personal.

Philippe picked up the small envelope. It was postmarked Marseilles. He knew no one in Marseilles. He turned it over, then studied the front again. His name and the address had been typed on a dirty machine that made some letters splodgy. The 'e's were filled in and also the 'a's. His eye ran from that envelope to the other. The solicitor's was a professional job, the one marked personal was not.

Philippe shrugged, slid a finger beneath the flap and ripped it open. Inside was the ransom demand.

Philippe sighed and opened his eyes. Red rose petals had splashed the windscreen like blood. Leaving the keys in the ignition, he dashed to the churchyard gate, a foot slipping on wet leaves and his sleeve smudging lichen from the gatepost. He cursed, softly.

The church door was ajar but his entry was noisy: heavy breathing after the exertion, a clattering of leather soles on stonework, a hand fumbling with the swinging inner doors. The light was poor. For a moment he thought he was wrong, the building seemed empty. Then a figure stepped back from the wall near the altar, came to stand in the centre of the chancel and peered at him. 'Philippe? Is that you?'

'Yes, Father.' His voice was harsh and irritable. He attempted to moderate it. 'I came to find you.'

'I'm not lost. I don't need anyone to find me.' But the tone was less testy than ironic.

'It's pouring out there.'

'That's why I'm in here. Mind you, if the roof isn't attended to it will be pouring in here before long. I was noticing, there's a stain.' He was indicating a spot above the altar.

'The car's outside. I'll drive you back whenever you're ready.' Philippe smelled damp plaster blended with the usual odours of ancient stone and old wood.

Maurice Devereux was in no hurry. He lifted his hat from a chair and ambled towards Philippe, his eyes taking in the simple wooden carvings, the plain lines of buildings and contents. Despite the memories it thrust at him, it was a soothing place.

Philippe looked at his wrist watch. 'I don't want to rush you, Father, but someone's coming to see me.'

'For lunch?'

'No. Afterwards.'

'Well, then, there's plenty of time.' Quite deliberately, he made a detour to ponder the Latin of a memorial plaque.

Philippe gave up. He sat in the final row, on the edge of a chair, leaning forward and folding his arms on the back of the one in front. 'Did you bring flowers?'

'A few. There wasn't much to be had. The garden isn't what it used to be.'

Neither, thought Philippe ungraciously, was his father. Mooning about, picking flowers for a graveyard when there was a business to be run. He wondered whether Maurice was ailing.

Maurice said: 'I can remember when we could go out into the garden and gather flowers for the house every day of the year.'

'That kind of gardening is very time consuming. People don't bother with all that these days.'

'It's a great pity they don't.'

'Things change, Father.' Philippe began to tap his foot but the sound was unpleasantly loud and he stopped.

'People say that when things are perfect they're too good to last. They forget that bad things don't last either.'

Philippe did not reply. Maurice dropped on to a chair a few rows ahead of him, sitting sideways and facing his son diagonally across the aisle. He twirled the old brimmed hat in his hands.

'You know, Philippe, I catch myself thinking about that child. When an adult dies you have memories of who they were and what they were like and how they fitted into the family pattern. But a baby as young as that . . . You have nothing except conjecture. The only question to which I have an answer is that if she hadn't been stolen from us and murdered, she'd be a young woman now.'

'It was a long time ago.' He spoke with finality, wishing to get off the subject. The murder was one of the bad things that could be left in the past. Good things had happened to them since then: his own marriage to Margot and the birth of David.

'Well, yes,' said Maurice, getting to his feet with laboured movements, 'you're thinking I'm being sentimental. Why shouldn't I be? A first grandchild's an important step in one's life. Your mother and I felt it very keenly when she died. You had Margot and your own happiness to make, the child's death wasn't central to your life the way it was to ours. But come on, enough of that.'

Philippe held the swing door for him as they went out. The shower was dying and they deviated from the path to reach the family plot. Devereux stones were sleek, the words hard and black with flourishes of gold. Maurice stopped in front of the child's. There were no flowers there. He saw Philippe cast around.

'Yes,' Maurice told him. 'I laid them on your mother's. Today is one of our anniversaries, the day we first met.'

The flash of pink and yellow petals of the chrysanthemums seemed out of keeping in the setting of sombre stone, but the rain had done its best to destroy them. Philippe moved away, trusting his father to follow. He did not know what to say to him.

In the car Philippe broached the matter of the couturier who wished the House of Devereux to produce a perfume to be marketed under his name. 'We have to reach a decision. I'm afraid we've already kept him waiting a discourteous length of time.'

'But Philippe . . .'

'Yes, Father, I know you don't want to get involved in this kind of thing but it *is* profitable.'

'For him, certainly. For us? It could be.'

'We'd make sure that it was.'

Maurice was trying to find somewhere to put his soggy hat. It was horrible to hold it on his knees but the dashboard shelf was too small and he was reluctant to set it on the floor, where his shoes had deposited churchyard mud.

Terse, Philippe said: 'Behind the seat.' And as his father obediently thrust the hat there, Philippe went on: 'I do see there's a danger of him paying us for a top-quality product to establish his brand name, and perhaps later cutting his costs by going to another company if he decides to extend his range.'

'He says he doesn't want a range, just one fragrance.'

'I know what he says. Now we must settle what we say to him.'

'As a matter of fact, Philippe, I've told him we're ready to do business.'

The car swerved. Maurice's hand flew for the grab-handle.

Philippe was icy. 'You've already told him?'

'Well, yes. And I believe we've struck a deal.'

Philippe drove on in silence. He left the vineyard in his wake, swooped along between the trees that flanked the dead-end road to the château. Travelling much too fast, he reached the bend shortly before the archway and the courtyard. He was fuming. As he braked and juggled the gears, his father spoke again.

'It's a good deal, Philippe. I think so.'

The car shot spray across the puddled paving. Bitterly, Philippe said: 'Perhaps you could tell me about it.'

He drew up close to the back door to save them another soaking from the shower's final flurries. The spicy honeysuckle framing it dropped pearls of water on their hair as they opened it. Once they were inside the passage, and Maurice was sticking his hat on a peg for it to drip harmlessly on to the tiles, Philippe said: 'Does David know about this?'

'He's in Milan now, finalizing it. I promise, Philippe, he's come to a very satisfactory arrangement.'

'Aren't you forgetting something, Father?'

'Yes, yes, yes,' Maurice grumbled, leading the way down the passage to the room Philippe used as his office. 'You wanted consultations, you wanted us all to sit around and chat about it. Well, what you must remember, Philippe, is that I remain the head of this business and I'm entitled to delegate as I think fit. David offered to go to Italy and I approved. He's young but he's capable, he understands what the future of the House of Devereux must be.'

They entered the room. Philippe shut the door. He waited to see what his father might do. Maurice went to the window, where Philippe had earlier watched for him to pass by the gap in the trees. Philippe hesitated, then took his usual seat behind the ornate *bureau-plat*. Ormolu satyrs' masks stared out from long cabriole legs that were inlaid with engraved brass on tortoise-shell. It was extraordinarily elaborate, extremely valuable, a benchmark for excellence.

Maurice strolled over to take a chair opposite him. 'Listen, Philippe, this couturier, he isn't rubbish, you know.'

Philippe gripped the edge of the ebony desk top. 'Father, I *do* know. He's been eminent for most of my life, he's top of the market and he's no fool.'

'Well, then.' Maurice leaned back, crossed his legs, pinching the dampened cloth of a trouser leg to ease it. 'Neither business will be compromised by association with the other. We're both, in our separate fields, the best.'

'For heaven's sake, these are the arguments I put to you weeks ago! *You* were the one holding back, saying we oughtn't to dirty our hands, that we'd be putting ourselves in the position of a food factory making own-brand lines for supermarkets.'

'I needed to consider it, Philippe. You were right.'

'Then why didn't you say . . .' He subsided. 'Oh, never mind.' Never mind, because the answer was plain: David had done the persuading he was incapable of doing himself. 'I simply wish you'd told me that your thinking had changed.'

And he wished he was half as confident as his father that David's deal was a good one for the House of Devereux and not a good one only for the Italian couturier. The telephone rang. A female voice from the kitchen warned Philippe lunch was almost ready.

Maurice uncrossed his legs. 'I must say, that outing has given me an appetite. It's *escalopes de veau cauchoise* today, did she tell you? She knows it's one of my favourites. And she's using the Calvados this time. Do you remember last time, when she had to substitute *marc*? Delicious, too, but not exactly my favourite dish of the *Pays de Caux*.'

Philippe produced a wan smile. Maurice's appetite was unwaveringly healthy, if favouring rich and old-fashioned dishes could be termed healthy. Left to himself, Philippe preferred to skip lunch and work through the day, but he lacked the heart to make Maurice eat alone and there was frequently only the pair of them at the house.

Maurice rested his hands on kneecaps. 'Well, now, one other thing before we go through. The perfume for our Italian friend.'

'Exactly. That was your other reason for resisting having anything to do with him. We don't have a new fragrance to offer.'

'But that's been solved too. The laboratory has the new one ready. David took a sample with him.'

Impish, delighted with himself, the older man's eyes twinkled. Beneath the marvellous desk Philippe's hands clenched.

Maurice sauntered in the direction of the dining room. 'Don't be long, Philippe. The escalopes make me too eager, I mightn't be able to wait for you.'

Philippe wrestled a moment with his temper. Then he flicked open the folder his secretary had set out for him. A history of the House of Devereux, its developments and its triumphs. And who but he cared that behind them, as far back as he could remember, there were squabbles? Weary, out-manoeuvred yet again, he shut the folder and went, devoid of appetite, to eat his *escalopes de veau cauchoise*. Perhaps all families are like this, he thought. But that was one of the imponderables. One never knew.

She was not at all what Philippe Devereux expected. On the telephone she had sounded older and when his secretary ushered her into the room he felt his eyebrows lifting in surprise. She was in her twenties, with that supreme assurance that English women of a certain background acquire very young. And she was unflawed: a slight pinkness enlivened her unblemished, delicate northern skin; her hair was perfect, in so far as the casual style demanded perfection; she was well proportioned and a good height. When she sat, her skirt slid back to stress the prettiest pair of legs seen at the château in years.

He began by offering her coffee, which she accepted. Philippe then took a sheet of paper from the folder and skimmed it over the desk to her. No rings, he noticed as her hands lifted it. Unmarried, although these days that could never be safely construed as unattached. Divorced? He hoped not, for her sake. She was too young to have been down that trail of woe, too wise to make the mistake of an early marriage.

'Those are a few basic facts,' he said as she read. 'I asked my secretary to set down the key points and some dates. I believe you'll find them helpful.'

'That was thoughtful. Thank you.' She put the sheet on the desk.

He liked her voice, too, and her accent. Although her French, as far as he had tested it on the telephone, was competent, her accent played those endearing English tricks. When the coffee came, he asked for the tray to be set down on a low table across the room.

She produced a tape recorder and placed it beside the tray. 'You don't mind this?'

'Not at all. But tell me, have journalists completely abandoned shorthand and notebooks?'

'Oh, no. My shorthand's in good working order, I promise you. And if we were going to talk English I'd probably not bother with this.' She pressed a button, ran back the tape, played herself saying 'in good working order', ran it back further and stabbed the record button.

Philippe sipped his coffee. The new seating arrangement was better, there was no intervening desk to cut off his view of her legs. He waited for her first question.

She was a good interviewer, he granted her that. During the telephone call she had explained she was writing a series of profiles of leading European companies for an international news magazine soon to begin publication. The Devereux profile was the first of them. And she had done her homework. The line of questioning was intelligent, she was searching without over-stepping the bounds of politeness. When he manoeuvred away from questions, on the grounds that answers would reveal secrets his competitors would love to know, she backed down without protest.

Any misgivings he entertained about agreeing to the interview were dispelled. It was altogether more enjoyable to spend the afternoon discussing the business with her than to be fretting about what his father and his son might be up to behind his back.

She declared herself impressed with the château, which the family had owned for several generations, and inquired about the vineyard. They went to the window to see the ribbed fields, gleaming damply, asleep until spring stirred the vines to activity. Gamay grapes, they produced a red wine. Description led to the offer of a glass. By the time it was poured he had forgotten exactly where they had reached in the conversation before the verbal diversion into the vineyard.

He kept his eyes on her as she took her first sip. He wanted to see her fingers cosseting the stemmed glass, the parting of her lips, the bob of her perfect throat as she swallowed. Her eyes were not on him, she was looking down, away to one side, as people do when they concentrate. Then she lowered the glass. Her lips parted again, in a smile. 'Good,' she said. 'Very good. Who makes it for you?'

The taste filled her head with visions of women wearing dresses of faded floral linen, sitting on wicker chairs in dappled shade, a lacy cloth lapping a round table. Was it a half-remembered holiday? Or garbled memory of an advertisement? Both or neither, for her Château Devereux had the flavour of summer.

'A man called Giles makes it,' said Philippe. 'We say he's the château's finest treasure.'

She laughed at his joke, she had laughed at them all. He liked that.

He said: 'He's been with us forever. Lives in one of the cottages in what's left of the village. The truth is he's growing fragile and the work has to be done by his helpers. But old Giles is a tyrant, he makes them obey him. We dread to think what will happen on the day he gives up or they rebel.'

She laughed at that too. 'Oh, you needn't worry. There'll be someone to take up the baton, there always is. You've probably got a man down there now, desperate for his chance to take over and prove he's every bit as capable as Giles.'

'What a comforting thought.'

And from wine-making they moved to the other family interests: the racehorses and the art collection.

'Those are more my father's concerns than mine,' he explained.

But she did not leave the topics. 'I believe they're both supported financially by the company.'

'Well, in effect, yes. And the horses have been named after the fragrances. Did you know we had an Arc winner?'

She said she did, and asked how well the stable was doing.

He answered with: 'It's an expensive matter, horse-racing. Perhaps we've been lucky, perhaps we spend more on our horses than we ought. But we're doing well.'

They talked on for a while. Gradually, Philippe felt the first uncertainties. His voice remained relaxed but inside he was growing wary. Each time he tried to edge the conversation back to the running of the perfume business, she coaxed him away from it.

Then she focused on the art collection, the way it had been established and the strategy to develop it. When Philippe underlined that this was kept separate from the business, she said that yes, she knew the running of it was separate but the financial link was crucial.

She was expanding but he cut her off, talking over her and sounding to his own ears brusque. 'I assure you this is an irrelevance. The fund is excessively well endowed. It flourishes, as does the perfume business.'

His tone jarred her. For a moment she looked at him, unflinching. He sensed his facial expression hardening and made an effort to smile, but he knew it was not successful. He feared he made it obvious she had strayed into a sensitive area.

'Very well. Everything is flourishing,' she encapsulated. 'So may I ask you why you're currently selling?'

Philippe gave up the attempt to smile. 'I, personally, can't explain why we might be selling one artist and purchasing another. That's the responsibility of the man we've appointed to be the director of our collection. Perhaps his taste has changed, perhaps the market demands another approach. You'll have to ask him.'

She dodged saying she had done so, that the director replied he was not allowed to answer questions and that, in any case, the decisions were not his and he did not have the information she wanted.

Instead she told Philippe: 'You're selling but not buying. Is there any particular reason for this?'

'You've been misinformed. Since my father began to collect, it's been the intention to establish a major art collection and we've never veered from that.'

She flashed a teasing smile. 'Then perhaps I should be talking to your father instead, as the collection's his creation.'

'No,' he said quickly. 'No, I don't think so. My father doesn't shop around. We have a fund and we have a director who dips into the fund and acquires what takes his eye.'

'Then I wonder why . . .'

He raised an impatient hand. 'Look, if you're trying to concoct a story that the House of Devereux is in ruins and we're having to sell off the art collection to rescue it, then I swear to you that you're wrong.'

A whining warned that her tape had run out. He said not a word as she swapped it for a fresh one. When she looked up, ready for the interview to resume, his face told her that her time had run out too.

'I have another appointment,' he said. 'I thought you realized that.'

Once she had dropped the recorder into her bag and was ready to go, he returned in a roundabout way to the subject. 'Perhaps you'd be good enough to tell me where you picked up this idea about us selling.'

She got her own back. 'Sale rooms in London, New York, everywhere.' Then she stuck out her hand, obliging him to touch it. 'Thank you so much, M. Devereux. I'll see myself out.'

And she was gone.

Philippe listened to her footsteps over the marble of the hall. He picked up the telephone. Beside it on the ebony desk top lay the sheet of details Rose Darrow had declined to take away with her. Philippe crumpled it as he waited for his call to be answered.

THIRTEEN

Ellie's parents' flat in the Prague suburb of Braník was on the top floor of the block. Snatches of distant greenery showed from some windows but in the main the view was of identical blocks. A discoloured patch marked the kitchen ceiling, rings within rings, dark brown to fawn, showing where the rain had come in, repeatedly.

She recognized the battered kitchen table. Her father made it when her parents set up home together but it was never perfect. Solid, yes, but marred by knot holes from the outset and now a history of family mealtimes was written on its surface. Her father sat at one end of it, bent over the components of an electric iron he had dismantled and was endeavouring to mend. Ellie's mother had her back to them and was pouring water on to tea leaves.

The flat was compact and neat. Everything except the table was unfamiliar. When she and her mother went through to a sitting room, her eye checked for more mementoes of her childhood. None except a lace cloth spread over the faded mahogany of a table.

Ellie supposed they would talk now. It had been impossible in view of her father's dumb objection to her sudden reappearance. He was treating her like an unwelcome neighbour, the sort of nuisance who is always dropping in for company or to cadge what they were too poor to give.

'Drink it while it's hot.'

'Pretty china,' Ellie said, the words out before she could stop them. Ever since she had come, there was this trade in polite compliments. Yet how might they pick up the threads of family life when each of them, first Ellie and later her mother, had chosen to snap them?

Her mother was dutifully responding to the remarks about the china, saying how she came by it. In Ellie's head a voice was complaining about the futility of it all. They spoke like strangers because that is what they were. No wonder her mother took out the best china to serve her tea and left the family's day-to-day things in the cupboard.

'Tell me about New York, Ellie.'

But that really meant tell me about Sam, this artist you say you live with. And if you do live with him, then why are you in London or here or anywhere except New York?

Ellie talked about New York, the touristy stuff, which was a waste of breath because that was what her mother saw on television. She switched to explaining about London, her home there and her work but not too much about the book on neglected women artists. From deep within her came the warning that taking feminist theory into the art world was a concept beyond her mother's grasp. A woman who lived as her mother had lived, stifling self-expression, imagination and potential, had no idea of the joy of challenging received opinion. Her mother had challenged nothing. She had kept her head down and raised her children and survived. But she had not challenged and she had certainly not encouraged them to.

Her mother said: 'You used to write to me about a young man in London who helped you when you decided to study art. He was a writer, too, I think.'

'John Blair? He became a journalist.'

And she found it easier to speak about John Blair than about the other aspects of her life. He provided the link they needed, he was a strand that ran through her life, from the time she reached London and her job in his cousin's home, right up until the present. A vital link, and she was glad of it and did not spoil it by revealing that this thread was also snapped because he was dead.

Ellie had missed her younger brother by a day. He did not live in Prague any longer but had travelled to the city in connection with his work and called in to see his parents. Her mother produced photographs of him, with an overweight wife and children all of whom looked like the fat wife.

'You wouldn't know him now, Ellie.'

Patently true. For one thing, he looked older, much older, than she did herself. Maybe it was a poor photograph but she found none of that brother-and-sister likeness that used to make the relationship obvious.

'And this . . .' Her mother was holding out another of the photographs from the stash in the cupboard.

The other brother, the elder one. He was wearing uniform.

Ellie looked sharply at her mother, the unavoidable glance a demand for information. Her mother's face was closed, the feelings obscured.

The policeman in the photograph stared straight ahead, mouth unsmiling but a sardonic glint in his eyes. How cold, how unemotional, how terrible he was.

Ellie cleared her throat to attempt to speak. Her mother reached for the photograph, saying: 'I thought that would surprise you, Ellie.'

'Yes. Yes, it does rather.' Then the question that mattered: 'Where's Pavel now?'

It meant does he live in Prague? And it meant did he lose his job after the revolution as many of them did? And am I in any danger of running into him?

Her mother gathered the photographs into a tidy heap and sat holding them on her lap, edges lined up, the man in uniform on the top. 'On the other side of the city. We don't see him very often. He'll be sorry he missed you. He used to be so fond of you, Ellie.'

Ellie's brain was flashing her pictures of herself, drying her long blonde hair by the fire, kneeling there and fluffing it out, dangerously, in front of the electric bar and willing it to be dry because she wanted to go out and meet her friends. An insistent hand drew her back, fanned out her silkiness, then pulled her comb through it, the touch of the teeth on her scalp and the threat of pain as it teased away the snags, disturbing and delighting her.

Her mother brushed imaginary dust from the border of the photograph of the policeman, the gesture distracting attention from the centrality of her question.

'Why did you stay away from us, Ellie? You never explained, you know.'

'But, Mother, you know why.'

'The political situation? I don't think so. Besides, you couldn't have known in the summer of 1968 how the next twenty years would be.'

Ellie gave a self-mocking laugh. 'Well, that's always been my answer.'

'It was a rapid decision for a young girl, if that's the true answer.'

Russian tanks had rumbled across the square and within hours Ellie knew she was not going back, that history had handed her the excuse she needed. When John Blair came to talk to her in the garden of his cousin's house, the decision had hardened in her mind.

'Mother, I've been happy,' she said carefully. 'There was more for me there. And that's what I needed. More.'

Her mother pursed her lips. 'If you'd been a political creature, a protester, then it would have been understandable. But you were a quiet girl who liked looking at pictures. You'd have been all right here.'

She was wearing a piercing look Ellie had not seen before, except on the face of her grandmother when the time arrived to unearth a truth. Ellie was amused.

'You look exactly like Granny when you do that with your eyes.'

'What did I do?'

'You dropped your eyelids and you stuck your nose in the air. Like this. No, it's no good, I can't do it. But believe me you had that look she used to have when she thought one of us had been misbehaving and ought to own up.'

175

Her mother put the photographs back in the cupboard and shut the door on them. 'Perhaps I was telling you, Elena, that you can't fool me. I noticed you dodged my questions. I can't force it out of you but you needn't think I don't know I haven't had the truth.'

Ellie felt the redness sting her cheeks. Her mother *was* just like Granny, an old tyrant who never let up until she got her way. Somehow, in her absence, her mother had transmuted into her own mother. Physical resemblance had been predictable but not traits of character.

Floundering, Ellie said: 'I'm not sure how to reply to that.'

The woman was standing against the window. It made her seem bulkier, taller. In the twin block of flats over her left shoulder a light was switched on in an identical room. It probably had the same orange plastic-covered cushions on the easy chairs.

'You don't need to reply, Elena. You've set yourself free of any responsibility for what happens in this family. It's not as though you were the only child, not even a special one like the eldest or the youngest, just the middle one. The rest of us are still a family wherever you are.'

'Mother, I had to take decisions.'

'Yes, I know. And you were very young. This may surprise you but I thought you behaved wisely.'

'*Wisely?*'

'In the circumstances, yes. At the beginning, I mean. I didn't expect it to be permanent. After all, what youngster doesn't want to see something of the world? For you it was a good time to take a look at it.'

There had been no resistance to her plea to be permitted to go to London and learn English. In retrospect that was odd but at the time she enjoyed the quirk that meant her small desires were trampled but the greedy one indulged.

'Elena, you were too close, too intense. It needed one of you to break away. I'm glad you had the good sense to see that and to do it.'

The older woman's face was in shadow. Her daughter searched the gloom for an alternative to the obvious meaning of the words and did not find one. A familiar tension gripped her, her breath came fast. She wanted to rip undone her tight clothing, gasp air into her resisting lungs. Her hand went to her throat but the shirt was not buttoned high, there was no constriction except within her own body.

Silently, she ordered herself: 'Control it. It's nerves, nothing else. Calm down.'

Attention always made her worse but fortunately her mother was turning aside to light a lamp and draw curtains and she missed Ellie's breathy panic. Ellie took a handkerchief from her bag, blew her nose, busied herself with minor activities. Sometimes the ploy worked, this time it failed. All she could think of was that her mother knew. Had known. Yet how could it be? How had she coped with the knowledge, with seeing her daughter impelled to behave 'wisely' and flee her home?

Drawn curtains limited the room. Walls pressed in. The ceiling, its stains twinned with the kitchen's stains, thrust down. Ellie was frantic to get away. That was her nature, she saw it plainly. It was the way she was: when threatened, she ran away.

Ellie said, and her voice was thick: 'It was a long time ago, not worth troubling about now.'

A voice in her head screamed: 'Liar! How can it be consigned to the past, written off to experience? It was a ruining, hateful episode that shaped your attitude and your life. And now, the crowning cruelty, you discover that your mother, that peaceable accepting woman, knew.'

She got to her feet, determined to leave. She had already prepared the way for brevity by inventing an appointment in the city centre. Now she was desperate to get out before she seized her mother and shook the answer from her. The question screamed inside her: 'How could you leave your own daughter to such misery, leave her unprotected, unbefriended?'

Her mother said: 'You were discreet and not many girls are. I was grateful for that. You know how people like a story.'

The hysterical voice inside Ellie was suddenly wordless. Her internal space was filled with a wail of disbelief.

To her astonishment the words she spoke were delivered in a normal tone. 'Yes, they do, don't they? But tell me, Mother. This story they might have heard, who told it to you?'

Her mother's face relaxed in an affectionate smile, the kind parents use to comment on the mild follies of good children. 'My dear, it was Pavel, of course.'

'Pavel?' The word was mouthed, soundless, it could not pass her lips.

'He was very concerned about you going to England. I said to him, if she wants to go then it's for the best because she's in such an emotional tangle. Anyone could see it, Ellie, but you were secretive, you didn't confide in any of us.'

Ellie's bag was in her hand, she was backing to the doorway. She saw her father, head bowed over the pieces of the broken iron, his quietness interrupted only by the metallic click of screw-driver and rivets. She guessed the thing was ruined, he had wrenched it apart and would not succeed in putting it together again. Some things that broke could never be repaired. Thinking that, speaking the words of goodbye, she escaped and stumbled down flights of dank concrete stairs to the featureless world outside.

The earth had shifted beneath her. Pavel's appalling behaviour could be blamed, in her more forgiving moments, on youthful lust but she saw no possible excuse for her mother's attitude. Whatever feelings she concealed at the time, to congratulate Ellie on wisdom and discretion showed the wickedest insensitivity.

She took a wrong turn. For a good few hundred yards she marched on, racked with the knowledge that her mother had known her shame. Nothing in all her varied experience, nothing she had heard of or read about, had prepared her to face this.

She faltered. A car parked ahead of her. It had approached

from the other end of the street but stopped twenty yards away on her side of the road. She recognized the two men who got out and went up the path to the flats. Krieger and Zak.

Alert now, she noted the number of the car and followed the men. Inside the building she paused to catch the sound of two pairs of feet going up the flights overhead. She mounted the stairs, glad of her quiet soles. There was an exchange of words, confirmation she had not been misled. Zak was asking Krieger to speed up, Krieger was telling him not to fuss. Ellie peeped around a landing door and saw them at a standstill outside a brown door. There was no key. Krieger knocked four times. Theatrical, she thought; a signal.

Out in the street again she realized she was lost and begged directions from a young man carrying an upholstered chair, spewing its stuffing, on the way to the mender's. Twice she tried to telephone Rose but Rose was out.

People looked at foreigners on the Metro. Unlike London or New York, where foreigners were commonplace, there was an element of mystery about them. Ellie knew herself to be wondered about. She thought of speaking, an inquiry to confirm Forum station was the one maps continued to list as Gottwaldova, and letting her tongue reveal they were fooled by appearances. But the staring would continue. Hybrids are mysterious too.

At Wenceslas Square she joined the wandering groups where sightseers mingled with young people savouring the freedom of the streets; and theatre-goers streamed in and out of performances; and window-shoppers ogled the satellite dish; and older people puzzled over election posters; and high up the slanting square a knot of figures bowed their heads where candles burned for martyrs.

She was about to enter the foyer of the Hotel Ambassador, had her hand on the door, when she saw the man lying in wait for her. Her cry was stifled to a gasp. She jumped back, brushing against the sables of a Russian woman, regained her balance and darted up the square. If she was lucky, the press of people would obscure her but if not . . . A road crossed the square and she slowed for a car to go by. Over her shoulder, she saw him in pursuit. She raced down a side street. Reckless, because there were fewer people and she was exposed. An alley let her double back. In the square again she concealed herself in a crowd. Then there was an arcade, the way to shops and the Rokoko Theatre. The people she had attached herself to filtered into the theatre. Two remained, reading posters, looking at stills of the show. A play, by Milan Uhde, former dissident and now Minister of Culture. A play about Marx and Engels in London, a bedroom farce demonstrating how small lies grow into enormous ones. Another time she might have smiled at it.

The couple moved away from her. She continued to the end of the arcade, seeking an exit. It was a cul-de-sac. A trap. She had to go back out. Cautious, she approached the entrance, looked up the hill where she had last seen him. Clear. Then down the hill. Clear too. Ellie blessed her luck and set off for the hotel.

This time he was waiting in the street outside for her.

'Ellie!' His arms were open, welcoming.

'No,' she said, her voice high and sharp. People's eyes were on them. He appeared not to notice.

'Ellie.' He came right up to her. Her position was hopeless. A lamp post, a flock of tourists, one obstruction after the other. She could not escape.

He was close enough to touch her arm. She almost dared him to, was afraid how hard she might strike him if he risked it. But his hand fell away.

He said: 'You've come back to us.'

Uş. He presumed to speak for her family. She was aghast at his temerity, at his determination to foist himself on her.

'No,' she said, at the same uncontrollable pitch. 'No, Pavel. I have nothing to say to you. Go away.'

He shook his head. His spurious smile was the one in her nightmares.

180

Summoning a fragile dignity, she said: 'Then *I* will go.' And she strode off.

If the tourists noticed, they did not show it. If the window-shoppers thought the scene worth attention, they hid it superbly. Yet Ellie was convinced the whole of Prague was aware of the bitter confrontation, that everyone saw she was the mouse in a game only the cat ever won.

He caught her easily. Their mother telephoned, he said, to pass on the news she was in Prague.

'She told me where you were staying. She thought you would be pleased to see me.'

'She's mad,' Ellie snapped, believing it. 'She must be absolutely mad.'

'Wait a minute.' He dragged at her arm.

Ellie lashed out with her bag. The blow was high, it ought to have caught his head but his reaction was immediate and the weapon bounced from his shoulder. Her vehemence halted him long enough for her to break free. There was a taxi and she scrambled into it. Through the back window she saw her brother gaping after her.

'*Kam chcete jít?*' the driver asked.

'Malá Strana,' she said. 'Please.' The address of Rose's borrowed flat came tripping off her tongue.

Malá Strana was good, it was across the river, a reasonable distance away. It had pleasant memories for her, of meeting her first love and walking uphill to art and her future. There were numerous sensible reasons as well as sentimental to head for Malá Strana. She was happy in the choice. All the way, the tears ran over her cheeks.

Ellie stood inside the wooden doors of the archway and figured out which doorbell on the iron gate was Rose's. She rang several times, frequently looking round to make sure Pavel had not traced her. After a while she rang the bell for the flat upstairs and a child skipped down to ask what she wanted. Ellie denied her identity, spoke English and then German with the boy and his mother. Cunning, she acted the visitor, a surer way of talking her way in as Rose's friend. A spare key was produced and the door was opened for her.

Her story was that Rose was expecting her and would be along any time. Alone, Ellie ripped off her boots, threw her coat on a hook in the tiled entrance hall and raided cupboards until she found some *borovička*. Not Rose's, the flat owner's presumably, but Ellie could not care less.

After three drinks and two hours she searched for clues to Rose's whereabouts. Suspicion that Rose had left the flat for good was confounded by clothes in a cupboard and papers on a table that was being used as a desk.

There was food but not much. She ate what there was, too nervous to venture out to one of the nearby bars. She was prepared to believe Pavel had followed her over the river, guessing where she had gone or asking her taxi driver. Anything, however far fetched, seemed plausible, and especially that there was danger outside the magic circle of the flat.

After eating, it occurred to her to telephone to check whether there were any messages for her at her hotel. Quite possibly Rose had rung her. Rose had not.

'But we have a message from New York,' the receptionist told her.

'New York?'

It took a second to slot Sam back into her memory. She was not tempted to ring him. She persuaded herself it was because of the unfairness of using a stranger's telephone to make expensive international calls. But it was a thin excuse when there was no difficulty about owning up and paying up.

The deeper reason for not ringing New York was that she had nothing to say to Sam. She did not want to report on her search for the Frans Hals woman; she had no date for her return, except the familiar pledge to be in time for his exhibition; and she did not care to share with him any of the painful things happening to her. Also, it would be beyond her to arouse interest in another of his calamities involving defunct fridges and the like.

Drowsy, she made up a bed on the couch in the living room where she settled down in moderate comfort, prepared to spring up full of welcome and explanations when Rose came. Next morning she woke early to find herself alone.

Late in the summer of 1969, two weeks after Philippe Devereux threw away the ransom demand, a second one arrived.

He realized this before he opened the envelope. The sender had used the same typewriter with the blobby filled-in 'e's and 'a's, the address was set out in an amateurish fashion and the postmark was Marseilles. Philippe's secretary included it without comment among his pile of mail. She opened the rest but this one was marked personal. The word was typed in red and underlined, twice.

Sickness gnawed at him as he lifted the envelope. How could anyone be so cruel as to taunt a bereaved family with offers to sell their dead child back to them? Then he ran a finger beneath the flap and took out the sheet of paper. Something shone and fell on to the desk. Philippe recoiled but it was only hair, a twist of dark fine curling hair.

It came to land on the creamy surface of a heavy-laid paper on which a managing director's secretary had typed an invitation for Philippe to speak at a conference. He would not accept, he would pass it to a subordinate. Philippe declined to attend such events himself. He was a private not a public man.

He heard his breath wavering as he bent over the letter of invitation. Nicole's hair. One of the soft curls that grew behind her ears and, when she tipped her head, could just reach her shoulders.

'Impossible.' He rejected the hair, getting away from it and going to the window, reasoning that the hair had come from another child, that it was proof of nothing except the warped mind of the sender. A ransom demand needed to be backed by evidence that the sender held the victim but this particular hank of hair did not qualify.

'Impossible,' he repeated. 'Nicole's fate is known, this is a wicked game. But thank God the letters are coming to me and not to her parents.'

When he read the note his confidence was shaken. The first one had been a short statement. 'We have Nicole. She will be returned safely on payment of half a million francs. Instructions for payment will be left in a *cave*.' There was an address, a date and a time.

The second note began with a complaint. 'You did not come and your failure endangers Nicole's life. She will be returned alive on payment of half a million francs. Go to the *cave* where instructions will await you.' An address, a date and a time followed. And then a final line: 'Minette sends you a memento.'

If the hair proved nothing, the name did. It was Nicole's pet name, something her baby babblings had coined for herself. Something no writer of malicious letters could know unless he also knew Nicole.

'No, steady,' thought Philippe. 'Lots of people know that pet name. Family servants, they're all familiar with it. The people who can't know it are the outsiders relying on press reports for their information. All right, then. So the letter writer is connected in some way with the château, as Laroche has always suspected. Therefore, there's an accomplice to post the envelopes in Marseilles. Wresting half a million francs from us requires conspiracy, one person couldn't achieve it alone. Well, I don't see how.'

He put the hair and the letter in their envelope and hid it in his pocket. Soon his secretary came into the room and they discussed what action he wanted taken on a series of matters that had come up. But the thought running through his head was that however pointless the pretence that Nicole was alive and recoverable, the people playing the evil ransom game ought to be stopped. Call in the examining magistrate, Judge Georges Laroche? Or the police? Having thrown away the earlier demand, and suspecting the police would bungle, Philippe shrank from doing either. Instead, he decided to keep the rendezvous.

He knew the place, not one of the big names but a modest wine cellar in a country lane. It was about half an hour's drive from the château, a short distance beyond a crossroads. Philippe used to take the road out that way to visit a friend before she married someone else, otherwise the area was unfamiliar.

A late summer, a reluctance to let autumn in. The sky was clear and the countryside dedicated to another hot day as Philippe set out for the *cave*. He was early, very early, intended to be there long before six. He recalled a clump of trees, a track through them to an old *vigneron*'s cottage, some shacks and the wreck of the house. If it was unchanged, he could conceal his car there, approach the *cave* on foot and spy on the people who intended to spy on him. He was convinced of their intention to spy.

As the crossroads came in sight he felt the first qualms. Up to this stage it was an intellectual contest: could he see through their ploy, outwit them, learn more about them than they would like him to know? He wondered whether one of the gardeners his mother had sacked in the spring was behind it. The recalcitrant young man was months gone from the château but his sweetheart had been one of the village girls who worked in the house. Easy to guess at the pair plotting revenge on a too-demanding employer. And the gardener was from the south, wasn't he?

Philippe slowed at the crossroads but his was the only vehicle. A short distance more, that was all. He did not pick up speed again, he dawdled, nervous now it had come to it. No one around, no witnesses, no help if he was blundering into a trap.

Then he was close to the trees. Even in summer foliage their protection was skimpier than he remembered. The *vigneron*'s cottage was more tumbled, the shacks fewer and nearer the road. Anyway, he had to turn in, there was nowhere else to go. He rocked the car along the track, positioned it between the ruined house and the largest of the shacks and trusted that it was screened from the road. With mounting doubts he got out of the car.

'I ought to have turned it round,' he thought. 'If I have to get away fast . . .'

A sound set his nerves jangling. Involuntarily, he took a step back to the car, a degree nearer safety. With his hand on the door handle he looked about, not knowing what to expect or which direction the noise came from.

Again, a scuffling sound. This time he was sure, it was coming from the cottage.

Philippe's fingers tightened on the handle. His palm was sticky. 'Go,' he thought, 'get out of here.'

A cat sprang over a fallen lintel, tossed the mouse it was carrying in its mouth, pounced and pawed the dying creature. Philippe freed the door handle and dried his palm down a trouser leg. A cat. That was all, a mere cat to cause such a fright. He moved away from the car, and the cat was in turn scared and fled, leaving the twitching mouse to die alone by the wall.

Philippe poked his head in the doorway, careful not to dislodge more stone. The front wall looked especially precarious. A room was littered with roof shingles and heaped dust that had once been plaster of ceilings and walls. Creeping plants were colonizing. At the back of the cottage a shrubby tangle barred his way. A cat might slide through but Philippe was afraid of snagging his trousers and, besides, he could see all that was necessary. There was no car tucked away there, no sign of the place being used as a hideout, just a waist-high wilderness leading up to a boundary wall. A pair of yellow butterflies flirted above the nettles. Tilted against the wall were the rusting handle bars of an abandoned bicycle.

A vehicle was coming. He ducked down and scurried into the trees for a view of the entrance to the *cave*, some yards along on the other side of the road. A grey car was approaching, an ordinary family saloon sitting squat in the centre of the road. It passed the *cave*, it passed the trees, it went over the junction and away, leaving a tang of acrid exhaust.

Philippe flapped at the flies that fussed around him, and checked the time. Almost half-past five. He was not a man who liked hanging around, but he schooled himself to be patient.

'Concentrate on what comes next,' he thought. Yet he could not anticipate it. Everything hinged on the identity of the person leaving the message for him. If it were someone he recognized, he would accost and accuse. But if it were not, he hoped for a vehicle registration number to pass on to Laroche. He wished he had brought a camera.

A van passed without reducing speed. Twenty to six. Should he wait any longer? The note said six, it was precise and maybe precision mattered. He delayed. And the delay gave space for a new fear.

'What if it's a plot to kidnap me?' He felt naive not to have admitted the possibility before. 'Nicole's dead. If this has any purpose it's not to arrange the return of Nicole.'

Alarmingly, it was slotting together. People stole the child, killed her by accident, now they were luring another member of the Devereux family to an unfrequented spot to snatch him in her place. Throughout Philippe had assumed the letter-writer had confused his name with his brother's. Suddenly it seemed there was no mistake, that the intention was to abduct Philippe himself.

He marshalled objections to this but they were unconvincing. He was not the natural alternative to Nicole? No, but he was attainable whereas the child's mother was never alone because of her neurotic state and the father was busy in Paris. The grandparents? No again: the kidnappers had already had one vulnerable victim die, why risk the oldest members of the family? Especially if the kidnappers were connected to the château and knew the ailments that undermined the grand-parents' health? However improbable at first sight, he was their best option.

He was tempted to run away. Pride held him there. Having come this far, he wanted to know who or what was in the *cave*. If he were abducted, overpowered when he entered the wine cellar, then the ransom note in his bedroom was a powerful clue. He was not utterly exposed, there would be hope of the police tracing him.

Ten to six. His impatience triumphed. Returning to the car, he wrote a line or two explaining he was responding to a false claim that Nicole could be ransomed, and he was prepared to be kidnapped himself. He anchored it with a stone inside the ruin, a spot the police might be relied on to examine if there was a search for him.

A few of the flies that pestered him while he was in the trees went up the road with him, circling his head, their buzzing a persistent irritation. Otherwise there was nothing to disturb the air except the dusty tread of his shoes.

The *cave* was open. The door gave at a touch. He pushed it back as far as it would go. Philippe looked up and down the road, saw nobody and no movement, and then crossed the threshold. Switching on a light, he closed the door. Fear of attack evaporated. He was alone in a long windowless room.

The air tasted of fermented grapes. Crates of wine were stacked on pallets around the walls. Chairs and tables showed where buyers tasted before choosing. Philippe went to the table, expecting a message. Nothing. He ventured further, to a ramp descending to a cellar. Another light switch illuminated more bottles, thousands of them leading back into the hillside.

He ran up to ground level. 'A trick,' he thought. 'No message, no instructions. A trick after all. Well, I'm getting out of here.'

Then, going for the door, he knew with miserable certainty that it was locked from outside. He had seen no key, not inside or out, and one did not leave thousands of francs' worth of good wine unguarded for the casual passer-by to lift a few bottles or the calculated thief to haul away in trucks. The openness was suspicious, threatening, but he did not realize it until now.

In his haste, his foot slipped on the smoothness of stone. He skidded the last yard and smacked against the door. Recovering, he tugged the handle, and threw himself off balance again as the door shot open. Unlocked. Nothing made sense. At a loss, he stared down the room, swung his glance from side to side. The table and chairs, the overhead light bulb, the crates of bottles, the ceiling with a few spiders' webs swinging, the slippery stone slab floor . . . An arrow was chalked on the stone, four feet inside the doorway and pointing to a crate on the left. Philippe followed the line of it. Beneath a bottle he found the note.

The same typewriter had been used. Philippe scanned the note, put it in a pocket and let himself out into the sunshine. The day was still. Late swallows were mewing as they quartered the sky. Flies that had been his escort formed up for the return journey. He waved them away but they went with him anyway, wheeling about close to him like security men protecting a politician. He led them all the way back to the trees.

Brave now danger was past, he wished someone would appear so that he could have the satisfaction of confrontation. He was not feeble, he thought, he stood a chance of getting the better in a fight if it came to that. But no, people who grabbed him would be armed and only a fool resisted. Had Nicole done that, in a childish way? Had she screamed or tried to run off?

Philippe blotted her out of his mind. He needed to concentrate on getting safely to his car, a few yards but enough in time and space for success to turn to disaster. Holding his breath, he moved from the trees, over rough ground and around the side of the cottage. His car was untouched. He was alone. Reaching inside the ruin he recovered his own note and crumpled it, dropping it in the well of the car.

There was room to shunt the car around rather than reverse to the road. Manoeuvring, he heard the rear end clip something and cursing softly got out to investigate. His paintwork was scraped low down on the offside. The shrubby patch concealed rubble and he had backed into it. As he straightened, he noticed that the rusty bicycle that had leaned against the wall had gone.

Ellie was a fugitive, bunkered down in the basement flat, jumping each time the telephone rang, not answering it, knowing it could not be for her as she had no right to be there. By mid-morning, hungry and feeling idiotic, she convinced herself she should get out, not to wander the streets of Prague and risk colliding with her brother but to resume the chase after the portrait.

She wrote a note for Rose, telling her about seeing Krieger and Zak in Braník and giving the number of the car Zak was driving. Then she paused, pen hovering above the paper. Gone to Bohemia? Going to Bohemia? Going: she settled for that. Ellie left the note on the table where it would be impossible for it to be overlooked.

She took a taxi from the rank in the lower square to her hotel, her safest way of avoiding Pavel if he were lurking. Given the sunny morning, she would have preferred to stroll over the bridge and let the rushing water, the gilded buildings and the autumnal park raise her spirits. Cooped up too long, depressed at her predicament and annoyed with herself for succumbing, she needed that uplift.

Bohemia dangled in front of her like a promise to a child. The tawny forest seen from the aeroplane, the fantasy castles, the air of possibility as suppressed culture shook itself free. She needed to experience it.

No one waylaid her in the hotel. Although her pulse quickened when she was handed a message, it was not from her brother but from the man who had abandoned her in the *kavárna*. He offered a telephone number and would, she presumed, add an apology.

'Ellie, I'm sorry about . . .'

'There's no need, honestly.' She felt girlishly excited to be speaking to him.

'But I shouldn't have . . .'

'Please. It doesn't matter.' She could overlook anything, he had been in her dreams again.

'I'll help you in your hunt for the Hals picture. Not that I think you'll find it but I can get you into the castle. Without help it won't be possible.'

'Oh, that's wonderful. I was going to ask you but it was an awful lot to ask.'

The previous day he had made it sound an obstacle course but something had changed his attitude. 'I'll take you there,' he said.

That was more than she had dared hope. What she had in mind was door-opening, string-pulling. 'That's even more wonderful. But I don't want this to be a dreadful nuisance. Are you sure you want to do this?'

'It's arranged. I have an excuse to return and you'll accompany me. Can you be ready tomorrow?'

She agreed. They made plans. Before he rang off she sought directions to the new art space where she could see the current work he disparaged. Once she had hired a car for the next day's journey, she would have time to kill. And the risk of running into her brother in any kind of art gallery was negligible.

The place smelled of potatoes. It was built as a mausoleum, carved out of the hillside beneath Hradčany, but it had stored potatoes. Despite the reverberation of rock music and the exuberance of the paintings and sculptures, it was the sour smell of potatoes that was the abiding impression. Pony-tailed, leather-jacketed men, cheated of their youth in the 1970s, were making up for it. Their clubs had been closed down by authorities who dubbed them dens of immorality and drugs. Since those authorities were swept away, the clubs were thriving. Ellie expected to recognize faces, people of her generation whose lives had been shelved. She was relieved not to see any of them, she did not know how to begin a dialogue.

Open to influences and visions from around the world, she hesitated to complain about the standard of what was crowded into the potato-scented tunnels. A plant needs water, an artist is nourished by ideas. Without, neither can produce anything of its own.

She was standing in front of a dotted canvas, pale splashes on a rich background.

'What do you think of it?'

He was short, dark, his glasses had gold-coloured rims and his hair was tied back. She prayed he was not going to try and sell the thing to her.

He said: 'It's rain, you see. Or maybe it's refracted sunlight. The colours were different. If you saw the whole sequence, you'd see what he was getting at.'

Inside her head a New Yorker was grumbling. 'They always want to know what the goddam thing is. Why can't they just experience it? You tell them it's elemental but they can't get that far, they don't have a little sticker in their mind that they can slap on it. And if they don't have a sticker, then they don't want to know. What you don't do, *ever*, is give them *Untitled*. They just cannot handle that.'

Ellie cocked her head on one side, looking hard at the dotty painting. 'A pity the sequence was broken up,' she said at last and took a discouraging pace away.

She moved on, careful not to be hooked into further discussions. But when she came up against *Gulag*, a collage of staples and rubber bands, it took all her presence of mind not to erupt in laughter. Not at the artist, who was making a legitimate reference to a famous work of art, but at the whole absurd notion of art.

'There isn't any Art until someone points it out,' she once, provocatively, argued with a painter. One of Sam's predecessors, although Sam adopted the line and confounded interviewers with it. There had been several predecessors, men whose vision she believed she was destined to share. Or, if not precisely that, whose vision she was happy to be publicly identified with. In practice, it had meant not competing with their opinions, waiting in the wings while critics savaged and sniped, and binding up wounds and salving egos when the reviews were all published and the All Clear sounded.

For an independent, intelligent woman who had made her way in this man's world, it was a questionable position to hold. She questioned it but she held it. Sam, she told herself, ought to be the last of the line. She was thirty-eight – oh, all right, she was almost forty – and bed-hopping was unfashionable if not a serious risk to health. She knew herself well enough to expect the next man to be the same as Sam, just as Sam was like the others. Naturally enough, because her needs were unaltered. Unless she underwent a fundamental change, her next man needed to be the same, give or take.

Stay with Sam, then? Settle down, as the phrase went. Ridiculous to put it that way; when was Sam ever settled? He was more moody, more dependent than the predecessors. She was the sheet anchor in his life, as his three married wives had been before her.

'No,' Ellie told him. 'No marriage. You're not a good bet.'

He accepted her conditions. That was in the days when he was glad to and she was persuaded she was running life on her own terms. A common misconception, folk believed they did that and were badly shaken when the truth broke over their heads.

'I'll stay with you,' she promised, the day he thought she would not.

'Of course I love you,' she said the day he asked. But, of course, the of course undermined it. What was predictable about love? She had sat on a river bank one day when she was very young and wondered about love: where did it come from and where did it go? Like the water she was watching, it was fluid, it was not a constant and sometimes her heart was full of it and sometimes it ebbed away.

When her love for Sam ran out she ought to stay. She was too experienced, too old to flit. Flitting was for the young and blindly optimistic. Time to take a longer view. Not Sam in slippers, but an acceptance that he was her type and he was a good example of the type and, therefore, what more ought she to ask, being the way she was?

So Sam was busy being a famous artist and Ellie was busy being with Sam and writing her books that poked at the received notions of art. And here, in a catacomb that stank of sprouted potatoes, a frustrated Czech artist hung a collage that was a translation of Sam's *Exile*. The world was very odd indeed.

Without warning she felt her face crumbling. A softness, a tearfulness flooded her. Flustered, she hurried on, afraid to be thought moved to tears by what prompted hilarity. But she reached a dead end and had to come back. She clutched a handkerchief to her face, pretending a cold.

Rose Darrow did not return to the flat in Malá Strana. Ellie tried several times to call her before going to bed at the hotel, and tried once more in the morning. She was loath to leave Prague without a word and decided to drop another note in at the flat.

A man leaving the building held the iron gate open for her and Rose's door swung at her touch, its lock broken. In the brown-tiled entrance hall, Ellie called out. No answer. The rooms appeared as she had left them, except that her first note had gone.

She left a new message and went back to the hotel to await the man who had been her young art lover. He had never been her lover in the physical sense; he was no longer young; and he had relinquished art. Neither was he hers. The handbag on the chair, the blouse on the hanger kept her notions in check. Today, on the long journey through the forests, she meant to extricate from him his past and his present. By the end of it, he would be a vague relation to the person she remembered from her teenage summer.

'You're extraordinarily good at shutting things out,' she had accused Sam, or one of his forerunners.

But she was also excellent at tamping down curiosity or knowledge when it was painful. She had learned it young and learned it well, and it stood her in good stead. Today, though, she was going to tweak at the curtain concealing the past.

'This is a quest for identity,' she said brightly as they drove out of the city and the land spread before them. Jet stream scored the sky and lazy pigeons flapped towards orange-leaved sycamores.

'Your Frans Hals woman?'

'Later. Your identity first. Everything. Tell me everything.'

She was driving. He twisted in the seat to look at her. Side-long, she recognized the smile: bemused because she had said something immature or inept.

Ellie laughed a teasing laugh, her bell of blonde hair shimmering. 'I mean it. You're my first mystery. I can't proceed to the next round until I've solved the puzzle of you.'

'I'm not the least puzzling.'

'How long before we reach the castle?'

'Hours. Many, many of them if you drive at this snail's pace.'

She jabbed the accelerator. 'You have a long story to tell. Twenty-odd years' worth. You'd better begin. I don't want to be parked outside the castle gates waiting for you to finish.'

He demurred but she was not to be dissuaded. He began to tell her the things he supposed she wanted to hear.

That it was dissimulation came to her later. She woke, the weight of his head against her arm, her pillow sliding off the edge of the hotel bed. Her first thought was that it had been one hell of a long way to come for a fuck. The second was that he had lied to her.

FOURTEEN

'So your friend is looking for Krieger?' he asked.

'She found him,' said Ellie. 'Found him and lost him and I found him again.'

'Did you return him, like lost property?'

'I left her a note but someone removed it from the table in the flat she's using. Did you say turn right here?'

'Yes. Then we stay on that road for several miles.'

The roads were getting narrower and rougher. Their route was hiding them in the heart of the country. Very few vehicles passed, the forests were empty, dying and empty. Although the map confirmed towns and industrial centres within easy reach, it was hard to believe in them. Ellie felt estranged. She was sliding through peaceful forests in a dimension of timelessness. Already she had stepped outside her own normal life and she was forgetting the centuries too. It was exhilarating but a little alarming.

Dark and deep, the woods closed in behind her, contained her. They were a warming, smothering presence. She had stood in front of paintings featuring vast forests, ancient ones that held pagan secrets, and she had marked the artists' minute human figures wandering with unconcern among the trees. They were too little to appreciate the scale of the things that stretched before them. Ellie had wished to enter with them, be enfolded and protected. But she was glad too when the spell broke and the compelling painted forests freed her to turn her eyes to other visions in other gilded frames.

'He's supposed to be connected with a drugs racket,' he said.

'Oh?' After a moment of blank puzzlement she realized he was still thinking about Krieger.

'A rumour. There's a story that the authorities want to question him about drugs coming in from Bulgaria.'

She was sceptical. 'If Rose Darrow and I have been able to find him, then the police can't be trying very hard.'

'As I said, it's only a rumour.' He opened a window an inch or two. Biting coldness fanned the car. 'I think he's one of those people that rumours attach themselves to. No man has time to do all the things attributed to him.'

When he told her his own story the day before, he had described a life lived without touching the sides, like a man falling down a chute. No detail, no irresistible digressions, no personalities to make it vivid. No reason to trust it.

He was still fiddling with the window. The winding handle did not work properly, the glass slipped and wedged at an angle. He could not close it.

He said: 'I hope your friend Rose persuades him to tell his tale, it would make fascinating reading.'

'Provided he tells the truth.'

He said nothing. In a few minutes he worked out the trick of closing the window.

They had left Prague late the previous day. They were delayed and then took a diversion and finally, almost without preamble, booked into the hotel. There was a neatness and an inevitability about sharing a bed with him. She was not in the habit of making love to strangers but she wanted him for what he had once been to her.

A jolly man and his fluffy, giggling wife were staying overnight, the man's voice too loud in the dining room and on the stairs. Ellie heard them coming along the landing as she stood in the dark, amidst folds of discarded clothing, her arms circling her lover's neck, her cheek against the darkly curling hair of his chest.

The jolly man was cheerfully drunk, his wife chirruping. 'Oh God,' Ellie prayed. 'Not in there, please not in there.' But the door of the next room thudded and then the couple were laughing through the wall, the dull roar of his voice and her trilling response.

Ellie shut her ears to them and stroked the nape of her lover's neck, pressed her mouth to his, led him through the gentle routine of love. He was impatient for her, whisking aside the orange bedcover and pushing her down on the firm mattress. She wanted to savour him, to experience what she had imagined, to keep her eyes open this time and see his face as her body brought him to joy. But he needed her quickly and did not allow her to play.

There was no lamp in the room. They had not switched on the harsh overhead light bulb beneath its plastic shade, and they left the window uncurtained. The night was starry, moonless, his face a dark orb above her.

Through the wall came the sounds of other bedsprings. The jolly man moaned: 'Oh, oh, oh!' And his fluffy wife echoed a few octaves higher: 'Oh, oh, oh!' They woke Ellie with a repeat performance very early next morning.

Her lover's lying – more accurately, his secrecy – did not count for much, she could almost ignore it. Partly, she felt debarred from the truth. If he dodged her questions or fobbed her off with inadequate answers, she let him. If his stories gaped with omissions, then so be it. It was not her right to press, interrogate. If he said life had been so-and-so and such-and-such, then because she had not stayed to share the experiences she was in no position to demand full knowledge.

Physical intimacy did not draw them closer. The gap was unbridgeable. When dawn light shadowed his face, she woke, shifted her arm with its pins and needles from beneath the weight of his sleeping head. He rolled away from her. A sadness settled as she faced up to his evasions. The young man who taught her about beauty and truth had grown into a different sort of man who used another language.

When she woke later he was gone. She met him downstairs, making a telephone call neither of them referred to.

'We could be there by lunchtime,' he said.

But he bought a bottle of wine and when it was lunchtime they left the car at the roadside and walked between the trees. Far off a chainsaw was whining. Birds crackled in undergrowth. He drew her on and she realized they were taking an indistinct path. When it broadened slightly, he reached for her hand and brought her alongside him.

'I shall show you something, Ellie.'

But he would not say what and her guesses were laughed away. Then there was a break of blue where there had been trees. They had come to the edge of the hill. Up the valley, rising from its nest among autumn gold, was a castle.

She gasped. 'Oh, that's beautiful. Is that it? Where we're going?'

Her childish delight amused him. 'Do you want it to be?'

'Yes. Oh, yes, *please*. It's perfect.'

'From a distance. We won't get a better view of it and we certainly won't get a more flattering one.'

She squeezed his arm. 'Don't spoil it. I want to enjoy this exactly as it is.'

'Or appears to be.'

'Hush! I'm not going to listen to anything like that. Oh, if I'd known, I'd have brought the camera from the car.'

'Does it look like a place where a mysterious Frans Hals woman might be hiding out?'

Ellie groaned. 'The suspense is killing me.'

Yet the suspense had not made her rush to her goal. Instead, she had been sightseeing, making love, squandering time and emotion, clutching at every diversion that offered itself. To get to the castle was to find out the reality, and by any calculation that was far more likely to be disappointment than success.

He opened the bottle of Melnik while she was gazing up the valley at the stone fantasy. He passed her the bottle. 'Someone should have thought about glasses.'

The words whisked her back across time, as he knew they would. Another al fresco drink, a river bank, a bottle cooling in among the reeds, an investigative mallard and, when the temperature was right, no glasses.

Ellie did what she had done then. She took the bottle and raised it to her lips. The wine was cool, a little ran down her chin and she rubbed it away with the back of a hand as she passed him the bottle.

Wryly she said: 'We don't progress much, do we?'

'It's a better bottle of wine.'

They drank only a mouthful or two. The point was not the drinking, it was playing let's be young and carefree. They carried the remainder back to the car and she drove on towards the castle.

The saw mill came and went. A farm cart, driven by a hunched old woman bundled in layers of winter wear, slowed them by plodding in the centre of the road until it veered down a forest track. They drove on.

He started to tell her things about the castle, unpromising things. 'You'll no doubt have to listen to a lot of boring stuff about his family. Humour him, Ellie.'

He was right about distance lending enchantment. Close up, the gingery trees were dying, the dilapidation of the castle was painful. She consoled herself with the thought that at least in one way the owner had hung on to what was his.

The old man was hawk-like, aloof, a combination of suspicion and deafness. He told her about his family, the Stehlik family into which Abetz married. For a long hour she listened and tried to worm her way into his confidence. But it was no use asking him directly whether he owned any paintings that might possibly be by Frans Hals. She had to skirt around it, murmur oblique suggestions that she be allowed to study the collection.

She wanted support from the man who brought her but he did not provide it. He hung back, letting Ellie struggle with old Stehlik alone. At last, exasperated, she drew him into the conversation with a heavy hint about his need to discuss his own business at the castle. The hint was a mistake. The owner became tetchy, they both became irritated with her. Stehlik stamped out of the room.

Ellie looked anguished. 'This is awful.'

'I did warn you. You have to humour him.'

'And I have been, for an hour. Why can't you discuss your business with him and then we can come back to mine?'

'If you lose your temper we'll both be thrown out.'

But she was losing it. 'I thought you'd arranged this visit but he was astonished to see us. And he doesn't want us here.'

'Wheedle him, Ellie.'

'But . . .'

'He's coming back.'

Half the afternoon passed in tedious conversation, with the owner content to recite facts and fantasies about the Stehliks and parrying any attempt to view the remaining paintings. Ellie grew intrigued by the possibilities of hours of speech that conveyed nothing of substance. She wondered how long he could keep it up. He behaved like a man trained to go on speaking without actually saying anything.

And he was not a man she liked. The thin erect figure, the unfortunate manner that was only in part attributable to his aloofness, the rancour that broke the surface civility whenever she tried to steer the conversation . . . There was nothing to like.

Crazy ideas were rattling around in her brain. Could she play a trick and race through the castle spying out the paintings before he realized she had left the room on a ruse? Could she plead to be shown portraits of the tiresome Stehlik family in the hope that on the way to them she would pass those more relevant to her own interests?

His story was a jumble of Habsburg princes, battles, riches and patronage. Things that no longer meant anything. Ellie's desperation ebbed and flowed. But she caught a chronological thread and it gave her hope, until the next time the thread was severed and he fell back a generation and meandered off down another track. What did it matter to her which of the Stehliks built a village or established a saw mill or died a hero's death under arms? The *paintings*, damn it; all she cared about was the paintings.

Then his knobbly hand stopped beating time on the wooden arm of his chair and the sing-song voice ceased. Her turn to speak, apparently, and she was tongue-tied. Beside her she heard a voice. 'My friend would be most grateful if she could be allowed to look at your paintings.'

The old hawk inclined his head in a bow. 'I wish there were more beautiful things in my house to show you.'

Because one of her legs was numb from sitting so long, she was slow to rise. But she managed gratitude and then, bewildered, made for the door from the anteroom into the great hall. The owner did not follow. He remained in his chair, awaiting their eventual return.

Out of his sight Ellie threw back her head, raised her eyes to heaven. 'Dear God, what was all that about?'

'I warned you he needed to be humoured. He was remembering, Ellie. He's the last of them and he has no one to pass all that family history on to.'

'Does he do this to everyone?'

'Few people come. But yes, he does it. It's a formality, and perhaps in a country that's been dedicated to forgetting, it's an understandable quirk.'

She choked off a derisive laugh. 'One old man in his dotage stemming the tide of government propaganda by musing on his ancestors?'

The silence that answered her was a reproof.

She backtracked. 'You think I'm being harsh. I don't mean it. I'm half-battered to death with anecdote. All right, it's absurd, but I'll accept it as his small means of defiance. Just tell me this, though: are there similar formalities to be observed before we get out of this place?'

They were walking around the hall, peering up at the portraits and the vast battle scenes. There was a massive fireplace, half a forest had burned away in the grate and deposited its soot over the pictures. They went into an adjoining room. Another battle scene, someone doing something indeterminate to someone in a flowery bower, then a glum man in a cocked hat. They moved on.

Some of the rooms were empty, some had a smattering of furnishings, all were cold and dreary. Some paintings were damaged with damp, some were torn, some were possibly good, and some impossibly bad. They went on.

Each picture was an attempt to show a fresh view, an invitation to the viewer to step, momentarily, from his own world into a parallel one. There was a glade she was content to walk along, a tree whose leaves she heard the wind ruffle, but few were as enticing as those. Maurice Denis' lines from *Theories* came to her, putting an end to her romantic games. 'Remember that a picture – before being a horse, a nude or some sort of anecdote – is essentially a flat surface covered with colours assembled in a certain order.' She was not to be waylaid by dreamy Italian landscapes, she must search among the darkest and dingiest for the sombre men and women of Haarlem.

Thoughts flitted through her head but she avoided speaking them. Once she almost remarked, sarcastically: 'Not quite the Narodni, is it?' But she held back because why ever should the rump that nobody had bothered to loot be up to national gallery standard? It was interesting enough that it was here at all.

He said: 'That's the end of the ground floor. We can get upstairs this way.'

A mark on the stair well showed where a picture had been removed. Ellie asked. He said: 'I don't know. He told me a rope broke and the picture dropped down.' And he added slyly: 'He said it happened in nineteen twenty-something when . . .'

She clapped hands over her ears, made a show of refusing to listen to any more Stehlik history.

Upstairs, here and there, they came upon rather better paintings. He pointed out work by Jan Kupecky, a Bohemian painter of the baroque period. 'That's worth a place in one of the public collections. So are the Canaletto and the Dürer we'll come to later.'

There was nothing remotely like a Frans Hals woman. Ellie ran a finger along a frame, furrowing decades of dust. 'I wonder how long since anybody inspected the paintings, before you came?'

He said the owner had mentioned showing them to someone before the war and claimed nobody took an interest since.

Wiping the dust from her hand, she mimicked the old man's delivery. 'In 1989, in the year of the Revolution, the peace of our quiet little castle was disturbed again, this time by the intrusion of an individual from Prague who came to evaluate the Stehlik collection.'

'No, no reference to revolutions, Ellie. I don't think the news has impinged yet. And when it does he won't know what to make of it.'

They went up another staircase to a floor where the rooms were lower and meaner. Water had dripped through a ceiling and rotted floorboards. Wind found a way around cracked window glass. Paint had degenerated to a crackled surface along skirting boards and door frames. She ached at the neglect.

She said: 'This could all be so good. Imagine, if the house was repaired and the grounds tidied up it could be a showpiece. Instead of which it's heading for total collapse.'

He said there were other priorities than restoring country houses that had outlived usefulness. Through her mind flashed the country houses of England, not the grand and stateliest homes but the modest gems that adorned the countryside wherever one travelled. She said nothing because to make comparisons there had to be some similarity in the cases. Anyway, how many good houses had England lost? How many was it still losing?

They opened the door of the next room. Unlike the first it was not totally empty: a broken-backed kitchen chair stood near a window and leaning against one leg was a dustpan that had lost its brush. On the seat of the chair lay a couple of wooden clothes pegs.

'God knows about the paintings,' she said, with wild laughter. 'But I know an art gallery in New York that would be proud to handle that. Not as *Still Life with Dustpan, Chair and Pegs*, you understand. The title would have to be fancier.'

'*The Return of the Exile*?' he suggested with a side-swipe at Sam.

'Mmm. Yes. That's good.' She waggled a hand at the 'sculpture'. 'It's got pathos, and the things are what you might find if you stumbled into the humble peasant's hovel you left behind for a life in the New World.'

He fumbled in Ellie's pocket for her camera and began to snap away at the clutter of oddments. 'We could have a line in the catalogue caption about the symbolism of back-breaking practicality.'

She had another idea. 'Actually, I see it as a feminist piece. I could concoct a fairly heavy argument along those lines.'

He lowered the camera and pleaded. 'Not now, Ellie.'

She pretended to be petulant, tutting and saying: 'Oh, all *right*.' Then she held out her hand for the camera, thinking that she was short of film and ought not to waste it on tomfoolery. But when she had it in her palm, she focused on him *contre-jour* with the crumbling damp wall and the rectangles of the window frame behind him. He let her take two shots and then walked away.

'I ought to be glum,' she said, trailing him into the next room. 'My quest founders in a clammy attic but I'm peculiarly cheerful. What do you think it is? Hysteria?' As she entered the room across the landing she ended with an 'Oh!'

There were pictures. On the walls, leaning against the walls, lying on the floor. Wherever there was room to put one, a painting had been put.

'These,' he explained, 'were to be taken away when a member of the family claimed his share but it never happened and, as you see, nobody bothered to hang them again. If the old chap

205

downstairs would sell the Veronese or the Rubens he could restore the house for you.'

'Tell me, if he's the last in the line, what happens to all this when he dies?'

'Perhaps a scrabble of exiles claiming title to his property. And I dare say some officials will flutter down like ravens to pick over the pieces.'

There was less light on this side of the house so they hurried, taking the next couple of rooms, where a few pictures were scattered, and then reaching a dim corridor ending in a locked door. She felt that blundering down culs-de-sac was becoming an inconvenient habit. At the Rokoko Theatre when she was dodging her brother, in the potatoey mausoleum that was an art gallery, and now here.

She asked: 'Did you go through the door when you were here before?'

'Yes, it was completely empty, unless you count bird droppings and a heap of ceiling plaster.

'Where did you get the key?'

'It was unlocked.'

As though she did not trust him, she tried the door handle for herself. 'I'd really like to get in there. If I have to go away empty-handed, I'd like to know I've seen every inch.'

He said he would ask for a key. 'Don't go away, Ellie, I'll see you here.'

Once alone she wandered back the way they had come, dreaming about the life the Stehlik family had led there. Then her head filled with random thoughts. For a few minutes she heard his footsteps diminishing over the uncarpeted surfaces on the staircases and the floors below. Then nothing.

She was seized with the idea he had abandoned her, that this time he was the one going and she was the one consigned to a place she was not permitted to leave. A flurry of images troubled her. She was walking past the saints and kings on the bridge to meet him, and he was looking down into the water until, when she was close, he raised his head and smiled. Or

206

they were passing through art galleries together, with him explaining what she did not expect to know. And finally, the scene she had often imagined: he was waiting on the bridge for her but she never came.

Coldness, guilt, made her shudder. She rubbed her hands, but the sound was loud and papery so she put them in her pockets instead. Ellie walked back in the direction of the locked door. Somewhere she went wrong. The corridor had become a different one, darker if anything and without a door at the end although she saw one on her left. This opened on to a plain wooden stairway that servants might have used. A very small window shed light, enough to entice her to go down. Ellie tested the banister. It held. She gathered the skirt of her leather coat in one hand to prevent it sweeping the dirty treads, and she descended.

The door on the landing below opened into a low room with a shutter across the window. The room was about eight feet square. Opposite the door she came through was a locked one.

For the second time her exploration was brought to an abrupt end by a locked door. There was no choice but to go up again. Turning, she saw something hidden in the darkness on her right. A patch of greyish white. No, two patches. One above the other, like a face above a white collar.

FIFTEEN

She was light-headed with excitement.

'I've found her. *I've found her!*' she kept saying.

He cautioned. 'You don't know for sure, Ellie. It might not be by Hals.'

'I do know. I am sure. Oh God, of course I'm not. But I feel it ought to be, I feel it so strongly it makes it true.'

They were in the forest, a mile from the castle. She was too elated to drive on, needing to move around, stride about among the trees, take celebratory gulps from the bottle of Melnik, and say anything that came into her head. He was being indulgent, offering the gentlest of curbs.

She said, and not for the first time: 'I noticed a paleness on the end wall. And I felt a frame. What I would have given for a torch! When we go back I'm going to take the biggest lamp in Prague.'

'Let's see what's on your film first.'

'Oh, it'll be terrible, a splodge if I'm lucky. The battery ran out on the flash. I never dreamed the castle would be without electricity, I couldn't have anticipated any of it. That crazy old man reciting his family history and harbouring all those filthy pictures, and . . . He didn't suspect anything, did he? He doesn't realize I want to get her out of the place and have her inspected properly.'

'Ellie, I've warned you all along, he isn't easy.'

And it was true. He often used that word, warn, to her. But she had taken no notice and the problems faded away. Oh, yes, it sometimes took patience and hours of boredom but they disappeared in the end and she reached her goal. To be cheated of a proper look at the portrait after enduring all that would be . . . Well, she had no words for it.

'Come, Ellie.' He moved towards the car.

Reluctant, she slipped into the driving seat. Her headlamps flicked on to illuminate encircling tree trunks, pine needles, weird night-time colours.

He said: 'We have a long way to go.'

And there was no suggestion of another night in a hotel together. They were taking the direct route and a stop was unnecessary.

'What time will we get to Prague?' she wondered.

'Midnight? Perhaps later.'

She drove very fast. There was nothing to delay her. He rested an arm on the back of the seat and his fingers played with her hair. After a few miles she said, in a changed and sober voice: 'The old man, he'll hate it, won't he?'

'He'll hate people going to look and he'll hate the portrait being moved, even from that black hole to a room with a decent amount of light.'

'I doubt whether he'll ever forgive us.'

'*Us?*'

'Well, you started it, barging in and demanding to see what he was hiding. If it wasn't for that, I wouldn't have known it was worth going there.'

He tweaked her hair. 'It's unfair but, all right, we'll share the blame.'

'To him we're both outsiders, intruders with fancy modern notions. I'm sure he won't think there's much to choose between us.'

'Then he must think himself lucky he was so little intruded upon in the past.' It was obvious he did not mean the house, he meant the life.

Ellie drove without replying. She recognized the bitter tone that had heralded her being stranded in the *kavárna*. Although her questions welled up, although he could not escape her if she put them into words, she vacillated. None of it was her business. Yet, on the other hand, she feared a connection. Suddenly she decided that this was not only the best chance but possibly her last one.

'I'm going to ask you something.' It was not the tentative, teasing approach she made on the journey out when she claimed the right to his life story.

She said: 'I went to see my parents.'

His fingers tightened in her hair. 'But you didn't mention this?'

'No. Well, it wasn't a great success. The point is, while I was there I learned about my brother being in the police force. I had no idea before and . . . You referred to him the other day and I'd like to know what contact you had with him.'

He had wound her hair around his fingers, was drawing her head back. He released her, withdrew his hand.

'You remember me telling you I had to leave university because there were difficulties? Your brother made those difficulties.'

She thought he wanted to leave it there and urged him: 'Go on.'

'After you went away, he threatened me. Later, he carried out the threat. He said things and left other people to act.'

He spoke with that air that assured her there would be no elaboration. When she tried for more, all she got was a line from Anouilh. 'Man's breath is fatal to his fellow man.'

She sighed. 'I could tell you I'm sorry but that would sound as though I felt responsible for his behaviour.'

'Of course you aren't.' A pause. 'You didn't like him, did you? You were scared of him.'

She sought a convincing but concealing answer. 'He liked to control people.'

When he asked exactly how Pavel had controlled her, she shuffled away from the subject. She looped the conversation round to something else that occupied them most of the way to Prague: Krieger. They swapped stories about him, old and new, marvelled that a man supposedly in hiding should allow himself to be seen on the streets of the City of Rumours.

The connection with drugs was credible because Krieger had been known to raise funds for his political activities by selling drugs, although those stories dated from before his defection to East Germany. But one tale that was completely fresh was that he had been seen in Prague with the youngest of the Devereux men, David.

Ellie said: 'I don't know much about David.'

'He's the green one. He attended an international conference in Prague to discuss what's to be done about pollution, particularly in the Bilina valley. Until a year ago it was hushed up, now it's admitted that where we once had healing mineral waters we now have open-cast lignite mines, inefficient chemical plants, toxic-waste dumps, old-fashioned coal-burning industries – in other words, we're the most environmentally damaged country in Europe and we're injuring our neighbours.'

'Why was David Devereux at the conference?'

'Because he's involved with the Greenworld charity. The whisper is he fitted in a meeting with Krieger.'

Ellie was intrigued but sceptical. 'How loud is this whisper?'

'I heard it from a man who claimed to have seen them together.'

The man, he said, was a taxi driver who took David Devereux from his hotel to the conference on the first day. Next afternoon David left the session and asked to be driven to an address across the river.

'When they arrived David seemed somewhat nervous and asked the driver to wait until he was inside the house. So the driver sat there and watched David on the doorstep. When the door opened, there was Krieger.'

Ellie's scepticism persisted. 'How could he be sure it was Krieger?'

'By chance Krieger was pointed out to him a week or two earlier.'

'But what on earth can Krieger and young Devereux have to discuss?'

'Whatever it was, Ellie, I don't think it can have been saving the planet.'

'Whatever it was, Rose, I don't think it can have been saving the planet.'

Ellie was sitting in the Malá Strana flat with Rose. She had called round shortly after Rose's return from interviewing David Devereux's father, Philippe.

Rose was bewildered and tired. She uncorked a bottle of Melnik, said: 'I'm trying to keep a grip on this Devereux story but it keeps slithering away from me. Each time I have a decent theory, something crops up to make nonsense of it.'

She broke off while pouring, then: 'You're right, Ellie. David's a saver of planets, a rich young Frenchman aiming to take control of a perfume business and cut out his father. Krieger's a one-time East German spy with a reputation for skulduggery, not least of which is drug running as a means of raising money for his political cohorts. He's no saver of planets.'

Ellie sipped her wine. 'I wish I'd brought you a solution instead of further confusion.'

Rose laughed. 'Actually, you're proving useful, more useful than the people I'm employing. You've already come up with two addresses used by Krieger, a link with the Devereux family, and confirmation that the family is selling off its art collection.'

'Not bad for an amateur, eh?'

'Not bad for anyone.' Rose smothered a yawn. 'I'm convinced David's the one selling off the art collection. I can't pretend I liked Philippe Devereux but I believed him when he denied any knowledge of the sales.'

Ellie suggested it could be the old man, Maurice, who was breaking up the collection. But Rose discounted that as he had spent years building it.

'The director, then?' suggested Ellie.

'I don't see how. He's a tight-lipped fellow who isn't prepared to criticize his employers but all the same he made it plain there's no money going into the art fund these days and his orders are to sell, starting with the modern stuff.'

'Sam's *Exile*, for instance.'

They sat quietly for a few minutes, casting around for credible explanations. Then Ellie said: 'You will be careful, Rose, won't you? If proving a Devereux involvement with drugs cost John Blair his life, then you're running terrible risks.'

'The Devereux people think I'm writing a profile of the company for my magazine. I'll be fine.' As soon as she said it she realized how feeble it was.

And Ellie picked her up immediately. 'John had a cover story too.'

Rose rubbed a hand across her eyes. This time she could not suppress a yawn. 'I promise not to take a single decision about anything until I've had a good night's sleep and am perky and clear-headed.'

'Give yourself a day off. There's a painting in a castle out in the sticks I could show you.'

Rose brightened. 'Your companion piece. Yes, now that *is* good news.'

'Will you come, then, Rose? I've acquired a lamp. It's taken most of the day but I've done it. Unfortunately, I have only one pair of hands.'

But Rose shook her head. 'Alas, I fly to Paris tomorrow. There's an editorial meeting I couldn't wriggle out of even if I wanted to. Come to think of it, I do want to. As I haven't done a deal with Krieger yet I'll be less than popular.'

Another yawn. Rose leaned back in the armchair and closed her eyes. If the wineglass in her hands were not so steady, Ellie would have thought she was sleeping. There was the sound of a distant bell as someone at the iron gate rang the flat upstairs for admittance. Then the noisy fridge jerked to life and drowned all exterior sounds.

'You're right,' said Rose, as though she had been criticized. 'I ought to make one more attempt with Krieger before I leave for

Paris. How far is it to the house where the taxi driver saw him welcoming David Devereux?'

Ellie said it was walking distance.

They walked.

'German or Czech from me this time, Rose?'

'German, please, Ellie.'

But the plotting was wasted because when the door was opened, by a young East German man with a squint, Krieger's stocky figure was visible at the end of the hall and he called out to Ellie in Czech.

'*Vstupovat*, Ellie. I've been expecting you.'

She was shocked he knew her name, ashamed of her ruse in letting him think she was not a Czech speaker. Obediently, she stepped into the hall. The fellow with the squint was holding the door.

She said: 'I've brought Rose Darrow.'

Krieger beckoned them on. 'So I see.' He shook hands with both of them, his cuff sliding back to allow a glimpse of the thick gold band of his watch. This evening he was playing at being affable.

Rose did not refer to his vanishing act after they arranged to talk a second time at the flat in Budj. Neither did he. She told him the truth.

'I'm going to Paris tomorrow. I want to tell them we have a deal and what it is.'

He looked sympathetic, a brindled middle-aged uncle showing concern for the petty troubles of a niece. 'They're getting impatient.'

And so was she although it was smoother to put the onus on them. 'Well, then?'

'Forgive me, Rose, if we don't discuss this now. I'm expecting some people. In fact, when the doorbell rang I imagined it was them arriving early.'

The familiar disappointment crept over her. She had hung around on a bridge for this man, wasted time at an empty house, chased him through suburbs and now, once more, he was squirming from her grasp.

But she kept her smile in place as she asked: 'Can we talk tomorrow before I set off?'

'I'll meet you in the Waldstein Gardens. Do you know the *sala terrena*?'

'I'll be there.'

Then he was saying goodbye, the man with the squint was ushering them out. Rose had a time, a place and a contained hope.

Ellie asked her: 'Do you think he'll be there?'

'I can't say. But *I* will.'

Ellie shivered. 'He knew about me. They've been checking up, Rose. God, it reminds me of . . .'

But no example was required. Her incomplete thought encompassed all the checking up, the state nosiness, the lack of freedom to possess secrets.

Staying away, she missed the worst of it. When the country was being remade as the most severely repressed of the Stalinist countries in the Soviet bloc, Ellie was in art school, at Rolling Stones concerts, sharing a London flat with a gang of friends, taking cheap holidays through Europe and all the way to India. She lived in a world of hope and youth and energy which appeared, at the time, to promise that all things would be well. Meanwhile, the friends she was at school with were banned from contact with foreigners and from any chance to see for themselves.

After they walked some way, Ellie burst out: 'I couldn't have done it, Rose. It would have destroyed me. They weren't all heroes and dissidents, you know. Mostly they were people getting by, hoping not to be too miserable and to keep out of trouble. When I came back I was worried about meeting my old friends on the streets. Well, I needn't have been. They wouldn't know me.'

Rose took her arm to cross a busy road, murmured encouragement to go on.

Ellie said: 'There was a girl, Nina, who was my friend at school. We were very close, for years and years. And it was Nina who had the idea of going to work in London to learn English.'

'What became of Nina?'

'Nothing. Nothing at all. She became nothing. And when I think of her I remember her being pretty and academically bright, far more than I was. I used to wonder about her, until I forced myself to stop looking over my shoulder. My mother told me the other day Nina's still here. She married, had children, lives in a block of flats in a suburb and works in a supermarket. On the checkout. Have you seen those shops, Rose? The tills have mirrors angled so that everybody can see that the money goes into the tills and not into the pockets of the staff. If I'd stayed, Rose, that would have been me.'

They reached the flat. Once they were inside, their coats hanging on the pegs in the tiled hall, Rose sat down opposite Ellie, tipped her head on one side and with a shrewdness that Ellie could have done without asked: 'What's brought on this attack of guilt?'

Ellie barked a laugh. She was not short of reasons. The man who took her to the castle was one answer. She offered Rose another.

'It hasn't been brought on, it's been there all the time. For years. It's why I didn't come haring back the moment Havel and Dubček stepped out on the balcony together.' She bit her lower lip, not trusting herself, afraid of revealing matters better kept to herself. 'I'm sorry, Rose. I must seem ridiculously sensitive.'

'I thought Krieger had something to do with it. Not just the business of him bothering to find out who you are, but he always makes you edgy.'

Ellie scraped her silvery blonde hair back with both hands, twisted it into a knot high on her head. The slanting grey eyes, the high cheekbones were emphasized, strikingly beautiful.

'Hmm. Edgy. He does, yes. I don't know him but I dislike him. Intensely.'

'Why not? said Rose, carelessly. She had botched it, meaning to coax more about the trip to the castle. Something strange had happened on that ride into Bohemia, she was sure of it. Ellie was distracted, her mood unsteady.

Rose ticked points off on her fingers. 'Krieger's been a terrorist, a spy, a drug runner.'

'What sticks in the craw is that he's going to get away with it.'

'And that *he* isn't afflicted by guilt.'

Ellie laughed again, but this time it was her warm chuckle. 'Yes, most of all that.'

The absence of the rusty bicycle was unnerving. Philippe had not been alone when he followed the kidnapper's instructions to go into the *cave*. The machine was not abandoned among the snaggled shrubs behind the *vigneron*'s cottage, it was someone's means of escape.

Hours later, sitting in his office at the château, a report on the desk in front of him, he was unable to concentrate. Over and over he read the page without the sense penetrating, because each time he was interrupted by the image of handlebars tilted against a wall. He had seen them and when he returned from the *cave* they were gone.

He pushed the report away and went out into the garden. His mother and two helpers were dead-heading roses, tidying away nature's rubbish. Musk wafted towards him. He watched them bent-backed beneath the sun, slaving to keep the garden in bloom as long as climate and constant human attention permitted. She loved flowers, his mother. One could always step into her garden and gather an armful. It was a matter of pride with her that each room always had its display of blooms. She did not begrudge the time or the cost but she was fierce about laxness. That was why she dismissed the young man Philippe considered a candidate for suspicion.

His mother straightened her back, a hand easing a twinge low down. She looked about her. Spotting him, she waved but he did not go over. Instead he took the path towards the vineyard.

The *vendange* had been early, in September, and now the fields had a sleepy left-over atmosphere. The grapes were sound and the quantity satisfactory but the year would be remembered as the one when the harvest happened automatically, without the family's involvement. Staff at the château and helpers from the village were summoned, seemingly by instinct, and carried out their annual tasks. Maurice, Philippe's father, put in one brief appearance although it was his habit to oversee everything, to prowl among the vines pointing out overlooked clusters of grapes and to lend a hand whenever help was needed. Perfume was his business but this vineyard was his hobby.

Walking along, Philippe was considering telling his father about the ransom notes and the business at the *cave*. Alone, he was finding it impossible to know what to do next. Each decision he took revived the original question: should he go to the police?

His resistance was intact. To admit to the police or to Judge Georges Laroche what he had withheld, and what he had done, was unthinkable. He had publicly criticized them over the missing child inquiry and was no kinder when reporters sought his opinion on lack of progress in the murder hunt. How could he expect anything but contempt when he turned up with a tale about concealed ransom demands and an assignation in a wine cellar? Philippe squirmed at the thought that *their* contempt would be public too. He had no hope that Laroche would refrain from feeding the story to the press. The man had precious little else to feed them, he would not waste the story of Philippe's meddling.

Ahead, across the vineyard, lay the church but Philippe swung around away from it and its dreadful memories of Nicole's funeral weeks earlier. If anything persuaded him to evade the attention of the press, that funeral did. The family escaped that day by running home and slamming the gates on the world. But if Laroche breathed a word about ransom demands and Philippe's failure to divulge them, then the press would besiege the château and make life misery until he exposed himself to them and their misinterpretations of behaviour and motive.

He could not guess his father's reaction if he shared the secret with him. Philippe did not have the same closeness to Maurice that his brother Claude did. Claude always understood precisely his father's attitudes, predicted his responses, but Philippe was unable to do so. From childhood and into his twenties he needed to ask Claude: 'Do you think Father would like such and such?' And Claude's yes or no was swift and confident, invariably correct.

Sun-gilded windows rose above him. Philippe crossed the terrace and entered an open door. On the day of the funeral he met his mother in this room. 'Thank God that's over,' he said. And she replied with a doubt: 'Do you think it is?' She was right, the funeral concluded nothing. That was also the day Philippe acquired his secret, the day the first ransom note came.

His mother was easier than his father but he refused to burden her with his story, her heart was giving her trouble. If he did not share his secret with Maurice, there was no one he could tell.

Philippe went into his office. He picked up the report from the desk and began to read. One paragraph. Two. Then the bicycle again. A pattern of thought was established. Each attempt to read ended in his brain flashing him pictures of rusty handlebars against a wall.

Annoyed with himself, he sent for coffee and asked the girl who brought it: 'That gardener, the one who left a few months ago. Was he from Marseilles?'

'No, m'sieu. From Languedoc.' She set the tray on the desk and hovered, anticipating further questions.

'And he's gone back there, I suppose?'

'No, he has work at a hotel.'

He probed for details.

Dismissed, she left the room, a slight heightening of her colour showing that the questions discomforted her. The young gardener was her sweetheart.

219

For Philippe the conversation settled much. She looked guilty, and the village she named was about twelve miles from the château but a mere handful from the *cave*. True, Marseilles was inexplicable unless the young man had a compliant friend there. Next time Philippe pictured the bicycle against the wall he also saw the gardener jumping on it and pedalling away while he himself was inside the *cave* finding the note that coaxed him on a futile journey south.

Philippe did not mention ransoms or vengeful gardeners to anyone but he made the journey south. No longer worried about kidnap, because they could have snatched him at the *cave* if that was their aim, expecting only extortion, he followed instructions. Instead of a bundle of bank notes, his bag contained paper cut to size. Otherwise he did as he was told. He drove to the town and went to a bar in the main square.

Market day, with autumn fruits and vegetables blushing on sunny stalls, sharp-eyed shoppers pinching them seeking perfection, and batting away wasps drawn by the sweet sharp scents. Philippe sat at a pavement table, the bag on the table top beside his beer glass. Tourists at the next table leaned over and asked in careful French for directions to somewhere he had not heard of. He resented the distraction and was brusque. Then a trio of ample farmers' wives came together to gossip right in front of him and instead of vigorous vendors, scrabbling shoppers, a church and a town hall, all he saw was acres of cloth stretched tight over acres of flesh.

Move? No, for all he knew . . . One of the trio swayed back, rested her bag on the edge of his table. Philippe was ready for the pudgy hand with the embedded wedding ring to lift his bag into her bigger one. And it was going to be so easy. Protected by her companions, no one else would see what she was doing and her face was hidden from him.

The woman raised her bag, hitched it over her arm and told her friends that she really must get to the olive stall, one never had enough time, did one? Philippe's bag remained undisturbed beside his glass.

According to the note, the chime from the church tower was to be his cue. When it started he sprang like a cuckoo from a clock but felt foolish and then struggled to look natural. He signalled the waiter.

'One moment, *m'sieu*.'

The man attended to other tables, then went inside. A couple of minutes were lost. Then the waiter reappeared with a tray from which he dispensed glasses and cups of hot chocolate. Philippe's repeated claim on his attention was ignored. The waiter skipped indoors. It was fully ten minutes after the chimes that Philippe was allowed to pay his bill.

He strolled, pretending not to be late and nervous. In among the stalls a dog tripped a man, the man stumbled into a stall, apples toppled. The mêlée impeded Philippe, who was forced to gather up and return a few apples before passing on. A crush around the popular cheese stall blocked his route and he skirted round another way to reach the vegetable stall on the corner. Here, as he was bid, he bought aubergines, green peppers, onions, and lay them on top of the package in his bag. Then he turned left into the church.

Mingling scents of dust, incense, flowers and candlewax reached him but he was blinded by sunshine and it was a second or two before his eyes confirmed where he was. Then flowers, banners, the freshly dressed patron saint proved they were celebrating the saint's day. Women with shopping bags came swishing by and he followed them, counting the rows of chairs until he reached the one sixth from the back. He moved down the row to the sixth chair, went through the motions of praying and then sat and waited.

The note was absolutely specific. Sixth row, sixth chair, put the bag on the floor by your right, when another person comes into the row from the same end wait a couple of minutes and then leave from the other end of the row, leaving the bag behind.

The arrangements pleased him, doing away with doubts about his own abduction and promising a glimpse of one of the extortionists. Philippe touched the bag with his right foot, kept discreet contact with it, wishing to know the moment anyone touched it.

Behind him the religious came to converse with the saint. Candles were lit. Occasionally there were voices, subdued murmurings of the devout or the broken-off laughter of tourists entering unready for the contrast between market and place of prayer. No one joined Philippe in the sixth row.

He expected the sacked gardener to come himself, or, if not, a friend of his. Philippe planned to linger at the back of the church, hidden by a pillar and look out for a man carrying his bag. He intended to pounce, accost the man. What came next, he was not sure.

After a while someone entered the row on his right. He saw the profile of a middle-aged stranger, a man with a worn collar, intensity in the lines of his face. The stranger sank to his knees, buried head in hands.

'Two minutes,' Philippe reminded himself and measured it against his wristwatch. Just after one minute, the man shuffled from his knees and backed on to a chair. Obliquely, Philippe studied him as the man gazed up at the saint, the altar, the banner. A twitch on the side of his face developed into silently mouthed supplication or complaint.

When two minutes were up, Philippe had still not decided whether this was an overwrought Christian who had haphazardly settled in the sixth row, or whether it was a cunning pose calculated to disguise the extortioner's true business in the church. He was inclined towards the accident theory. The pose was altogether too attention seeking and elaborate to be part of a clandestine transaction.

Philippe sighed and tapped his foot against the bag. '*Now* what? Change rows? No, the orders are specific. But it's late, surely the man's here by now? Back there watching me?' And the tiny hairs on his neck rose in objection.

On his left, a movement. A young woman in a headscarf took the final seat in the row. She stood a deep tote bag on the floor.

It seemed empty, its sides leaned in towards each other, and it was big enough to contain his bag.

He disobeyed instructions and glanced round. Several people were seated, others stood. None of them took notice of him. He guessed that, finding the sixth row occupied on his right, his contact was improvising and had approached from the left. Philippe began to move in the direction of the tote bag. He went half a dozen paces before a voice hissed at him.

'M'sieu!'

Jumpy, he looked back. The intense stranger was leaning over, pointing.

'Your bag, m'sieu.'

'Oh . . . er . . . thank you.' Philippe added a smile more grateful than his words and collected his bag. Movement released the earthiness of vegetables into the air, to blend with the spiciness of incense and flowers.

As he neared the other end of the row, the woman in the scarf raised her bag and placed it on the chair beside her. Briefly, he wondered whether this was a hint for him to drop his bag inside it, then realized it would make the switch obvious. She swung her legs out into the aisle and let him pass.

Near the pillar earmarked as a vantage point for spying, he came to a halt. Still nobody was taking any interest in him. His bag felt huge and suspicious, his behaviour peculiar and yet people seemed unaware. He did not know what to do, except wait for the intense man in row six to leave and then try again.

For twenty minutes he feigned fascination with paintings, memorials, architecture, and kept an eye on the fellow in row six. At last the man rose. Philippe bobbed out of sight as he headed for the street. During that twenty minutes there was a change of cast, everyone who saw him in the row earlier left. Among the new faces was a group of four Americans, young women who mooched around the memorials with him, remarking on antiquity and quaintness. Philippe had hardly sat down when he heard them sliding into the row behind.

A voice from Georgia drawled: 'I tell you, Paige, if I don't rest a while I shall surely die.'

'Marsha, it's those pumps. Sightseeing, you gotta have comfortable shoes.'

'OK. Tomorrow I wear my trainers. Promise.'

Philippe heard the clatter of Marsha's pumps being kicked off. She was a tall, big-boned girl with fair sun-dried hair and a reddish nose. He heard her ripple with pleasure as her sore feet met the cold stone.

Within a minute or two a young man sat in row six. Philippe registered his dark looks and alert demeanour and was satisfied that this, after all, was the contact. Sidelong, he saw the man flicking glances to left and right, taking stock of who was around and what they were doing. Philippe memorized the sharp profile, long eyelashes, line of moustache, tinny watch on plastic strap, slightly curling hair reaching down to meet the neck of the sweatshirt. Philippe got up and left.

A priest entered. A service was about to start. Front rows were filling with the elderly devout. Casual onlookers were sidling away. A hand touched his arm. He met Marsha's blue eyes. 'You forgot your bag.'

'Oh. Thanks.' He swallowed hard. 'Thanks very much.'

'You're welcome. I was in the row behind, I saw it sitting there kinda lonesome.' Close up, her nose was very red.

'That's very kind of you.'

He was holding the strap with two hands, swinging the bag slightly between himself and this maddeningly helpful American woman. She wanted them to talk, to walk out of the building together. He hoped to detach himself as her friends came up, but instead they all stopped and spoke to him. They asked him to name a good place for lunch. Philippe pleaded ignorance, said he was a visitor to the town himself. Marsha's eyes dropped to his bag of aubergines, peppers and onions. She did not believe he was a stranger, she thought he was giving her the brush off. He held the door as Marsha and her friends went out into the market place.

He stayed inside, right by the door, trying to see between the heads whether the man in row six was waiting for him to return with the bag. A couple who were arguing about whether to stay or to go were blocking his view. They reached their decision. Go. Row six was empty.

Disappointment was shortlived because the young man in the sweatshirt was plodding towards the exit. When he was close, Philippe moved forward a fraction and, with discreet movements of hand and eye, proffered the bag. He was getting a good look. The face was broad, eyes pale and deep set. Philippe did not know him but would recognize him in future.

His gesture was ineffective, the man was about to pass. Philippe moved more positively, offered the bag again. A look of alarm crossed the man's face. He sidestepped and skipped out into the market place.

Onions. Aubergines. Green peppers. And beneath them a wad of paper masquerading as a ransom. Philippe carried them all back to his car, tossed the bag into the boot and drove home.

Krieger was waiting for Rose Darrow in the *sala terrena* of the Waldstein Gardens, smoking.

'You're late, Rose,' he said with an ironical smile. 'Thirty seconds late.'

'I forgot how steep the hill is.' In fact, she had decided he was going to be provocatively late if indeed he bothered to turn up at all. Overnight her optimism had diminished to vanishing point. To discover him standing there, surrounded by frescos of the Trojan wars, was rather a surprise.

'Have you a taste for Homer, Rose? Or shall we stroll among the statues? They're mostly fakes, of course.'

'Reproductions. The originals became spoils of war and are in Sweden, or so my guidebook says.'

'Mine too. Well, let's skip these doubtful statues and head up the hill.'

She fell in with this, taking the role of a niece indulging a middle-aged uncle from whom she means to extract future favours. When they reached a meeting of paths and he turned left, saying: 'We'll walk this way, shall we?' she turned automatically.

'Fewer people this way?'

'But more dogs. Rose, isn't this the most splendid of cities?'

River mist again. Autumn trees. Sun streaks through cloud lighting red roofs and the golden tips of spires and green cupolas.

'Mesmeric. Is this why you stay here?'

'Perhaps. And you?' He finished his cigarette, stubbed it out and, with action formed of habit, put the butt in his jacket pocket.

Rose said: 'Now I've discovered Prague I'll keep coming back. Once I have your story, I'll find other reasons to come. But I shall come.'

They began to climb again, more steeply. Twice he stopped, joking about growing old and unfit. She talked, letting him get his breath, ignoring his folly in lighting another cigarette.

He said: 'I used to be athletic, you know. If there was a wall to be scaled, then I was the one who scaled it. As a boy I was fast on my feet. I trained myself to move without sound, like a cat in the night. These were useful things for the life I chose.' He puffed at the cigarette. 'But they slip away, those skills don't last. Nothing lasts.'

He was ready to move on again. Rose walked beside him, on his right to avoid the slipstream of tobacco smoke.

Out of the blue he named a figure. High but not astronomical. Rose told him she expected a lot in return. By the time they reached the end of the path, swung round to join a higher one, sloped upwards towards the castle, the deal was struck.

'Rose, there'll be no changing of minds. What I offer is a promise.'

She shook his hand with mock formality. 'I'm glad to hear it.'

'Today Rose, you may fly to Paris and astonish your colleagues with your outstanding success.'

She demurred, saying they expected nothing less of her. And he laughed.

A terrorist, a drug runner, a spy, a notorious man who dedicated his life to forcing change by fierce methods, and yet she found herself enjoying a few jokes with him, sorry they had to break off soon. He had mentioned an appointment, not a meeting but a telephone call, he needed to be home for. She noted the word. Home. Krieger described the house in Prague as home. Significant, or loose translation? Difficult to know.

They stopped to lean on a wall. The weir was a white fleck, a tram toy-like, the rich diversity of the city was laid out for their amusement. Over there the medieval Old Town, crumpled up around the jagged towers of the Týn Church. Then the newer districts, red roofs spreading more spaciously. On the river bank the national theatre, a cushiony shape in green and gold. She wondered how long you had to live in Prague before you gave up being stopped in your tracks by its beauty.

A reddened leaf rattled along the wall beside her. She cradled its brittleness in her palm and then tossed it into the air, watching it sail across the sky, the hill, the red roofs, dipping and twisting down the hillside before the wind. Change did not have to come Krieger's way, violently, dishonestly, and in 1989 it had come like autumn leaves. The promise had always been held out to anyone in Prague who cared to read Avigdor Kara's lines in the Jewish museum, a fifteenth-century poet recounting Hussite victory over German knights:

At midnight, all of a sudden, frightened shouting was heard in the very centre of the large forces of Edom who had put up their tents along three miles near the town of Zatec in Bohemia; in the distance of ten miles from Cheb. And all of them fled from the sword, driven out by the voice of falling leaves only, not being pursued by a single man. And they left behind all their riches and property and they did no more harm to this country.

'Rose, have you had breakfast?'

Krieger's question was unexpected, down to earth. She said no, she had not eaten.

'Well, we can get coffee here.'

The clocks of the city began to strike. He was too late for his telephone call. Guessing her thoughts, he said: 'The telephone will be unanswered and he'll have to try later. Or perhaps he won't be able to get through, anyway. That happens, rather often.'

The café was buried inside the ramparts, a spiral staircase led down. The room had a window with the wonderful view and the *cappuccino* was the best Rose had tasted since coming to the city.

They were the only customers but it was not ideal for the kind of private conversation he promised for later, so he asked her: 'What else are you working on for your magazine?'

'A piece about the Devereux family.' She spoke without thinking. Inside her skull a warning light began to flash.

He spooned the froth on his coffee. 'Well, there's always plenty to be said about them.'

'I should say it's about the business, rather than the Curse of the Devereux and that type of thing.'

Krieger licked the froth from the spoon. 'I don't see how you separate them.'

She armed herself against a diatribe on the questionable morality of the perfume industry and the unjustified riches of the private individuals who ran it. But what he actually said to her was: 'Don't bother with the old man, Maurice, or with his son, Philippe. It's David, the grandson, who calls the shots now. Whatever the others might choose to tell you, David's the one.'

'I hear you've met him.'

His eyes registered a shift of mood. He waited for her to go on.

Rose said: 'He was seen with you, here.'

He agreed to it with a slight bow but offered no elaboration. He ate another spoonful of froth.

The warning light in her head was still blinking but her mouth took no notice. 'I doubt if he was appointing you the Prague sales rep for the House of Devereux.'

'Therefore you have an alternative theory?'

'One or two.'

'It's simple, Rose. We were discussing Greenworld and the future of the planet.'

'That's the one theory I won't accept.'

They stared at each other, neither of them willing to break the silence that followed.

Back down the hill she went, alone. Sunshine had been killed with coldness, dark clouds were switching off the light. Rose turned her coat collar up, thrust hands deep into her pockets and watched her footing over the treacherous broken cobbles.

The flat was empty. Ellie, who had spent the night on its sofa, had left a note saying she would take Rose up on the offer to use it while Rose was in Paris.

Ellie wrote: 'I'm going back to the castle today to look at the painting. Keep your fingers crossed for me.'

Rose made the gesture immediately. Then crossed them again to wish herself luck with Krieger. She put belongings into a bag and dashed round to the square for a taxi to the airport.

She did not notice the man, stock still, in the deepest shadow beneath the arch. When she shut the gate behind her and went through the wooden doors into the street, he listened to be sure her footsteps continued, that she was not doubling back having forgotten something. Then he undid the gate and entered the flat in one unbroken movement. Before her taxi left the square, he was going through her possessions.

SIXTEEN

After the fiasco in the church there were no more ransom demands, no more pretence that Nicole was alive.

'Just someone playing a senseless cruel prank,' Philippe decided. 'And I frightened him off. Excellent.'

The end of it then, except that he did not destroy the notes. He kept them in a sandalwood box in a drawer in his room at the château. There they stayed during the years he was married to Margot and lived in Paris. They were undisturbed when he returned to the château after the divorce. By then his brother and Andrée had been killed in the car crash down the valley and his mother was becoming an invalid. Her heart was weak. The garden was too much for her. She could not do it herself and each year it grew more difficult to employ helpers prepared to match her standards. She simplified and began to let it go. No one was astonished when she died.

What would she have thought of him, he asked himself, if she knew about him concealing the ransom demands? He thought of them that way although they were not true attempts at ransom. Quite what form of extortion they were he never clarified. A peculiar one when the family knew, and anyone who read a newspaper or switched on a television set knew, that the Devereux baby was found dead weeks before the first demand was delivered to the château. It would have pleased him to get to the bottom of it. Over the years he often wished for the release of discussing the predicament he had been in and his response to it. It was not to be.

Two things kept the story alive for him: the media's fascination with the 'Curse of the Devereux', particularly the unsolved child murder, and the money tied up awaiting the return of Nicole. His son, David, was scathing about both.

'Look,' said David one evening, sprawling on a gilt and white chair in the salon, 'you shouldn't give these interviews. It only feeds their fire.'

'I don't give interviews, I tell them they exaggerate. They get their facts wrong.'

'I mean you shouldn't speak to them at all. Refer everything to the company's press officer. She knows how to handle them.'

Philippe swilled the wine around his mouth before answering. 'I dare say you're right, David.'

'You know I am. They never get anything out of Grandfather so they don't bother him any more.'

David refilled their glasses. Philippe thought how typical it was for David to look to Maurice for example. Those two understood each other. Yet again, he felt isolated. Perhaps it was this isolation that made him dig his heels in when David raised the question of Nicole's money. Philippe knew it was coming, David had remarked that they needed to discuss it when there was time and this evening he made time.

David said: 'There's a lot of cash swishing around in Nicole's piggybank and if the company doesn't want it, I do.'

Just like that he asked for her money. Philippe's face stiffened.

'David, we can't do it. You know that.'

'Correction. We can do what we want. *Anything* we want.'

'No, the terms of the fund . . .'

'I know, I know. The money's supposed to stay there for fifty years in case Nicole comes home. Well . . .' He ended by rolling his eyes towards the chandelier.

'It would be bad . . .'

David pounced. 'Bad luck? Is that it? Oh, so you believe in the family curse, do you?'

'I was going to say bad faith. My brother and his wife made that provision for their daughter and it would be breaking faith with them to alter it.'

His son shook his head in bewilderment. 'They're dead. Nicole was dead when they set the money aside for her. It wasn't rational at the time and it's even sillier now. That money could pay for things to be done in the world. Do you realize how much there is? It's a fortune.'

Philippe wriggled on his chair. David's enthusiasm for the environmental movement was not fizzling out like his earlier passions, and its financial demands were infinite. Yes, Nicole's money was invested where it multiplied and, yes, it was valid to argue that it was wasteful not to use it. And yet he resented David dragging him towards the brink of a dangerous drop. Spend Nicole's money this year and when that was gone might David not expect the House of Devereux to dole out more? Philippe was also fearful of sponsorship deals, the company's name degraded and politicized. He wanted nothing to do with it. How David squandered his own cash was his affair but he ought to keep his hobbies and the family business apart.

David said: 'Grandfather's quite sympathetic. He's well on the way to becoming green.'

This was doubtful. 'That doesn't mean he's willing to dispense Nicole's money.'

David admitted with a look that this was true. 'Not yet,' he murmured. And it was understood he was not giving up.

In a while Philippe went up to his room, brooding. He was proud of the energy David was putting into the company, proud of his talents, but he wished he could rid himself of the suspicion of collusion between Maurice and David. Maurice was susceptible to David's persuasion, and Philippe frequently found himself having to argue against the pair of them, and losing the argument too. Yet he doubted David would succeed in getting his hands on Nicole's money.

Philippe opened the drawer. After twenty years the sheets of notepaper were scented with sandalwood, they were brittle. In the envelope with them were other documents. A newspaper cutting about the murder hunt, although after two decades he could not recall why he singled it out to file away with the ransom demands. A photograph of Nicole, the one taken a couple of weeks before she was abducted, the one the press published during the search for her. A page from a notebook on which he had written the name of the sacked gardener.

Philippe held the photograph close to the lamp. A sweet little face smiled at him, wavy hair twisted into ringlets below each ear. If there was a likeness to his brother Claude or to any of the Devereux family, it eluded him. Neither was she a diminutive replica of Andrée. In her brief span Nicole had been herself.

He lay the skein of hair on his palm, remained unconvinced it matched the coiling hair in the photograph. Then he put away all these sandalwood-scented relics except the photograph, which he placed in his wallet. For some months he had been mulling over an idea. The time was ripe to act.

He was not good at lies but the situation demanded secrecy. In France the ruse would fail but in America people would believe he was whoever he said he was.

The woman worked in New York. He told her he was Swiss. He said he wished to trace a daughter not seen since his marriage broke down.

'It doesn't come cheap,' the woman said, but he did not look like a man with financial worries.

'I know that.' He admired her directness. She was a plain, big-boned woman wearing a serious pair of glasses and he sensed he could trust her.

'And it doesn't guarantee results,' she said.

'I know that too.'

She held out a hand. 'OK, show me what you have.'

Philippe gave her Nicole's photograph. She said it was a good clear image and offered her plenty to work with.

'How old was she when this was taken?'

'Two years.'

She pulled a face, rueful, sympathetic. 'And you haven't seen her since? That's bad.'

'My ex-wife changed her name, they disappeared. I've used detectives, of course, but I couldn't trace them.'

'Your daughter mightn't know you're her father.'

'She probably isn't aware of her true name.'

The woman warned: 'Could be she doesn't want to be found.'

'I've thought about that but there's family money. I owe it to her to try.'

Philippe was nervous of ploughing further into this fiction. If discrepancies crept in the woman might lose confidence in him and reject him.

He asked: 'How long will this take you?'

'Well, I can't promise it tomorrow. I have a lot of work on right now. Do you know this country loses one and a half million kids every year? Anyone who's in the business of finding them is going to keep busy.'

She watched his eyes widen at the alarming statistic. Before he could speak she backtracked.

'OK, so most of those cases clear themselves up: 100,000 are runaways, say up to 750,000 are snatched by a parent in a custody fight. But that leaves anything between 4,000 and 20,000 kidnapped by strangers.'

He wondered where the figures came from.

She said: 'The National Center for Missing and Exploited Children came up with that set. Chilling. The Center gets their faces on television, on milk cartons, grocery bags, any place. They see to it that when you open your electricity bill, a missing kid falls out.' She raised a cautionary finger. 'But, I have to say, the FBI is more conservative. They reckon around seventy a year are grabbed by strangers.'

She showed him some of her work, successes. Several of the cases were familiar to him, he had learned about her through magazine articles. Most impressive was the chubby baby aged on her computer until it was such an accurate depiction of the boy several years on that he was discovered.

'Where can I contact you, M. Brelade?' She expected a smart business card.

'I'm travelling,' Philippe said. 'I'll be in touch with you in a few weeks.'

He went from the computer artist's studio to a business lunch, then to a meeting at the House of Devereux's Manhattan office, and on to the airport. A missing child looked out at him from a highway billboard, others were posted in the airport concourse. He kicked the shocking figures around in his head. Up to 20,000 a year or around seventy? And how many of those were already dead and how many still alive? And which was Nicole?

The pictures that came out of the studio in New York were of a young woman with the immobile features of a plastic doll. He had offered the snapshot of a giggling toddler and been returned this substitute, a creature lacking warmth or animation. It did not remind him of anybody he knew. In fact, it conjured up those police posters where they resort to photographing the victim's corpse.

Philippe showed it to the private detective. The ferret-faced little man had worked for him once or twice before on minor matters that were best snuffed out without attention from the police. Philippe relied on his discretion and paid well for it.

'Not a soul, not even members of the family,' Philippe stressed.

The man sniffed and pocketed the photograph. 'No one will know who my client is or why I'm seeking her.'

'Of course, I don't expect you to find her.' Immediately Philippe thought this was a rash statement. The man might do nothing at all except send in his bills. 'What I mean to say is . . .'

Possibly clients had previously accused him of doing nothing but submit bills, because the detective cut in: 'Forgive me, M. Devereux, but I must ask you what prompts this action now. Is there any suggestion of a case of mistaken identity? It will help me very much if I have all the relevant information, whether or not you believe it to be genuine.'

Philippe kept quiet about the ransom demands, the incident with the rusty bicycle at the *cave* and the bungled rendezvous at the church. Looking sad, he shook his head.

'Unfortunately, all that's new is this marvellous technique of updating photographs with the aid of a computer. But . . .'

'Yes?' The bead-bright eyes were urging more.

'There's nothing that amounts to information, I'm afraid. You'll have to accept you're relying on your client's instinct.'

'Instinct, *m'sieu*? Instinct must have a basis.'

'Oh, it has. It arises from my dissatisfaction at the way the affair was handled at the time. Nothing was resolved, you see.'

The detective did not see, not exactly. There had been a murder and a body and a burial. He sniffed. 'You mean no one was convicted.'

'No one was even charged, not with abduction and not with murder.' He saw the ferrety little nose lift as if scenting a clue, and he went hastily on. 'I'm not asking you to attempt to replicate months of police work at this impossible distance in time. If this remarkable photograph performs the miracle of bringing Nicole home alive, I'll be more than content with that.'

The detective permitted himself a cunning smile. 'If that miracle's performed, it will also be a short cut to solving the mystery of her abduction.' He narrowly avoided saying murder. One always humours one's clients.

Philippe stood at his window and listened to the man drive away. Six months, he thought. Let him ply his trade for six months, then call him off. If no likeness stepped forward in that time he would shrug off guilt about concealing the ransom demands and he would set about freeing Nicole's money.

Through the gap in the trees below the vineyard, he saw his father's bent figure pass on his way to the churchyard again. Maurice's hands were free, no flowers on this occasion. He did not always take them, sometimes when he wanted to there were none to be picked.

'I go for the walk, Philippe,' he would say, defending himself. 'The exercise does me good.'

There were other walks, pleasanter ones through the trees or around the other side of the vineyard, but he preferred this one.

'Maudlin,' Philip murmured at the window pane. 'Maudlin, foolishly repetitive, pointlessly trying to hang on to a bit of the past. Maddening.'

He looked forward to the day he sided with David and they outvoted Maurice over the matter of what David flippantly called Nicole's piggybank. No, he would not let David have control of it and squander it on one of his hare-brained schemes to save the world, he had a use for it himself. For the benefit of the business, naturally.

There was a Greek island, Kios, where jasmine of a superior fragrance grew. Philippe intended to buy up land there and secure an excellent supply for the future. The traditional fields of roses and jasmine around Grasse were dwindling because of property development and home-grown supplies would become more difficult as the years went by. Yes, he wanted to own fields of Greek jasmine and he wanted a new laboratory too. Maurice and David knew his dreams. They could hardly condemn them as undesirable, but they argued they were too costly.

Philippe was convinced the expenditure was justified because improving their working methods and their product ensured the company's future as leader in the perfume business. He did not want Nicole's money for his personal hobbies, as Maurice earmarked company money for his art fund or David craved it for environmental projects. He wanted it to make the House of Devereux better. It was unfair that they obstructed him.

As he stepped away from his window, his face darkened by shadow, Philippe looked smug. He had set events in motion. Before long, when the six months were up, he would be able to flourish the detective's report and the updated photograph in front of Maurice and prove it was time to shake the money out of the piggybank and go shopping for fields of jasmine. Anticipating, he relished victory over his father, having his own way for once, a pleasure he seldom enjoyed.

The six months stretched. Seven. Eight. Nine. Unfortunately, the detective was reporting progress, which made it very hard indeed for Philippe to call the man off.

SEVENTEEN

Ellie had a headache and, if she were honest, a high temperature. It was enough to make the long drive to the castle tiresome and to account for her mood the evening before. She thought Rose had coped well.

Stopping for coffee, she swallowed painkillers and peered at her flushed face in the mirror above a cracked washbasin. She wished she had postponed the journey. But the car was hired and she was twenty miles along the route before she realized how her joints ached, how she longed to be in a peaceful room with nothing to do but doze.

Her snatched photographs of the painting were as vague and unhelpful as expected. They confirmed the figure was probably female and clad in black with the high-necked white collar familiar from Hals's portraits. Beyond that it was impossible to go.

For the umpteenth time she twisted her neck and checked that the precious lamp and its batteries lay on the rear seat of the car. They had cost much time and money.

'When I get there,' she thought, 'I'll be exceedingly careful. Even if it means sitting through the Stehlik family history again, I mustn't blow it.'

She was sorry to be travelling alone, a second pair of hands would be useful while she photographed and if, miracle of miracles, the owner allowed her to lift the painting down and take it away to be identified. She was disappointed Rose could not come and had then thought of asking the man who took her to the castle before. But a woman answered the telephone and said, rather shortly, that he was not there. The female voice conjured the blouse on the hanger and the handbag on the chair.

The journey was dreary, the day dull, all colour wrung out of it. The thrill that had made her too excited to drive away from the castle was diminished by the sheer impossibility of knowing what she had discovered. An old painting, yes. A painting of a woman, probably. A missing Frans Hals companion piece to the Washington man? She would be a fool to believe it.

Once more she checked the back seat. Good. Her tape measure was definitely there. It had not sneaked out of the car while she was minding the road ahead.

The painkillers were wearing off. Ellie stopped at a bar where she ignored the food and drank more coffee to wash down a second dose of tablets. In a cracked mirror above a basin, she worried about her reddened skin. Her natural fairness played up the effect of what, on a brunette, could be flattering pinkness.

A couple came into the bar and sat near her. They were hoping to buy a business, she could not help overhearing. The government was selling off a batch in the New Year and these two were calculating their chances. The man reminded his wife it was not straightforward but it was worth trying. She agreed, reminding him in return that if they acquired a shop this way it was a better prospect than attempting to set up from scratch.

They were in their thirties, a few years younger than she was. What were they obliged to do with their working lives under the old regime? How extraordinary, when you came to think of it, that they were denied the opportunity of becoming *shopkeepers*. And, more extraordinary when you came to think of this, how had they nurtured the courage to risk it now? Ellie wished she felt well enough to edge into conversation with them and find out.

The forest around the castle was dark and dead, the dilapidation of the building depressing. Could she really have daydreamed about resurrecting this pile? The words that came unbidden to her this time were 'Too late. Too late.' Instead of scaffolding and a team of men with hods and trowels, she pictured nothing more encouraging than a bulldozer bearing down on it.

Waiting for an answer to her clanging of the bell led to feverish fantasies that the owner was lying stricken in the darker recesses and she must force her way in and save him. The door opened, a ragged motion caused by the wood having dropped on its hinges and nobody having bothered to rehang it. She parodied Stehlik.

'In the year 1781, when Joseph the Second abolished serfdom, the grandest of balls was held at the castle and it was then that the great door sagged upon its hinges, an event that came to be known in the family as the Sagging of the Great Door.'

Old Stehlik was standing before her, his hawk-like features pale and troubled. He was a changed man, the aloofness gone, but she did not see this at first. He and Ellie stared at each other. She tried to speak, garbled her words, tried again. He was not listening, her muddle did not matter. She repeated herself, especially the part about bringing her lamp to take a better look.

He shook his head. Anguished, she argued with him, not wheedling but plaintive, protesting that she had driven all the way from Prague specially. She held up the lamp although if argument failed then mime would not help her case.

His head shook again. 'No,' he said. 'You're too late.'

Too late. Too late.

Hysterical, Ellie tried to hang on to facts. He was not going to disappear before her eyes. There was no bulldozer charging up the drive. What did he mean by too late?

Once more she started on her blundering speech but he shut her up. He said: 'The painting's no longer here. They took it yesterday.'

'Took it? Who took it?'

'They came from Prague. They said it was important and made me agree they should take it.'

'Who?'

'They had a van. They promised me they'd be careful. They

240

laid it flat in the back of the van, on a blanket. There was room to do that.'

'Yes, yes, but who were they?'

'The woman said she works for the national gallery.'

A hammer was pounding in her skull. 'Oh, God.'

'The man was the one who came with you.'

'Oh, God,' she said again.

She set the lamp down heavily, did not notice when it toppled sideways. She clutched at her head with both hands. If only the pain would subside, not just the headache but the pain of what had happened.

She felt a hand on her arm. His grip was powerful. 'You'd better come in. You look ill.'

Ellie let him haul her inside. She murmured about having flu. For an hour she stretched out on a couch in a warm room. A younger man appeared and brought her hot drinks, a tisane – it tasted like sage – that he promised would reduce her temperature, something else for the pain. They were kind and concerned. Their kindness made her cry. Tears washed her red cheeks, hotter than the burning skin that was too tender to touch. She lay there, helpless, scalded by her own tears.

Part of the time her mind drifted. Sleeping or not, she could not tell. Once she thought Sam was in the room with her and she had something pressing to tell him about the fate of *Exile*, but the sense of what she said was distorted in its journey from her brain to her mouth, and the man was not Sam, in any case. An hysterical woman raged about the room reciting lines of Kafka at her. '*What do I have in common with Jews, I who have nothing in common with myself?*'

By early evening she felt rather better, although weak, and fancied she ought to get herself out of there into an hotel. Driving back to Prague was out of the question. But old Stehlik assured her that patients often felt better at that time of day although they were far from cured, and that she would be unwise to move. She swallowed more of the sage tisane and heard the two men discuss which room to put her in.

There was an area of the castle she had not explored, the few rooms where they lived. Plumbing was antiquated but it worked and there was electric light. Despite her worst fears, the mattress was new, unlike the bed itself, which was an elaborate relic from a grander age. Ellie slept through until morning.

Breakfast arrived on a tray. She was limp but without pain or fever and improved for having eaten. She went to locate her host.

'Ah, you're looking much better.' He struggled up from his chair as she entered the room.

'I can't thank you enough.' Of course she tried and, of course, he demurred and said any work involved had been done by his staff. The staff, which is to say the younger man, was equally reluctant to be thanked.

The owner said to her: 'The people who came were most persuasive but as they didn't inform you they were moving the painting I'm very concerned. Could you find it for me, do you think? I shouldn't like it to be lost. It has belonged in this house for many years.'

Ellie replied that she fully intended to trace it and to let it be known that he wanted it back.

They went to the door. He picked up her lamp and handed it to her, watched her put it in the back of the car with the batteries and her tape measure. Gathering her wits, she took the lamp and batteries out and gave them to him.

'They aren't much use to me now and they're all I have to offer as a thank you.'

As she drove down the drive she saw him in her rear mirror, on the front door step, waving with one arm, the lamp held in the other.

'That's great, Rosie.' Larry, the brash one in the Paris office, could not fault her this time.

Steve, the softly spoken one, echoed the praise.

Rose brushed it aside. 'We have to complete the interview yet.'

'Krieger's not writing the stuff himself?' Hard to tell from Larry's face which he hoped for.

'No,' she said. 'That way it would take for ever and heaven knows how it would read.'

'Good,' said Larry.

They moved on to the next topic, inching down a scribbled agenda made up of stories to cover and administrative problems to solve, and all before the first issue hit the streets of Europe's capital cities.

Joelle, who had been caught on the telephone, sidled into the room and perched on the edge of a desk next to Rose. She whispered: 'Have you met any of the Devereux family yet?'

'Philippe. I went to the château.'

'Well, David's in Paris now. He's involved in a publicity stunt Greenworld are staging tomorrow.'

'Rosie,' said Larry, raising his voice and breaking in on her *sotto voce* discussion with Joelle. 'Do you want to add anything to that?'

'Yes,' she said, improvising, having no idea what he had been talking about. 'But later.' She got a laugh, from Larry too.

Then he said: 'We're talking about the Vatican story. Have you picked up anything fresh on it?'

'Afraid not. All I know is what we had from our people in Rome last week.'

Larry said he would get back to them. Rose suggested he speak to Patricia, who was significantly brighter than her colleagues. Larry said fine, he would do that.

When they straggled away to the main office, Joelle said to Rose: 'I'll give you what I have on the Greenworld thing.'

She offered a press release, outlining plans for a flotilla on the Seine. Rose laughed. 'Seems a curious place to Save the Whale.'

But she went along. She wormed her way into the crowd and was close when an impassioned young man with mousy brown hair and an athletic shape seized a microphone and made a speech about pure water and a pure life and a pure planet. She turned to the person nearest, another journalist as it happened.

From the side of her mouth she asked: 'Who's that?'

A withering look made it clear she was the only person in Paris not to know. 'That's David Devereux, of course.'

But it reminded her of someone. His intense look was familiar. No, not like his father, Philippe, not like that at all. There was no similarity in their appearance. Yet somehow or other, she had seen David's face before.

'The Devereux file,' she begged, back at the office.

Joelle produced the originals; Rose had left her copies in Prague.

'What did you make of David, Rose?'

'I'm not sure. He was . . . unexpected.' She looked up and caught Joelle's quizzical expression. 'Go ahead, tell me what I'm supposed to say.'

Joelle giggled. 'You're supposed to say he's crazy. That's what everyone else says.'

'Do they now?'

'Yes, because he's over the top. Did he make a speech today?'

'A brief one. And yes, I suppose it was a fraction over the top.' She flicked on through the cuttings. 'Joelle?'

'Hmm?'

'There aren't any photographs of David in here.'

Joelle pretended the complaint put her in a huff. 'Oh, sorry about that. Could it be because he's only recently gone public about his Greenworld involvement?'

'Ah, I see.'

'And before that he was just the grandson of a man running a business, so who cared about him anyway?'

Rose lay the file on Joelle's desk. 'All yours.'

'Why did you want a photograph of him? To check the fellow today wasn't an impostor?'

'Gosh, I wish I had your fertile mind.'

'I know, I'm a great loss to journalism.'

'Well, if *I* get lost too would you report I was last seen heading for the Paris office of the House of Devereux and a tête-à-tête with David?'

Joelle said some people got all the luck.

'*Luck?* Joelle, this is the guy you tell me is crazy.'

'Ye-es, but mega-rich and crazy.'

David was charm itself. Rose sensed herself slipping under the influence and ticked herself off. She was supposed to be interviewing him to discover something, *anything*, about the story that had begun with the Devereux family and ended with John Blair being killed; but she had to maintain the pretence that she was only concerned with writing a profile for the Euromagazine; and she had no business succumbing to the personality of her rich, amusing subject.

First Krieger, now David Devereux. What on earth was wrong with her? Her taste in men was taking a nose dive. She was letting herself enjoy their company, when cool professionalism and false friendliness served better. Oh, she knew what was wrong with her. She needed a new man, that's what.

It had been too long. The break-up with John Blair, then the frantic pace of the new job, the teasing relationship with colleagues and with Willi from Frankfurt, but no one and nothing to fill the space.

David did not offer her wine, as his father had done at the château. Instead he offered polemic. Pure this, pure that, pure . . . 'Baloney?' she asked herself at one point. But her features remained firm and interest gathered in her eyes. 'Put up with a bit more of this, Rose,' she thought, 'and then hop across to the art market.'

She hopped. David was reluctant to hop too. He told her what she already knew to be a lie: that the decisions about the direction of the art collection were made by his father, Philippe.

Rose clarified. 'Not your grandfather, then?'

'No. He started the collection, it's true. But now there's a director who takes instructions from my father.' He smiled his quick, dazzling smile. 'I'm sure you appreciate that my involvement with the running of the business and the struggle to protect the environment leave me short of time to concern myself with the collection.'

'On a day-to-day basis, yes. But are you also saying you have no control over the funding of it?'

'None at all. There's a fund and there's a director, and all questions related to them should properly be addressed to my father.'

Rose nodded and made a note on her pad. The note read: 'Liar.'

By the time she left his office she had a fresh perspective on the Devereux family's relationships and the effect of those relationships on the future of the business. She also had an invitation to dinner.

'Idiot,' she chided herself, as she riffled through the rack in a clothes shop. 'Your old black dress will do very well.' But she bought a new black one all the same.

Joelle spotted the bag immediately Rose rushed from the taxi into the office. 'Hey, you've really been spending.'

She was right. The dress was hideously overpriced, especially as there was so little of it. Rose tossed the bag over for Joelle to ogle the contents. She heard a 'Wow!' and an 'Mmmmm!' The 'Mmmm!' was Steve, who peered across to see what was going on.

Joelle said: 'I must meet this guy sometime. Anyone who can send you off to spend this amount of money on a frock must really be something special. He sounds great on the phone, but not *that* great.'

Rose's forehead puckered in a frown. 'Did a man ring for me?' The worst thought was that David was cancelling, that she would not wear the dress that evening after all.

Joelle folded the wisp back into the bag. 'Willi rang to say he'll be in Paris this evening and hopes you're free. Didn't you spot the note I put on your desk?'

Rose's face tried out several expressions before it settled into blank stupefaction. Willi any other time was fine but Willi when she was about to be dined by David was not.

She asked: 'Did he leave a number?'

He was out. She left a message at his hotel to say she would meet him there for a drink in the early evening.

The hotel was the kind favoured by businessmen, which is a way of saying the bar was full of men with nothing to do except watch her and wait to see whether she was genuinely meeting a friend or whether she was hoping to be picked up. One or two opened conversations with her and rather than encourage false hopes she was impolitely frosty. Apart from anything else, how could they be stupid enough to imagine that a tart as well dressed as she was would hang around that particular hotel when richer pickings were to be had at the classier ones?

When Willi at last appeared, she gave him a rapturous welcome. Relief, genuine pleasure at seeing him, and an eagerness to demonstrate to those tiresome watchers that she had been waiting for a friend, made it the warmest welcome Willi had received from her.

'Rose, the dress is wonderful.' He disengaged himself from her arms and stood back to admire it.

'Ah. The dress. Well, I'm afraid it means I have a dinner date and this can only be a drink before I move on.'

His disappointment was touching. 'And tomorrow I must leave for London. There's too much work, Rose. We never stand still, you and I.'

She smiled, tenderly. 'I'm sorry.'

He attracted the waiter, ordered drinks. 'But perhaps I'll see you in Frankfurt soon. You've never been, have you?'

'No. That's perverse because I get to so many places. I must seek an excuse to go there.'

'And I must avoid all temptations to be in Prague or in London or in Paris when you succeed.'

Mention of Prague took them neatly to Krieger. Rose told Willi what had taken place, how she had begun a series of interviews and planned to run the introductory article in the magazine's first issue.

'Rose, you're paying him too much.'

'Maybe. But sometimes you pay heavily for what you get and

other times something wonderful falls into your lap and costs you nothing. Don't you agree?'

He pursed his lips. 'It's still too much.'

She teased him. 'So if Krieger asks about reopening discussions with a German publisher, I should warn him the money will be a disgrace?'

'No, you should let me know and I'll tell him face to face what a mean bastard I am.'

'I promise.'

After they talked a while he asked her: 'What time is your friend expecting you?'

'It isn't social, I'm interviewing him.'

Willi looked pleased about that, and as lies went it was an inoffensive one.

For the second time that evening, she found herself waiting for a man who was late. David telephoned an apology but she felt she had fulfilled her quota of good-natured hanging around and she was annoyed. Yet when he came, weaving through the tables to her, a flapping waiter in tow, she was instantly cheered. His apology was convoluted and funny. She forgave him.

'The television people,' he said, and pulled a face that consigned them all to a sad fate for their incompetence. 'They want me to do this, do that, and then this again. Why do I bother with them, Rose? I should be here with you and they're waving their arms about and clapping their boards and shouting Take This and Take That, and I thought one more time and then, whatever they shout, it's time for me to Take Off.'

He was making her laugh. 'And?'

'I Took Off. They're still there, shouting Come Back and We Haven't Finished Yet. Well, let them. I tell you, I'm finished. All I asked was ten minutes of their time to allow me to say a few words about the demonstration on the Seine today and it leads me into hours of chaos.'

With a glance he beckoned a waiter. The restaurant was the kind that takes a pride in attentiveness and high standards, and selects its patrons from moneyed folk who never notice the wildness of its pricing. David ordered fish for both of them and champagne. Rose managed not to blink at his high-handedness. She was used to her escorts consulting her, even if they offered recommendations she could not reject for fear of hurting feelings. But then, David was an original.

It would have been so simple to bask in his comic tale-telling all evening. With Willi there was a gentle vein of humour, much smiling and warmth. David was outrageously funny. Her role was strictly that of audience.

A stray thought recurred. He reminded her of no one, she had been wrong. And it was hard to remember him as the intense young man who harangued the riverside crowd on the perils of polluting the world's oceans. That was, though, the only subject on which he did not regale her with witty anecdote. When she brought it up, he could not treat planet-saving with hilarity.

'Even now people pay only lip-service to the ideal,' he said. 'Governments, rich individuals, ordinary people who're not prepared to alter their habits significantly – none of them is willing to do enough to make a difference. They refuse to grasp that the natural balance has gone and very soon the situation won't be reversible.'

She licked sorbet from her spoon, hearing his words, marking the abrupt switch in tone from entertainer to fanatic. He was talking about the destruction of the rain forests, damage to the ozone layer, depletion of fish and fauna because of pollution of the waters of the earth, industry poisoning the air . . . And she was the audience, present only to applaud. Each attempt to say 'Yes, but . . .' or 'That's all very fine but how can we . . .' met with an impatient rebuff.

There was one tiny concession. 'Rose, I know what you're thinking. They say it to me often. If I'm committed to the seriousness of protecting the future of our world, how can I associate myself with something as inconsequential as perfume? Well, it's a fair question. My only answer is that the Devereux

249

name, and the position it gives me in the international business community, is an asset I use for the cause. Breaking away, I'd be merely another determined and outspoken individual struggling to be heard. As head of the House of Devereux, I can guarantee attracting attention to the issues.'

'And money.'

'Yes, Greenworld can't survive without money. Can you imagine what it costs to keep ships ploughing the seas to monitor threats to the purity of the oceans? Or what it costs to undertake the ecological research we do? It's beyond figures, Rose. And the value of what we can achieve is beyond price. The money must be found. Cajoled out of people who find their consciences easier because they support us. Twisted out of governments who need a spot of whitewashing. Grabbed wherever and whenever we can get it.'

Rose told him: 'Greenworld is always cagey about its finances, David. You must realize there are rumours about where it gets its supply.'

He did not wait for her question. 'Stupid rumours, Rose. We get it from sources that rely on our discretion. You know, it's a cockeyed world. We have to go grubbing around for donations for a cause of supreme importance while there are women in France who fritter 80,000 francs on a suit from Chanel or Yves St Laurent and then come to the House of Devereux asking us to create them an individual perfume. We don't come cheap: once the formula is finalized, a litre of fragrance costs around 20,000 francs. To these women – or, I should say, to the men who pick up their bills – this gross extravagance seems quite reasonable. But try asking them for a donation to Greenworld and you'll get nothing.'

A waiter interrupted his flow. When he had gone Rose took David up on his remark about being head of the House of Devereux. But he was back to joking, she could not draw from him anything definite about his future at the family firm. If David and his grandfather had decided to bypass his father and put control into David's hands, then it was being kept secret.

'We'll go elsewhere for coffee,' he told her. And it was a means of shutting down the conversation as well as showing her the Devereux house in the Bois de Boulogne.

The house had been bought by his great-grandfather. He pointed him out among silver-framed photographs clustering on a desk. Rose looked for a family likeness, something that linked David with the rest. But they were generally dark, usually with long solemn faces, rather heavy people like his father. In older age they stopped appearing ponderous and became distinguished. Maurice, his grandfather, looked particularly distinguished. But she could not believe David would achieve that. She trawled for him among the frames.

He guessed. 'You'll find me aged about thirteen. After that I took to dodging cameras.'

'Who's this?' She knew the answer.

He took up the photograph and put it into her hand. 'That's Andrée. She was the wife of my Uncle Claude, my father's brother. Rather beautiful.'

He lifted up another photograph, this time Andrée with her child. 'This is her daughter, Nicole. She was kidnapped from the château and murdered. You must have heard the story.'

'Yes, a terrible story.'

'Andrée never recovered. They sent her to a clinic in Switzerland but she drove everybody there mad by wandering around singing all night. Too disruptive, the clinic sent her home again.'

'She was an opera singer, wasn't she?'

'I didn't say she wasn't singing in tune. Apparently she had a thing about Gounod's *Faust* and kept giving them chunks of Marguerite. Nice stuff, but all the same. Oh, if you're not *au fait*, Marguerite's the one Faust falls in love with. She has his illegitimate child and is raised by the angels into heaven.' He put the photograph back in its place. 'Well, Andrée wasn't raised into heaven. At least, not like that. She killed herself, my uncle too.'

Rose said she understood it was an accident.

He shrugged. 'Oh sure, an accident. A wide road, no other

traffic and she goes tearing off the road at tremendous speed and smashes into a tree. The family don't believe it was an accident.'

A servant carried in a tray with their coffee and brandy. When he withdrew, David said: 'Andrée wouldn't accept the baby was dead. They prevented her seeing the body and consequently she refused to believe it was Nicole they buried.' He shook his head in wonderment. 'Do you realize, all of that happened before I was born, but it's such a familiar story I feel I lived through it too. When journalists write about us, it pops up every time, pretty well unrecognizable, but growing and growing.'

'The Curse of the Devereux?' And, self-deprecating: 'Well, you know what journalists are.'

'Did you know one from London called John Blair?'

'Did you?' Her cup shook as she set it in the saucer; the question was utterly unexpected.

'He sat where you're sitting now, Rose.' His eyes narrowed to slits. 'He was also writing about the company, only in his case for a British newspaper.'

She opened her mouth, behaved like a goldfish and shut it again. Then: 'I last saw him in the spring. When did he come here?'

David gave her an approximate date. 'I'm afraid he had a wasted journey. I think he was hoping to discover the bottom's fallen out of the perfume business. I had to tell him that, absurd or not, we're thriving.'

She knew she was looking odd, an explanation seemed necessary although not desirable. Lulled by her brandy she told David: 'John was killed, during a street demonstration in Spain. It's difficult to come to terms with that.'

'He was your lover?'

'We split up.'

'Then you have two separations to come to terms with.'

She managed a watery smile. They had hit a low note, a bad way to conclude what, on the whole, had been a jolly evening.

252

Ever since meeting David earlier in the day she had been pick-ing her way around the course John Blair's inquiries had taken, but she had hoped to reduce suspicion by not introducing his name. Having it flung at her like this was distressing. She did not want to share anything about him with David Devereux.

David said: 'But you must come to terms with them. Don't be like Tragic Andrée.'

'No danger, I can't sing,' she replied, with a shot at humour.

After a pause he said, making himself deliberately mysteri-ous: 'I'll tell you what I'm going to do when I'm at the helm, Rose. I'm going to do something my father refuses to do, some-thing he says mustn't be done for another thirty years.'

She was grateful for a change of subject. She raised an inquir-ing eyebrow.

He said: 'I'm going to put an end to this nonsense about locking up money in the name of Nicole Devereux. Andrée believed that one day her daughter would walk through the gates of the château and claim her inheritance.'

'Good heavens. And your uncle?'

'I suppose he agreed to it to humour Andrée. Anyway, it was arranged. My grandfather doesn't like to talk about it. I thought old people were fond of reminiscence, but he's very selective. Some things he ignores. No, he doesn't forget people. He goes to the graves, too often in my father's opinion. One thing they agree on, though: it would bring bad luck down on our heads if Nicole's money were to be touched.'

'But you, David? You're prepared to risk a further manifes-tation of the Curse of the Devereux?'

He warmed her with a wicked smile. 'You read too many newspapers, Rose. The curse has more to do with journalists than with me.'

The meeting was stormy. Maurice and David lined up together and Philippe attacked.

'Impossible,' he shouted, and brought a fist down on the table. 'We are *not* going along with this.'

Maurice tried to put up a defence but David leapt in. 'We can't prevent it but it isn't a bad thing anyway. He has his own name to consider, he won't be involved in anything that's detrimental to ours.'

Bitter, Philippe retorted that the last thing on the Italian designer's mind appeared to be the good name of the House of Devereux.

David said: 'We have to move with the times. There's no market value in being old-fashioned.'

Maurice could not decide whether to demur or nod in agreement; his head wobbled indecisively. But Philippe knew what he believed himself: 'Our business is built on the premise that we attain a high standard, in everything, and stick to it. No cutting corners. No diversification into areas other than the production of excellent perfumes. You're wrong, David. Our segment of the market is all about being old-fashioned. Going downmarket will ruin us.'

A pause while Philippe struggled with an anger that was straining to fever pitch. He had begun icily, treating David and Maurice like defiant boys who had done what they were warned against and were now in a mess. But Philippe had not been able to keep it up. His voice had risen and he banged the table. They were not a volatile family, he could not remember anyone banging a table during a business meeting.

David flopped back in his chair, a calculated way of settling his own tension. He infuriated Philippe by grinning at his grandfather. Maurice looked blank.

'Poor Father,' Philippe thought. 'He's too old for this sort of thing.' But he did not mean tussles over the business, what he meant was anything to do with it.

The Italian couturier with whom David, with Maurice's blessing, had done a deal was being wily. There were things he had failed to reveal to David and they made all the difference. Apart from the perfume bearing his own name, he was planning to launch a range of travel goods and women's underwear. Equally undesirable, at the same time he was to introduce a less expensive, which is to say less exclusive, range of clothes.

David said to Philippe: 'You're making it into a problem that doesn't necessarily exist. Now that we know about the other lines . . .'

'Knickers. Shopping bags.'

'Yes, all right, all *right*. Now that we know exactly what he has in mind we can prevent him using our name on the perfume bottles.'

Philippe looked to heaven to give him patience. 'How can you be so naive?' He encompassed his father in this, too. 'How can you? All he's ever wanted is the right to put Devereux on the bottles along with his own name. *That's* what he's been buying, our name. There's no hope we can wriggle out of it.'

David got as far as 'But . . .' before Philippe skimmed the contract across the table to him.

'Read it,' he snapped. 'Read it, which is what you should have done before you forced this situation upon us.'

Maurice stirred to say: 'We took a joint decision, Philippe. As we always do.'

The anger was out of control. Philippe sensed the words on his lips, heard them only as he spoke them. True words and wounding. 'We rubber-stamped a decision already taken by the pair of you. As we always do.'

He got up, unsteadily, and went out of the room. Nobody had ever banged a table. Nobody had ever walked out. Everything was wrong, irrecoverably wrong.

He reached the door of his office before retracing his steps and going upstairs to his room. His breath was fast and jagged. He saw his flushed face in the mirror above the mahogany chest. Everything burned. His skin. His flesh. The breath in his throat. Philippe sat down on the edge of the bed and waited for it to pass.

This had not happened to him before, he thought of himself as a fit man. In a minute or two it was easing. He poured a glass of water from the jug on the table and sat at the desk, sipping, wishing it cooler.

The day had begun with disturbing news. The detective had sent his monthly report. Like the earlier ones, it began with the man writing: 'Unfortunately I have as yet had no success . . .' But each time he reported progress of a sort. Today he was able to tell Philippe: 'As a result of placing the photograph in an advertisement in the press, a man has now contacted me suggesting that he knows the woman and is prepared to sell me information about her.'

The detective described a telephone call he received, a conversation that withheld the caller's identity and a meeting arranged for later that week. Philippe had tried to ring the detective to discuss the caller's credibility and how much, if anything, ought to be paid for his information. But the line was engaged. He had left the report in its envelope in his bedroom and gone down to the meeting with Maurice and David.

Back in his room, Philippe read the report again, a way of taking his mind off the scene downstairs. There were no nuances to pick at, no hints about the value of a meeting with the man who claimed he recognized Nicole Devereux. Philippe pushed the pages half-way into their envelope and went into the bathroom to freshen his face with cold water.

When he emerged, David was in the bedroom, his hand on the door knob. 'Are you all right, Father?'

Gruff, Philippe said he was fine. He felt confusingly grateful for the attention while disliking that sort of fussing. 'I'll be down directly.'

'No hurry, we can continue whenever you like.'

'I told you I'm fine.'

'We think you ought to see a doctor.'

This irritated Philippe because all they knew was that he had lost patience with them, they knew nothing of his shortness of breath, the tide of anxiety that engulfed him. With an effort he avoided a repetition of ill temper. 'Yes, perhaps I will. Let's go down.'

As he drew the door to behind them, he spotted the envelope on the table. He was relieved to see it undisturbed.

It was evening before he telephoned the detective and sanctioned payment, in stages, of several thousand francs if the informant appeared genuine.

'He'll want cash, of course,' said the detective.

'And I shall require receipts.' He cut off a sarcastic 'of course'. Because 'of course' he had no means of knowing whether the caller was a figment of the detective's imagination, a way of milking the client. Receipts proved nothing either way.

As if he were mind-reading, the detective said: 'If you didn't need total secrecy, you could come along and see him for yourself.'

'I shall rely on your judgement. Call me immediately after the meeting.'

But the meeting did not take place that week. It was delayed for a further week and by that time Philippe Devereux was in hospital.

EIGHTEEN

A cat was screaming in an alley beneath her Paris flat. Rose Darrow turned over in bed, resettled herself, turned back, gave up and got out of bed. Too much to drink, too much to think about. A bad night.

She flicked back the curtain and peered down. The cat screamed, unseen. She shivered. Just out of her sight something terrible was happening.

Rose went into the living room and uncapped a bottle of mineral water, the brief *pht* warning her it was flat. She did not care, she emptied it into a tumbler and gulped. It was exactly that time of night when everything seems worse than it reasonably could be. She stood there, listening to the night sounds of Paris: a faint whine of traffic a few streets away, electrical clicks from inside the flat, dying bubbles in her glass and the intermittent agony of a cat.

David Devereux had slipped away from her. She had failed to create the right moment to probe his link with Krieger in Prague, and she had let him skip away from the question of Greenworld's finances and his own contribution. It was inefficient and it was unlike her.

'But he threw John Blair at me,' she thought, defending herself against her own accusations. 'I wasn't ready for that, it changed everything.'

Then she blamed herself for seeking excuses, inadequate ones. 'No, the bit about John came later. Something – I don't know what but something – held me back. I did make opportunities to raise Krieger with him and to push him about Greenworld, but I didn't take advantage of them.'

Instinct, then. But what might he have done if she had persisted? Flounced out and left her with the bill? Refused to be drawn? Oh, what did it matter anyway? The point was she was no nearer understanding the intricacies of the House of Devereux.

She swallowed the rest of the water and decided to go back to bed, to put out of her mind everything but the need for sleep. As usual, there was a packed day ahead. A conference to look in on, a lunchtime interview with a writer, a backlog of mail, a meeting with a freelance journalist who promised an unmissable story worth her first issue.

But outside the bedroom door there was a cupboard and on impulse she whisked a camera from one of its shelves and hovered, in the soft light of a lamp, twisting it in her hands. Her fingertips stroked the lines scored on the surface. She rubbed a thumb over the bruised corner, where it had hit the ground.

'Why?'

The word was savage, loaded with all the questions about John Blair, his life with her and the manner of his death.

Then she plucked from the shelf the notebooks, the photographs, the bits and pieces that were what she had left of him. Anger took over from all the other jumbled emotions.

Her fascination with his Devereux story fluctuated from day to day but her anger at the loss and the waste was fixed. Whoever else came into her life, John Blair was a crucial, irreplaceable part of it.

For a long, long time she sat at the table reading his notes, staring at key words such as Ramírez, Gib, cover up and snow, with a concentration that suggested she believed concentration would force them to yield their meaning. Yet she penetrated no further than the transparent meaning she had shared with Ellie: John Blair's theory was that the Devereux art fund was used to launder drugs money.

Rose spread the photographs out. Without a magnifying glass the one of the French newspaper cutting was indecipherable, although previous examination showed it to be a court case from Marseilles featuring a petty thief called Deschamps. She could not place the old man emerging from the chauffeur-driven car, his hat threw shadow across his face. The naked young woman on the sandy beach and the two old men at the pavement café were equally strangers. Obviously, the blurred building was in the town where Blair died because that was his final shot.

The telephone rang. She jumped as though guilty, let it ring twice more before lifting the receiver.

'Rose?' A woman's voice was racked with sobs.

'Yes. Who's this?' An accent, but which?

'Oh, Rose, I need to talk to you.'

She got it then. 'Maria?' A little Spanish songbird, a waif-like beguiler phoning all the way from London in the middle of the night to cry on her shoulder.

Maria did not answer, she sniffled.

'Maria, tell me what's wrong.'

'There was a bomb . . .'

'Yes, I know. I was with you, remember?'

'It's different.'

'*Another* one.'

'No.'

Rose dragged at her hair with her free hand. Maria was hysterical, Maria had been drinking, Maria could probably keep this nonsense up for hours. Rose tried to calm her, to get her to focus on reality.

'Why don't you explain what you'd like me to do?'

'Rose, you don't understand.'

Quite possibly not, Rose thought. Aloud she said: 'Then tell me again, Maria. I'm listening.'

'No, no. The bomb, Rose. You remember the bomb?'

'Yes?'

Maria struggled on with her story, breaking off to snuffle and weep. It irritated Rose that the tale kept going full circle, to Maria's criticism of Rose's failure to understand. Rose did not argue, instead she mouthed objections into the silence of the Paris room.

'Rose, you say it was to do with the neighbours.'

'Oh, now hold on, I'm not accusing your neighbours of planting the bomb.'

'No, I don't mean . . . But you say it was because of the people who lived there before me. I mean *here* before me. Rose? Are you there?'

Reluctantly she confirmed she was.

'And the newspapers, Rose, they say it too. Everybody says it was because of that actress who married a politician.'

'That's right. The bombers thought he was living there. Their information was out of date, it often is.'

'No, no, no!' Maria's voice soared to a wail. Drunk or not, there was no mistaking the frustration, the pain, the fear.

Rose attempted to stem the panic. 'Look, Maria, it's over. It was awful and it was scary, but those people know they hit the wrong target. They won't bother you again.'

Rose heard an abandoned crying. She shouted down the phone, demanding Maria's attention. Then there was a pause before Maria recovered sufficiently to speak.

'Rose, *please*, you must believe me. They are trying to kill me. The bomb was in my car *because it was mine*.'

'Who are, Maria?'

In a broken voice. 'I don't know.'

'And why should anyone want to harm you?'

Again, higher and more desperate. 'I don't know.'

Rose reasoned with her but Maria retreated into hysteria, muddling up the story of the bomb blast with another one about being followed around London by strange men. When Rose pinned her down, Maria had enough. She yelled at Rose for not trusting her and hung up.

For five minutes Rose waited beside the telephone but it did not ring again. Then she went back to bed. Down below, the cat was still screeching.

When the last sob had shaken free of her body, Maria put Beethoven's *Fidelio* on her CD player, curled on her sofa, screwed up her reddened eyes and withdrew from the world.

She went in through the layers, losing her sense of time and place, reaching her core where life could not hurt her. Comforting warmth flowed over her, she relaxed, her head filled with the encouraging words of an inner voice. It promised she could not be harmed, she was successful, she need not be upset by inconsequential matters, she would thrive. The voice used her secret name. Maria hugged herself and mouthed the secret name.

Summer. The black shadows of kestrels on a yellow sweep of ground. Maria is looking through a schoolroom window, the birds themselves are out of her line of vision. The shadows go round, round, the birds free to leave but held by invisible threads. She thinks that if she could fly like a bird she would fly free.

The teacher shouts, makes her pay attention. Children are laughing at her. She is odd, different. They often laugh. Maria runs home ahead of them, alone. The kestrels circle above, she runs through the shadows, lifting her feet high to step delicately and not damage them.

That summer she visits the ruins on the hill. In the theatre cut in the red-gold rock, her whisper rings clear to the highest tier. Nobody is watching as she skips along the stage, whispers a verse of a song and throws her arms wide to embrace her audience. Then she runs to the head of the hill, to where it falls sheer away. Below her fly the kestrels. Twenty, two dozen of them, their wings drawing shadows across the land. She lies on her stomach on the cliff edge and looks down on their brown-gold feathers. Her arms reach forward into space, her fingers flex and she plays the kestrels like puppets on invisible strings.

Her mother scolds her and drags her back where it is safer. 'That one has no sense of danger,' her mother grumbles to a friend. But Maria is not upset. She has seen freedom and she means to make herself free.

Fidelio reached its climax. The Kensington room fell silent and Maria opened her eyes. The night had fled, she was revived and did not need sleep. She took out her writing pad, sat at her dining table and began a new letter to the man who never replied. After her usual greetings to him, her hopes that he was well, she jiggled the fountain pen, seeking words. Then she bent over the page and, in a rush, her thoughts became script.

I am a tight bud, holding in. Music releases me. I become a flower unfolding petals to the rhythm of my own sounds. I hear no other sounds. People say I move them but I keep them still and steal my strength from them. I take the strength to be free. Not for long: for a half-hour, for a song, for one moment of silence before I release them. My heart is a bird, my music sets it free.

She sucked at the pen and then wrote:

Writers snare me with words. They want to name parts, distribute praise and criticism. I have no interest in naming or praising or blaming. Artists are the same – they want to 'catch' the expressiveness of my voice in the tilt of an eyebrow, the line of my nose. I cannot be pinned like a butterfly to a board. Musicians, too – they fret that I know nothing of arpeggios and fugues. My singing is not an arrangement of terms, it is a shedding of pain, a blossoming of love.

In the clubs they know. They wait, with the forgotten meal, the broken sentence, the disregarded lover. I sing and the world changes. That is my gift to them. Peace.

She pulled at strands of her short dark hair, teasing them into a curl around her forefinger. For a little while she was thoughtful. Then she lay down the pen and left the letter unfinished.

Her day was busy. She drank coffee with a man she was wooing for a recording contract. Skipping lunch, she shopped for swinging silver ear-rings and shoes in her tiny size. Then she went to the television studio.

'Maria, love, could you just put a teeny bit more life into it?'

The producer demanded a flight of steps, the director required her to skip down them on to the stage. She went back up and skipped again, for the fourth time.

'Ye-es, all right,' the director called grudgingly, realizing he would get no better from her. 'All right, everybody?'

Grunts of assent. Maria stood, feeling *de trop*, while technicalities were discussed. Someone had a problem with a faulty lead, or a light bulb or something. They were taking no notice of her, far more interested in the mechanics than in a singer guesting, as they put it, on an afternoon show. Maria sat down on the bottom step, wrapped her arms about her knees, tipped her head on one side and waited for life to resume.

Winter. Rain is slashing the coast. Water rushes from the mountains, thrusting roads and bridges from its path. She is in a car, hitching with tourists, pretending her home is a coast town. All the tourists have cars, smart ones, lots of money.

'Bloody hell,' the driver says, putting a hand to his mouth. 'The fucking road's gone.'

Through urgent windscreen wipers the three of them can see slurry sliding over the edge of a precipice. The rest is a miasma of silver shapes and water.

The other young man, the one called Keith, says: 'Have we got room to turn round?'

'Are you kidding?'

'Well, what are we supposed to do?'

'How do I know? It doesn't teach you this in the bloody *Highway Code*.' The driver turns to Maria in the back seat. 'I thought you said it would be all right.'

She makes a face. Yes, she said it but she has not been down this road before. She knows the village the giant squashed into the crevice, she knows the mountain town her parents moved to when she was growing up, but she does not know the coast nor the way to it.

When she fails to answer, the driver bangs the steering wheel with his fist and shouts. 'Fucking hell! We come here for the sun and we get stuck up a mountain in a raging fucking torrent. I'll have that tourist company for this. It never said nothing about this in the brochure.'

'No, that's right, it never,' says Keith.

They sit in quiet petulance while the windscreen steams up under their breath and white water crashes on to the bonnet from a rock rearing beside them. On the other side there is nothing, not for hundreds of feet down.

'You want me to reverse it?' asks Keith.

'You kidding? How are you gonna do that? You can't see nothing out the back, it's worse than this lot.'

'Yeah, all right, but there's a road out the back and that's more than we've got out the front.'

'Well, you just watch you don't reverse us over the fucking edge, OK?'

Keith dashes round and gets in the driver's door. The driver kneels on the back seat beside Maria, saying he will guide Keith. They are both drenched. Maria squeezes into the corner to keep away from his wetness. Every time he turns his head to warn Keith, spots of water flick off his hair and sparkle her dark clothes.

They arc round a hairpin bend, discuss whether there is room to turn the car and decide not. 'There's a better bit further back,' says Keith. He is managing well and not afraid to go on.

'Yeah, all right. But you want to watch out for some stuff on the road, mud and that.'

He gives Keith inch-by-inch directions to steer between the scree and the edge of the precipice. His hand is smoothing Maria's thigh, its warmth penetrating the cloth of her skirt. She cannot move away and so she lifts his hand. It dives beneath her skirt, stroking her skin, each stroke going further than the previous one. She clamps her thighs together, struggles to tear his hand away. He is talking to Keith, all the time, as though nothing is happening except a car teetering along a shattered mountain ledge while wind and rain conspire to throw it off.

His hand is rough, his short thick nails are ragged and his skin calloused. His hand tears into her tender smoothness, fumbling its way, separating her legs. She clamps them again, wanting to give way, *not* wanting to, but his hand is between them, kneading, working its way up to where the hair begins and she is eagerly damp.

The car skids, losing grip on mud. The back slews and then

the front end swings out. The hand grabs at Maria's flesh, nails gouging.

'Jesus Christ!' says Keith. And then, anxious to dump the blame elsewhere: 'Are you looking out for me or what?'

'It's mud. I told you there was mud. Take it slower and don't swing the wheel about.' His grip on Maria slackens, the nails stop digging but he pushes further between her legs.

Keith mutters and reverses away from the edge.

Maria, resisting, struggling to resist, struggling against the feeling that she does not want to resist, feels the hand pinch the inside of her left thigh. She bears it at first which makes him do it harder until she gives in and lets him force her legs apart. His fingers are on the damp crotch of her knickers, then they hook at elastic and slide inside to her sticky warmth. She is leaning back in the corner of the seat, her eyes shut and her head turned away as though she is looking at the rain streaming over the pane. He is talking to Keith, all the time.

She feels the fingers searching among her hair, spreading her tender pink flesh, discovering the way to the heat within her. He thrusts into her without kindness. The jagged nails nick her, sending out thin spiky pains that she enjoys. Then he hurts her, pinching all the soft sensitive parts. She leans into the corner of the car and she lets him do it. He does not look at her, his eyes are on the road and he is talking to Keith.

Around the bend they are sheltered from the wind. The rain seems less now that it is no longer whipping them. The men decide they have sufficient room to turn the car around and head back to the top of the mountain. The one who felt her is leaning on the back of the front passenger seat, discussing everything with Keith. They have given up asking her for advice or directions, what she told them before was wrong.

She pulls her skirt down to cover her legs. Her knickers feel uncomfortable, wet and dislodged, but she will not hitch them up with Keith looking her way. When they decide to turn the car, the other man stands outside and directs Keith. Maria gets out too.

'Right,' Keith shouts against the roar of the rain. 'You stand on that side, Maria, and watch I don't get too close to that.' He means a spot where the edge of the road has crumbled.

She backs off a few yards. He has to move the car in the other direction first, and while the two men are engrossed in that, she begins the long trudge downhill to the coast.

It takes her two days. On the second one she is seen by a woman at a *finca* that has become a foreigner's holiday home. The woman, a housekeeper, is in the garden looking at the damage the storms have wrought. She gives Maria food and a shower, and makes her son drive Maria the rest of the way to the town. Maria is lucky a second time: that same day she talks the owner of an English bar into giving her a job as a singer.

To get the job she adds several years to her age and pretends she has previously worked at a bar in another town. The owner shows her a room she can sleep in until she finds somewhere of her own. Her singing is terrible and she realizes she will lose the job. She makes plans to move on.

In the television studio in London, the light bulb had been swapped or the lead changed, and the crew were ready to continue.

'Maria, love, can we do that bit where you make a joke with the band?' The director knew the producer liked those 'guest-ing' to contribute a joke, although the director was not sure what was amusing. He adjusted his granny glasses and beamed encouragingly. 'That crack about the drummer's bald patch would do nicely.'

Maria got up from the bottom stair and smiled back. She recited the line to prove she had learned it.

'Great, love. Now can you go over there? Yes, to the left and . . . Right, that's it, love. Stop there. That's fine. Start walking from there and say the line as you go. OK? OK, everybody?'

The nonsense went on most of the afternoon. Maria posed and walked and ran and tried to make a pathetic joke sound like a spontaneous quip. She did not sing but mimed to a recording of one of her songs. The whole experience was divorced from reality, and yet it was the reality of the world she desired. She had done a lot of laughing at pathetic jokes and flattering a man in granny glasses to get herself on the show.

From the television studio she went home. The mess caused by the bomb had been cleared but the garden wall was not rebuilt nor the sapling replaced. She let herself into her flat and stood, her back against the door, ears cocked. All day she had felt followed, each time she came home she suspected someone was there before her.

The tick of a clock. Nothing else. Maria went through to her living room, kicked off her shoes and sat down at the dining table. She wrote some concluding lines to her letter and signed it with her secret name.

They had gone on for years, these letters. A friend, when she was working in Barcelona, told her about him. He was one of hundreds in a Moroccan prison, abandoned there for political reasons that were, to the friend and therefore Maria, obscure.

'If you can write songs, Maria, then I'm sure you can write letters.' The woman gave her an address, a description of him, a smudgy photograph taken years before his arrest. 'They can't write back, mind,' the friend revealed once Maria had promised. 'Think of it as a lifeline.'

The lifeline was spinning out across the years and, no, there were no replies. She wrote to him from Barcelona and from London, queueing for her stamps and casting her messages into the void of his silence. No one told her how he lived or when he died.

As she had run out of stamps, she did not mail the letter that day. She left it on the table, its envelope beside it, and took her taxi to the club. The journey was smooth, she was there early. Before doing her make-up or taking her dress from the cupboard, she wrote down a verse of a new song.

> My heart is a bird.
> When I sing it flies free.
> My soul soars.

Where are the words
To tell of my joy?

Then she lay the pad aside and opened the cupboard door.

NINETEEN

When Rose Darrow walked into Ramírez's office in Marbella, the first thing she noticed was John Blair's lap-top computer. Ramírez had denied ever having seen it, he had denied ever having any contact with John Blair.

'Very nice,' said Rose, going up to it and smoothing her hand over the case. 'A friend of mine owned one very like that.'

Her sarcasm was not wasted. Ramírez moistened his lower lip with the tip of his tongue. 'Look,' he said, nervousness in word and gesture. 'I don't know what you want but . . .'

She snapped back at him. 'Yes you do.' A finger jabbed at the computer. 'I want that and I want the truth.'

He brought off one of those neat Latin shrugs, a comment on her audacity in demanding either.

She pressed him. 'I asked you on the telephone about John Blair and his computer.'

He was not ready to give in yet. 'A woman's voice on the telephone? How was I to know whether you were who you said you were?'

Feeble enough but she had to allow him an escape route if she was to win help rather than antipathy. 'Well, now you do know, let's go over the ground again.'

Ramírez was more or less what she anticipated: young, cocksure, vain, ambitious. If he proved difficult she could dangle the prospect of freelance work for her Euromag. He proved difficult and she dangled it.

The difficulty arose because he was drawing a line between information he regarded as John Blair's, and therefore available to her, and what he ferreted out himself and refused to share.

'This is beginning to sound like a story we'd want to buy,' she said. It did not but no matter, he had not played fair with her.

Ramírez did not fall for it, maybe he had been cheated by foreign journalists before. He took a lot of persuading before he finally accepted he could not shake her free. Rather than spill out details of his own work, he let himself be guided back to the John Blair affair.

'He came here one day,' he admitted. 'He walked in here the same way you did. A journalist in Madrid gave him my name. He looked tired, he'd driven a long way. We went out for a beer while he told me what he wanted. Everybody knows about our drugs problem – British gangs bringing hashish in from Morocco on its way to London, South American cocaine dealers, Turkish heroin gangs . . . John was hoping to make a connection with a big French company, although he was vague about which drug was involved. He thought the French people launder profits through Gibraltar, using a company there as a front. Well, if they do it will be hard to prove because of the banking secrecy laws on the Rock. He asked me for contacts in the drugs scene.'

'Do you have contacts?'

'Sure. I've written several pieces about drugs, the journalist in Madrid told him that. But I don't know of the French link he was looking for.'

'Give me the names you gave John.'

Ramírez declined. 'He didn't speak to them.'

'You once assured me he didn't speak to you either. The names, please.'

He recited two names. 'But he didn't get in touch. One was in hospital and the other was away on business.'

She was inclined to believe him this time because the names did not feature in John Blair's notes. But she demanded more. 'Addresses? Phone numbers?'

Ramírez provided them. Rose, writing them down, looked up sharply at the second address. It was a small inland town. A nothing sort of place. The place where John Blair was gunned down.

'Well, now.' She flipped her notebook shut. 'Your car or mine?'

He was horrified. 'Hey, now hold on. I've got work to do.'

'And I'll pay you handsomely for it.'

'Rose, I can't walk through those streets with you.'

'Afraid of getting shot? Or afraid your contacts in the drugs world won't like you helping me? Both, perhaps?'

'I don't want to . . .'

His face told her the rest. She finished the sentence for him. 'Get involved? Señor Ramírez, you *are* involved. How long will it take us to get there?'

The coast road through the architectural disaster that is the Costa del Sol was treacherous and crowded, as usual. Flabby north Europeans overlapped the stools of English bars and watched the traffic trundle by. Shop staff ripped out window displays and changed them for fresh ones with the same goods at higher prices. Restaurants were also coping with inflation by hiking prices and wondering at the fall in customers. The town was busy. It had been busy for years milking the foreigners and, now the free fall of cash was drying up, it was busy wondering why.

She stopped at a traffic light. A gaggle of old people with Birmingham accents limped across the road. Winter breaks in the sun for pensioners. Long-stay holidays at cheap rates. She could practically see the advertisements that lured them.

Suddenly she asked: 'What places did John visit on the coast?'

Ramírez did not bother to break off watching the gyrations of a lithe young window dresser. 'He was here, in Marbella. He came to my office.'

'But did he say he'd been down on the beach?' She was addressing the back of his head.

'No. I told you, he walked in looking tired out from a long drive.'

'And you went to a bar together.'

'Close to the office, not near the beach.'

The light changed and Rose drove on. She willed herself to enter John Blair's mind, discover how he went about the inquiry. Did he truly drive straight to Ramírez's office? Was it not more likely he stopped, if only to get his bearings, maybe ask directions? All right, he may have given Ramírez the impression he drove without a break but that did not make it true. It was probably not. He was not a man to divulge more than was necessary. If Ramírez ran away with the wrong idea, he might not have corrected him.

And if John Blair was cautious about how much he revealed to Ramírez, then she should be too. She decided against flashing the photograph and asking him to identify the beach where it was taken. Instead, she parked near shops, left him in the car while she showed the picture to a man in a newsagent's.

'Sí, San Pedro,' he said, a nicotined finger indicating the roofline, the hill, and then pointing the way to San Pedro.

Rose bought a copy of the *El País* and went back to Ramírez. San Pedro de Alcántara was straight ahead on the coast road.

On the way they talked about the tourist trade and drugs, about the improbability of a link between a French perfume-maker and drugs, about Blair's conviction that there was indeed a link and Ramírez's mystification. Over and over, without either of them giving away more than they had already admitted knowing.

'I need petrol before we head inland,' she said, and went past the turn and into San Pedro.

Ramírez sighed. 'It's a very long way, Rose. Why don't you make the journey another day?'

But she dared not. She did not want him losing interest or making telephone calls to warn people she was on her way, or any of the other things he might get up to if they did not push on immediately. Having begun with the advantage of surprise, she was loath to lose it. It was a juggling act, trying to impress him with her determination to reach the inland town while also checking up on what John Blair did on the coast.

Once the tank was full she surprised Ramírez again, saying: 'I have a feeling he came here.'

'To San Pedro? No, I'm sure he didn't come this way.'

She drove towards the sea, conscious of his bewilderment.

She said: 'It won't take a second, I just want to look at the beach.'

This time he followed when she left the car. She kept an eye on the building the man in the newsagent's pointed out as a distinguishing feature and when she had it lined up so it looked much as it did in the photograph, she came to a halt and stared about. A mountain rising above a red-roofed town, a curve of beach although, in November, no sunbathing nude. A road beyond the beach.

Give or take a few feet, she was where John Blair took his photograph. There was no café, it was not an idle shot between sips of a cooling drink. It seemed he walked purposely to this spot and aimed the camera.

At her shoulder Ramírez said: 'You see, Rose? There's nothing here. When the sun shines there are many people without their clothes on but today there are none.'

They began the long, long climb into the mountains. Up past foreigners' villas pimpled with burglar alarms; up where reddish rock thrust through brittle greenery; up and away from English pubs and English prostitutes who advertised their services in the back pages of *Sur*.

The road she travelled was a writhing snake, flinging back on itself, rearing and coiling up the mountainside. Edges crumbled above rocky gorges and the ghosts of earlier fallen roads.

Once, Ramírez encouraged her to stop, to see how the grey arm of the Rock reached out for Africa, how the hideous hotel blocks joined the old fishing villages into a linear city of seventy miles, how fast and how high they had climbed to escape the ersatz Spain of the coastal strip.

Higher, she stopped again, keen to see where the Pillars of Hercules held up the sky, thinking about myths ancient and modern. Ramírez said: 'That's Morocco. The Rif mountains.'

And as soon as her head filled with amateur productions of *The Desert Song*, as soon as she saw her uncle swashbuckling about on stage to the 'Song of the Rifs', Ramírez was telling her about the present-day threat.

'They grow hashish there. Most of what's sold on the streets of Britain comes from those mountains. They smuggle it across in speedboats, hide them in marinas like the ones at Estepona and Puerto Banus. It goes north in lorry loads of fruit and veg.'

'You talked to John Blair about all this?'

'I told you, I couldn't help him. I've never come across anything that ties in with what he was hoping to hear.'

She restarted the engine and drove into the wild emptiness of the *serranía*. Ramírez made the occasional remark, emphasizing his reluctance to go where they were going and his inability to assist John Blair. Rose was only half-aware of him. In her head, a different discussion was going on.

She was weighing the chances of the photograph being a random snapshot of a pretty woman against those of her being germane to the Devereux drugs inquiry. Could she be a drugs courier or dealer? Off duty, as it were, because there were precious few means of concealing a cache of illegal drugs or anything else, undressed as she was and with only a towel and a tiny beach bag.

Was she connected to the Devereux company or family? Rose thought she did not look Spanish, or maybe she thought Spanish women shied from stripping off with the abandon of northerners. If they did not have a different attitude to nudity, they certainly had a different one to the sun.

Fleetingly, she pictured John Blair somewhere undefined, laughing at the amount of mental effort she was putting into it. What did the woman's identity matter, or the reason for the photograph, or the eagerness with which he delved into the Devereux business? How important were they in the long run? They were hardly a matter of life and death.

Or they ought not to have been.

Rose realized she had missed a question. Ramírez was awaiting a response. She changed gear as the gradient changed, admitted: 'Not listening, try again, please.'

'I said what do you expect to do when we arrive? You don't

tell me your plans, Rose. How can I be of help if I don't know the plans?'

He had not shown any concern about this before. Rose doubted he particularly wanted to help, she guessed he wanted to avoid trouble.

'I think,' she began slowly, not sure where the sentence would run, 'we should take a look at the two men you say John didn't meet.'

'No, he didn't. But I don't know whether they are there, this might be a wild goose.'

My life is a flock of wild geese, she thought. But said aloud: 'I don't think so. I feel lucky. I feel certain it's going to be all right.'

'That's what John . . .'

She let the silence stretch. Then: 'I wonder at what moment he stopped feeling lucky.'

Beside her Ramírez turned his head away to stare across infinite miles of unpeopled mountain. In the furthest of far distances a yellowish sky leaned down against the earth, there were clouds that might have been mountains and mountains that might have been clouds. A landscape for dreaming, fantasizing about life without limits. High above the humdrum, raised above the petty constraints of ordinary life, it freed the mind and the imagination. Yes, a wonderful place for day-dreaming, unless you had troubled thoughts. Rose noticed his shoulders hunch in a shudder beyond his control.

They reached the no place town late, in the lull between the shops closing and people flooding on to the streets for the *paseo*. Any Andalusian town: scents of warm olive oil and petrol fumes, geraniums tumbling from window sills, dogs lounging in shadow, disorganized building work, anarchic car parking, shop girls dressed like film stars and young men with eyes only for skittish motorcycles.

Rose stepped out of the shadow of a narrow street. Sun sloped across a dusty square, a tall building rose opposite. And her ears were full of imagined sounds, her eyes were inventing a mêlée of people and, right in front of her, a figure was jogging the elbow of a man taking a photograph, the camera was forced upwards, staccato sounds of gunfire were echoing off buildings and the photographer was falling, a rush of people were kicking the camera over the ground as they fled gunfire. When they were gone, a figure lay in the dust.

Rose passed a hand over her eyes, swallowed hard, pretended to be searching in her bag for her sunglasses. But as her eyes went to the ground, they instinctively sought bloodstains, fragments of plastic chipped from a camera, clues to what happened.

Being there was shocking. It scared her with her own mortality and it made sense of what had been incomprehensible at the ceremony of Highgate: John Blair was dead.

Ramírez touched her arm. She leaped. But he was not gauging the depth of her feelings, he was looking obliquely across the market square. 'That bar's the best one. We could do with a drink.'

She tried to reply but her voice was absent. She sat near the window of the bar, had a clear view of the square and sipped brandy. When Ramírez disappeared into the background to make a telephone call, Rose looked at the photograph of the woman on the beach.

A nude young woman on a towel by her beach bag. A road. A mountain. Fly-on-the-wall stuff, no one in the photograph taking notice of the photographer, probably unaware he was there. The woman's eyes were closed and the three figures on the road ignored her, intent on where they were going.

A press photographer's trick, perhaps? Pretending to concentrate on one subject, he had stolen a shot of another? Rose took the photograph into the street for better light and studied the figures passing to and fro on the road in the background. And then she understood.

Ramírez was at their table, watching her. She tossed the print down in front of him.

'John took it, Paco.'

'At San Pedro. So this is why we went there.'

277

'I couldn't believe he took time off from an assignment to photograph a sunbather.'

'She could be somebody he knew.'

Impatient, she shook her head. 'Do you recognize any of the people?' She studied him closely as he scrutinized the figures before saying no.

He said: 'He drove here immediately he left my office. If he took this shot, it was before I met him.'

Putting it away in her bag she said: 'Supposing he stopped in San Pedro on the way here, as we did.'

But he was adamant. 'No, he came straight here.'

'I see.' Rose looked at him hard. 'Why didn't you tell me before? On the telephone weeks ago? Or today when I insisted on coming here?'

He gestured to the waiter for another beer. 'What does it matter?'

She fought down a frightening degree of annoyance. 'Because as you brought him here, you know what happened to him. You were with him, weren't you?' She meant when he was killed.

Ramírez understood. 'Look, Rose, it was difficult . . .'

'*Difficult?* He was killed. Shot. Over there. Look at it. Three feet from the pavement, right in front of the pink building. That's the place, isn't it? That's where my friend was shot. And all you can say is that it was difficult.'

He eased back his chair, away from her anger. He quietened her with frantic hands criss-crossing the air between them. 'No, no. You mustn't say this, Rose. It was dangerous. That's the word I want, dangerous.'

The rest of her anger was expelled in a sigh. She felt foolish at having picked him up on the misuse of a word. The issue was not the quality of his English, it was the degree of his duplicity.

She made another, calmer, attempt. 'It isn't the word that's important, it's the way you've misled me. Ever since I telephoned you from London when they sent me John's things, you've been obstructing me with half-truths. Helping but not helping.'

She offended him. Her pointless outburst changed the atmosphere, and her measured criticism did nothing to rectify it. Little by little, she had been building his co-operation, or at any rate his compliance, and now she had spoiled it. How stupid, how incompetent, but this was not a normal inquiry. Possibly it was not journalism at all, her personal involvement precluded objectivity. The hurt ran too deep.

Paco Ramírez set his jaw in a proud determined line and looked past her through the window. Shadow divided the square, the near half was dull while the other glowed. *Sol y sombra*. People walked about, a couple of cars drove through, sparrows picked around tables for crumbs until a cat slithered between chair legs. Rose wished to say something to make matters all right again but did not know what. She decided to leave it for him to gather up the threads.

He continued to stare out. She declined to notice. But it was ridiculous, she thought, to have her day peter out with a sulky young man in a bar. They ought to be outside, chasing up the leads that drew her to the town. She wondered how long he could keep this up.

He touched her forearm and whispered: 'The car.'

Rose leaned closer to him, her eyes on a big black car as she listened for the confiding breath of his words. She had been wrong, confusing silent concentration with sullen objection.

He said: 'This is one of the men John Blair hoped to meet. He was away on business. John never met him, I promise you.'

A short, solid man was struggling out of the car. Elderly, greyhaired and dressed in black, he looked like a prosperous businessman in any southern European city. A pillar of the Church, possibly, a mayor, anything worthy and wealthy. But Antonio López's business was drugs.

López went into a house. Once he was out of sight Ramírez beamed at Rose: 'I thought we might see him if we waited here.'

'Does he live there?'

'No, but his mother does. He calls to see her and then he goes up the hill to his house.'

'We could follow him.'

'We wouldn't see anything. There are security gates, dogs patrolling the grounds.'

'Well, I want a closer look at that car, anyway. Do you know the number?'

'No.'

He stayed where he was while she strolled past the car, apparently pausing to hunt for something in her bag before haring back to the bar.

He was grinning as she rejoined him. 'That was really good, Rose. You were like a woman who'd forgotten something.'

'That *was* the idea.' She wrote the car number in her notebook, added a couple of points. Then: 'Paco, what makes you certain López was away on the day John was killed?'

'That's what the company told the press. He's one of the owners of the factory whose strikers were causing the trouble. It's his legitimate business, the cover for his real money-making. The offices are along there, to the right. The strikers were outside, backed up by political activists from all over the region. You must understand there were several hundred people here.'

'But apparently Señor López wasn't. Where was he?'

A lift of the shoulders. 'The strikers demanded he meet them, they were told he was away.'

She went on a different tack. 'Were you beside John all the time?'

'No, we split up. When the shooting began I ran into a café. We'd said we'd meet up there when we'd finished.' He was reluctant to continue.

Quietly she pleaded. 'I must know.'

'Everybody in the café was very excited. There were rumours about a number of people being wounded, then a man said several were shot dead. Nobody knew what to believe. The shooting stopped but the stories were growing and growing, people were making things up. I decided to go out. There was a lot of shouting and milling around, but no evidence of dead or injured people. I assumed the police fired into the air which is what they later claimed.'

'Where was he?'

'They'd moved him. I came round a van and he was on the pavement. Three or four people were fussing over him. There was a lot of blood, he was obviously dead.' An uncomfortable pause before he burst out, defensively: 'Look, Rose, there was nothing I could do.'

'You left.'

'There was nothing I could do.'

For a minute or two they sat without speaking, her mind empty of thought. Then she asked: 'You've never believed the police did it, have you?'

'No.'

'Then who?'

He tipped his head towards the big black car in the square. 'I suspect he was warned John was asking questions.'

'But . . .' She did not go on with it although the explanation was flawed. López was widely known to be involved in drugs, the journalist she was with was one among many who knew. Why should it concern López if another of the tribe learned about it?

Floundering, unsatisfied, she went back to the beginning. 'Paco, are you absolutely sure John didn't succeed in proving a connection between the Devereux family and drugs?'

'Perfectly sure. One of the last things he said to me was that he had a feeling he was wasting his time.'

She pounced. 'Hold on. He said he felt lucky.'

'He said that too but that was on the way. When he got here and saw the demonstration he changed his mind. He said: "This isn't the way I want it. I have a feeling I'm wasting my time." '

They left the bar and went down the square. Ramírez showed her the place the body was found, a few yards to the right of the spot where she calculated the final photograph was taken.

Her questions came like gunfire. 'What was happening immediately before the firing started? Who were the people near him? Did you see the police shooting? Where were they standing? How did you get hold of the camera?'

He picked up the last one first. 'The camera? The strap was around his wrist. I unhooked it. All his other stuff was in my car and I knew if I didn't take the camera somebody would steal it.'

'Yet you didn't get the film developed.'

'No, but he said he'd put a new film in and we hadn't stopped on the way so I knew he hadn't photographed anything until he was here.'

Rose deduced that, for a journalist, Paco Ramírez was unwisely fond of making assumptions. For one thing, he was happy to assume the factory spokesman was telling the truth when he denied López was in town. She resurrected one of her questions. 'The shooting. What happened before it?'

His description was vivid. Strikers parading with placards outside the company's offices. Groups of political supporters orchestrating chants. Hotheads drowning them out with their own more urgent demands accompanied by threats. Police stamping around and fingering their weapons. And faces pressed to the first-floor windows of the offices.

Rose said: 'But not López? You're convinced of that?'

'Completely. I've met the man, I'd know him. No, there was a woman up there with López's brother who owns the other half of the business.'

'And deals in drugs too?'

'Strange if he didn't but there isn't any proof. The brother opened the window and came on to that balcony. That's when the guns were fired. Of course, he dashed inside. Now don't push me for details of what came next, Rose, because I was running like hell for the café.'

Without a word she set off for the café, Ramírez padding behind her. He skipped a couple of steps and caught up. 'Rose, I don't know what you expect to see . . .'

They were outside the building where the strikers had massed; they were passing the place where Ramírez said he found the body; they were at the spot where John Blair was shot. Ahead of them was the café, an uninspiring sort of place with a window on to the square. Rose stopped directly in front of the window.

Tables were arranged in the café window, in fine weather they flowed out over the paving. She asked: 'Was it warm, the day of the demonstration?'

'Warm?' He frowned at the absurdity of the question. Southern Spain. Autumn. Of course it was warm.

'Were there tables out here?'

'I don't remember. What difference does it make?'

'I'm trying to picture it, everything.'

She wanted to understand what he had seen from inside. People at outside tables might have leapt to their feet to see what was happening or taken cover indoors and grabbed the best viewpoints before Ramírez got there.

He helped her piece it together. 'When I heard the shots, I was over there talking to a couple of strikers.'

'Where did you think the shots were fired from?'

He pointed. 'That's where the police were. As you see, I was between them and the demonstrators. The police were staying back, or most of them were. There was a kind of corridor separating them and the demonstrators, and a lot of other people – journalists and ordinary people – were in that corridor.'

He said there were about a dozen shots. He had looked behind him, saw police running forwards, guns in their hands. 'I was between them and the target, it wasn't a good place to be.'

'No, I think I'd have run too.'

She also thought that from inside the café he could not see where John Blair fell; neither could he see the body carried away to the spot where he found it. In so far as she could test his story, he was telling the truth.

Down the square a door opened, a man in a dark jacket got into a black car and drove away. Ramírez drew her attention to it but Rose refused to pursue López to the house with the patrolling dogs and the security fences. She preferred to talk to the police.

'It's all right,' she added, 'you needn't come.'

He was relieved. A dark fear disappeared from his eyes. 'You needn't tell them I'm here.'

She left him in a bar while she traced a policeman Ramírez said might be willing to talk and had something to say. Rose lied about writing a profile of John Blair because he was a famous British journalist, and claimed it was essential to have details of his death.

There was always a gamble, paying someone to talk, that cash influenced what they said. But the man's account tallied with Ramírez's in all important respects: he described a similar scene, a dozen shots and the discovery of the body at the same place.

'Firing into the air was necessary,' he said, 'because the demonstrators refused to disperse.'

She avoided challenging the validity of the tactics, afraid of alienating him, but wondered aloud what the demonstrators had been doing that called for such measures.

'Not the strikers,' he explained. 'The political elements attached to the strikers. They caused the trouble. We had intelligence that they intended to turn the strikers' protest into something fiercer. A riot was threatened.'

'Were any of them armed?'

'I speak only for myself, but I saw no weapons. One officer believes he saw a man in the crowd raise a gun.'

'Can he describe him?'

'Oh, yes, a dark-haired young man in a dark jacket. Average height, average this and average that. What kind of description shall we call this?'

Rose conceded with a wry smile. She probed about the police inquiries into the death. They were far from complete but she gained the impression they would be allowed to run into the sand. The police did not wish to admit responsibility but had no evidence that anyone else fired shots. The bullet came from a gun of the type the police carried.

Careful not to criticize, she left unasked the obvious questions about comparing the fatal bullet with those fired from police guns. Each barrel leaves distinguishing marks, bullets can be attributed to individual weapons.

The police officer looked regretful. 'A ricochet, a very sad incident but . . .' He ended with a shrug that underlined that a journalist who gets involved in the rough and tumble of public disorder runs certain risks.

'We made extensive inquiries,' he said, although she doubted that extensive was accurate. 'Nobody saw Señor Blair fall, nobody saw a shot fired at him.'

So much for police work. That left pathology. Distasteful as it was, Rose begged to see the pathologist's report.

If you are President of the United States of America, you expect every detail of illness and death to be published. If you lead a public life in other countries, you allow for a degree of exposure. And victims of violent death have from earliest times forfeited the right to privacy. Corpses used to go on display for wounds to be inspected: the Romans put Julius Caesar on show, and a physician announced that only one of his twenty-three wounds was fatal. On one level, Rose did not believe her request was reasonable but on another she was determined not to leave town without getting access to the pathologist's findings. Within the hour a document was in her hands.

There are people who suppose getting shot is neat. They are taken in by those old-time Westerns, those television thrillers with the high body counts but no agony of splintered bone and ripped flesh or life flooding away on a red tide. The Kennedy stuff should have taught them about the comparative sizes of entry wounds and exit wounds, about the mess a bullet makes of a human body. Even so, they go on thinking getting shot is neat.

The bullet that killed John Blair was not a ricochet. It was a direct hit and it was fired at close range.

TWENTY

'That's funny,' said Joelle, without meaning to speak aloud.

'What is?' Rose Darrow was half-hearted in her interest, her mind on Krieger. He had said yes but now he was saying no to each date she proposed for them to continue.

'This.' Joelle was holding up a German magazine.

'It's months out of date. See?'

Joelle gave her a pitying look. 'I know. It's meant to be out of date. I'm going through the back numbers for an article Steve wants to reread.'

'And?'

'This picture. I think I saw it the other day.'

Rose went over, determined to be good-natured about the interruption. Joelle was a chirpy dogsbody, a rarity and a treasure. So what if she was being tiresome for once? Rose leaned over her shoulder and looked at the photograph of a young woman. 'Who is she?' the title asked. It was an advertisement.

'Who is she?' Joelle also translated the lines beneath the picture. 'If you think you recognize her, please telephone this number.'

'You think you know her? Ring the number, maybe there's a reward.'

'No, I don't think I actually know her, I think I saw her photograph the other day. If not this identical picture, a similar one.'

'Young woman with vacuous gaze and long black curly hair? Could be half a generation. She's a type, that's all.'

Joelle screwed up her elfin face, thinking hard. 'It's going to drive me crazy until I remember.'

Rose was back at her desk when Joelle yelped. 'Got it! The one I saw had cropped hair.' She began scrabbling through newspapers on a shelf. 'Right, this is it. Look. Don't you see the resemblance?'

She was all bouncing excitement, eager for Rose's response, pushing the magazine and the newspaper towards her, demanding her agreement. 'Oh, you must be able to see it!'

Rose did not, she could not even concentrate on seeking a likeness. All she saw was a very familiar face watching her from the foreign page of *Paris Soir*.

'Joelle, give me that.'

Her tone snuffed out Joelle's excitement. 'What is it, Rose? What's wrong?' And then: 'Oh God, you didn't know her, did you?'

Joelle lay the newspaper on the desk in front of Rose. Rose cupped her mouth in her hand. A one-column picture, a face, what journalists call a mugshot, on a foreign page, a few lines encapsulating a tragedy, a headline that distilled it further: 'Singer dies in London blast.'

'You were in Spain,' Joelle said gently. 'That's why you missed it.'

Rose got her emotions under control. 'I didn't know her well, we met a few times.'

'It's always a shock when someone you know dies, especially someone young when you're young yourself.'

Rose shut her eyes. The pictures in her mind were vivid, pictures of a side street in Kensington and a bomb blast ripping through a parked car, uprooting a sapling. Pictures of Maria drenched in blood that turned out to be milk. Of Maria, a survivor, picking her way over wreckage to her front door in defiance of the police. And the sounds came back to Rose too: Maria howling until Rose struck her and shut her up; singing from the depths of a soul brimful of sadness; hysterical in her night-time call to Paris. Maria's words butted in, excluding what Joelle was saying and the replies Rose was marshalling: *They are trying to kill me. They are trying to kill me.*

Rose forced the words away, paid attention to Joelle and the photographs side by side on the desk. With a gesture of her neat brown hand Joelle was inviting Rose to compare them.

'Forget the hair,' Joelle instructed her. 'If you can do that, they are rather alike.'

Not enough, not for Rose. There was more than a hair-style to discount. Maria's photograph was a skilful publicity portrait, she was wearing make-up and a sweet smile. The other one was eerie.

Rose startled Joelle by saying: 'I think this woman's dead. It doesn't look like a genuine photograph of a living person. The eyes, look at them.'

Joelle's theory was collapsing. How could the one published earlier in the year in Germany be a corpse if the subject was alive until a week ago? She tried to salvage something. 'Well perhaps it shows a sister.'

'Maria didn't have one.' And then she deflected the discussion by suggesting Joelle rang the telephone number in the advertisement. 'Say you've spotted a likeness, ask if they have identified the woman yet.'

Without waiting for the outcome of the call, Rose faxed friends in London and begged details of Maria's murder. Before long, she was talking to Mike Lowry, the television presenter Maria took up with. He declared himself fed up with answering questions about her.

'They were all on, Rose – the papers, television reporters. God, what a revelation it is when you find yourself on the other side of that particular fence.'

'I'm sure you handled it superbly, Mike. Anyway, it's publicity, isn't it?'

'Too cynical, Rose. I'm actually rather picky about the type of publicity I court. By assigning me the role of boyfriend in this sorry tale, the media do me no favours whatsoever. Besides I can't tell them anything.'

'Didn't she have an inkling she was in danger?'

'She was neurotic, we all knew that.'

'Nothing more specific?'

He caught on. 'Rose, you're hiding something.' But when she did not own up, he went on: 'No, Maria didn't spell it out to me but she grew ridiculously cautious. Always looking around, as if she expected danger to be creeping up on her. It was silly. In restaurants she insisted on a table where she could sit with her back to the wall. And she put extra locks on her door at the flat and installed an alarm. I kept thinking: "Who does she think she is? Why does she imagine anyone would attack her? She's not a politician, she's not connected to anyone influential." No, Rose, it was paranoid behaviour and, I can tell you, I was tired of it.'

'You're saying you dropped her?'

He took a moment to decide how much to admit. Then: 'Look, Rose, I would have wriggled out of it weeks ago but how could I? She was in such a mess and I didn't have the heart to be tough. I kept telling myself I'd ease out of it once she was over the worst. Besides, she was a treat in bed, Rose. Worth putting up with a bit longer.'

Rose worried away at it. 'Mike, are you absolutely sure she didn't tell you she was being followed? That people were trying to kill her?'

'Of course I'm sure, it's not the kind of thing I'd forget. Obviously she felt threatened – her behaviour, all those door locks . . .'

'And then they got her at the nightclub instead.'

'Yes but did they intend that? You know the sort of people attracted to owning clubs, they carry trouble around with them.'

'But a bomb in her dressing room? If they wanted to get the owner . . .'

'Please Rose, spare me the Sherlock stuff. I've heard more theories about this than Maria knew songs to sing. And one of them is that by putting a bomb in a dressing room you damage business, and make the owner, and all the other club owners, more compliant with whatever your unpleasant underworld plans may be. Presumably he wasn't employing the firm of bouncers he was told to employ, which is to say paying protection money.'

'All very well,' Rose countered. 'But she was the victim of a bomb blast at her home too. How does that square with the protection racket theory?'

He conceded it did not. 'Don't beg me for an explanation, Rose, I don't have one. And the police aren't any the wiser.'

The fax machine spewed out words from London, a few people telephoned instead. Each one helpfully muddied the waters until Rose had listened to a great many unconvincing theories but still understood nothing about Maria's death. When she broke off, to keep a lunch date, Joelle was ready with a story of her own.

'A woman at the Frankfurt telephone number referred me to a Paris number. She said I needed to contact a detective agency here. So, Rose, the story has come home to us.'

She was relishing her own role as *flic*, taking more time over the tale-telling than Rose had to spare. Rose tried to speed her with an encouraging: 'And?'

'Well, the agency is called Paul Martin Investigations and I spoke to Martin himself. He said any information was welcome and asked me to meet him. In an hour.'

'That's very . . .' She faltered. Interesting? Yes. Quick? Yes, positively eager.

'Now what's wrong? I'm only going to tell him about the similarity in the photographs.'

Rose advised her to be cagey, to feed him her own information slowly while drawing out of him what he knew. She was willing to go in Joelle's place but that was impossible as Joelle had spoken to him and he knew her voice. Rose rehearsed a few questions with her and wished her luck.

When Rose returned to the office after lunch Joelle was still away. Her absence made the normally placid Steve tetchy because he was waiting for an article she was looking up when the advertisement side-tracked her. Rose soothed him but became anxious. She believed the woman in the advertisement was dead, Maria was definitely dead, and Joelle was missing too long.

Clockwatching, she thought: 'Heaven knows what she's blundered into. Or whether she's capable of extricating herself.'

And a while later she decided: 'I can't stand this, I'm going over to that agency.'

But when she ran out into the street, she collided with Joelle. Joelle was pink from hurrying, her eyes glittered. 'Rose, you won't believe this, but . . .'

Rose steered her into the relative privacy of the magazine building. 'You look like a woman who's stumbled on the year's biggest news story.'

Joelle tried to suppress her excitement but it was no use. She bubbled. 'I did what you said, I didn't give anything away easily.'

They reached a secluded corner where they could talk without being overheard. Nevertheless Joelle whispered. 'The woman in the advertisement isn't dead. That's a computer mock-up, an updated version of the photograph of an abducted child. Paul Martin – he's a ferrety little chap, looks just the type to sniff out the facts – well, he's protecting his client's confidentiality and won't give me a name, but he says a member of the child's family had the computer photograph done and asked him to use it to trace her.'

'Hence the advertisement.'

'Yes, he placed advertisements in magazines in several countries. He did other things too, but we didn't go into that because all the response came from the advertisements. An Italian woman claimed it was her granddaughter and a Dutch woman said she sat next to her on a flight to London this year. There were others too.'

Joelle reported that Paul Martin traced the woman on the airline but she was of no interest to his client. The Italian granddaughter was ruled out straight away. None of the others could possibly be the grown-up missing child either.

She said: 'Martin didn't spot the *Paris Soir* picture of Maria Flores but he certainly saw the resemblance when I showed him. He practically whisked the paper out of my hand and he kept staring at it. He said: "In *London*", twice, as though that was the most peculiar thing about it all.'

The showing of Maria's photograph had come at the very end of the conversation. Before that Joelle winkled out that his client was French-speaking if not actually French, that there was no reward on offer for reuniting child and family although the family was rich.

She sat across from Rose, crossed one leg over the other, clasped her hands around her knee and spoke the words she had been saving up.

'I think the Devereux family are looking for little Nicole.'

Rose almost laughed before realizing Joelle was not teasing.

'Rose, I know more about them than I do about my own family. Putting together your Devereux file made me an expert. The timing's right. Paul Martin says the photograph's updated from a picture of a two-year-old, and the advertisement says the woman is twenty-three. Several things fit, Rose. We have a rich French family, a baby girl abducted twenty-one years ago . . .'

'But, Joelle, the Devereux baby was murdered. The cuttings include a harrowing funeral in the church near the château. Nicole Devereux is dead.'

'Then why does someone in the family think she's alive?'

'They can't, Joelle.'

'A man. Paul Martin's client is a man, he gave that much away.'

One of the Devereux men. Maurice, Nicole's grandfather? Philippe, the uncle? Or David, the cousin born after her disappearance?

Ellie crackled down the line from Prague. The flat in Malá Strana had been entered, someone had interfered with the Devereux file. Cuttings were no longer chronological and one had dropped under the table, giving away a search she might not have noticed but for that.

'Twice, Rose,' she said, and her voice was high with tension. 'Once the door lock was smashed and now this.'

Rose floundered for an explanation. Ellie butted in. 'Krieger. It must be Krieger.'

'Why ever should it be? No, we're on good terms, he'd have no reason.'

Ellie scoffed. 'People like that don't need reasons the way the rest of us do. It's second nature to him. Anyway, are you coming back?'

'I'll let you know,' she said.

And to Joelle: 'Would you call the House of Devereux and fix an appointment for me to see David? Pretend it's to do with the art collection. Say I want to talk to him specifically about auctioning *Exile*.'

Joelle did not get through to David. 'They say he's gone to make a speech on behalf of Greenworld at an environmental conference.'

'Oh, damn.'

'Could be convenient. It's in Prague.'

Rose caught a flight later that day. There was rain and cloud, the earth an occasional smudge. She had a mad idea that she did not want the plane ever to land, that she wanted to rise higher and higher, spiralling away from the planet, freed from its unreasonable pressures and miseries. There were thoughts she refused to think, ideas too appalling to formulate. Later, she said inside herself. And later became soon.

Fantasy painted the bits Ramírez and the pathologist's report spared her. The gouts of blood, the streak of red in the dust where the too-late helpers dragged the body to a kind of safety behind the parked van, the sticky stains on their clothing as they struggled to find a life no longer there. But perhaps not. Death need not be abrupt, it could pump away for minutes while Ramírez was fleeing . . . She shook herself, adapting a shudder into a rebuttal of fancied horrors.

Foolishly, in a shady corner of her mind, she had hoped the journey to the no place town in Spain would end in the revelation that it was not, after all, John Blair who had been shot, been mourned by his colleagues and interred at Highgate. She accused herself of conjuring professional reasons for him dropping out of sight, unaware of mistaken reports of his death. Awake, she was sensible but her dreams were undisciplined. The shot, the falling figure, the wound, people running to help and turning the figure over. And always and ever the face she dreamed was the face of a stranger.

The plane cut between heaven and earth. Higher, she thought, *away*. She wanted to spin away, not plunge back to do what she must do. She was burdened with suspicion and knowledge. Then the plane was losing height, there was to be no magical escape from responsibility. An inner voice spoke the words: 'I know why he was killed.'

She went directly from the airport to the house Krieger called home. He was taken aback but not unwelcoming. Last time she had seen the entrance hall, now she was taken to a sitting room overlooking a garden. The house was well furnished, a mixture of French antiques and more recent good-quality pieces. Whoever owned it had not had to stint, to settle for enamel cupboards or plastic and plywood chairs.

Krieger poured her a beer. 'You're cross with me, Rose, aren't you? We're making slow progress with our talks.'

Her hand waved away his excuses. 'You went to my flat. You looked through my things. I'd rather you explained that first.' She made it sound like proven fact rather than guesswork.

He raised his hands in surrender, the cigarette jammed between his fingers coiling smoke. '*Mea culpa*. A habit, Rose.'

'A bad one.'

'No doubt you're right.'

'But why? What did you think you'd find there?'

He drew on the cigarette and regarded her severely. 'You demand my confidence but how do I know you're to be trusted?'

Exasperated, she blurted: 'Old newspaper cuttings, that's what you got for your trouble. It must have been very disappointing for you.'

But even as she was speaking she remembered sitting across

the table from him in the café near the castle, recalled his special interest when she said she was working on a story about the Devereux family. A warning light had flashed in her skull yet she had ignored it, answered his questions and let him advise her. *'Don't bother with the old man, Maurice, or with his son, Philippe. It's David, the grandson who calls the shots now.'*

Well, that was one way of putting it.

Ellie had returned from her Bohemian castle with a story about Krieger and drug running; John Blair had died proving the Devereux family were involved with drugs; Krieger had been seen in Prague with David; therefore . . . Rose set about getting Krieger's confirmation.

He attempted to play the affable uncle who had met her in the Waldstein Gardens and walked uphill with her, but the act was a failure. The guarded look in the eyes, the contrived good humour, gave him away. She attacked and he parried. It was gentle stuff. Too fierce and she would lose her deal regarding the life story.

He stubbed out the cigarette, stopped his hand on the way to his pocket with the stub and dropped the stub into the ashtray. His hand eased his neck where the pain ran down into his shoulder.

'David's in Prague,' she said. 'Will you be seeing him?'

His eyes answered. Surprise, followed swiftly by concern.

Rose told him: 'He's speaking tomorrow at a conference at the castle.'

'Why should that interest me? You've already told me you don't believe I share his passion for saving the planet.'

So he too was thinking of their previous conversation. She said: 'No, I don't think you discuss that. I had dinner with him in Paris, I have a clear idea what you two do talk about.'

'Ah.' He lit a cigarette. She sat without stirring and watched the screwing up of his eyes against the smoke, the puckering of the forehead as he worked out whether it was worth stringing her along or whether to admit the relationship was about buying and selling drugs.

Krieger said: 'Proof?'

Circumstantial evidence, John Blair's notes and photographs, Ellie's second-hand rumours. 'Yes, proof.'

He exhaled smoke, a grey screen that hovered between them and made it impossible for her to read his eyes again. She was tempted to reach forward and hold on to him, in case he disappeared as the smoke dispelled. There was unreality in the air.

'In that case . . .' he said.

She could not prevent herself leaning forward, keenly.

He said: 'I was thinking of telling you when we resumed our interviews. Undecided. But, as you know about it, then yes, by all means, let's fill in the details. You can't have learned those. I was the only one who ever knew them.'

The smoke tasted sour to her, it was tainting her jacket, her hair, her skin. She continued to lean into it, quietly triumphant, awaiting his confession.

Krieger said, with a harsh laugh: 'If I keep it to myself, it makes nonsense of my spell in France. A guessing game has its attractions but why shouldn't I take the credit? One day someone else will if I don't.'

Rose grunted agreement. She did not understand what he meant.

He sucked on the cigarette again before saying: 'Once more, *mea culpa*. I stole the Devereux baby.'

She had the wit to quell her reactions. No drugs, none of what she was prepared for. Instead, a thunderbolt. And she dared not put him off by showing astonishment or alarm. She sat rigid, offering murmurs of encouragement, as he told her how he did it.

Krieger mentioned the shadows of poplars, a long wait, the odd cigarette to cheer him, rooms darkening as family and servants went to bed, his dash from trees to house, the secret gliding of the window of the salon.

'When I was a boy, I taught myself to move without a sound, like a Red Indian in the films.'

She nodded. Yes, he had said something similar on the walk up the hill. *'Like a cat in the night.'*

'I knew her room. No, I hadn't been inside before but servants' gossip filtered through and I knew enough. She was asleep. I placed the sticking plaster over her mouth while she was asleep. In three and a half minutes I was carrying her through the trees.'

'To a car?'

'A bicycle.' He laughed at her disbelief. 'A car's noisy but a bicycle sneaking along the footpaths in the night doesn't disturb anybody. The car was a mile away. We drove fast.'

'South.'

'A long way south. She was left with a couple posing as holidaymakers in a cottage on a hillside. Local people didn't know them, they weren't capable of saying Nicole didn't belong to that family.'

Krieger had been an agitator, a money raiser. He was not mentioning money. Rose put it to him: 'Why was there no ransom demand?'

'There were two. But I was far away by then, my role was over. I went to Italy, as a matter of fact. Other people were to care for her and extract the money from her family.' He gestured, his cigarette writing smoky shapes in the air. 'It became a fiasco. The demand was delayed, I don't know why. And then the police discovered a body they persuaded everyone was Nicole's. Utter fiasco.'

His laughter was chilling, he might have been describing an inconsequential muddle rather than the unreported murder of an unnamed child and the ruin of Nicole Devereux's life. Rose fought to conceal her disgust.

'Nicole went to Spain,' she prompted.

'Look, I didn't take these decisions. If it had been up to me, they'd have left her somewhere. One phone call and she'd have been home. But other people have different ideas. They thought they could wait and try again for the money. They arranged for a family to take her, poor people who agreed because it promised them an income. They were told she was an illegitimate child from northern Spain being hidden away, it wasn't so rare as to be unbelievable.'

Krieger said that for him the story ended there. As a means of raising money for the political cause he had been involved with, the Devereux kidnapping was a disaster but he had been too busy to dwell on it and moved on to other things. He meant spying.

Rose looked disbelieving. 'A famous mystery, and you never bothered to ask what happened next?'

Her sarcasm brought a flare of annoyance. 'Those idiots. I did all the work for them. The idea was mine, I went in and got her. What was left for them? A letter to be written and sent off, a plan to be followed for the money to be collected and the child dumped. They didn't have to think, just stick to the plan. But they couldn't even manage that. Do you know the name of Deschamps? From Marseilles? He persuaded them. I never wanted him involved in the job, he was always stupid, he's spent his life in and out of prison. Why did they want to listen to a man like that? Anyway, I was in Italy and I was thinking why is there nothing in the papers about the ransom, about the Devereux baby going home? And then they told me. *Spain!* A long-term thing, not a quick raid on the Devereux bank account. They were crazy. I said the longer they sent the money through their chain of contacts to that Spanish family, the surer it was they'd give themselves away.'

She filled in the next part for him. 'They stopped sending the money.'

With a movement of the cigarette, he agreed. She said: 'Then Nicole was abandoned. Or did they ever try and get her back?'

The notion of recovering her appeared to amuse him. 'Too risky,' was all he said.

She brought him sharply up to date, not giving him time to realize he was mistaken in thinking she knew about him discussing Nicole with David Devereux. 'Did you go to him, or did he come to you?'

'He came. He said my name's linked to the case. A man in Paris wrote a book about me and hinted I carried Nicole away. It wasn't proof, I don't think there is any. But David asked me whether it was true.'

Krieger entertained himself by making her wait to know whether he lied or owned up. Then: 'I told him I did it.'

'And told him about Spain.' Not a question, she knew the answer.

He rubbed out the cigarette and fanned the smoke with a nicotined hand. 'A happy ending to our story, Rose. David will trace her and take her home.'

His complacency appalled her. He was sitting there, in an armchair facing hers, a smug smile on his uncaring face. She did not know how a man could recite such wickedness and then joke of happy endings.

Her words would not come. In her bag, beside her chair, was the photograph that she believed David Devereux paid a computer artist to create to help his search for his missing cousin. Beside it was the newsprint photograph of the dead singer Maria. And Krieger could speak of happy endings.

She said: 'The detective David hired . . .'

'Detective? He said he'd go himself. As I knew which village and the names of some of the people, he said it was easy. Anyway, he wants as few people as possible to know. Perhaps you're right, though. Perhaps he is using a detective.'

'He did,' she said firmly, stopping short of naming Paul Martin Investigations but creating the impression she had spoken to David Devereux about the search. 'I was going to ask . . .'

Her question petered out. Suddenly there was no point in putting it because things no longer added up the way she thought. David hiring a detective to place advertisements in magazines across Europe did not tally with a secretive David choosing to go alone to Spain armed with information from Nicole's abductor.

She was stumped but Krieger helped her out. 'Money? Of

course the help I've given David is to be paid for. My circumstances have changed drastically in the last year, and he's an exceedingly rich young man who can afford to pay for information.'

Rose latched on to this. 'That sounds as though you haven't seen the colour of his money yet.'

He looked uncomfortable, persuading her she was right. 'David isn't a fool, he's paying on results. Something for putting him on the right trail, more when he finds her. Up until now he hasn't found her.'

'How do you know? He could trace her and not bother to tell you.'

Krieger laughed, like an uncle chafing a favourite niece for stupidity. 'Rose, when the Devereux family reclaims Nicole the whole world will know.'

'But only if David wants them to.'

'Don't forget Nicole, or whatever she calls herself.'

'I haven't.' She dipped into her bag and held out an envelope to him.

He blew a scattering of ash off the table and tipped out the contents. The bigger photograph landed facing away from him. Rose saw the dead eyes that were the best the computer could do. Krieger spun the photograph around, straightened it, pushed the magazine advertisement up beside it. He sat there, looking down at the evidence. The hair was thin over his crown, Rose had not noticed this before. She seemed to sit a long while looking at this thinness before he moved back in his chair and lifted his face to hers. She had dented his complacency.

'You never knew him,' Ellie said. Her voice was unexpectedly bitter. 'Oh, yes, I know you lived with him, you were around the places he was around. But believe me, Rose, you never knew him, not really.'

Shaken, Rose managed: 'We knew him in different ways. We knew different things about him.'

She was thinking she had never been curious enough to ask

300

precisely what Ellie's relationship with John Blair had been, and that after this she would never be told the truth.

Ellie did not reply. Rose knew she ought to let it drop but, forced on to the defensive, added: 'We all know people differently. We take different things from them.'

'Yes,' said Ellie without conviction. 'I expect that's what I meant.' She scraped back her chair and got up.

The flat was too small to contain them both. The noisy fridge dominated the kitchen, the overactive boiler made an inferno of the rooms nearest it, they were forced into the living room crowded by Ellie's makeshift bed on the sofa. Rose wished she would hide the duvet and pillows when not actually using them. A lot of things rankled.

Ellie strode though to the bathroom. Her boots clumped over the tiled hallway and she started back to the living room. On the way she stopped off at the kitchen and the hinge of a metal cupboard shrieked, a tap ran.

Rose gritted her teeth and wished it was morning and they could go their separate ways. She had expected to be on her own at the flat and found Ellie encamped. And when she began to share the astonishing developments in the Devereux story, Ellie stuck at the point where a motive for John Blair's murder surfaced. As Rose, unaware how much tact was required, insisted on moving on to Maria's murder and Krieger's reaction, Ellie reached flashpoint.

Angry, beautiful, with her slanting grey eyes and swing of silvery hair, Ellie looked a woman capable of saying and doing whatever she chose, one who knew her way in the world and had grown into that. In contrast, Rose felt diminished. Not because of the spoken accusations but because Ellie challenged her in various ways. Ellie's own fought-for identity undermined Rose's confidence in her own easy route through life. Given Ellie's unelaborated hardships and disadvantages, how would Rose herself have survived? Because Ellie was, in an unemphatic way, a survivor.

And something, Rose thought, had happened to Ellie since

she came to Prague. Something deeper and more damaging than a spat with a brother, an uncommunicative meeting with her parents or trickery over the fate of a potential Frans Hals woman. Suddenly it was obvious to Rose that whatever the truth of it, John Blair would have understood. He and Ellie had been that close.

Rose put down the book she was pretending to read. She went and stood in the doorway to the kitchen. Ellie was perched on a stool, a glass of water in front of her. Rose said: 'I have to confront him. I'd like you to come with me.'

Ellie was crisp. 'Your French is better than mine.'

'I don't mean I need a translator, what I want is a witness.' And when Ellie looked doubtful: 'It's quite normal. Journalists do it all the time, when things are sensitive they go around in pairs.'

'I'm no journalist.'

'No, but I'd rather trust you than root around for the woman who counts as my Prague staff. She moves in mysterious ways and I haven't time to play games.'

Ellie capitulated. 'When can we see him? I have a meeting at the art gallery tomorrow afternoon.'

'We'll catch him at his hotel early, before he has a chance to do anything else. He's addressing a conference after lunch. I don't know what he has lined up for the morning but we're going to alter his plans. Do you have a tape recorder?'

Ellie said not. Rose fetched her own. 'I'd feel safer with two but we must make do. Carry it in your bag. He'll take less notice of you because I'll be the one attacking.'

Rose opened the recorder and spilled the batteries into her hand. 'I wish I had replacements.'

'They are a problem here, hard to come by. If people are lucky they own rechargeable ones.'

Rose slid the batteries into the case. 'We'll have to manage.'

But that was what her work was, always, eventually, a business of compromise. A guessing game, making leaps of faith, being stung by a sudden thought. Watching out for details, coincidences, tell-tale gestures and the curious omission of words. Following a lead she hoped would reveal one thing only to find it told her another that pointed her in a fresh direction. Amassing information, contradictory facts. Building a story without possessing all the building blocks. Finally, having to make do.

Ellie took the tape recorder. 'I presume my role as witness is to work this and support your version of the encounter if he later denies it.'

'And to stop me getting killed.' It was meant to be a joke.

TWENTY-ONE

The hotel was a modern brick and concrete calamity on the river bank in the heart of the city. Rose and Ellie trekked along cream corridors, catching the glimmering river through landing windows. The feeling was international, the hotel belonged to every city and none.

David Devereux had a towel tied around his waist, his hair was wet and his skin gleamed. Once he spotted Ellie and grasped that Rose was not there to play audience to his entertainer, far less to slip into bed with him, his smile grew several degrees cooler.

'Rose, I hope it's Greenworld this time, not nonsense about art sales. I'm speaking this afternoon, you should come. If you haven't fixed it, I'll arrange for them to let you in.'

'Not art. Not Greenworld. The Curse of the Devereux.'

He turned away allowing her further into the room. Ellie closed the door and joined them nearer the window. She was not sure of the range of the tape recorder. Rose introduced her as a colleague but after the briefest politeness David ignored her as Rose had predicted.

'Unfortunately,' Rose began, 'the Curse of the Devereux doesn't confine itself to messing up Devereux lives. It's branched out and it's harming people who look into Devereux affairs.'

He took up a hand towel and rubbed at his hair. 'You're supposed to be a better class of journalist, Rose, not a scandal monger.'

'Oh, I can be any kind that's required.' She was cross that he was not granting her full attention, anxious he was moving out of range of the recorder. She stepped towards him. He turned his back and considered his wet hair in the mirror. Her eyes met the reflection of his. She saw the hard expression, the intensity she had sought in vain during their evening together.

David flung the hand towel aside. 'I have to get dressed, I have a busy day and I really can't fritter any of it on nonsense.'

'John Blair's murder isn't nonsense. Nor is the death of a singer who probably never knew her true name was Nicole Devereux. Nor is . . .'

He discarded the last vestige of good humour. 'I'm not going to listen to this. You dare to accuse me of . . .' He dried up.

'Go on, of what? What are you afraid I'll say? That you paid her abductor for information about Nicole? That you traced her to Spain? To London?'

He was breathing fast, gripping the towel at his waist. All his security and confidence had fled. He repeated that he must get dressed, that he refused to hear any more. But Rose and Ellie were between him and the bathroom and he was compelled to face the allegations.

'This is untrue. All of it. Nobody knows who abducted Nicole.'

'You and Krieger do. It's useless lying, I know what you did. Krieger thought you wanted to fetch your cousin home, but it wasn't like that, was it?'

'You've talked to Krieger?'

She let him absorb the fact she had details directly from Krieger.

'All right, Rose. So Krieger and I had a conversation. His name's in a book, a long shot by the author. An officer in the security services claimed he was seen in the region the year Nicole was taken. Everyone knows he was responsible for a raid on a French bank, among other fund-raising activities. The author dropped a hint he was behind the Nicole business, said it was a failed ransom attempt. When Krieger came out from behind the Wall, I asked him. That's all.'

She asked what Krieger said to him.

David told her: 'He could easily have denied it, but he didn't. Don't ask me why. No, not the money. He isn't a man who's governed by money. He told me how he took Nicole away, handed her over and left for another of his jobs in Italy. That's it, Rose. I don't know about Spain or any singers in London.'

Rose tossed the blown-up prints over the rumpled bed. David with two men in the background of a shot of a nude sunbather in San Pedro de Alcántara. David as a shadowy figure in a car with a man that Ramírez had pointed out as a Spanish criminal. David hurrying past two older men drinking at a pavement café in the town where John Blair died.

The face in the photographs was cruel. Meeting him for the first time she had scoured her memory for that look, wondered who he reminded her of. But David had reminded her of himself, in the photographs, in this other mood.

He swung away from the evidence of the pictures, pushed past to the bathroom. 'They could be anywhere. What are they supposed to prove?'

'Not anywhere. I've been there and checked, and I know when you were there and who you were with.'

He slammed the bathroom door. The key turned.

Ellie let out a sigh. 'The photographs really threw him. He can't talk his way out of evidence like that.'

Rose gathered them up. 'We'll wait downstairs.'

He did not come down. They sat watching the lift and the stairs. Ellie asked: 'Can you actually prove anything?'

Wryly Rose replied that a confession would help no end.

Tourists making a commotion near the doorway caught her attention. Beyond them David was commandeering a taxi.

'Quick, Ellie.' Rose was on her feet and running.

His taxi was queuing to join the traffic. She raced towards it. Futile. David saw her and crouched lower in the seat. He spoke to the driver who edged to the front of the queue and then forced his way into the stream.

Behind Rose a rattling sound ended in the blast of a horn. She side-stepped, then changed her mind and lunged at the car.

'*Please*,' she begged. 'Please follow that taxi.'

'Rose Darrow?'

'Yes.' She did not know him, was relieved he spoke English.

'I'm a friend of Jiří. You don't know me, he pointed you out one day.'

Rose was climbing into the front passenger seat. 'Please,' she repeated, 'it's very urgent. That blue taxi, I must catch up with it.'

'How exciting.' The anonymous friend of a Czech acquaintance let in the clutch and the vehicle lurched out into the road. 'Did you see which way it went?'

'Left. It's held up at those lights.'

Her driver thrust at the accelerator pedal, eager to get there before the lights changed. Rose flung a glance over her shoulder. Ellie, hands on hips, was standing outside the hotel utterly perplexed. Then Rose concentrated on the road ahead and the frisky Renault second in the line at the lights.

She had never, in her maddest moments, imagined that if ever she hijacked a car for a high-speed chase she would be rash enough to grab a Trabant.

They were pushing her around, stone-walling her questions. Years ago, a week ago, she would not have been equal to them. But anger was a powerful commodity. It strengthened her will wonderfully.

Coming from the castle in Bohemia, empty handed, weak after her fever, she felt thwarted and inadequate. But now she knew what to do. The years of playing games were over. She was going to teach them that.

She was sorry her part in Rose Darrow's adventure with David Devereux was finished because it was an interesting digression, but its abrupt end set her free for the morning. Ellie assumed Rose could take care of herself. She shrugged off Rose's troubles and set about resolving her own.

Although she could not guarantee success, she was certain of making a nuisance of herself. If they refused to give in to her, they would waste much time in regret. Ellie strode through the lanes, planning her attack.

She was getting used to it, to pedestrians outnumbering motor traffic, to human voices and footsteps emerging from lanes into operatic squares. Sights no longer impressed themselves on her quite so passionately, they were losing the power to make her marvel and fear. A dash of moral superiority gave her all the confidence she needed.

The corridors that she now marched down were undaunting. Watchers at the corners looked away rather than hold her determined gaze. She raised her voice when she was denied, and things became possible. All morning she lobbied and protested. After lunch she kept her appointment at the gallery.

Milena Hobzek of the wintry smile intended to keep her waiting but after five minutes had elapsed, Ellie threw open her door. The woman was seated behind her desk. Her suit was unchanged: neat, with the blouse collar arranged high, the stone in the brooch on her lapel and the ring on her finger, an exact match. She might never have left the office since Ellie last saw her there.

Mrs Hobzek was piqued. 'You're not allowed to burst in like that.'

'I was told you were busy. That seems to be untrue.' Ellie sat down uninvited.

'I'm waiting for a colleague.' She rested one hand on the other and contemplated a fingernail.

'It's you I've come to see. You took the decision to remove the Frans Hals painting, you can explain and tell me where it is now.'

'It's really none of your business.' She spoke in an end-of-the-matter voice.

Ellie said: 'But I found the picture . . .'

'One might well argue that it was never lost.'

Ellie ignored this interruption. 'It's a painting that deserves examination by experts on the work of Frans Hals. You've taken it away from the condition in which it's happily survived for centuries, you've humped it across the country in the back of a

308

van and you're no doubt allowing a bunch of incompetents to poke it and prod it. That does you no credit at all.'

'You have no claim on that painting. If it's proved to be of any value then it'll be moved to a gallery here.'

'You're not qualified to judge it. No one in this country is. You've been isolated too long and art's an international affair. The experts are in Holland and America, not here.'

Milena Hobzek's reply was cut off by the telephone ringing. 'Yes,' she said into the receiver. 'Yes.'

To Ellie she added: 'The painting stays here.'

Behind Ellie the door opened. A man walked past her to stand beside Milena Hobzek. He did not say hello or speak Ellie's name, he looked at her with the kind of disinterest with which he might examine a not very accomplished portrait.

Ellie's surprise at his presence was momentary. Once, he had introduced her to the world of art but now he was joining with Milena Hobzek in rejecting her. It hurt that they had colluded in getting her into the Stehlik castle, in whisking away the painting from beneath her nose. But the damage was done, his presence now made no difference. It did not escape her that he had been referred to as a colleague. Perhaps his reward for betrayal was a new job.

Milena Hobzek wore a look of unpleasant satisfaction. 'Naturally we're grateful for your assistance in drawing our attention to the painting, but I may say that until it's been cleaned it'll be impossible to verify the artist. The Stehlik documents prove only that the collection included work by Hals, they can't confirm that this portrait is one of those mentioned.'

Ellie agreed. She asked whether cleaning had begun. Mrs Hobzek said it would begin soon. Ellie replied that it was preferable to invite one of the experts to examine it in its current state.

The woman argued. 'We don't share your enthusiasm for surrendering our responsibility to outsiders. The painting belongs here and it'll stay here. It's our affair and no one else's.' She looked for support to the man beside her, and he made a slight, dutiful nod.

Ellie rose to leave. 'I believe you're wrong and you must expect me to act accordingly. You might not wish to alert the art world to the possibility that you have an important Frans Hals in your grasp, perhaps even the true companion for the man in the National Gallery of Art in Washington. But it doesn't really matter, I've done it for you.'

The blouse collar quivered above the neat suit. Crimson suffused Milena Hobzek's cheeks. 'How dare you? It's not permitted to . . .'

'Think?' Ellie threw back at her. 'Use a little imagination?' She shifted her gaze to the man. 'Seek the truth?'

Then she left, quietly, leaving the door wide, forcing on them a clear view of her triumphant exit.

She went out of the building and became entangled with tourists before she heard footsteps speeding after her. She had been wondering whether he would come. He caught at her arm. He was agitated. 'Ellie, for God's sake, what are you trying to do?'

'I told you, both of you. I've done it. Everybody who matters knows now. There's nothing more to say.'

She was walking on, if he wanted to talk he had to keep pace. She did not care where she was going. She strode forward, cutting through parties of tourists, declining to give way to posses of soldiers.

'You don't understand, Ellie,' he was saying.

But she had done with deferring to his opinion. 'I've made my decision. It's different from yours and Milena Hobzek's, that's all.'

'For heaven's sake, what exactly *have* you done?'

She did not explain. She did not need him any longer, he was only an unreliable link with her past.

They had been welcoming and interested in what she said, the new officials and the government people. The Minister was especially keen to ensure the matter was properly investigated. He joked about inducing her to stay. She blushed to think of the days she had wasted feebly supposing the Hobzeks and the time-servers counted. Going over their heads, she met with enthusiasm and co-operation, and they would hate it.

Stay on? Well, yes, because she could not bear to fly back to London without so much as a tentative identification from one of the experts. The American could not be in Europe for another six weeks but the Dutchman was on his way. If his answer was no, it would come quickly but he could spin out a yes over weeks of testing and comparison.

But stay on?

The Minister's remark was meant to entice her and it did. The new order appealed strongly, both in theory and in reality. How many countries could boast they drew their government from the world of the arts? They welcomed her, she was not like those writers who had claimed to be a culture in exile, those professional Czechs who lost touch and fell into a gap between cultures. There was work for her in Prague, engrossing worthwhile work. She need no longer skitter over the surface, dodging questions about herself and the people in her life. Somewhere between the cathedral and the courtyard she was seduced by the idea of staying on.

The man tried to force her to pay attention but she refused to stop and turned aside through the south doorway, the Golden Gate of the cathedral, passing beneath portraits of Charles IV and Elisabeth of Pomerania and a fourteenth-century Last Judgement. She came to a standstill, schemes and dreams diminished by the scale of the building. An unbidden memory provided some figures: 28 piers, 21 chapels, 407 feet long, 197 feet wide, a nave 108 feet high. Meaningless figures, conveying nothing of the effect of the place on the human spirit.

An English couple, a businessman in a navy reefer coat and a younger woman inexpensively dressed, perhaps his secretary, blocked Ellie's view up the nave as they argued over the guidebook entry. She moved away before she was asked to mediate. Cold from the marble floor was creeping up her legs.

There was one thing troubling her about a future in Prague, one piece of information she needed before her mind was easy.

She looked over her shoulder. The man was several yards behind, by a pillar. She beckoned him to join her. He came, hoping she had relented and was going to reveal what she had done about the painting.

She said: 'What were the rumours when I went to London?'

That bemused smile she remembered. His surprised laugh echoed among the columns, drifted high into the nave. 'Nothing that was near the truth. Rumours seldom are.'

But they often were, that was the point of them. 'You do remember, though?'

'You can imagine what they were. A teenage girl leaves home suddenly, after a summer of secret outings . . .'

'They said I was pregnant? Who said?'

He laughed again but more uncertainly. 'Ellie, what can it matter now?'

'Tell me who told you?'

In the instant before he spoke she saw how it had been. After she had left him waiting on the bridge, he had sought out her friends, especially Nina, who was closest and knew her family well.

'All right,' he said, resigned. 'I was on my way to your house and I met Nina. She told me you'd gone to London and said I'd better not call on your family as they believed you'd left because of an unhappy love affair. And then she said your brother was claiming you'd told him about it and thought you were pregnant. Pavel hadn't mentioned my name but I took Nina's advice and kept well away.'

He gave her a searching look before adding: 'I've always thought it very odd the rumours originated with him. I'd have expected him to protect you, defend you, if he'd believed any of that to be true.'

'Just Nina's story,' she said with a shrug, to avoid giving credence to his suspicion.

So she had the missing piece of information. Pavel, who had tried but failed to possess her, had pretended that another man had done so. And her mother had accepted what he told her, not recognizing the subversion of truth. When she spoke to Ellie about the wisdom of breaking free, the man she had in mind was not Pavel after all. Even that was turning out all right.

'I have to go now,' said Ellie. She moved away from him, over the death-cold marble, between the red and the gold.

David Devereux's taxi stayed in sight, the Trabant trundling in its rear and scattering dozy pedestrians who regarded Smetanova Nabř as a viewing point for castle and cathedral rather than as a main road. Then they got stuck behind a tram and all Rose could see was red and cream coachwork.

'This is very exciting,' said the tweed-jacketed man who was her driver. 'But I'm not sure we can catch up.'

'Overtake, then,' she urged.

The Trabant nosed out, and nosed back in as a bus rumbled towards it. At the third or fourth attempt the car laboured alongside the tram, passengers looking down with disdain on its efforts. Rose thrust forward in her seat, her foot pressed against a non-existent accelerator pedal. 'Go on, go on,' she begged under her breath.

Her driver laughed. 'It's from East Germany, this car. Not the best, I think.'

As they passed a bridge Rose sought the Renault. No sign of it crossing the river so with luck they were in its wake. Their road was long and straight. Far ahead she noticed a flicker of blue.

'There,' she said, and stubbed a pointing finger against the windscreen.

The blue car crossed a bridge. The Trabant followed, minutes behind, Rose unsure whether she had the quarry or an imposter in her sights.

Until this drive, Prague had struck her as a city with a remarkably low level of traffic. Now it all appeared to be out on the roads at once, on the route the taxi was taking, blocking her, holding her back, helping David escape her.

She was disappointed with the confrontation in his hotel room. People faced with proof of calumny tended to confess and excuse themselves. He had not. She had spilled out what she knew but he had given little away. The tape would provide evidence of allegations but not of guilt.

A traffic light delayed the Trabant. A flash of blue rounded a corner and went out of sight. Her driver tapped the steering wheel with an impatient hand. The wheel bounced dangerously. The ticking, choking engine continued to make its sewing-machine noises. Shutting her eyes, Rose pretended she was an old lady treadling away at a Singer.

The driver let the clutch in. It snatched and stalled. He restarted at the fourth attempt and, in slow motion, wheeled the car right. A junction lay ahead. Right or left?

'Right,' Rose hazarded. They lumbered around a corner. There was a square, a hill. A steep hill. A steep, winding hill.

The driver slammed the engine into bottom gear, jarring her teeth, turning the heads of women milling outside a baker's shop with vicious elbows ready to do battle for their share of bread.

The car dashed across the cobbles, launched itself at the hill. Unwittingly, Rose was trying to make herself as light as possible, almost hovering above her seat, her foot still flattening a fictitious pedal.

The driver cut precious fractions of seconds by taking bends on the wrong side of the road, zig-zagging up the incline. In this fashion they manoeuvred through two bends, their pitted fawn bonnet rearing up ahead of them, blotting out a view of broken cobbles and slithering grit, of tangled scaffolding on the blistered façades of gentlemen's eighteenth-century houses.

Then the car conked out. The gear stick jumped from where it should have been, and the vehicle slid back yards before the brake held it.

'Ježíšmarjá!'

'Damn,' said Rose. She looked at the man for a moment, daring him to say how exciting it was.

'Can you restart it?' Improbable but it was churlish to abandon him without asking.

When he tried, the engine sputtered and died. The only course was to run the car back and let it wedge itself against the kerb to stop it rolling all the way down to the river.

'Go,' he insisted. 'If you're quick, perhaps you can . . .'

They looked at the hill. It assumed the proportions of a precipice. She said: 'I'll get a taxi in the square.' She was already on her way, grateful for his persuasion, hoping he had not gallantly wrecked his car for her. A car was a car, even if it was a Trabant. As she loped downhill, the fumes from its inefficient engine thickened the air.

Traffic fumes, the debris of lignite from domestic fires, industrial pollution borne miles on the wind to catch at her lungs – a suitable city for a conference on cleaning up Europe's environment.

There were no taxis. She crossed back over the bridge thinking that as David Devereux had eluded her, she ought to find Ellie. For a while she waited for a bus, then sought a Metro station. Soon she realized she was being followed.

There were two of them, young men she had seen before. Not in Prague, though. In Paris. She saw them at the Greenworld demonstration on the Seine, spotted them another time with David Devereux, and one of them she was sure had been caught by John Blair's lens in Spain. Lean, athletic, dressed in sporty clothes, they were equipped for a chase.

She jumped on a tram and they jumped into the second carriage, alighting when she did, not allowing her the ghost of a chance to shake them off. They chased down the Metro steps after her and dodged in and out of the train as she did, and when she raced across a platform to catch a departing train on a different line, so did they. They did not quite catch her, make physical contact, but she feared it was only a matter of time.

Moving rapidly, she wove through alleyways and crowds, went into a church by one door and left by another. The pair stuck close. She slipped into the old Jewish cemetery and found a huddle of American tourists among the twenty thousand jutting tombstones, a scene of mossy sandstone with a few dashes of pink and white marble. She pressed forward, as though to get closer to hear the guide. Pretending attention, she half-heard about Rabbi Jehuda Löw ben Bezalal who created Golem, the first artificial human being, from the mud of the Vltava. When the compliant party studied the carved lions on his sarcophagus, and several of the men lay pebbles on it, her eyes ranged beyond to one of her pursuers inadequately concealed by a sycamore. Pigeons mocked her with their cooing contentment.

The guide led his party along paths narrow as sheep runs. He shepherded them around him, his entourage elbowing in among the crammed-together tombstones whose jumble recorded burials up to nine tiers deep. Rose stayed with the Americans, nice Jewish folk from the East Coast, but it was hopeless. When she came out, her pursuers were waiting.

They were content to follow. Several times she was within arms' length but they did not grab, their orders appeared to be to follow and intimidate. They were efficient.

At the house in the Old Town where she first met Zak, she rang the bell. The men hovered at the end of the lane. When she gave up and moved on, they did too. She led them around the vegetable and fruit stalls of Havelská Street, past an orange garbage truck with its revolving orange light, along streets boasting rococo palaces and streets ashamed of builders' rubble. Everywhere she went, they went too.

A game but not a game, because she knew what happened to people who played with them. Maria was dead. John Blair was dead. The thought turned her blood to ice. She lengthened the space between them, lost what she had gained, fooled them at a junction and made headway. In a department store she confused them, riding up escalators out of their reach, going to ground amongst the women's coats.

Customers, queuing passively for the handful of shop's baskets, their passports to the shoe section, welcomed the diversion. She bent her knees and lost height, waddled between racks and peeped around the ends of them. Retreated, strode swiftly away.

The store was spacious because it was far from full. Racks and counters were sporadic, often with hardly anything displayed on them. Garments came in drab uninviting fabric, tea towels required the customer to hem them for herself.

From a window Rose looked down into a square surrounded by modern buildings like the one she had strayed into. Buses, people, a horse pulling a cart with an old man and an empty sack in the back. And right in front of the store's exit stood the two young men who were trailing her. They shuffled around, not much, a hand dipping into a pocket or scratching an ear, that sort of thing. They did not drop their guard on the exit.

Krieger was right. He had warned against tackling David, especially against doing it solo. Having Ellie as witness did not count, David was dangerous.

'If you insist, Rose,' Krieger said, 'meet force with force. Guile and wit won't help against a man who employs people to do the strong-arm stuff for him.'

Krieger meant well but his advice was impractical. What did he expect her to do? Hire henchmen of her own?

But she did not make a joke of it, he was too livid for that. David had tricked him. Krieger did not care about the broken pledge to pay for his information leading to Nicole, but he was outraged that David arranged to have her killed rather than rescue her.

'An old villain,' Rose thought, 'taking pleasure in doing good for once in his life. And it turns into a greater evil because he's conned by a younger villain.'

Krieger furious was a daunting spectacle. He might not be an active man any longer but Rose did not doubt that David Devereux would suffer for incurring his bitter enmity.

She seized the moment of Krieger's fury to draw out of him what he knew about David. One day he had tantalized her with the assertion that David was effectively in control of the House of Devereux, then denied her details. After betrayal, he was free with them. They were shocking.

In Paris, in London, in Madrid and New York Rose's friends

and colleagues were running checks for her. If what she knew and deduced dovetailed with what Krieger believed, then she had uncovered scandal on a serious scale.

Rose used a staff exit to leave the department store and hired a taxi to take her to David's hotel. The two young men were still in position outside the store's main entrance.

At the hotel, she took advantage of new arrivals confusing the receptionist and requested a key. She let herself into David's room. The simple lock on his briefcase gave way easily. She lifted out the papers, careful to keep them in order. His speech for the conference that afternoon was in there, a straightforward plea she assumed would be delivered with passion. Beneath it were other documents he would die to keep secret. She photographed them.

Time was short. Unless he was carrying a copy, he would return to collect his speech. She replaced the papers, locked the case and went out on to the landing. She met him as she stepped out of the lift.

Lots of people were around, he was charming to her. Equally charming, she delayed him so the lift went up without him and they had to talk.

In public recognized by strangers and delegates to the conference, he had to project the David Devereux personality they knew from their television screens, the one with the friendly smile and honest determination to save the planet. He managed it with disarming ease and Rose felt twinges of doubt that he was capable of what she believed. But in her bag was a camera containing one aspect of the truth.

'David, I shan't be fobbed off.' She matched him for playfulness. 'My questions this morning were serious.'

'Slanderous.' His smile did not shift, no one could possibly guess the substance of their conversation. 'I'm sure you won't publish anything of the sort.'

'Is this why a couple of your men are following me around?'

He shook his head. 'I'm a simple perfume-maker, Rose, with a penchant for campaigning.'

A delegate broke in on them and David snatched the opportunity to say goodbye to her and go with him. She travelled to her flat by taxi, looking back every few hundred yards although nobody was chasing after it. A brief shower had dampened the cobbles and speckled the pile of builder's sand near the entrance to the archway. With a nervous glance up and down the street, she went through the high wooden door in the coach arch, entered the tunnel of gloom, felt where to insert the key in the iron gate. She was braced for attack.

Rose examined the bathroom, the kitchen, all the rooms. She peered behind the sofa where Ellie slept and under the bed. Persuaded she was alone, she rechecked the lock on the door and got to work on the telephone.

First Paris. Joelle was breathless. Information was pouring in and she barely had time to assimilate it.

'Tell me how you got on yourself,' suggested Rose, seeking a starting point.'

To Joelle that seemed the least interesting part. 'Oh, I sat around a few bars with that detective, Paul Martin, and pecked away until he admitted I was right about his client being one of the Devereux. He said the client arranged for the photograph to be updated. In New York, he thought. Well, I bullied him into finding out. He talked a lot of rot about it being unethical to spy on his own client, but he did it. He spoke to the artist and she provided a description of her customer.'

'And we know what he got: a rundown of David Devereux.'

'Wrong. He got a description of his client, David's father, Philippe.'

'*What!*'

Joelle relished Rose's astonishment before asking, tongue in cheek, whether this news spoiled her carefully constructed theory.

'No-o,' said Rose, rearranging the puzzle pieces in her head. 'No, actually it fits better. It explains why your Paul Martin was advertising in northern Europe while David was secretly in Spain which is where Krieger told him to go.'

'Both David and Philippe were searching for Nicole. Coincidence?'

'No, not that. You remember Krieger saying there were two bungled ransom demands? David wasn't born then, he can't have been the one with the suspicion that Nicole was alive.'

'But why go looking for her now?'

'Money. David told me he was nagging his father and grandfather for the money in what he terms Nicole's piggybank. If nothing else did it, then David's demand for her money revived the mystery of what became of her.'

'OK,' said Joelle briskly. 'That's enough of that. Ready for the rest?'

TWENTY-TWO

The noise made by the worn-out motor of the fridge covered the sound of the door being forced. The man was in the room with her before Rose knew it.

She heard a scream, her own. And she was up, backing away from the table that served as her desk. The padded arm of a chair jammed up against her thigh, the corner of a sideboard jabbed into her other hip. She was in a trap constructed of walls and furniture.

The man was one of the pair who followed her that morning. Athletic, full of energy and no way to spend it. He ignored her and went to the table.

'Don't touch anything,' she said stupidly, knowing he would do as he liked.

He lifted a sheet of paper, looked at it. The same with a second one. She calmed her breath, holding it in, steadying herself for violent reaction. But no reaction came. He was reading about David Devereux subverting the Devereux art fund and channelling it and the proceeds of art sales into Greenworld coffers; about him ordering the shooting of John Blair under cover of a street demonstration in Spain, and the killing in London of a singer who called herself Maria. The pages recounted how a rich young campaigner turned into a murderous fanatic. Explosive, but no reaction.

Then she realized. David's sporty young Frenchman could not read English. She gave a silent sigh of relief and relaxed a shade, sagging her weight against the arm of the chair. Respite.

The chair shifted and the man looked over at her. They were about the same height but she was no match for his strength. His hands flexed and he stepped nearer. Trapped, she had no space to manoeuvre.

'Stay here,' he said with enough menace to make leaving the room unattractive.

He moved away, an arm scooping her papers on to the floor, throwing her computer after them.

'Stay here,' he ordered a second time. And left.

For a minute she did as she was bid, to the extent of not leaving her trap in the corner of the room. Then she pulled herself together, went to the doorway leading to the kitchen, checking that the faint sound had been the front door closing behind him.

Alone again, jumpy, she picked up the computer and papers, put the sheets in order in an envelope, hid it under her clothes, scattered other typed pages on the table in their place. If he returned with a translator, the pair would learn about the comical doings of a couple of priests at the Vatican.

Rose opened a window and stuck her head out. To her left she could see part-way into the darkened tunnel of the coach arch. For the rest, there was a concrete and grass area about thirty feet square, littered with washing lines and watched over by buildings on all sides. She climbed out on to the window sill.

Nothing moved except a dingy tea towel on one of the lines flung between a wooden scaffolding pole and a rickety balcony on the first floor. Where there might have been shrubs, flower tubs, a pleasant area for sitting out, there was neglect and the odour of damp. The scaffolding was years old, mould grew on it, weeds lodged where it met the ground. She delayed, testing whether the Frenchman would challenge her. Then she dropped to the ground.

Close to the wall, she edged towards the coach arch, straining to make out shapes in its darkness. But beyond the iron gate half-way along it, there was a black void. It took all her courage to keep moving towards that mysterious patch of ground where a killer might be lying in wait. John Blair's photographs, Krieger's information topped up with confirmation from far-flung colleagues, indicated this was the man who fired the shot in Spain. He had the reputation, the contacts, the gun. All he lacked was a conviction for murder.

Her nails were slicing her palms. With deliberate effort, she eased her hands, wriggled shoulders knotted tight as the tension seized her. She felt the envelope against her skin, revived her determination to survive and do what she must do, for the sake of those who had died, and for those countless others who were being misled and misused.

Rose's fingers touched an iron rung of the gate. She released the lock, stepped through. Her eyesight adjusted, she saw blacker patches in the gloom but none looked like a man poised to pounce. She opened the wooden door to the street.

It took five steps to get clear of the corrugated-iron sheeting protecting building materials, and then she saw him. He was in a car. He shifted, she ducked back. Rose had the wooden door open and was unlocking the iron gate before she knew what her decision was. Ashamed of her trembling panic, she threw back the broken door to the flat and reached the room where he had told her to stay.

'Crazy!' she said, beating a fist against her forehead. 'The worst place to be. He can do anything in here and nobody will even hear. Get out, get out into the open. It's the only chance.'

She ran to the entrance hall, heard the metal gate moving. Skidding, she whirled round, reached the living room. By the open window she listened. No footsteps mounted the curving stone staircase to the other flats. Rose climbed out again and dashed into the street. Nobody was in the car. She ran uphill.

A figure that might have been the second of the men appeared round a corner. She slipped into a passageway that led into a square. As she neared the end of it she heard running footsteps behind her. The baroque church of St Nicholas filled most of one side of the square. Rose sprang up the steps and found a hiding place among the monuments and frescos.

If she could just get her bearings, if there was another exit that would deposit her beside the taxi rank in the lower square . . .

She saw the second man enter, glance around, stand feet apart like a border guard near the doorway.

'For an intelligent woman,' she thought, 'you're taking some absurd decisions.'

Blaming herself, she began to fret about wasting time. She had to make it, there was a chance today to do what she might never be able to do again. Fate was offering her this opportunity, she must grab it.

She touched the envelope, safe but for how long? If she were overpowered . . . Down the nave the man stood guard. The word struck her as particularly apt. Guard. If his orders were to harm her, she would be injured or dead by now. No, the pair were guarding her, trying to keep her away from someone or something. Grasping this much, she guessed the rest.

Practised in the trick of latching herself on to knots of strangers, she wandered out into the square in company with a few Germans who marvelled loudly at the frescos. Then she strode off at a tangent, uphill, skipping from Néruda to another street, and back, zig-zagging, making pursuit tiresome. Once, she emerged in front of a car driven by the man who scared her in her flat. She increased her speed, walking not running, keeping ahead of the car and within earshot of other pedestrians, although doubtful that the man walking with a moth-eaten hound or the woman on the way to the bar with a jug for beer amounted to protection.

A shout. The car stopped, the other man was haring after it. When he leaped aboard, the vehicle surged forward. It would have caught her easily, if it were not for a slit of an alley between the huge houses. She darted down it, heard car doors slam in her wake, found herself in another of those backyards of washing lines and scaffolding. Nowhere to hide. Unless she went up.

Her hands slid on slimy wood but she got a grip, got the knack. Up she went, as far as a dangerously tilting balcony on the first floor. A rug hung over a rail, shielded her as the men crashed into the square and cursed that they had lost her. Their altercation left her in no doubt.

'We ought to put a bullet through her. I've had enough, dodging round after her.'

'We can't do that. You know what he said.'

The other one spread his jacket to reveal a gun. 'Yes, I know what he said.'

Rose wormed her way to the end of the balcony, wondering how long before they worked out she could only be up there. The envelope dislodged, she pushed it back in place. Then she fantasized about a friendly face peering out of a room and rescuing her, providing safe conduct off the premises. Fantasy petered out in the information, floating up from below, that one of the men was to stay guard by the street entrance to the alley as they were convinced she had run in there. The other one was to drive up the hill and investigate further afield. It was the one with the gun who elected to stay.

She peered out through ornamental ironwork as they left the square. Then she climbed on to the scaffolding. Between this building and the next was a narrow linking section, the sort formed when a passage is covered over. Red tiles sloped away from her. Rose trusted them with her weight.

Once she was on the roof, she saw the folly of it. The section ended with a wall as high and inviting as a cliff. She squatted there, her clothes sucking up pools of rainwater and bird droppings. She moved her arm out of shadow to read her watch. Late. She was not far off, geographically, but if she were stuck on a roof she was no more use than if she were in Paris.

The pattern of shadow was changing, the warm colour of terracotta tiles intensifying at the end of the roof. Rose gasped and crawled forward. Within a yard or so she saw an opening at a right angle to the cliff. A roof sloped down to meet the one she was on, presenting her with a gentle gradient. It was fan shaped and she was at the point. She squeezed on to it between high walls and saw another street, a glimpse of orchard below Strahov Monastery, gardens close by and castle walls.

Rose slithered from the roof to a wall and jumped down into a lane. Up, she had to keep going up. Paths turned into steps and she broke into a trot. People were perplexed by her, pausing in the midst of trying on Russian army hats at makeshift stalls on the steps to wonder at the mad creature rushing by. At the top she pelted flat out towards the castle entrance. She was nearly there, so very nearly there.

She hitched at her clothes, forcing the envelope back in place. There were crowds of people. Pushing through them she met a barrier. A trumpet sounded, soldiers stamped to and fro in the new uniforms the President insisted on as a break with the past. Until the ceremony was over, no one could come or go. Rose squirmed back through the crowd.

Running round, teetering along a wall, she discovered an alternative way in. Late, she was very late. Probably too late. She ran faster. Through courtyards, around happy people on holiday and others solemnly about their work, she ran.

The gates came in sight and she slowed, catching her breath, smoothing her hair, checking the safety of the envelope. At the entrance she cleared her throat and prepared to sound impressive.

They let her in, because she allowed them no option by speaking up firmly, and to hang with her appearance. The way was signposted and she sped along corridors until she came to the hall. With one hand on the door she shut her eyes tight, steeled herself to face disappointment or whatever was demanded of her on the unknown side of that door. Then she pushed it open.

He was on his feet. She recognized the passage from the speech, he was into the final part of it. Cameras and microphones were banked around the hall, he was the highlight of the event. For a sickening moment her plan seemed foolhardy, unworkable.

David, in the spotlight, did not see her. When the climax of his speech was a few sentences away, she plucked the pages from the envelope and suddenly ran up to the front, on to the stage and challenged him with his hypocrisy and deceit.

A number of television companies were broadcasting the conference live. Before she was manhandled from the platform they sent out into the world her accusations and, most telling of all, David's reaction. Utterly shocked, he lost control, ripping up the documents she held, switching from the personality who enthralled an audience into his frightening *alter ego*.

Conference organizers dragged her out of the hall amid the hubbub. Then she was in an office, being harangued in Czech. Next, she was alone, eavesdropping on an argument outside the room, partly in Czech, partly in German. She was trembling. She had done it and it had exhausted her. The emotional cost as much as the physical effort. She had done her best and now it was up to other people to make what they could of it. She could only . . . The door opened and the men who had shouted at her beckoned her out. With mistrust, they pointed to the exit. Turning from them, she saw her rescuer, a fair man in a dark coat. Willi.

She started to ask why he was there instead of at his desk in Frankfurt, but he butted in.

'Come, Rose. I think we should leave here quickly before they change their minds.'

And when they were in his car and driving out of Hradčany Square he said: 'I was going to let you think I had second thoughts about publishing Krieger's memoirs but as this is apparently a day for the unvarnished truth to be told, then I'll confess. I came especially to see you Rose. Your Paris office told me you were here. I spoke to a charming young woman called Joelle.'

Rose did not doubt Joelle was very helpful. 'She mentioned the conference?'

'She believed you'd be there. I'd almost given you up when you made your spectacular entrance.'

They began to laugh. She said: 'I must have looked extraordinary.'

'It was very wonderful, something for David Devereux to remember while he languishes in jail.'

'Oh, I doubt whether I've got him into jail. He comes of a rich and powerful family and he's not short of cunning. But I've discredited him, Willi, and people won't forget. It'll become another episode in the long running saga of the Curse of the Devereux. He can escape the law but he can't escape that.'

'And Greenworld?'

'I expect they'll tear up his membership form right now.'

David Devereux was found in his hotel room next morning with his throat cut. There was no weapon by the body.

'Krieger,' said Rose when she heard.

Ellie, straightening the duvet and pillows on her makeshift sofa bed, said over her shoulder: 'Suicide, surely. You destroyed him.'

'Krieger,' Rose repeated.

She hurried round to the house Krieger called home. Locked. He had moved on in the way he would always have to, never settled, never free, always paying the price.

'Willi rang while you were out,' Ellie reported when Rose returned. 'He has to change the plans you made.'

Rose felt all the pleasure drain from the day. She did not know until this moment how much she had been looking forward to being with him, how much her happiness depended on it. She had spent the night with him, comforted, loved.

Ellie was looking at her closely. Too defiant, Rose said: 'Maybe it *was* a matter of life or death whether or not I helped finish what John Blair began with the Devereux story, but I honestly can't see it any longer. I've done what I can to get at the truth and now I'm giving up guilt. If that seems heartless I'm sorry, but I won't be burdened by a tragedy that can't be undone.'

'Guilt?' echoed Ellie, who had not known Rose felt that. And then: 'Of course you can't be tied down by memory, none of us can.'

'Sorry, I'm stirring up all the old clichés about life having to go on.' She lifted the coffee pot. 'Is this fresh?'

'I made it two minutes before you walked through the door.'

The metal cupboard squeaked as Rose took out cups.

Behind her Ellie said: 'Ring him, Rose. I'll pour the coffee.'

Ellie stayed in the kitchen while Rose spoke to Willi. When she came back Rose was bright-eyed and laughing.

'He wasn't cancelling, just changing the venue. Why have I come to expect the worst?'

Rose did not know of Ellie's plan to live in Prague, she knew she was waiting to meet the Hals expert from Holland but no more. Ellie hugged her secret. Neither had she shown Rose the photographs taken in the Bohemian castle, except for the shots of the portrait.

After Rose left to keep her rendezvous with her new lover, Ellie looked at them again. The murky Frans Hals companion piece. The broken wooden chair with the dustpan and pegs, so splendid she earmarked it for the cover of her book. And the portrait of the man who was her first love. The exposure was wrong. She had tried for a mysterious *contre-jour* effect but his face was completely obscured. The result was a memento of evasion.

Her fingers stroked the space where she had intended his features to be. She wished she could fix them in her memory, recall his voice, think how his skin felt as his body moved above hers in the hotel bed. For years she had carried in her heart his face, his voice, the touch of his hand. Strangely, she had now lost him.

Frustrated, she blurted out: 'All I wanted to do was . . .'

And then, clearly as if he were beside her, she heard John Blair's voice, teasing her with his mock profundity, joking about 'the gap between intention and achievement, which is where we spend our lives'.

She laughed, sat reflecting for a few minutes. Then she made a call to New York.

'Sam? I'm coming home,' she said. The words sounded right.

She snatched up her coat, her boots clattered over the cobbles. On the bridge wealthy Russians clustered around a guide distorting history, stallholders were packing up their offerings of kitsch, a girl in shimmering tights sang love songs. Near St

329

Wenceslas a man was catching the clamouring gulls, seducing them with bread cast on the wind. They wheeled about him like unanswerable questions.